# ALL THE MISSING GIRLS

*a novel*

## Megan Miranda

"A twisty, compulsive read—I loved it." **—RUTH WARE**, author of *The Woman in Cabin 10*

Praise for
*All the Missing Girls*

---

*ENTERTAINMENT WEEKLY,*
Thriller Round-Up

*THE WALL STREET JOURNAL,*
5 Killer Books for 2016

*THE HOLLYWOOD REPORTER,*
Hot Summer Books . . . 16 Must Reads

---

"Miranda convincingly conjures a haunted setting that serves as a character in its own right, but what really makes this roller coaster so memorable is her inspired use of reverse chronology, so that each chapter steps further back in time, dramatically shifting the reader's perspective."

—*Publishers Weekly* (starred review)

"[Gillian] Flynn's meta-literary crime fiction deconstructs crime fiction. . . . Megan Miranda's novel *All the Missing Girls* also exults in this new tradition in crime fiction . . . twists it, creating a new reading experience. . . . *All the Missing Girls* is set to become one of the best books of 2016."

—*Los Angeles Review of Books*

"Looking for the next *Gone Girl*? *All the Missing Girls* is its heir apparent. . . . A book that you can't help but whip through, and Miranda is a master of leaving just enough tantalizing clues to keep you from pausing between chapters . . . It becomes increasingly difficult to tear your eyes from the page."

—*Refinery29*

"Darkly nostalgic . . . Miranda takes a risk by telling the story backward, but it pays off with an undroppable thriller, plenty of romantic suspense, and a fresh take on the decades-old teenage-murder theme."

—*Booklist*

"A twisty plot, unreliable narrator, and high-concept hook (the story unfolds backward, present to past) is drawing comparisons to *Gone Girl*."

—*The Hollywood Reporter*

"*All the Missing Girls* is a smart, suspenseful, and emotionally complex thriller. Told in reverse, this story will make you want to lock the doors, turn off the phone, and read until the last satisfying page."

—Alafair Burke, *New York Times* bestselling author of *The Ex*

"As original as it is addictive, this story puts a knot in your gut from the opening pages. Then, through the wizardry of its unconventional structure, that knot tightens and tightens and will not let go until the final pages—and even then the story continues to haunt you."

—Tim Johnston, *New York Times* bestselling author of *Descent*

"*All the Missing Girls* keeps you off balance in the most perfect way. I was held hostage by the book from the first page to the stunning conclusion. This literally backward tale is a winner."

—Lisa Lutz, *New York Times* bestselling author of
*The Passenger* and *How to Start a Fire*

# ALL THE MISSING GIRLS

*A Novel*

# MEGAN MIRANDA

**Simon & Schuster Paperbacks**

New York   London   Toronto   Sydney   New Delhi

Simon & Schuster Paperbacks
An Imprint of Simon & Schuster, Inc.
1230 Avenue of the Americas
New York, NY 10020

First Simon & Schuster trade paperback edition February 2017

SIMON & SCHUSTER PAPERBACKS and colophon are registered
trademarks of Simon & Schuster, Inc.

For information about special discounts for bulk purchases,
please contact Simon & Schuster Special Sales at 1-866-506-1949
or business@simonandschuster.com.

The Simon & Schuster Speakers Bureau can bring authors to
your live event. For more information or to book an event, contact the
Simon & Schuster Speakers Bureau at 1-866-248-3049 or
visit our website at www.simonspeakers.com.

*Interior design by Lewelin Polanco*

Manufactured in the United States of America

9   10

Library of Congress Control Number: 2015022237

ISBN 978-1-5011-0796-2
ISBN 978-1-5011-0797-9 (pbk)
ISBN 978-1-5011-0798-6 (ebook)

*For my parents*

# PART 1
*Going Home*

Man . . . cannot learn to forget, but hangs on the past: however far or fast he runs, that chain runs with him.
—FRIEDRICH NIETZSCHE

t started with a phone call, deceptively simple and easy to ignore. The buzzing on Everett's nightstand, the glow of the display—too bright in the bedroom he kept so dark, with the light-blocking shades pulled to the sill and the tinted windows a second line of defense against the glare of the sun and the city. Seeing the name, hitting the mute, turning my phone facedown beside the clock.

But then. Lying awake, wondering why my brother would call so early on a Sunday. Running through the possibilities: Dad; the baby; Laura.

I felt my way through the dark, my hands brushing the sharp corners of furniture until I found the light switch in the bathroom. My bare feet pressed into the cold tile floor as I sat on the toilet lid with the phone held to my ear, goose bumps forming on my legs.

Daniel's message echoed in the silence: "The money's almost gone. We need to sell the house. Dad won't sign the papers, though." A pause. "He's in bad shape, Nic."

Not asking for my help, because that would be too direct. Too unlike us.

I hit delete, slipped back under the sheets before Everett woke, felt for him beside me to be sure.

But later that day, back at my place, I flipped through the previous day's mail and found the letter—*Nic Farrell,* written in familiar handwriting, in blue ink; the address filled in by someone else, with a different, darker pen.

Dad didn't call anymore. Phones made him feel even more disoriented, too far removed from the person he was trying to place. Even if he remembered whom he'd been dialing, we'd slip from his mind when we answered, nothing more than disembodied voices in the ether.

I unfolded the letter—a lined journal page with jagged edges, his handwriting stretching beyond the lines, veering slightly to the left, as if he'd been racing to get the thoughts down before they slipped from his grasp.

No greeting.

*I need to talk to you. That girl. I saw that girl.*

No closing.

I called Daniel back, the letter still trembling in my hand. "Just got your message," I said. "I'm coming home. Tell me what's going on."

# DAY 1

I took *inventory of the* apartment one last time before loading up my car: suitcases waiting beside the door; key in an envelope on the kitchen counter; an open box half full of the last-minute things I'd packed up the night before. I could see every angle of the apartment from the galley kitchen—exposed and empty—but still, I had the lingering feeling that I was forgetting something.

I'd gotten everything together in a rush, finishing out the last few weeks of the school year while fielding calls from Daniel and finding someone to sublet my place for the summer—no time to pause, to take in the fact that I was actually doing this. Going back. Going *there*. Daniel didn't know about the letter. He knew only that I was coming to help, that I had two months before I needed to return to my life here.

Now the apartment was practically bare. An industrial box, stripped of all warmth, awaiting the moderately responsible-looking grad student who would be staying through August. I'd

5

left him the dishes, because they were a pain to pack. I'd left him the futon, because he'd asked, and because he threw in an extra fifty dollars.

The rest of it—the things that wouldn't fit in my car, at least—was in a storage unit a few blocks away. My entire life in a sealed rectangular cube, stacked full of painted furniture and winter clothes.

The sound of someone knocking echoed off the empty walls, made me jump. The new tenant wasn't due to arrive for another few hours, when I'd be on the road. It was way too early for anyone else.

I crossed the narrow room and opened the front door.

"Surprise," Everett said. "I was hoping to catch you before you left." He was dressed for work—clean and sleek—and he bent down to kiss me, one arm tucked behind his back. He smelled like coffee and toothpaste; starch and leather; professionalism and efficiency. He pulled a steaming Styrofoam cup from behind his back. "Brought you this. For the road."

I inhaled deeply. "The way to my heart." I leaned against the counter, took a deep sip.

He checked his watch and winced. "I hate to do this, but I have to run. Early meeting on the other side of town."

We met halfway for one last kiss. I grabbed his elbow as he pulled away. "Thank you," I said.

He rested his forehead against mine. "It'll go fast. You'll see."

I watched him go—his steps crisp and measured, his dark hair brushing his collar—until he reached the elevator at the end of the hall. He turned back just as the doors slid open. I leaned against the doorframe, and he smiled.

"Drive safe, Nicolette."

I let the door fall shut, and the reality of the day suddenly made my limbs heavy, my fingertips tingle.

The red numbers on the microwave clock ticked forward, and I cringed.

It's a nine-hour drive from Philadelphia to Cooley Ridge, not counting traffic, lunch break, gas and restroom stops, depending. And since I was leaving twenty minutes after I said I would, I could already picture Daniel sitting on the front porch, tapping his foot, as I pulled into the unpaved driveway.

I sent him a text as I propped the front door open with a suitcase: *On my way, but more like 3:30.*

It took two trips to drag the luggage and remaining boxes down to the car, which was parked around the block, behind the building. I heard the beginnings of rush-hour traffic in the distance, a steady hum on the highway, the occasional honk. A familiar harmony.

I started the car, waited for the air to kick in. *Okay, okay,* I thought. I rested my phone in the cup holder and saw a response from Daniel: *Dad's expecting you for dinner. Don't miss it.*

Like I might be three hours later than I'd claimed. That was one of Daniel's more impressive accomplishments: He had perfected the art of the passive-aggressive text message. He'd been practicing for years.

—

WHEN I WAS YOUNGER, I used to believe I could see the future. This was probably my father's fault, filling my childhood with platitudes from his philosophy lectures, letting me believe in things that could not be. I'd close my eyes and will it to appear, in tiny, beautiful glimpses. I'd see Daniel in a cap and gown. My mother smiling beside him through the lens of my camera as I motioned for them to get closer. *Put your arm around her. Pretend you like each other! Perfect.* I'd see me and Tyler, years later, throwing our bags into the back of his mud-stained pickup truck, leaving for college. Leaving for good.

It was impossible to understand back then that getting out wouldn't be an event in a pickup truck but a ten-year process of excision. Miles and years, slowly padding the distance. Not to mention Tyler never left Cooley Ridge. Daniel never graduated. And our mother wouldn't have lived to see it, anyway.

If my life were a ladder, then Cooley Ridge was the bottom—an unassuming town tucked into the edge of the Smoky Mountains, the very definition of Small Town, America, but without the charm. Everywhere else—anywhere else—was a higher rung that I'd reach steadily with time. College two hundred miles to the east, grad school one state north, an internship in a city where I planted my feet and refused to leave. An apartment in my own name and a nameplate on my own desk and Cooley Ridge, always the thing I was moving farther away from.

But here's the thing I've learned about leaving—you can't really go back. I don't know what to do with Cooley Ridge anymore, and Cooley Ridge doesn't know what to do with me, either. The distance only increases with the years.

Most times, if I tried to shift it back into focus—*Tell me about home, tell me about growing up, tell me about your family,* Everett would say—all I'd see was a caricature of it in my mind: a miniature town set up on entryway tables around the holidays, everything frozen in time. So I gave him surface answers, flat and nonspecific: *My mom died when I was sixteen; it's a small town at the edge of the forest; I have an older brother.*

Even to me, even as I answered, it looked like nothing. A Polaroid fading from the edges in, the colors bled out; the outline of a ghost town full of ghosts.

But one call from Daniel—"We have to sell the house"—and I felt the give of the floorboards beneath my feet. "I'm coming home," I said, and the edges rippled, the colors burned: My mother pressed her cheek against my forehead; Corinne rocked our cart gently back and forth at the top of the Ferris wheel; Tyler balanced on the fallen tree angled across the river, stretching between us.

*That girl,* my dad wrote, and her laughter rattled my heart.

———

*I NEED TO TALK to you. That girl. I saw that girl.*

An hour later, a *moment* later, and he'd probably forgotten—setting aside the sealed envelope until someone found it abandoned on his dresser or under his pillow and pulled my address from his file. But there must've been a trigger. A memory. An idea lost in the synapses of his brain; the firing of a thought with nowhere else to go.

The torn page, the slanted print, my name on the envelope—

And now something sharp and wild had been set loose inside my head. Her name, bouncing around like an echo.

*Corinne Prescott.*

Dad's letter had been folded up inside my purse for the last few weeks, lingering just under the surface of my mind. I'd be reaching for my wallet or the car keys and feel a sliver of the edge, the jab of the corner, and there she would be all over again: long bronze hair falling over her shoulders, the scent of spearmint gum, her whisper in my ear.

*That girl.* She was always *that girl.* What other girl could it be?

The last time I'd driven home was a little over a year ago—when Daniel called and said we had to get Dad into a facility, and I couldn't justify the cost of a last-minute flight. It had rained almost the entire trip, both ways.

Today, on the other hand, was the perfect driving day. No rain, overcast but not dark. Light but not bright. I'd made it through three states without stopping, towns and exits blurring by as I sped past—the embodiment of everything I loved about living up north. I loved the pace, how you could fill the day with a to-do list, take charge of the hours and bend them to your will. And the impatience of the clerk inside the convenience store on the corner near my apartment, the way he never looked up from his crossword, never made eye contact. I loved the anonymity of it all. Of a sidewalk full of strangers and endless possibilities.

Driving through these states was like that, too. But the beginning of the drive always goes much faster than the end. Farther south, the exits grow sparser, the landscape just sameness, filled with things you're sure you've passed a thousand times.

I was somewhere in Virginia when my phone rang from its spot in the cup holder. I fumbled for the hands-free device in my purse, keeping one hand steady on the wheel, but eventually gave up and hit speaker to answer the call. "Hello?" I called.

"Hey, can you hear me?" Everett's voice crackled, and I wasn't sure if it was the speakerphone or the reception.

"Yes, what's up?"

He said something indecipherable, his words cutting in and out.

"Sorry, you're breaking up. What?" I was practically shouting.

"Grabbing a quick bite," he said through the static. "Just checking in. How are the tires holding up this time?" I heard the smile in his voice.

"Better than the cell reception," I said.

He laughed. "I'll probably be in meetings the rest of the day, but call me when you get there so I know you made it."

I thought about stopping for lunch, but there was nothing except pavement and field for miles and miles and miles.

———

I'D MET EVERETT A year ago, the night after moving my dad. I'd driven home, tense and uneasy, gotten a flat tire five hours into the drive, and had to change it myself underneath a steady drizzle.

By the time I'd gotten to my apartment, I was hovering on the edge of tears. I had come home with my bag slung over my shoulder, my hand shaking as I tried to jam the key into the door. Eventually, I'd rested my head against the solid wooden door to steady myself. To make matters worse, the guy in 4A had gotten off the elevator at the same time, and I'd felt him staring at me, possibly waiting for the impending meltdown.

Apartment 4A. This was all I'd known of him: He played his music too loud, and he had too many guests, and he kept nontraditional hours. There was a man beside him—polished, where he was not. Smooth, where he was rough. Sober, where he was drunk.

The guy in 4A sometimes smiled at me as we passed in the hall in the evening, and one time he held the elevator for me, but this was a city. People came and went. Faces blurred.

"Hey, 4C," he'd slurred, unsteady on his feet.

"Nicolette," I said.

"Nicolette," he repeated. "Trevor." The man beside him looked embarrassed on his behalf. "And this is Everett. You look like you need a drink. Come on, be neighborly."

I thought the neighborly thing would've been to learn my name a year ago, when I moved in, but I wanted that drink. I wanted to feel the distance between *there* and *here*; I needed space from the nine-hour car ride home.

Trevor pushed open his door as I walked toward them. The man beside him stuck out his hand and said, "Everett," as if Trevor's introduction hadn't counted.

By the time I left, I'd told Everett about moving my dad, and he'd said it was the right thing. Had told him about the flat and the rain and everything I wanted to do over the summer, while I was off. By the time I stopped talking, I felt lighter, more at ease— which could've been the vodka, but I liked to think it was Everett— and Trevor was passed out on the sofa beside us.

"Oh. I should go," I'd said.

"Let me walk you back," Everett had said.

My head was light as we walked in silence, and then my hand was on the doorknob and he was still nearby, and what were the grown-up rules for this? "Want to come in?"

He didn't answer, but he followed me in. Froze in the galley kitchen, which looked out into the rest of my studio loft, one room with high windows and sheer curtains hanging from the exposed pipes, segregating my bedroom. But I could see my bed through them—unmade, inviting—and I knew he could, too.

"Wow," he said. It was the furniture, I was sure. Pieces I'd mined from thrift stores and flea markets and had stripped down and repainted in bold colors to match. "I feel like I'm Alice in Wonderland."

I slid off my shoes, leaned against the kitchen counter. "Ten bucks says you've never read it."

He smiled and opened my refrigerator, pulling out a bottle of water. "Drink me," he said, and I laughed.

Then he pulled out a business card, placed it on the counter, leaned forward, and brushed his lips against mine before backing away. "Call me," he said.

And I did.

———

THE DRIVE THROUGH VIRGINIA had turned endless, with its white farmhouses in the hills and the bales of hay dotting the surrounding grass. Then the pass through the mountains—guardrails and signs issuing warnings to turn on the fog lights—and the static as the radio stations cut in and out. The longer I drove, the slower I seemed to go. *Relativity,* I thought.

The pace was different back home. People didn't move as fast, didn't change too much over the course of the decade. Cooley Ridge, holding you to the person you'd always been. When I pulled off the highway, went down the ramp, and hit the main drag, I bet

I'd still find Charlie Higgins or someone like him leaning against the beat-up side of the CVS. Bet I'd still find Christy Pote pining for my brother, and my brother pretending not to notice, even though they went ahead and got married to other people.

Maybe it was because of the humidity and the way we had to fight our way through it, like syrup sticking to the bottom of our feet, sweet and viscous. Maybe it was from living so close to the mountains—a thousand years in the making, the slow shift of plates under the earth, the trees that have been here since I was born and would be here when I was gone.

Maybe it's the fact that you can't see anything beyond here when you're in it. Just mountains and forest and you. That's it.

One decade later, a hundred miles away, and I cross the state line—*Welcome to North Carolina!*—and the trees grow thicker, and the air goes heavy, and I'm back.

The blurred edges shifting back into focus, my own mind resettling, remembering. The ghosts of us gaining substance: Corinne running down the side of the road in front of me, holding out her thumb, her legs shiny from sweat, her skirt blowing up when a car passes too close. Bailey hanging off my shoulder, her breath hot with vodka. Or maybe that was mine.

My fingers uncurled from the wheel. I wanted to reach out and touch them. Have Corinne turn around and say, "Pull your shit together, Bailey," catch my eye, and smile. But they faded too fast, like everything else, and all that remained was the sharp pang of missing her.

One decade, twenty miles away, and I can see my house. The front door. The overgrown path and the weeds pushing through the gravel of the driveway. I hear that screen door creak open, and Tyler's voice: *Nic?* And it sounds a little deeper than my memory, a little closer.

Almost home now.

Down the exit, left at the stoplight, the pavement cracked and gray.

A sign freshly staked into the ground at the corner, the bottom streaked with dried mud—the county fair, back in town—and something flutters in my chest.

There's the CVS with the group of teenage boys loitering at the side of the lot, like Charlie Higgins used to do. There's the strip of stores, different letters stenciled in the windows from when I was a kid, except for Kelly's Pub, which was as close to a landmark as we had. There's the elementary school and, across the street, the police station, with Corinne's case file stored in some back closet, gathering dust. I imagined all the evidence boxed away and tucked in a corner, because there was no place else to put her. Lost in the shuffle, forgotten with time.

The electrical cables strung above us on the roadside, the church that most everyone went to, whether you were Protestant or not. And beside it, the cemetery. Corinne used to make us hold our breath as we drove past. Hands on the ceiling over the railroad tracks, a kiss when the church bells chimed twelve, and no breathing around the dead. She made us do it even after my mother died. Like death was a superstition, something we could outwit by throwing salt over our shoulders, crossing our fingers behind our backs.

I took my phone out at the stoplight and called Everett. I got his voicemail, like I knew I would. "Made it," I said. "I'm here."

———

THE HOUSE WAS EVERYTHING I imagined those last nine hours. The path from the driveway to the front porch now overtaken by the yard, Daniel's car pulled all the way to the side of the carport beside the garage to leave space for mine, the weeds scratching my bare ankles as I walked from smooth stepping-stone to smooth stepping-stone, my legs stretching by memory. The ivory siding, darker in places, bleached from the sun in others, so I had to squint to look directly at it. I stood halfway between my car and the house, forming a list in my head: *Borrow a pressure washer, find a kid with a riding mower, get a few pots of colored flowers for the porch* . . .

I was still squinting, my hand shielding my eyes, as Daniel rounded the corner of the house.

"Thought I heard your car," he said. His hair was longer than I remembered, at his chin—same length mine was before I left here for good. He used to keep it buzzed short, because the one time he let it grow out, people said he looked like me.

It seemed lighter all grown out—more blond than not blond—whereas mine had turned darker over the years. He was still pale like me, and his bare shoulders were already turning bright red. But he'd gotten thinner, the hard lines of his face more pronounced. We could barely pass for siblings now.

His chest was streaked with dirt, and his hands were coated in soil. He wiped his palms against the sides of his jeans as he walked toward me.

"And before three-thirty," I said, which was ridiculous. Of the two of us, he was always the responsible one. He was the one who'd dropped out of school to help with our mom. He was the one who'd said we needed to get our dad some help. He was the one now keeping an eye on the money. My being relatively on time was not going to impress him.

He laughed and wiped the backs of his hands against the sides of his jeans again. "Nice to see you, too, Nic."

"Sorry," I said, throwing myself into a hug, which was too much. I always did this. Tried to compensate by going to the other extreme. He was stiff in my embrace, and I knew I was getting dirt all over my clothes. "How's the job, how's Laura, how are you?"

"Busy. As irritable as she is pregnant. Glad you're here."

I smiled, then ducked back in the car for my purse. I wasn't good with niceties from him. Never knew what to do with them, what he meant by them. He was, as my father was fond of saying, hard to read. His expression just naturally looked disapproving, so I always felt on the defensive, that I had something to prove.

"Oh," I said, opening the back door to my car, shifting boxes around. "I have something for her. For you both. For the baby." Where the hell was it? It was in one of those gift bags with a rattle on the front, with glitter inside that shifted every time it moved. "It's here somewhere," I mumbled. And the tissue paper had tiny diapers with pins, which I didn't really understand, but it seemed like a Laura thing.

"Nic," he said, his long fingers curled on top of the open car door, "it can wait. Her shower's next weekend. I mean, if you're not busy. If you want to go." He cleared his throat. Uncurled his fingers from the door. "She'd want you to go."

"Okay," I said, standing upright. "Sure. Of course." I shut the door and started walking toward the house, Daniel falling into stride beside me. "How bad is it?" I asked.

I hadn't seen the house since last summer, when we moved our dad to Grand Pines. Back then there was a chance that it was a temporary move. That's what we'd told him. *Just for now, Dad. Just till you're better. Just for a little bit.* It was clear now that he wasn't going to get better, that it wasn't going to be for just a little bit. His mind was a mess. His finances were messier, a disaster that defied all logic. But at least he had the house. *We* had the house.

"I called to have the utilities turned back on yesterday, but something's wrong with the AC."

I felt my long hair sticking to the back of my neck, my sundress clinging to my skin, the sweat on my bare legs, and I hadn't even been here five minutes. My knees buckled as I stepped onto the splintered wooden porch. "Where's the breeze?" I asked.

"It's been like this all month," he said. "I brought over some fans. There's nothing structural other than the AC. Needs paint, lightbulbs, a good cleaning, and we need to decide what to do with everything inside, obviously. It would save a lot of money if we can sell it ourselves," he added with a pointed look in my direction. This was where I came in. In addition to my dealing with Dad's paperwork, Daniel wanted me to sell the house. He had a job, a baby on the way, a whole life here.

I had two months off. An apartment I was subletting for the extra cash. A ring on my hand and a fiancé who worked sixty-hour weeks. And now a name—Corinne Prescott—bouncing around in my skull like a ghost.

He pulled the screen door open, and the familiar creak cut straight to my gut. It always did. Welcome back, Nic.

————

DANIEL HELPED UNLOAD MY car, carrying my luggage to the second-floor hall, stacking my personal items on the kitchen table. He swiped his arm across the counter, and particles of dust hung in the air, suspended in a beam of sunlight cutting through the window. He coughed, his arm across his face. "Sorry," he said. "I didn't get to the inside yet. But I got the supplies." He gestured toward a cardboard box on the counter.

"That's why I'm here," I said.

I figured if I planned to live here for the duration, I should start in my room, so I had a place to sleep. I passed my suitcase at the top of the stairs and carried the box of cleaning supplies, balanced on my hip, toward my old room. The floorboards squeaked in the hall, a step before my door, like always. The light from the windows cut through the curtains, and everything in the room looked half there in the muted glow. I flipped the switch, but nothing happened, so I left the box in the middle of the floor and pulled back the curtains, watching as Daniel headed back from the detached garage with a box fan under his arm.

The yellow comforter covered with pale daisies was still rumpled at the bottom of my bed, as if I had never left. The indentations in the sheets—a hip, a knee, the side of a face—as if someone had just woken. I heard Daniel at the front door and I pulled the comforter up quickly, smoothing out the bumps and ridges.

I opened both windows—the one with the lock that worked and the one with the lock that broke sometime in middle school, which we never got fixed. The screen was gone, which was no great loss; it had been torn and warped from years of abuse. From me pushing out the bottom, crawling onto the sloped roof, dropping into the mulch that hurt only if you misjudged the distance, night after night. The type of thing that made perfect sense when I was seventeen but now seemed ridiculous. I couldn't climb back in, so I'd sneak in the back door and creep up the stairs, avoiding the creak in the hallway. I probably could've sneaked out the same way, saved myself the jump, saved my screen the damage.

As I turned back around, the room now bathed in light, I noticed all the little things that Daniel had already done: A few of the pictures were off the walls, the yellow paint discolored where they'd hung; the old shoe boxes that had been up high in the closet, stacked neatly against the wall in the back corner; and the woven throw rug that had been my mother's when she was a child, out in the middle of the floor, pulled from under the legs of my bed.

I heard the creak in the floorboard, Daniel in my doorway, box fan under his arm. "Thanks," I said.

He shrugged. "No problem." He angled it in the corner and flipped the switch. Heaven. "Thanks for coming, Nic."

"Thanks for starting my room," I said, shifting on my feet. I didn't get how other siblings had such an easy relationship. How they could ease back into childhood in a heartbeat, dropping all formalities. Daniel and I were about to spend the day tiptoeing around our empty house and thanking each other to death.

"Huh?" he said as he turned the power up on the fan, so the low hum became a steady white noise, muffling the sounds from the outside.

"My room." I gestured toward the walls. "Thanks for taking the pictures down."

"I didn't," he said, pausing in front of the fan and closing his eyes for a second. "Must've been Dad."

Maybe. I couldn't remember. I was here a year ago, the night after we'd moved him out, but the details . . . the details were lost. Were the shoe boxes down? Were the pictures off the wall? I felt like I would've remembered that. That whole night was a blur.

Daniel didn't know I had come back here instead of driving straight home, like I told him I had to—*I have work, I have to go.* I came back here, wandering from room to room, dry-eyed and shaken, like a kid lost in the middle of the county fair, searching the crowd for a familiar face. Curling up on the sheets in the empty house until I heard the engine out front and the doorbell I didn't answer. The creak of the screen, the key in the door, his boots on the steps. Until Tyler was leaning against my bedroom wall. *I almost missed you,* he'd said. *You okay?*

"When was the last time you were here?" I asked Daniel.

He scratched his head, stepping closer to the fan. "I don't know. I drive by, pop my head in from time to time, or if I need to get something for Dad. What is it?"

"Nothing," I said. But it wasn't nothing. Now I was imagining the shadow of someone else in the room. Rifling through my boxes. Moving my rug. Looking. *Searching.* It was the feeling that my things were not where they should be. It was the uneven imprints of dust, revealed in the sunlight. Or maybe it was just my perspective. I grew, and the house got smaller. At my place, I slept

19

in a queen-size bed that took up about half my apartment, and Everett had a king. This full-size bed looked like it was meant for a child.

I wondered, if I curled up on the mattress, whether I would feel the indentation from someone else. Maybe just the ghost of me. I yanked the sheets off the bed and brushed past Daniel. The crease between his eyes deepened as he watched me.

By the time I got back upstairs after putting in the load of wash, the room felt a little more like mine. Like Daniel and me, the room and I took some time to grow accustomed to each other again. I took off the ring and placed it in the chipped ceramic bowl on my nightstand before tackling the bathroom and the dresser drawers. After, I sat on the floor in front of the fan and leaned back on my elbows.

Hour two and I was already procrastinating. I had to go see Dad. I had to bring the paperwork and listen to him talk in circles. I had to ask him what he meant in that letter and hope that he remembered. I had to pretend it didn't sting when he forgot my name.

Didn't matter how many times it had happened before. It gutted me every time.

———

I GATHERED UP THE guardianship paperwork to bring to Dad's doctor—to start *the process*. So that, in life's biggest irony, we would become guardians to our father and his assets. As I prepared to leave, I heard faint, muffled noises from outside—closing of doors, revving of a motor. I figured Daniel must've called someone about the yard. But then the screen door creaked, cutting through the noise of the fan.

"Nic?" I knew that voice like twelve years of history filed down into a single memory, a single syllable.

I leaned toward my window. Saw Tyler's truck idling on the

side of the road. Some girl in the passenger seat. Daniel's sun-scorched back facing me as he leaned against the open window of the truck, talking to her.

*Shit.*

I spun around just in time to see Tyler standing in front of my open bedroom door.

"Figured it'd be rude not to come in and say hi."

I smiled without meaning to, because it was Tyler. A knee-jerk reaction.

"Kind of like not knocking?" I said, which made him laugh—but *at* me. I was going transparent, and I hated it.

He didn't say *How've you been* or *What have you been up to* or ask if I missed him, joking but not. He didn't mention the boxes or the luggage or my hair, which was longer than last year and curled into submission. But I saw him taking it all in. I was doing the same.

Face just a bit fuller, brown hair just a bit wilder, blue eyes just a bit brighter. When we were younger, he had these dark circles under his eyes that never went away, even if he'd spent the entire day sleeping. They kind of added to his appeal, but now that they were gone, he looked just as good. More youthful. Happier.

"Dan didn't tell me you'd be getting here today," he said, now fully inside my room.

Daniel liked us both fine apart, just not together. When I was sixteen, he told me I'd get a reputation if I started hanging around a guy like Tyler—I'm still not sure whether the slight was against me or against Tyler—and he never seemed to get over the fact that he was wrong.

"He didn't tell me you were coming today, either," I said, cross-ing my arms.

"In his defense, I was supposed to drop the mower off on my lunch break five hours ago." He shrugged. "But I had to be in the area anyway. Two birds, right?"

21

I peered over my shoulder to check out the girl, but also for the opportunity to look anywhere other than at him. While it took Daniel and me days to slide back into some form of comfort with each other, Tyler and I took no time at all. Didn't matter how long it had been or what we last said to each other. He stands in my room and it's spring break two years ago. He takes a step forward and it's the summer after college graduation. He says my name and I'm seventeen.

"Date?" I asked, seeing a blond ponytail, a skinny arm hanging out the window.

He grinned. "Something like that."

I looked over my shoulder again. "Better get back out there," I said. "Daniel's probably warning her off." Daniel's upper body disappeared farther into the truck, and I jumped at the sound of the horn. "By the way," I said, "that wasn't your date."

When I turned back around, Tyler was even closer. "If I didn't know any better," he said, "I'd guess he didn't want me around his little sister."

I kept myself from smiling at the running joke, because this was the dangerous part. Didn't matter that there was a girl in his car or that he was heading out on a date this very second. Because every time I came back, this was what happened. Didn't matter that I'd leave again or that he wouldn't. That we never talked about the past or the future. That he'd give up something else for me and I'd pretend not to notice.

"I'm engaged," I said. I said it fast, forcing out the words.

"Yeah, that part he told me." He eyed my hand, my bare finger.

I ran my thumb against the skin. "It's on the nightstand," I said. "Didn't want to get it dirty." Which seemed ridiculous and pretentious and everything Tyler would hate about a girl and a ring.

It made him laugh. "Well, let's see it, then." Like a dare.

"Tyler . . ."

"Nic . . ."

I tipped the ceramic bowl over into my palm and tossed him the ring as if it weren't worth more than him and me combined. His eyes went wide for a minute as he turned it over in his hand. "No shit, Nic. Good for you. Who's the lucky guy?"

"His name's Everett."

He started to laugh again, and I bit my lip to keep from smiling. I'd thought the same thing when we met—my neighbor's Ivy Leaguing college roommate, partner in Daddy's law firm. I'd thought, *Of course that's his name. Of course.* But Everett had surprised me. He kept on surprising me.

"His name is Everett and he got you this ring," Tyler continued. "Of course he did. When's the date?"

"No date yet," I said. "Just . . . eventually."

He nodded and tossed it back the same way I'd thrown it to him. Like flipping a coin or tossing one into a fountain. *Heads or tails. Make a wish. Penny for your thoughts.*

"How long are you staying?" he asked as I dropped the ring back in the bowl.

"Not sure. As long as it takes. I'm off for the summer."

"I guess I'll be seeing you around, then."

He was halfway out the door already. "Anyone I know?" I asked, gesturing toward the window.

He shrugged. "Annaleise Carter."

That's why he was in the area. The Carter property backed up to ours, and Annaleise was the oldest Carter, but not as old as we were. "What is she, thirteen?" I asked.

He laughed like he could see right through me. "Bye, Nic," he said.

Annaleise Carter used to have these big doe eyes, so she always looked both innocent and surprised. I saw those eyes now—saw her leaning out the car window, eyes fixed on me, blinking slowly,

23

like she was seeing a ghost. I raised my hand—*hi*—and then the other—*not guilty.*

Tyler got into the driver's seat with one last wave to my window before pulling away.

What was she now, twenty-three? She would always be thirteen to me. And Tyler would be nineteen and Corinne eighteen. Frozen at the moment when everything changed. When Corinne disappeared. And I left.

——

TEN YEARS AGO, RIGHT around this time—the last two weeks of June—the fair had been in town. I hadn't been home for it since then. And yet for all the time and distance, this still remained my sharpest memory—the thing that came to me first, before I could push it away, any time Everett asked about home:

Hanging over the edge of the Ferris wheel cart, the metal digging into my stomach, calling his name. Tyler down below, too far to focus on his face, frozen with his hands in his pockets as people weave around him. Watching us. Watching me. Corinne whispering in my ear: "Do it." Bailey's laughter, tight and nervous, and the cart rocking slowly back and forth, suspended over all of Cooley Ridge. "Tick-tock, Nic."

Me, climbing over the edge though we were all wearing skirts, the shift in my weight swinging the cart even more, my elbows gripping the bar at the top of the cage behind me, my feet balancing on the waist-high ledge below. Corinne's hands at my elbows, her breath in my ear. Tyler watching as the Ferris wheel started to circle downward again. The wind rushing up with the ground, my stomach dropping, my heart racing. The ride screeching to a stop at the base and me stepping off a moment too soon.

The impact from the metal loading dock jarring my knees as I ran down the ramp, dizzy and full of adrenaline, calling back to the worker who was yelling after me, "I know, I know, I'm leaving!" Racing toward Tyler, faintly smiling, his eyes telling me everything he wanted in that moment as he stood near the exit. An *enabler*. That was what Daniel called him, trying to find someone to blame other than me.

*Run,* Tyler had mouthed to me. I was out of breath, not quite laughing but something close, as I raced toward him. His lips curled into one of his half-smiles, and I knew we wouldn't make it out of the parking lot. We'd be lucky if we made it to his truck.

But then a hand gripped me—"I said I'm leaving," and I yanked my arm away.

But it wasn't security. It was Daniel. He grabbed me, solid and forceful, and hit me. He hit me across the face with a closed fist, and the impact knocked me off my feet onto my side, my arm twisted on the ground between my stomach and the dirt.

Shock and pain, fear and shame, they all felt like the same thing in my memory, all tangled up with the taste of blood and dirt. He'd never hit me before. Not even when we were little kids, really. Ten years later and that moment hangs between us in every interaction, in every passive-aggressive text message and ignored phone call.

And later that night, sometime between the fair closing and six A.M., Corinne disappeared, and everything that had happened that day took on new weight, new meaning. In the weeks that followed, the potential for death became palpable. It was all around us, intangible yet suffocating, existing in every different permutation of events. She could always be dead, in a thousand different ways.

Maybe she left because her father abused her. Maybe that's why her mother divorced him and left town a year later.

Or maybe it was the boyfriend, Jackson, because it's usually the boyfriend, and they'd been fighting. Or the guy she was flirting with at the fair whom none of us knew—the one at the hot dog stand. The one who Bailey swore had been watching us.

Or maybe she stuck her thumb out for a ride home, in her too-short skirt and her long-sleeved, gauzy top, and maybe a stranger passing through town took her, used her, left her.

Maybe she just left. That's what the cops finally decided. She was eighteen—legally, an adult—and she'd had enough of this place.

*What happened,* the cops asked, *in those hours, with all of you?* Lay bare your secrets, the Who and the What and the Why, between the hours of ten P.M. and six A.M. The same cops who broke up our parties but then drove us home instead of calling our parents. The same cops who dated our friends and drank beer with our brothers or fathers. And those secrets—the *Where were we between ten P.M. and six A.M.*, the *What were we doing,* the *Why*—they wouldn't keep with those cops. Not at the bar, not in the bed, not in this town.

By the time the people from the state arrived to help out, it was too late. We'd already turned inward, already had our theories set, already believed what we needed to believe.

The official line: Corinne last existed to everyone who knew her just inside the entrance to the fair, and from there, she disappeared.

But she didn't, really. There was more. A piece for each of us that we kept hidden away.

For Daniel, she disappeared from outside the fair, behind the ticket booth.

For Jackson, from the parking lot of the caverns.

And for me, she faded to nothing from a curve of the winding road on the way back to Cooley Ridge.

We were a town full of fear, searching for answers. But we were also a town full of liars.

———

THE CAFETERIA OF GRAND Pines is a great deception—hardwood floors and dark-linen-covered tables better suited for a restaurant instead of a long-term rehab facility. A piano in the corner, though it seems to be more for decoration, and faint classical music playing in the background during dinner. The food, I've heard, is the best in any rehab facility in the South—well, that's what Daniel was told when he picked this place, as if that should make him feel better and make *me* feel better, by proxy. *Don't worry, Dad, we'll visit. And the food is to die for.*

Today the nurse near reception escorted me into the room, and I caught sight of Dad at a corner table for two. His eyes slid over the nurse and me, then refocused on his fork twirling in the pasta.

"He didn't tell us you were coming or we would've reminded him to wait," the nurse said, her mouth scrunched up in worry.

Dad looked up as she walked me to the table and opened his mouth like he was about to say something, but the nurse spoke first, her smile practiced and contagious—my own and Dad's stretching in return.

"Patrick, your daughter's here. Nicolette," she said, facing me, "it's been so nice seeing you again."

"Nic," I said to the nurse. My heart squeezed in my chest as I waited, hoping the name caught, contagious as a smile.

"Nic," Dad repeated. His fingers drummed on the table, slowly, one, two, three, one, two, three—and then something seemed to click. The drumming sped up, onetwothree, onetwothree. "Nic." He smiled. He was here.

"Hi, Dad." I sat across from him and reached for his hand. God, it had been a long time. A year since we'd been in the same room. Calls, for a time, when he'd drift in and out of lucidity, until Daniel said they were making him too agitated. And then just letters, my picture enclosed. But here he was now. Like an older version of Daniel but softer, from age and a lifelong appreciation for fast food and liquor.

He closed his hand around mine and squeezed. He was always good at this part. At the physical affection, the outward displays of good-fatherhood. Hugs when he stumbled in late at night, half drunk. Hand squeezes when we needed groceries but he couldn't pull himself out of bed. *Hand squeeze, take my credit card,* and that should make up for it.

His eyes drifted to my hand, and he tapped the back of my ring finger. "Where is it?"

Inwardly, I cringed. But I smiled at Dad, glad he'd remembered this detail. It made me happy to know he remembered things I told him in my letters. He wasn't losing his mind, he was just lost within it. There was a difference. *I* lived in there. *Truth* lived in there.

I flipped through my phone for a picture and zoomed in. "I left it at the house. I was cleaning."

He narrowed his eyes at the screen, at the perfectly cut angles, at the brilliant stone. "Tyler got you that?"

My stomach dropped. "Not Tyler, Dad. Everett."

He was lost again, but he wasn't wrong. He was just somewhere else. A decade ago. We were kids. And Tyler wasn't asking me to marry him, exactly—he was holding it out like a request. *Stay,* it meant.

And this ring meant . . . I had no idea what this ring meant. Everett was thirty, and I was closing in on thirty, and he'd proposed on his thirtieth birthday, a promise that I wasn't wasting his time and he wasn't wasting mine. I'd said yes, but that was two months ago, and we hadn't discussed a wedding, hadn't gone over the logistics of moving in together when my lease was up. It was an *eventually.* A *plan.*

"Dad, I need to ask you something," I said.

His eyes drifted to the papers sticking out of my bag, and his fingers curled into fists. "I already told him, I'm not signing any papers. Don't let your brother sell the house. Your grandparents bought that land. It's *ours.*"

I felt like a traitor. That house was going to get sold one way or the other.

"Dad, we have to," I said softly. *You're out of money. You spent it indiscriminately on God knows what.* There was nothing left. Nothing but the money tied up in the concrete slab and four walls and the unkempt yard.

"Nic, really, what would your mother think?"

I was already losing him. He'd soon disappear into another time. It always started like this, with my mother, as if conjuring her into thought would suck him under to a place where she still existed.

"Dad," I said, trying to hold him here, "that's not why I came." I took a slow breath. "Do you remember sending me a letter a few weeks ago?"

He drummed his fingers on the table. "Sure. A letter." A stall tactic—I could feel him grasping, trying to remember.

I pulled out the paper, unfolded it on the table between us, saw his eyes narrow at the page. "You sent this to me."

His gaze lingered on the words before he looked up, his blue eyes watery, slippery as his thoughts. *That girl. I saw that girl.*

I heard my heartbeat in my head, like her name, knocking around. "Who did you mean? Who did you see?"

He looked around the room. Leaned closer. His mouth opening and closing twice before the name slipped through in a whisper. "The Prescott girl."

I felt all the hairs, one at a time, rise on the back of my neck. "Corinne," I said.

He nodded. "Corinne," he said, as if he'd found something he was looking for. "Yes. I saw her."

I looked around the cafeteria, and I leaned closer to him. "You saw her? Here?" I tried to picture the ghost of her drifting through these halls. Or her heart-shaped face and bronze hair, the amber eyes and the bow lips—what she'd look like ten years later. Slinging an arm around me, pressing her cheek against mine, confessing everything in a whisper just for me: *Best practical joke ever, right? Aw, come on, don't be mad. You know I love you.*

Dad's eyes were far off. And then they sharpened again, taking in his surroundings, the papers in my bag, me. "No, no, not here. She was at the house."

"When, Dad. When?" She disappeared right after graduation. Right before I left. Ten years ago . . . The last night of the county fair. *Tick-tock, Nic.* Her cold hands on my elbows, the last time I touched her.

Not a sighting since.

We stapled her yearbook picture to the trees. Searched the places we were scared to search, looking for something we were scared to find. We looked deep into each other. We unearthed the parts of Corinne that should've remained hidden.

"I should ask your mom . . ." His eyes drifted again. He must've been pulling a memory from years ago. From before Corinne disappeared. From before my mother died. "She was on the back porch, but it was just for a moment . . ." His eyes went wide. "The woods have *eyes,*" he said.

Dad was always prone to metaphor. He'd spent years teaching philosophy at the community college. It was worse when he was drinking—he'd pull on lines from a book, reordered to suit his whim, or recite quotes out of context from which I'd desperately try to find meaning. Eventually, he'd laugh, squeezing my shoulder, moving on. But now he would get lost in the metaphor, never able to pull himself back out. His moment of lucidity was fading.

I leaned across the table, gripping his arm until he focused on my words. "Dad, *Dad,* we're running out of time. Tell me about Corinne. Was she looking for me?"

He sighed, exasperated. "Time isn't running out. It's not even *real,*" he said, and I knew I had lost him—*he* was lost, circling in his own mind. "It's just a measure of distance we made up to understand things. Like an inch. Or a mile." He moved his hands as he spoke, to accentuate the point. "That clock," he said, pointing behind him. "It's not measuring time. It's creating it. You see the difference?"

I stared at the clock on the far wall, at the black second hand moving, moving, always moving. "And yet I keep getting older," I mumbled.

"Yes, Nic, yes," he said. "You change. But the past, it's still there. The only thing moving is you."

I felt like a mouse in a wheel, trying to have a conversation with him. I had learned not to argue but to wait. To avoid agitation, which would quickly slide into disorientation. I'd try again tomorrow, from a different angle, a different moment. "Okay, Dad. Hey, I gotta get moving."

He pulled back and looked at me, his eyes roaming across my face. I wondered what version of me he was seeing—his daughter or a stranger. "Nic, listen," he said. I heard the ticking of the clock. *Tick-tock, Nic.*

He drummed his fingers on the table between us, twice as fast as the clock. There was a crash from the other side of the room, and I twisted in my chair to see a man picking up a tray of dishes he must've dropped while clearing tables. I turned back to Dad, who was focused on his plate, twirling his pasta, as if the last few minutes hadn't existed.

"You really should try the pasta," he said. He grinned, warm and distant.

I stood, stacked the edges of the paper against the table, matched his warm, distant smile. "It was really good to see you, Dad," I said. I walked around the table, hugged him tight, felt him hesitate before bringing his hand up to my arm and squeezing me back.

"Don't let your brother sell the house," he said, the conversation in a loop, beginning anew.

———

THE PORCH LIGHT WAS on and the sky almost dark, and I had a message from Daniel when I parked the car in the gravel driveway.

31

He'd be back in the morning, and I should call if I needed anything, if I changed my mind and wanted to stay with him and Laura.

Sitting in my car, watching the lantern move with the wind, the light casting shadows across the front of the house, I thought about it. Thought about driving straight across town and pulling out the blow-up mattress in the unused nursery. Because I could see us, the shadows of us, a decade ago, telling ghost stories on that porch with the dancing light.

Corinne and Bailey rapt with attention as Daniel told them how there was a monster in the woods—that it wasn't a thing they could see but a thing they could feel. That it took people over, made them do things. I could hear that version of me in my own head, saying he was full of shit. And Corinne tilting her head at Daniel and leaning back against the porch railing, sticking out her chest, placing her foot against a slat of wood, bending one of her long legs, and saying, *What would it make* you *do?* Always pushing us. Always pushing.

I hated that the ghosts of us lived here, always. But Laura was almost due, and there wasn't a place for me there, and even though Daniel had offered, it was implied that I would say no. I had a house here, a room here, space here. I wasn't his responsibility anymore.

I pushed the front door open and heard another door catch at the other end of the house, as if I had disturbed the balance of it.

"Hello?" I called, frozen in place. "Daniel?"

Nothing but the evening wind shaking the panes of glass in a familiar rattle. A breeze, thank God.

I flipped the wall light switches as I walked toward the kitchen at the back of the house, half of them working, half not.

Daniel wasn't here. Nobody was here.

I turned the deadbolt, but the wood around it was rotted and splintered, the bolt cutting through the frame whether it was locked or not. Everything looked as I'd left it: a box on the table, a used glass in the sink, everything coated in a fine layer of dust.

*The ring.* I took the steps two at a time and went straight for the nightstand, my fingers trembling as I reached inside the ceramic bowl, frantic heartbeats until my finger brushed metal.

The ring was there. It was fine. I slid it back on my finger and ran my shaking hand through my hair. *Everything's fine. Breathe.*

The bed was still bare, but the sheets were folded and stacked on top, the way Daniel used to leave them when he started taking over for the things Mom couldn't do. I moved the shoe boxes back to the closet and the rug back under the legs of the bed. I centered the jewelry box under the mirror, a dust-free square where it had sat for the last year, at least. Everything resettling. Realigning.

I felt the memories doing the same. Falling back into place. The investigation. All I'd left behind, neatly boxed away for ten years.

I looked around my room and saw the rectangles of discolored paint. I closed my eyes and saw the pictures that had hung in each spot.

My stomach churned, unsettled. Corinne had been in every one.

*A coincidence,* I thought. Corinne was so wrapped up in my childhood, I could probably find her shadow in anything here if I went looking for it.

I needed to find out what thought had surged and then faltered, driving Dad to a sheet of paper and an envelope with my name. What memory had been flickering from the dying portion of his brain, begging for attention before it faded away for good. Corinne. *Alive.* But when? I had to find out.

Everything was stuck here. Waiting for someone to step in and reorder the evidence, the stories, the events—until they came together in a way that made sense.

In that way, Dad was right. About time. About the past being alive.

I walked down the wooden steps into the kitchen, the linoleum shrinking away from the corners. And imagined, for a moment,

33

catching sight of a girl with long bronze hair, her laughter echoing through the night as she skipped up the steps of the back porch—

*Tick-tock, Nic.*

I had to focus, make sense of this house, and get out. Before the past started creeping out from the walls, whispering from the grates. Before it unpacked itself from that box, layer after layer, all the way back to the start.

# PART 2
*Going Back*

It is quite true what philosophy says; that life must be understood backwards.

—SØREN KIERKEGAARD

*Two Weeks Later*

# DAY 15

**I**f I kept my eyes closed, I could almost imagine that we were driving back to Philadelphia. Everett in the driver's seat and the backseat full of luggage and Cooley Ridge fading away in the rearview mirror—no missing girls; no unmarked cars circling town; nothing at all to fear.

"You okay?" he asked.

*Just one more moment.* I wanted more time. Another minute to pretend this wasn't happening.

Not here in Cooley Ridge. Not again.

Not another girl fading away in these woods in the middle of the night, disappearing without a trace. Not another missing poster stapled to the trees, hung in the storefront windows—another innocent face, asking to be found. *Please, not like this.*

But the back of my neck prickled as the world shifted into focus, and there she was, inescapable, her huge blue eyes staring out from under the red MISSING letters of the poster on the telephone pole: Annaleise Carter. Gone.

"Nic?" Everett said. God, a few days in this place, and apparently, he's calling me Nic, too. It got its claws in him already.

"Yeah," I said, still looking out the window.

My eyes caught hers again at the next stoplight, her face under the white painted letters of Julie's Boutique, right next to a display of handmade jewelry and a green silk scarf. Annaleise Carter, whose property backed to my own, who had been dating my ex-boyfriend the night she disappeared. Annaleise Carter, gone and missing for two weeks.

"Hey." Everett's hand hovered over my shoulder before he pressed down and squeezed. "You with me?"

"Sorry, I'm fine." I turned toward Everett, but I felt her gaze on the back of my neck, like she was trying to tell me something. *Look. Look closer. Do you see?*

"I'm not leaving until I know you're okay." His hand rested on my shoulder, his silver watch—steel, he'd told me—peeking out from his long-sleeved button-down. How was he not sweltering?

"I thought that was the purpose of the appointment." I raised the paper prescription bag at Everett. "I'll take two and call you in the morning." I mustered a smile, but his expression tightened as his eyes settled on my bare finger. I dropped my hand back to my lap. "I'll find the ring," I said.

"I'm not worried about the ring. I'm worried about *you.*"

Maybe he was talking about the way I looked: hair thrown back in a messy ponytail; shorts that had fit two weeks ago but were now hanging off my hip bones; an old T-shirt I'd found in my closet where it had been hanging for the last ten years. Meanwhile, his hair was cut and styled, and he was dressed for work like this was all part of the agenda: *Take Nicolette to the doctor because she hasn't been sleeping; follow up on paperwork re: future father-in-law; take cab to airport and prepare for trial.*

"Everett, honestly, I'm fine."

He reached over and brushed back the wisps of hair that had escaped my ponytail. "Really?" he said.

"Yes, really." My eyes burned as they drifted back to Annaleise's picture. Only a sane person would realize how close he or she was to the edge. Not like my dad, who didn't know when he was teetering too close to that chasm, didn't seem to notice the change in velocity as he went tumbling into the abyss.

But I knew. I knew how close we all were to that edge. And if I knew, then I was fine. Those were the basic rules of holding one's shit together, according to Tyler.

"Nicolette, I don't want to leave you here alone." A car behind us laid on the horn, and Everett jumped, revving the motor of my car as he sped through the green light.

I stared at the side of his face, watched the road blur past behind him. "I'm not alone. My brother's here."

Everett sighed, and I could hear the argument in his silence.

Missing girls had a way of working their way into someone's head. You couldn't help but see them in everyone—how temporary and fragile we might be. One moment here, and the next, nothing more than a photo staring from a storefront window.

It was a feeling that settled in your ribs and slowly gnawed at you from the inside—the irrational fear that people were slipping away right before your eyes. I felt it, lingering just under the surface, in the haunting monotone of Tyler's voicemail recording, and in Daniel's increasingly unreadable expression. I felt it with greater urgency every time I walked into Grand Pines. Two weeks back in Cooley Ridge and everyone in danger of disappearing.

Everett pulled into the gravel driveway, parked, and got out of the car without speaking. He was staring at the front of the house, like I'd done when I first arrived home.

"I need to get my dad out of Grand Pines," I said, walking toward him. Everett had stopped the cops from questioning Dad for the time being, but I knew it was only a matter of time before his ramblings about "that girl" earned him another visit from detectives desperate for a lead.

Everett put a hand around my waist as we walked inside. I felt him grasping the loose fabric of my shirt between his fingers. "You need to take care of yourself right now. The doctor said—"

"The doctor said there's nothing *wrong* with me."

Everett had insisted on coming into the exam room with me. First the doctor asked about my family history, which was depressing but unrelated. Then came the *When did it start* question, and Everett answering about Annaleise—my *neighbor*—who went missing, and the doctor nodding like he understood. *Stress. Fear. Either. Both.* He scribbled a prescription for some anti-anxiety medicine and a sleeping aid and issued a warning about my mind getting duller, slower, if I didn't start getting some more sleep. And the elevated risk for daytime blackouts the longer this went on, which was how Everett ended up with my keys.

*You try sleeping,* I wanted to tell the doctor. *You try sleeping when there's another missing girl and the police are trying to question your father, whether he's in his right mind or not. You try sleeping when you know someone has been in your house.* As if everything would settle down if I could just *relax.*

Everett was still holding me like I might float off into the atmosphere otherwise. "Come home with me," he said. But where was home, really?

"I can't. My dad—"

"I'll take care of it."

I knew he would. It was why he was here. "The house," I said, gesturing to the broken-down boxes in the corners, the back door that needed fixing, all the items on my list that I hadn't tackled.

He shook his head. "I'll pay to have someone help finish up. Come on, you don't need to be here."

But I shook my head again. It wasn't the organizing, or the fixing, or the cleaning. Not anymore. "I can't just leave. Not in the middle of this." *This* being the wide eyes of the girl in the poster, watching us all, on every telephone pole, in every store window. *This* being the investigation, just beginning. *This* being the darkest parts of my family about to be broken open yet again.

Everett sighed. "You called me for advice, and here it is: It's not safe for you here. This place, the cops are circling it like goddamn vultures, grasping anything they can. They're interviewing people without cause. It doesn't make sense, but it doesn't change the fact that it's happening."

Everett didn't get why, but I did: Annaleise had sent a text to Officer Stewart's personal cell the night before she disappeared, asking if he could answer some questions about the Corinne Prescott case. His return call the next day went straight to voicemail. By then she was already gone.

The cops were all from around here, had been here ten years ago when Corinne disappeared. Or they'd heard the stories through the years, over drinks at the bar. Now there were two girls, barely adults, disappearing without a trace from the same town. And the last-known words from Annaleise were about Corinne Prescott.

It made perfect sense if you came from a place like Cooley Ridge.

If the entirety of Corinne's official investigation existed inside that single box I pictured at the police station, I'd imagine this was all the evidence you would see: one pregnancy test, stuffed into a box of candy and hidden at the bottom of the trash can; one ring with remnants of blood pulled from the caverns; cassette tapes with hours of interview reports to sort through—facts and lies and half-truths, wound up in a spool; Corinne's phone records; and names. Names scrawled on ripped-up pieces of paper, enough pieces to pad the entire box, like stuffing.

Until recently, I imagined that this box was taped up and hidden in a corner, behind other, newer boxes. But now there's the feeling that all it would take is a simple nudge for it to topple over, and the lid to fall free, and the names to scatter across the dusty floor. The box is exactly like it is in Cooley Ridge. The past, boxed up and stacked out of sight. But never too far away.

Open the top because Annaleise mentioned Corinne's name and disappeared. Close your eyes and reach your hand inside. Pull out a name.

That's how it works here.

That's what's happening.

Yes, I had called Everett for advice. For my *dad*. He could've told me what to do about the cops who were ambushing my senile father at his nursing home, but he hopped a plane three days ago and paid a ridiculous amount of cab fare and set up his own base of operations in the dining room. He showed up at this house and stood on the front porch because he said I'd scared him, and I loved him for it. I loved that he came. But I couldn't dig through our history with him here. Couldn't figure out what the hell had happened to Annaleise without dragging him into it.

My advice to him: *Leave. Leave before we pull you down with us.*

"It's my family," I said.

"I don't want you staying here," he whispered, pointing to the backyard that stretched as far as we could see, disappearing into the trees. "A girl went missing from right there."

"I'll take that prescription, and I'll try to sleep more, I promise. But I have to stay."

He kissed my forehead and mumbled into my hair, "I don't know why you're doing this."

Wasn't it obvious? She was everywhere I looked. On every telephone pole. In every store window. The same places I'd hung posters of Corinne, stapling them with a knot in my stomach, handing them out faster and faster, as if my speed could somehow change the outcome.

Annaleise on those posters now, with her huge, open eyes, telling me to open mine. Everywhere I looked, there she was. *Look. Look. Keep your eyes open.*

———

THE TAXI COMPANY SAID a car would arrive in twenty minutes, but I guessed it would be more like forty. Everett was leaning against the laundry room doorjamb, watching me dump his clothes from the dryer into the warped plastic bin with half a smile on his face. "You don't have to do that, Nicolette."

I cleared my throat and balanced the laundry basket on my hip. "I want to," I said. I wanted to fold his clothes and pack them up and kiss him goodbye. I wanted him to get home and open his suitcase and think of me. But I also just wanted him to go.

He watched me fold his clothes into perfect squares on the dining room table. And then he watched me stack them in his suitcase, as if performing a delicate surgery. "See if you can break your lease," he said, striding toward me, wrapping his arms around my waist as I folded his last shirt. He brushed my ponytail to the side and put his lips against my neck. "I want you living with me as soon as you're back."

I nodded and kept my arms moving. It should be easy for me to say, *Yes, of course, yes.* It should be easy for me to envision: me, with my clothes taking up half his closet; us, cooking together in his kitchen, curled up on his couch with the red throw blanket over my legs because he kept the temperature about five degrees cooler than I liked it. Him, talking about court. And me, talking about my students as I poured two glasses of wine.

"What's the matter?" Everett asked.

"Nothing. Just thinking of everything I need to do here first."

"Do you need anything?" he asked, stepping back. He cleared his throat, tried to make his voice seem natural. "Money?"

I flinched. He'd never offered me money. We'd never even talked about money. He had it and I didn't, which meant we circled the topic like a fire that could quickly burn out of control and consume us both. It was why I never brought up the wedding, because then he'd have to mention the prenup that I knew his dad would demand I sign, and I would, but there it would be, out in the open, ready to burn. "No, I don't need your money," I said.

"That's not what I— Nicolette, I just meant I can help. Please let me help."

He'd told me, back when we first met, that I was the embodiment of everything he wished he could be. Setting out in a car by myself, working my way through school, self-made.

But as I'd told him back then, you have to come from nothing to have that chance. You have to pay your debts.

"Yeah, well, I have ten years' worth of loans," I'd said.

Sometimes I wondered if, when we got married, he would pay them off. If that would make me a different person. If he'd like me quite as much.

"Everett, thank you, but money isn't going to help." I zipped up his suitcase and leaned it against the wall.

I heard a car turn off the road in the distance. "Your cab's here," I whispered, bringing my arms around his waist and resting my head against his chest again.

"Think about it?" he asked, pulling back. I wasn't sure which he was referring to—moving in with him or taking his money—and I hated that he was bringing both up right *now*. That it took this— seeing me here, hovering near some indefinable edge—that made him seem to want me more.

"Okay," I said, and from the look on his face, I wondered if I had just unintentionally agreed to something.

"I wish I could stay longer," he said, pulling me into a kiss. "But I'm glad I got to meet your family."

I laughed. "Yeah, good thing."

"I'm serious," he said. Then, lower, "They're good people."

"Yeah," I whispered, and I let him pull me in so tight I'd probably have indentations from the lines of his collar on my cheek. "So are you," I said as he released me.

He dragged his hands down my arms as he backed away and lifted my left hand to his face. "I'll file a claim tomorrow."

"It might still turn up." I cringed. "It's probably in one of those half-packed boxes. I'll look again."

"Let me know if you find it," he said, pulling his suitcase behind him toward the front door. "And Nicolette?" My heart stopped, from the way he was looking at me. "If you're not home by next weekend, I'm coming back for you."

———

AFTER WATCHING HIS CAB drive off, I shut the door behind me, turned the lock, and twisted the knob to double-check. I circled the house, checking them all, closing the windows that Everett had insisted on opening, and wedging the kitchen chair under the handle of the back door with the broken lock. Everything felt slow and labored, even my breathing. It was this heat. The damn air-conditioning unit that still wasn't fixed. I dragged myself to the kitchen—I needed a drink. Something cold. Caffeinated. I bent over and stuck my head in the fridge, debating my choices.

Water. Gatorade. Cans of soda. I sank to my knees in front of the open door, breathing in the cold air—*wake up, Nic*—as the electricity hummed in my ear and the fridge light illuminated the space around me.

There was a sudden, high-pitched cry as the chair scraped against the floor. The back door swung open as I spun around, my back to the open refrigerator, my hands grasping for anything I could use to defend myself.

Tyler stood in the open doorway, his arms trembling, covered in sweat and dirt and something that smelled like earth and pollen. His body shook like he was wound tight with adrenaline and was fighting to keep himself still. He frowned at the chair, toppled on its side, and then scanned the room behind me.

"Tyler? What are you doing?" His brown work boots were coated in a thick layer of mud, and he braced an arm against the doorframe. I pulled myself upright and shut the fridge, and the house settled into an uncomfortable silence. "Tyler? What's going on? Say something."

"Is anyone here?" he asked, and I knew he didn't mean just *anyone*.

"He left," I said. His arms were still shaking. "It's just me."

He was not okay. This was Tyler at fifteen when we all went to the service for his brother, and the folded American flag was placed on his mother's lap, and he appeared to be sitting perfectly still, but if you looked closer, you could see his entire body was trembling. I was so sure he was on the edge of cracking into a thousand pieces, and all the strangers pushing closer and closer to him were making it worse. This was Tyler at seventeen on the day we got together for real, when I scraped my car door against his, and at first he looked so tense, all coiled-up adrenaline, before he noticed me holding my breath, waiting for his reaction. "Just a piece of metal," he'd said.

"It's just us," I whispered.

He took a step inside, and pieces of caked dirt settled on the linoleum floor. "I'm sorry," he mumbled, seeing what he was doing to the floor.

"Where have you been?" I asked.

But he was focused on his shoes and the mud on the floor. I was scared he was going to leave. That he'd leave and disappear and I'd never see him again.

"Here," I said, kneeling in front of him, prying at the muddy laces of his work boots. His breathing was ragged, and up close, I could see a fine yellow powder clinging to his pants. I concentrated on keeping my hands steady, trying to settle the growing unease. *Tyler. This was just* Tyler. I had one shoe unknotted when my phone on the table rang, making us both jump. Tyler watched me move across the room while he took off his other boot.

"It's my brother," I said, frowning at the phone display. Tyler's face mirrored mine. I held the phone to my ear.

"Nic," Daniel said before I'd even said hello. "Tell me where you are."

"I'm home, Daniel."

"Are you with Everett?" he asked, and I could hear wind through the phone. He was moving. Fast.

"No," I said. "He left. Tyler's here." I looked over at Tyler, who had taken another step closer. He was halfway across the room, his head tilted to the side, like he was trying to hear the conversation.

"Listen to me," Daniel said as an engine came to life in the background. "Get out."

My stomach dropped, and I looked at Tyler's boots once more. "Get out. *Now.*"

My hand dropped to my side. "Tyler?" I asked as the phone slipped from my hand, cracked as it made contact with the floor. *Pollen,* I thought. *Earth.*

"What? What did he say?" Tyler said, his words quiet and laced with panic.

I looked at his hands, at the dirt caked under the nails, at the thin line of dried blood running between his thumb and pointer finger.

"Tyler," I said. "What did you do?"

He leaned against a chair, his fingers pressing into the wood. "I'm running out of time, Nic."

And then I heard it—faint and far away—the high-pitched call of a siren.

*Tick-tock, Nic.*

"What happened?" I asked.

He squeezed his eyes shut, and a slow tremor made its way through his body. "They found a body at Johnson Farm."

The field of sunflowers. *Pollen. Earth.*

The siren, growing insistent.

Tyler, coming closer.

And time standing perfectly, painfully still.

It's just a thing we created. A measure of distance. A way to understand. A way to explain things. It can weave around and show you things if you let it.

*Let it.*

*The Day Before*

# DAY 14

**T**ime had gotten away from me. I'd been searching through the boxes of Dad's old books and teaching material while waiting for Everett to fall asleep, pulling scraps of paper from between the pages, checking the margins for comments. It must've been well after midnight, and I wasn't finding anything meaningful. Simpler and safer to trash it all. I stacked the boxes out in the hall to bring down to the garage in the morning.

The sound of rustling sheets carried through the open doorway, and I silently padded back to my bedroom in bare feet. Everett was sprawled across the middle of my bed, the yellow comforter discarded and crumpled on the floor beside him. He wasn't the deepest sleeper, but now his breathing was slow and measured. I placed my hand on his shoulder, and his back rose and fell in the same steady rhythm.

The clock on the nightstand said 3:04. Perfect. This was the empty gap—that time between when everyone went to sleep, when the last stragglers headed home from Kelly's Pub, and the earliest risers were up, when the newspaper delivery began. The world was silent and waiting.

I left the room, stepping over the piece of flooring that squeaked, tiptoeing across the wooden floor to my parents' old room, to the bedroom closet with the worn-out slippers and ratty shoes and work clothes that my dad would never need again. I slid my hand inside one slipper, where I'd hidden the key until I could check— until I could be sure—what it was for. I felt the imprint of a foot in the matted fake fur. The key was cold in my grasp, and in the dark, I couldn't see the intricate patterns on the rectangular metal key chain. But I could feel them, infinitely swirling, closing in on one another, as I tightened my fist around it. *Tick-tock, Nic.*

My sneakers waited beside the back door, and I felt a gust of chilled air brush against my arms. Everett must have opened the downstairs windows again.

I hopped on the counter and pushed the windows back down, flipping the locks.

And then I was gone.

———

THESE WOODS ARE MINE.

These were the woods I grew up with. They stretched from my home and wove through all of town, connecting everything, all the way down to the river and out to the caverns. It had been years, but if I stopped thinking so much and moved by heart, I could follow countless paths through them, day or night. They were mine, and I was theirs, and I shouldn't have to remind myself of it. But now there were too many unknowns. The scurrying of animals in the night, something so unsettling about the nocturnal, about things that needed the dark to survive. Things breathing and growing and dying. Everything in perpetual motion.

*These woods are mine.*

I ran my fingers along the tree trunks as I walked, as I repeated the words to myself. These were the woods I used to sneak through in the middle of the night to see Tyler, who'd park his truck in the lot of the convenience store and meet me halfway, at a clearing my brother showed me when I was younger. Daniel and I once built a fort there out of tree branches and lined the perimeter with thorny vines—*to keep the monster out,* he had said. The storm that had swept through when I was in middle school destroyed the fort, and Daniel was too old to care by that point, so the clearing became mine and mine alone.

But these were also the woods where Annaleise was last seen. These were the woods we searched ten years ago for Corinne. The woods we searched again last week. I was out here alone, in that empty gap of time when only the nocturnal and people craving the darkness roamed.

My flashlight skimmed over the shadows, the branches hanging low and the roots reaching up from the earth and something small and fast darting away as I approached. I stopped worrying so much about staying quiet, my footsteps growing louder as I moved faster.

I broke through the tree line, now firmly on Carter property. The studio, where Annaleise had been living while applying to grad school for the last year, was dark and set back from the main house. Neither was particularly large, but they'd been kept up well enough, if you didn't count the yard or the shingles. The main house had the outside lights on, as if they were expecting Annaleise to return at any moment.

Her place was once a stand-alone garage, before her father renovated it into an art studio years earlier—*My daughter has so much promise,* he'd told my dad. But that was before he lost his job—*downsizing,* he'd said, sitting on the back porch with my dad, drinks in hand. Before the divorce—*She gets the goddamn house; been in my family and she gets the goddamn house.* Before he left for a job in either Minnesota or Mississippi, I could never remember. Back when promise was a thing that felt real.

We'd almost done the same thing to our garage for Daniel, years earlier. Finding a place to live in Cooley Ridge wasn't as easy as it was up north—there's not a constant inventory of apartments turning over, and most rentals are occupied for years at a time. There were apartments over the stores on the main drag, and basements to rent out, and trailers you could lease and park on other people's land for a price. So when Daniel decided to stay, he thought converting the garage would be the cheapest option. Ellison Construction—Tyler's father's company—was going to do the job, but my dad and Daniel would help out to defray some of the cost.

They built a carport between the garage and the house before starting, and they got as far as laying a new concrete layer over the unfinished garage floor, leaving space for the pipes. But they never got to the insulation or the plumbing. Corinne disappeared, and the world halted. Daniel changed his mind about how to spend that money, opting to live with Dad until years later, when he purchased his own place with Laura.

I was guessing Annaleise knew better than to put down permanent roots in Cooley Ridge. She left once, after all. She left and came back, and I bet she and Cooley Ridge didn't know what to do with each other anymore. This apartment was hers now, but next it could belong to her brother, who was in high school. *Just for now,* I could imagine her saying any time it came up. *Just until the right opportunity comes along. Just until I find my way.*

A driveway snaked from the road to the side wall, from when it was a garage. Annaleise's car and two others were lined up under the extra-wide carport beside the main house.

I kept my flashlight off as I ran the remaining distance to her back door, the teeth of the key cutting into my palm. I took a breath and guided the key into the lock, each groove falling into place. My palm shook against the door as I turned the lock, the bolt sliding effortlessly open.

My whole body tingled with anxiety when I stepped inside. *I shouldn't be here.*

I turned the flashlight back on, keeping it low, away from the windows. The place looked a little like my apartment, with half-walls to partition the rooms but no doors. There was a queen bed with a white duvet in front of me, and an art desk pushed against the other wall, the supplies organized in containers, lined up in a perfectly straight row.

Through the partition, I saw a couch across from a television attached to the wall. The whole place was sparsely furnished but expertly done. Everything was understated and minimalistic except the walls themselves. They were covered in art, in sketches, but even those looked like they were done in pencil or charcoal, the whole place completely devoid of color.

I ran the flashlight from picture to picture. Framed sketches—Annaleise's, I assumed—though some of them appeared to be replicas of famous pictures. Marilyn Monroe, looking down and off to the side, standing against a brick wall. A little girl, her scraggly hair blowing across her face. I had seen this somewhere, but I couldn't place it. And there were some I didn't recognize at all. Didn't know whether they were copies or originals created by Annaleise.

Oh, but there was a theme: Girls, all alone, all of them. Girls looking exposed and sad and full of some longing. Girls passed over, passed by, staring out from the walls: *Look. Look at us.*

Girls, like Annaleise on the telephone poles, silent and silenced.

Annaleise had gone to some well-known art school, which wasn't surprising. Back in middle school she'd won a statewide photography competition, and that had made the local news. She looked the part—the girl on the other side of the camera. Timid and fine-boned, with too-wide eyes, every move tentative, careful, deliberate. The one creating, seeing, but never seen. The opposite of Corinne.

I knew the cops had been here, but the place looked completely undisturbed.

There obviously hadn't been a struggle in the apartment. Besides, we know she went out walking. If she had been hurt, it hadn't happened here. Her purse was gone, but that could've been because she had it with her when she left. Her car was here. That was the Big Sign. Who leaves without her car? They hadn't found her cell phone, so the general consensus was that it was with her, wherever that was. And it was powered off, since they hadn't been able to trace it.

The cops had been through here, and probably her parents, though I hadn't heard a thing about any evidence or clues. But this key was something real and solid and gut-twisting. This key was dangerous.

I went through her desk. Her closet. Her bathroom cabinets. Even the garbage can, remembering the pregnancy test they'd found at Corinne's, stuffed inside the box of Skittles.

There was nothing here. A tissue, an empty stick of deodorant, the wrapper from a bar of soap. Though it was possible that someone had swept through here before the cops, cleaning up after her, saving her the embarrassment, letting her keep the parts of her that should've remained hidden.

I checked her dresser drawers. Everything neatly folded and everything hers. No men's clothes. No spare toothbrush beside the sink. No notes on her desk. Nothing at all there except the sleek laptop next to a bundle of wires. I chewed the side of my thumb. They'd probably already been through it. I could have it back before anyone noticed. *I could.*

I grabbed it before I could change my mind.

I checked under her bed on the way out. There was a

suitcase—more potential evidence that she hadn't gone on a trip. And beside that, a white box that could hold a large photo album. I placed the laptop on the hard floor and slid the box out from under the bed. Lifting the top, I saw that it held the sketches that hadn't made it onto the wall.

I flipped through them rapidly, the flashlight cold and metallic between my teeth, wondering if she'd stuffed anything else amid the drawings. Something the cops missed, something she'd tried to keep hidden. But no, only art. More sad girls. Eyes open, eyes closed, all forlorn, somehow. I had to squint to see their faces, their outlines so faint. Drafts, maybe. Sketches to darken and shade and bring depth to later. All blurring together as I turned them over faster and faster.

But then I stopped, flipped back a few pictures. I took the flashlight from my mouth, ran the light over the familiar angles of the face, the curve of her smile, the freckle at the corner of her right eye. The bow shape of her mouth and the flowing peasant dress that hit just above her knees—

*Corinne.*

It was a sketch of Corinne. No, it was a goddamn replica of a picture that had hung in my room. We had been in a field of sunflowers. Johnson Farm. It was only a few towns away, practically a tourist attraction—people driving from hours away to take pictures there. It was Bailey's favorite shoot location.

This picture had been taken with Bailey's camera the summer before senior year. We'd taken at least a hundred shots that day, posing beside each other for so long that we forgot we were posing. Bailey liked to make us spin as fast as we could, and she'd set the camera for long exposure, and after she got the film developed, we'd look like haunting, blurred images. Like ghosts.

I never picked those pictures to keep—I hated how you couldn't tell us apart when we were spinning. I took the ones with us smiling, frozen-faced and happy, and I hung them on my walls, like proof.

I had been in this picture, too. Corinne's eyes were closed, and she had a small smile, caught between moments. She'd been telling us a story that I could no longer remember, her hand brushing the top of a waist-high sunflower. I'd stood beside her, watching her. Laughing.

This was my favorite picture of us. But Annaleise had sketched only Corinne. She'd left me behind when she transferred Corinne, and filled the white space I'd occupied with sunflowers. I was gone, removed from the memory. An unnecessary complication, easily excised. Without me in it, Corinne looked lonely and sad, like every other girl in this box.

I moved the page aside, and there was another behind it. Another sketch of one of my pictures, this time of Corinne and Bailey and me. Again, the sketch was just Corinne, staring forlornly to the side. We'd both been looking at Bailey in the picture, at her twirling with her head back and her white skirt flying up around her dark legs. Now it was Corinne alone in a field of sunflowers.

How the hell did Annaleise get my pictures? She must've been in my house. She must've been in my *room*. Who was this girl I'd lived beside for years?

Annaleise was five years younger, and we barely noticed her back then. Noticed her even less because she was a quiet kid, and the times I remembered her, she'd been in that awkward phase between kid and adolescent, skinny and unsure of herself.

This was all I knew of her: Her parents sent her over with food for a solid three months after my mother died, and she never seemed to know what to say when she brought it over, so she never said anything at all; she didn't have a lot of friends, I didn't think, because any time I remembered seeing her, she'd been alone; she won that photography contest, but I'd known about it only because Bailey had entered it, too; and she liked strawberry ice cream. Or she liked it enough to be eating it at the county fair ten years ago.

She'd been standing by herself near the entrance as I ran from the Ferris wheel; I hadn't seen her at first. I'd seen only Tyler, waiting for me. It wasn't until Daniel hit me so hard that I dropped to my side, until I untwisted my arm and turned my head away and saw her face frozen behind a melting scoop of strawberry ice cream, her tongue still out, halfway up the cone.

I heard a fist collide with flesh—something snap—and I didn't have to look to know exactly what it was. Annaleise's ice cream scoop fell off the cone, and she ran out the front entrance. I turned my head the other way in time to see the drops of blood collecting on the ground as Daniel bent over, his hands cupped over his nose, and Tyler cursing to himself, shaking out his hand.

I slid the box back under the bed. But I folded the sketches of Corinne and tucked them inside the laptop. They were almost mine, anyway.

———

"NICOLETTE?" EVERETT WAS SITTING on the side of my bed this morning as I stared at the empty space where the pictures once hung on my walls. "What are you doing?"

"Just thinking." I opened the top drawer and pulled out a change of clothes. I'd hidden the laptop and the sketches in my dad's closet, along with that damn key, before sneaking back into bed. But his eyes had opened as I slid under the sheets, and I'd felt him staring at the side of my face as I rolled over.

"Did you sleep at all? I woke up, and you weren't here."

"A little. I couldn't get to sleep for a while, so I did some more packing." I walked into the bathroom and turned on the shower, hoping Everett would drop it.

"I heard you," he said. He was standing in the doorway, watching me squeeze toothpaste on my toothbrush.

I started brushing my teeth and raised my eyebrows at him, buying myself some time.

"I heard you come in. What were you doing out there?" He gestured through the walls to the woods. Everett grew up in a city where a girl wandering the streets at night wasn't safe. Where woods were unfamiliar or dangerous or an adventure to be shared with friends and a tent and a six-pack of lukewarm beer.

I spat into the sink and said, "Just taking a walk. Clearing my mind."

I felt him in the room, taking up space, and I held my breath. He knew how to get to the truth. It was his goddamn job. If he wanted, he could push from every different angle until I cracked in half. He was very good at what he did.

But he let it drop. "I need to spend the morning at the library," he said. "Can I take the car?" Any time he needed the Internet, he had to go there. This house didn't even have a phone line.

"No problem. I'll drop you off." I watched the water circling the sink drain, my mind on the other side of the trees, searching through Annaleise's drawings.

Everett was beside me then, and he pulled my chin so I was facing him, the toothbrush sticking out of my mouth. I jerked back. "What?" I said.

His hand dropped, but his gaze held, the corners of his mouth tipping down. "You look exhausted," he said. "Your eyes are all bloodshot."

I looked away, put the toothbrush down, and started stripping for the shower, hoping he'd focus on something else.

"You know, you can take something to help. To sleep. We'll go to the doctor tomorrow."

In charge. Taking over. Making the plan. Averting the crisis.

The steam slowly began to fill the room. Even as he backed away, he was looking into my eyes.

———

I PULLED THE CAR up to the library entrance, which looked like a library only if you knew what you were looking for. It was once a Victorian home, two stories with bay windows and a wraparound porch. It had been partially renovated—walls knocked down to open up the spaces—but the creaky stairs and heavy banister and single bathrooms remained.

"How long do you need?" I asked.

"Sorry, I'll probably be most of the day. We go to trial next week."

"Didn't take the plea?"

He cut his eyes to me. "You're not supposed to know about that."

I'm never supposed to know. Didn't stop me from asking, though. A few nights before I left for here, I was trying to finish all the school counselor documentation for the end of the year. I'd sat across from Everett at the table while he worked, the contents of his briefcase strewn across the entire tabletop. I'd run my fingers across his papers, the highlighted lines, the notes in the margins. "Parlito case?" I'd asked. There was a phone trace he was trying to get thrown out. And if I was reading it right, there was a proposed plea bargain.

He had grinned and stacked the papers back up. Reached under the table, at my legs resting on the chair beside him, and squeezed my calf. I ask every time. It's a game at this point. He never tells. Truth is, I love that he doesn't. That he is both good at what he does and good down to the core.

"Call me when you're ready," I said, squinting from the glare through the windshield.

He grabbed my elbow before opening his car door. "Make an appointment to see a doctor, Nicolette."

———

SOMETIMES, WHEN I'M NOT focused, I'll end up someplace I had no intention of going. Like muscle memory. Head to the store but end up at school. Walk to the bank, end up at the subway. Drive to Daniel's but find myself in front of Corinne's old place. Which must've been what just happened, and how I ended up parked on the corner by Kelly's Pub even though I had every intention of heading home.

My eyes drifted over the storefront, over the awning, to the window a floor up with the air-conditioning unit hanging over the edge. The blinds were open.

I needed to talk to him about that key, anyway. And he wasn't answering my calls—not that I really blamed him.

I pushed through the entrance into the vestibule area of Kelly's Pub and cringed as the bell chimed overhead. At least at night, there was too much noise to notice. I could smell smoke and grease and something stale underneath as I passed the open doorway inside on the way to the narrow stairwell. "He's not here!" someone called, and the sound of laughter drifted out from the darkened room.

I took the steps two at a time to the alcove with a door on either side, facing the one on the right. I knocked rapidly three times, waited, and tried again, pressing my ear to the door. Then I called from my cell, my ear still pressed to the door, and heard the periodic vibration of his phone from somewhere inside, until the voicemail picked up: *Hey, this is Tyler. Leave a message.* Maybe he was in the shower. I tried to listen for the sound of water in pipes or any movement inside. I called again—the vibration, the voicemail, and nothing else.

Another round of laughter from downstairs. I checked the time on my phone: one P.M. on a Sunday. The new five P.M. I used to find my dad here during summer break. But not this early. Never this early.

I turned to go, but the creeping feeling that I was being watched started at the back of my neck, worked its way down my spine. The stairwell was empty. The door at the bottom was closed. I listened for movement somewhere nearby. A shuffling in the walls. A breath in the vents. There was a shadow in the tiny strip of light escaping from the apartment door across the hall, but it hadn't moved. I stepped closer, keeping my movement as quiet as possible.

Could be the angle—sunlight and furniture—but . . . I stared at the peephole, leaning closer, my own face distorting in the reflection. Like a fun-house mirror, too-big eyes and too-small mouth and everything elongated and sickly.

I knocked once, softly, but the shadow didn't move. The tiny hairs on the back of my neck stood on end. I closed my eyes, counted to ten. This was what happened during an investigation. You felt eyes everywhere. You became suspicious of everyone. Everything fell apart if you didn't hold yourself together. *Hold it together.*

I jogged back downstairs, my footsteps echoing in the hollow underneath the steps, and walked through the bar entrance. A crowd of faces I vaguely recognized glanced in my direction, and one man leaned over to say something to another. I watched his lips move—*That's Patrick Farrell's daughter*—and the other man tilted a bottle of beer to his lips.

I tried to catch the bartender's eye, but either he didn't see me or he didn't care. Probably the latter. I knocked on the bar top. "Jackson," I said, trying to keep my voice low.

He came closer, the muscles and sinew of his forearm straining as he cleaned and stacked the dishes behind the bar, before fixing his bloodshot green eyes on me. "Yes, Nic?"

"Who lives in the other apartment upstairs?" I asked. "Across from Tyler?"

The skin at the corners of his eyes tightened as he looked me over, and he rubbed a tan hand over the dark scruff on his face. "I do. Why?"

I shook my head. "No reason." I had to get home. Had to check the laptop. Had to get it back inside Annaleise's place before anyone went looking for it.

He narrowed his eyes as he gave my entire body a quick skim. "Sit down, Nic," he said. "You look like you could use it." Jackson poured a shot into a glass with lip smudge marks from the last customer visible on the rim. "Vodka, right? On the house."

My stomach churned, and I pushed it back in his direction across the sticky surface. "I gotta go."

He grabbed my wrist, tried to hide the grip under a playful smile. "There's a blue car," he said, facing away from everyone. "I've seen it pass three times in the last half hour. You're not the only one looking for Tyler. He's been gone all weekend."

*Gone all weekend.* Except his phone was here. "I was just in the area," I said.

"Sure you were."

I wondered if Jackson knew anything more, but his face gave nothing away. He tilted his head, his fingers circling my wrist.

A man at the far end of the bar raised his glass—a friend of my dad's, or at least someone he used to drink here with. He had a sprinkling of gray hair and cheeks that burned bright red like apples. "Regards to your father, hon. Are you okay?" His eyes slid to Jackson's hand, then back to me.

"Yes. I'm fine," I said, pulling my arm away.

Jackson frowned, downed the shot, and slammed it back on the counter. "Something's about to happen, Nic. You can feel that, right?"

Like static in the air. A net closing, a car circling. Two weeks of digging into the past, and all the lies were rising to the surface. Annaleise goes missing and the box of Corinne's evidence is shaken up, tipped over. All the names fall out again.

I was at the front door when I saw it. The blue sedan, tinted windows, rolling slowly down the block. I waited for it to pass before walking to my car.

———

ANNALEISE'S LAPTOP HAD NO password protection, which I found slightly odd, but maybe not unexpected if she lived by herself in the middle of nowhere. Or maybe the police had hacked in to it, leaving it unsecured. I scanned through the folders of college projects and grad school applications, sorting by date last modified to see if there was anything new or potentially relevant. Then I did the same with her pictures.

The photos weren't sorted by anything other than date, time-stamped from as long as five years ago to as recent as three weeks ago. I lingered on one of Tyler in his truck, his mouth slightly open, his hand slightly raised: *Smile, she says. He puts a hand up to wave or to block her shot.* A frozen moment. A hundred different possibilities existing all at once. And most recently, a few shots from this year's fair. The Ferris wheel looming, empty carts, lights glowing in the dusk. A child eating cotton candy, his mouth sticky with pink sugar, the wisps of cotton melting as soon as they touched his lips. Vendors reaching with change or hot dogs, their fingers starting to unfurl, and the people on the other side looking toward their children, or over their shoulders, already half turned away.

I could picture Annaleise standing there, like when she was a kid. A bystander to the story, watching other lives play out. I closed the images and quickly scanned the files and saw the discrepancy. The image file names were in numerical order, but there were a few jumps—a few *gaps*. The trash had been emptied. Could've been that Annaleise didn't like how they'd turned out. But I couldn't shake the feeling that someone else had been through here, checking for something he or she didn't want seen. I jotted down the date range for the missing files: a chunk from four or five months ago.

By the time Everett called to be picked up from the library, I'd searched every corner of the computer. Found the portfolios that she must've scanned in and photos of her artwork. I'd checked the list of last-visited websites, which were mostly school websites or job boards.

*Where the hell are you, Annaleise?*

I wiped down the keyboard and the rest of the laptop and slid her key into the front pocket of my shorts, the metal still hot from the sunlight. I'd store both in Dad's closet until it was night again, and the world was sleeping, and silent, and waiting.

———

I COULD PROBABLY FIT all of my conversations with Annaleise into the span of an hour, yet I had an odd intangible connection to her, tied to my sharpest memories.

Because in that box, the one I imagined in the corner of the police station hidden just out of reach, her name will forever be tied to ours. The cops had interviewed each of us, asking us about that night—about why Daniel had a broken nose, and why Tyler had scraped-up knuckles, and why I looked like someone had knocked me around. It was Tyler who remembered. "That Carter girl," he'd told the cops. "Begins with an *A*. She was there. She saw us."

I imagine they questioned her, and I imagine she confirmed our story, because they never asked again.

Annaleise had been our alibi.

# The Day Before

# DAY 13

**E**verett's here," *I said.* I stood facing the corner of the bathroom, mumbling into the phone, with the shower running in the background.

"Everett's where?" Daniel responded.

Steam filled the room, the mirror coated with a fine layer of fog. "*Here.*" I looked over my shoulder. "In my bedroom. I called him about Dad, and he showed up yesterday to help. He *is* helping."

I could hear Laura in the background—something about paint fumes and pregnancy and *open the damn window,* which made me love her a little in that moment.

"Okay, good. That's good." A pause, and I imagined him walking away from Laura. "What did you tell him?"

I cracked the door, and the steam escaped into my bedroom, wisps curling up toward the vents. Everett was still sprawled face-down on the bed; I had my money on a hangover. I eased the door shut, walked across the tiny bathroom, out through the other door to Daniel's old room.

"I told him the truth, Daniel. That the police were trying to question Dad in the disappearance of a girl ten years ago, regardless of his mental state. He marched down to the police station *and* Grand Pines, threatening legal action if it happened again."

"It's done? Is that it?"

"He needs to follow up on Monday. Get some paperwork from the doctor or something. But they'll back off until then."

"So he's staying through Monday?"

"Looks that way."

I heard Laura again: *Who's staying through Monday?* And then everything sounded muffled, like Daniel was covering the phone with his hand. He cleared his throat. "Laura wants you to bring him by for dinner tonight."

"Tell her thanks, but—"

"Great. Six o'clock, Nic."

———

I DIDN'T WAKE EVERETT until nearly noon, and only then because his work was stacked in the middle of the dining room table and I knew he had to make up for the time lost yesterday. I nudged him on the shoulder and held the over-the-counter painkillers in one hand, a glass of water in the other. He moaned as he rolled over, his gaze roaming around my room as he tried to orient himself.

"Hey there," I said, crouching beside the bed, trying to hide my smile. I liked Everett in the morning most of all, when he was lazy and malleable, when his thoughts lagged a few seconds behind; he always looked surprised while his mind caught up to what was happening. Before the caffeine hit his bloodstream and he sharpened into focus.

I liked him even better on the rare mornings he'd wake in

my apartment and sit up and fumble for the alarm on his phone, misjudging the distance to my nightstand, confused by the studio apartment and the painted furniture.

"Hey," he said, then winced. He propped himself up on his elbows and downed the painkillers before flopping back onto the mattress.

"Want to sleep it off some more?"

He peered at the clock, threw an arm over his eyes. "Ugh, no."

He'd been out for nearly twelve hours. Meanwhile, I'd been busy moving all the boxes from the dining room to the newly finished garage. Stacked them against the walls, organized them into piles: *For Dad; For Daniel; For me.*

Everything else must go. And everything else was heaped in the middle of the floor in garbage bags: cookbooks and glass figurines, magazines from a year ago and floral curtains that had seen better days, old credit card notices and pens that had run out of ink.

"Coffee's downstairs," I said. "When you're ready."

———

I POURED MYSELF A mug and stood in front of the kitchen window with the view over the back porch, straight to the woods. Everett brushed my arm, and I jumped. "Sorry, didn't mean to sneak up on you," he said, reaching around me for the coffeepot. I brought the cup to my lips, but the liquid seemed bitter and left a foul aftertaste. I dumped it in the sink as Everett filled his cup. "I'll make a new pot," I said.

The steam rose from his cup as he took a sip. "It's perfect. Nice view," he said, standing beside me.

We were down in the valley, so we didn't have much of a view other than trees, but I guessed it was better than the view in the city—buildings and sky or, from my place, the parking lot. There was also the hill that rose up behind us here, with a great view into the valley on this side, and the forest stretching to the river on the other side. I should take him there. Show him something worth seeing. *This piece of land,* I'd tell him, *it's been in my family for three generations.* It wasn't much, but Dad did have a point. Small though it was, it was ours. The Carter property jutted against ours at a stream that had dried out long ago and was now a narrow ditch that got shallower every year from leaves decaying, land eroding. The next generation would have to put up a fence or a sign if they cared to know where the line fell.

Everett didn't spend long at the window, slumping into a chair at the kitchen table and rubbing his temple as he sipped the coffee. "God, what do they put in the drinks down here? Tell me that was moonshine so I can maintain a little self-respect."

I pulled open a cabinet, surveying the cups. "Ha," I said. "This is the South. More bang for your buck. Not everything gets watered down and jacked up in price." I could bring my parents' wedding china to Daniel's tonight and be nearly done with the kitchen. I could leave the money for him before he could notice and say no. And since Everett was here, that was probably all I'd be getting done anyway.

"Daniel and Laura want us to come for dinner tonight," I said.

"That sounds great," he said. "Would be even better if they had Internet."

"I'm sure they do. But Laura's probably going to ask about three hundred wedding questions. Just so you're prepared."

He tilted his head back and grinned from across the room. "Three hundred, huh?"

"The price of Internet access."

"A fair trade, I suppose."

He walked to the dining room, where his laptop and briefcase sat on the table. It was a tiny alcove, visible from the kitchen, where I'd been organizing and storing most of the boxes. He glanced around the empty room. "You got a lot done. How long have you been up?"

"A while," I called, opening the rest of the cabinets so the room seemed even smaller, the walls closing in on us. "Look around. There's still so much to do."

"Yeah, well, I probably could've done that for you in half the time if you'd waited—"

"Everett, please," I snapped.

He tapped his pen against the dining room table. "You're stressed."

I grabbed a stack of plates, setting them down on the table across from him. "Of course I'm stressed. Imagine the police treating *your* father like this."

"Okay, calm down," he said, and I suddenly hated how practical he sounded. How condescending. He shifted in his seat, wood scraping against wood. "About your dad, Nicolette."

"Yes?" I stood on the other side of the wooden table, folded my arms across my chest.

"I can stop people from officially questioning him, but I can't stop him from volunteering information. You get that, right?"

My stomach twisted. "But he doesn't even know what he's saying! He's borderline senile. *You* get *that,* right?"

He nodded, powered up the computer, flicked his eyes to me and back to his screen. "Is it possible he did have something to do with it?"

"With what?" I asked.

He kept his eyes on the screen. Made like he was half working, but I knew him too well. "The girl. Ten years ago."

"No, Everett. *God,*" I said. "And her name is Corinne. She wasn't just *some girl.* She was my best friend."

He flinched, his gaze flitting over me, as if he'd just woken up in my roomful of painted furniture. "You're acting like I should know this, but you've never mentioned her. Not once. Don't get mad at me because you neglected to tell me."

*Neglected.* Like it was my duty. My failure. My fault. All the stories I hadn't told him: Corinne and me in the principal's office. Corinne and me in the kitchen with my mother, flour on our clothes, licking the sugar from our lips. Corinne and me in the back of Officer Bricks's car senior year, his first month on the job, trying to keep a straight face when he said, *I'm not a taxi service. Next time I'll bring you down to the station, make your parents come for you.* Nearly every story from my childhood included Corinne. And Everett hadn't ever heard her name.

Everett didn't like it when details surprised him. He was once blindsided in the middle of a trial—information his own client had kept from him—and he lost. It was an unforeseeable outcome for him, something he wasn't expecting, and it hit him with a ferocity I wasn't expecting. Behind closed doors, he became impenetrable. Closed off and borderline depressed. *You couldn't understand,* he kept saying, and he was right. I couldn't. Three days later, he started a new case, and he was back. Never mentioned it again.

If Corinne were here, she would've poked at this vulnerability over and over until she could expose it, and then it would be hers. And so would he.

I was more generous with people's flaws. Everyone had his or her own demons, including me.

"I don't know a thing about you from high school, either," I said. "Because guess what? It doesn't matter."

"My family wasn't part of a potential murder investigation." He didn't look at me when he said it, and I didn't blame him.

I leaned across the table, my palms sweaty on the surface. "Oh, I get it. This would look bad for you, right? Taint your perfect family image?"

He brought a hand down on the table, harder than either of

us expected to judge from the look on his face. He ran his hand through his hair and leaned back in his seat, taking me in. "This isn't you," he said.

It was my own fault. I wasn't sure Everett had ever got a real grasp of who I was. We started dating when I was off for the summer, so I spent most of the summer being Everett's girlfriend. I could be whatever he needed, whenever he needed it. I was the very definition of flexibility. I could bring him lunch at the office, say hi to his dad, stay out as late as I wanted, and sleep until noon. Could help his sister move apartments, browse the flea markets in the afternoon, always free by the time he got home from work, always willing to do what he wanted. By the time I went back to work the next month, we had crammed triple the time into the same amount of space.

I'd made myself small and unobtrusive, and I fit neatly into his preexisting life. One year later, and he knew things about me like a list of evidence presented in a case—everything removed from the scene, labeled and numbered in plastic bags: *Nicolette Farrell. Age twenty-eight. Father, Patrick Farrell, vascular dementia following stroke. Mother, Shana Farrell, deceased following cancer. Hometown: Cooley Ridge, North Carolina. Education: bachelor's in psychology, master's in counseling. Brother: Daniel, insurance claims adjuster.* Favorite foods and favorite shows and the things I liked and the way I liked them. My past just a list of facts, not something that ever truly existed for him.

"I didn't come here to fight," he said.

"I know." I took a deep breath. "Corinne was screwed up, and I missed it. Or I ignored it. I don't know. And the investigation was even more screwed up. But my dad didn't do anything."

"Tell me, then," he said. "Tell me the story." When I balked, he put his hands up, as if attempting to calm me. "This is my job. I'm good at it."

The story. That's exactly what it was now. A story with gaps that we attempted to fill with things that made sense. A story with different perspectives and different narrators and a single girl at the center.

"We were eighteen, had just graduated." My voice turned low, and even to me, it sounded haunting. Haunted. "It was this time of year, almost exactly ten years ago. The fair was here, just like last week. We were all at the fair that night."

"Who's 'we'?" he asked.

I threw my hands up. "All of us. Everyone."

"Even your dad?"

I flashed to this image—me on the stand and Everett asking questions. Getting to the truth. "No, not my dad. Daniel. Corinne and me and our other friend, Bailey—we went together in Daniel's car. Our friends were going to be there. All of our friends."

"And did you leave together?"

"Everett, are you going to let me tell the story, or are you going to cross-examine me?"

He folded his hands on the table. "Sorry. Habit."

My limbs twitched. Too much caffeine. I paced in front of the table, trying to wear it off. "No, we didn't leave together. Daniel and I got in a fight. It was kind of chaotic after that, keeping up with who stayed and who left, exactly. But I left with someone else when Corinne was still there." I shrugged. "That's my part of the story. Bailey couldn't find Corinne after, so she caught a ride home with my brother later. She assumed Corinne had made up with her ex—Jackson. But Jackson swore he never saw her that night."

Everett took a sip of his coffee, staying silent, waiting for more.

I shrugged again. "Her mom called my house in the morning, looking for her. Then Bailey's and Jackson's. By the end of the night, we were already searching the woods."

"That's it?"

"That's it." You couldn't explain the rest to someone who wasn't there. Who didn't know her or us. That a story is the most simplified version of events—something to file away into a sound bite, dulled and sharpened at the same time.

"I know how these things go, Nicolette."

I nodded, but I didn't sit down. Didn't get any closer. "Other than the sorry excuse of an investigation, it got ugly—people accusing each other, saying things about Corinne . . . Everyone's secrets out in the open, everyone's thoughts and suspicions. It was a mess. I left at the end of the summer, but nothing changed. We never found her."

Everett paused. The light on his face shifted as his computer screen turned black from disuse. "So who did it?"

"Excuse me?"

"I mean, if I go sit at the bar"—he shuddered—"after I recover from last night, at least . . . If I go sit at the bar and buy people drinks and ask, 'What happened to Corinne?', what are they going to say? There's always a name. Even if it never gets to an arrest or trial, there's always a common assumption. So who's the name?"

"Jackson," I said. "Jackson Porter."

"The boyfriend?"

*The one who mixed your drinks last night,* I wanted to tell him. But *The Boyfriend,* yeah, that was what the investigation made him. "Right," I said.

Everett took another sip, went back to his work. "It usually is. Are they looking at him for this other girl?"

"Annaleise," I said, staring back out the window. "I don't know. Maybe."

"What do you think? Did he do it?"

"I don't know." There was too much to explain, too much to whittle down into a testimony under cross-examination on the stand. "The thing is, Jackson and Corinne were always fighting. It was nothing new."

They spent at least half their time breaking up and the rest getting back together. If Corinne hadn't disappeared, I could imagine them caught in the cycle still. Her pushing him to do something he shouldn't have done; him getting fed up and leaving; her "forgiving" him; and him coming back for her. He always came back for her.

Didn't matter that she once sent Bailey after him when he was three drinks past drunk to see if she could get him to kiss her. Or that half the time, Corinne didn't show up when she said she would. Or she'd show up unexpectedly, swearing you had plans, and *How could you forget?* and *Did you have a mind-fuck or something?*

Didn't matter that she was constantly trying to get us all to prove our loyalty to her.

"She liked to test him," I said. "She liked to test everyone. But he still loved her."

Everett raised an eyebrow. "This was your best friend?"

"Yes, Everett. She was also fierce and beautiful and I'd known her forever. She knew me better than anyone. That counts for a lot, you know."

"If you say so."

He went back to his work, calm and contained, but I was wound tight with adrenaline.

Everett had never been a teenage girl—maybe there was some equivalent in the adolescent male, something that simmers under the surface of a friendship like that. But the simple truth was that when a girl like Corinne loves you, you don't ask why. You just hope it doesn't change.

Tyler never understood, either. Inevitably, he was the thing that changed us. Winter break, senior year, Corinne had dragged me to a party where I didn't want to be in the first place—mostly because my brother would be there. *Don't tell Tyler,* Corinne had said. *It'll be a surprise.* She told me to find a place for our jackets, and I watched from inside as she practically threw herself at Tyler, who was sitting in the back of his truck, tailgate down, legs dangling over the edge. He tossed her aside—it wasn't a hard push, but he was firm, and Corinne remained in motion until colliding with the car beside his.

"Domestic abuse, asshole," she'd said, rubbing her side as a crowd started to gather. I was already outside, had started moving the second I saw her lean in to him.

"Not interested," Tyler said, his eyes scanning the crowd, settling on me. He pushed through the crowd, into the house, while Corinne recounted the story to everyone who would listen.

"Were you really wondering what I would do?" he'd said to me. "I'm not one of her games. Don't play them with me, Nic."

"I'm not," I said. "I didn't know she would do that."

He cut his eyes through the crowd, and I saw where they landed. I watched as Corinne stared back. "You're friends with her, you're already playing."

*Truth or dare. Dare. Dare. Always take the dare.*

*Tick-tock, Nic.*

I confronted her as we were leaving, while Tyler waited for me at the front door. "What the hell, Corinne?" I asked.

"You needed to know," she said, smiling at me. "And now you do." She rubbed her arm, leaned close when she saw Daniel watching us. "But tell me, does he always push that hard?"

That was six months before she disappeared. I started to pull away, just a little. Eighteen, on the cusp of adulthood, and perpetually shaken by the feeling that at any moment I might burst from my skin. That I was trapped, and Cooley Ridge was the thing I had to escape.

I had missed something. That was what I'd told Everett. Ignoring her calls while I was with Tyler. Brushing her off when she showed up pretending we had plans, heading out with Tyler instead.

I hadn't been looking, and then she was gone.

———

PARTS OF THESE STORIES made it into that imaginary box—the official investigation—in witness statements, in people's suspicions.

Tyler pushing Corinne made it into the box.

Bailey kissing Jackson made it into the box.

But there were countless stories that never did. Things I held on to that felt too private, like her whisper in the middle of the night from the sleeping bag beside mine. Like the time the bird flew into the high living room window at her house, how she didn't flinch, just rolled her eyes and took a shovel from the garage and bashed the bird as its wings beat against the sidewalk, how the noise of the wings on the concrete haunted me for months. And so did her words: *You're welcome,* she'd said to it after.

Or the senior-year camping trip, how she dragged me with her into the outdoor shower—*Don't be such a prude*—making it seem like a show, our bare feet visible under the swinging door, hanging our clothes over the wall. *Soap my back?* she'd asked, loud enough for someone outside to whistle. She'd turned slowly so I could see the gash running from spine to shoulder blade and another below, fine and precise, as if made by a razor. I never said anything, just moved the bar of soap around, never too close. Never knew if it was from Jackson or her dad or something else, but she showed me, and I knew.

And when we walked out, our wet skin clinging to our dry clothes, I'd felt the heat of Jackson's glare—felt him watching me through the trees for the rest of that trip.

Corinne was larger than life here. Had become even larger because she disappeared. But she was just a kid, eighteen, and bursting out of her skin. Believing the world would bend to her will. Must've torn her up something good the first time she realized it wouldn't.

———

EVERETT PUSHED THE WINDOWS up, the edges scraping wood against wood in high-pitched resistance, his papers fluttering on the table, the sound hypnotic.

I spent the rest of the afternoon wrapping the china in old newspapers, my fingertips black and sooty, and loading the car with boxes for Daniel. When it was time to go to Daniel and Laura's, I shut and locked the windows Everett had opened.

"It'll be like an oven when we get back," Everett said.

"It gets chilly at night. You're in the mountains. Go ahead and start the air in the car," I called.

I heard the engine turn over, and I peered out the kitchen window once more. Then I dragged the chair from the kitchen table and wedged it under the handle of the back door. If someone tried to come inside again, I'd know. The chair would be moved. Or the windows would be unlocked.

I'd know.

———

THERE WERE BLACK SMUDGES under Laura's eyes as she greeted Everett, and Daniel was rubbing the back of his neck like there was a kink he couldn't work out, but Laura was nothing if not a Southern hostess. She'd reached the size where it was impossible to hug without coming at her from the side, which Everett was doing, her expression switching to a practiced glow. "I've heard so much about you," she said to Everett, her swollen fingers on the back of his neck as she air-kissed his cheek.

"You, too," he said, backing away, his hands shoved deep in his pockets. "I'm so glad I finally get to meet you."

"Same," she said. "I can't wait to hear all about the wedding! Nic's been too busy with the house since she got back." Playful grin in my direction.

Everett fought a smile as I raised an eyebrow at him. "When are you due?" he asked.

She ran her hands over the floral dress stretched across her stomach. "Three weeks."

"Do you know what you're having?"

Laura cut her eyes to me. "Girl," she said.

"Any names picked out?"

Again with the look at me as it became obvious that I had not actually told Everett much about her. "Shana."

"Pretty."

She cocked her head to the side. "After Dan and Nic's mom."

Everett nodded too quickly and Daniel waved his arm toward the living room, rescuing us both. "Nic said you needed to send some emails?" Daniel led him to the couch and Laura dropped the act, her shoulders slumping as she rested against the wall.

"Is this a bad time? Are you okay?" I asked.

Laura pulled me into the kitchen, eyes wide. "Oh my God, Nic," she said. She was like this—she believed that having the label of sister-in-law meant we were officially confidantes, neither of us having to earn it. Never mind that she'd ignored me all through high school and then after, until she'd started dating Daniel four years ago. It was like she'd suddenly decided we would become close, and was now determined to make it so.

"What's wrong?" I asked.

A timer over the stove started beeping, but Laura didn't seem to notice. "The *police* were just here," she whispered. She was nearly pressed up against me, and the timer was getting more insistent, and I felt a dull headache forming behind my eyes. Daniel finally crossed the room and hit the timer, frowning at the way Laura and I were standing.

"What did they want?" I asked, facing Daniel.

"Oh, you mean other than to push me into early labor?" She rubbed her stomach again, letting out a slow breath. "Have they been to see you?"

"Laura, what did they say?"

"Oh, they didn't *say* anything. They *asked*. They *demanded*. They treated me like . . . like . . ."

"Laura," Daniel warned.

Everett stood in the doorway, his laptop folded at his hip. "Everything okay?"

"You finished?" I asked, pulling away from Laura.

"It was just pressing send on a few emails." His eyes moved systematically from me to Laura to Daniel.

Laura shifted her weight. "You're a lawyer," she said. "So tell me, is it legal to question someone for no reason?"

"Laura—" I didn't want to drag Everett into this. I didn't want this dragged into my life with him.

"Back up a second," Everett said. "Are we still talking about your dad?"

Laura leaned back against the counter. "The police just came by here, asking me about Annaleise Carter. For no reason! Can they do that?"

His face tightened, then relaxed. "They didn't arrest anyone, so they don't have to advise you of rights. And you don't have to talk to them. But they can still try."

She shook her head at him. "Of course you have to talk to them."

"No, legally—"

She laughed. "Legally." She pushed off the counter, and she

moved her hands to her lower back. "If you don't talk, they'll think you had something to do with it. Even *I* know that."

"What did you say?" I asked Laura.

"There was nothing *to* say. It was Bricks, you know, Jimmy Bricks. Remember him? But also another guy, not in uniform. I didn't know him. He's the one who did most of the talking. He asked if we knew her, and of course we knew her, but not *well*. Bricks could've told him that. Then he asked when we last had interaction with her, and I wasn't sure. Maybe church a few weeks ago? Maybe she asked about the baby? I don't *know*. I barely knew the girl. Then he asked if Daniel knew her."

"They're just fishing," Everett said.

"What about you?" I asked Daniel. "What did *you* say?"

"I wasn't here," he said, his jaw clenched, when I realized what exactly the police were after. Why Laura thought they might come to me next. *Daniel.* His name was getting dragged out of the box.

"You know what I thought when they showed up? I thought something had happened to Dan," Laura said, her hands back on her stomach. She took a deep breath. "They shouldn't be allowed to do that." Her hands tightened into fists. "This is our *life.*"

Daniel rubbed her back. "All right. It's done," he said.

"It's not *done,*" Laura said, her eyes glistening as she looked up at Daniel. "They're just getting started."

Neither of us had any words of comfort after that. We'd lived through it once before, after all.

Even though Annaleise had been our alibi, had corroborated my story that Daniel and I were fighting and he hit me, that didn't clear him. In fact, that made it worse. By the time the story rolled through town, people wondered what else he did to me behind closed doors. Were those bruises on my back? What happened in that house without a mother, with a half-vacant father?

*Were he and Corinne ever involved?* they had asked. They'd asked him. They'd asked all of us.

*Never,* said Daniel.

*Never,* said Bailey.

*Never,* said I.

———

DINNER WAS BARBECUE CHICKEN and vegetables that Laura had grown herself. She'd also made the sweet tea, which Everett had obviously never tasted before. His eyes gave him away when he took a gulp, but he recovered well enough, and I squeezed his leg under the table.

"Sugar and liquor," I said. "We take them very seriously."

He smiled, and I thought maybe we would get through this all right. But it took only until the second gap of silence—knives sliding against the dishes, bread crunching in my mouth—for Laura to start up again.

"They should be looking at the workers from ten years ago, see if there's any working the fair. I told them that. Two makes a pattern, right?" The ends of her long blond hair were centimeters from brushing her dinner, and I motioned my fork toward her plate. "Oh," she said. "Thanks." She brushed it back behind her shoulders.

"Dinner's delicious," I said.

"Pass the butter?" Daniel asked.

"They're looking in all the wrong places," Laura went on. I tried to catch Daniel's eye, but he was focused on the chicken he was cutting from the bone, his expression unreadable. She pushed her chair a little farther out, twisting to the side. "Honestly, they should be talking to Tyler more." My hand froze, my knife over the chicken. She leaned closer, conspiratorially. "No offense, Nic. But he *was* seeing her, and I heard he was the last phone call on record—"

Daniel put his cup down on the table a little too hard.

"Who's Tyler?" Everett asked.

Laura laughed at him before she realized he was serious.

Daniel cleared his throat and answered for her. "A friend we grew up with. He was seeing Annaleise. He and his dad own a construction company, and they've been helping us with a few repairs."

"You know, Nic's Tyler," Laura said, like that should clear it all up.

"Oh my God," I said, rolling my eyes. "Ex-boyfriend, Everett. Tyler was my high school boyfriend."

Everett smiled tightly at Laura. "Nic's Tyler, huh?" Then to me, "And he's helping with the house?"

"Oh," Laura cut in. "But that was years ago. He's good people. You'd like him."

Daniel choked, coughed into the crook of his elbow, and Laura reached an arm for him. "Are you okay?"

My fork trembled over my plate, and I pressed my hands to my legs to still them. "You think he's involved in Annaleise's disappearance?" I asked. "Is that what you told the cops?"

"No, I didn't mean to imply *that*. I just meant they should be asking *him* questions, not us. He probably knows more— Oh!" Laura gasped, grabbed my hand, and pressed it to her stomach. I froze, trying to politely pull away, when something rolled, slowly and languidly, and I felt myself sucking in a breath, leaning closer, moving my hands, trying to find it again.

"You feel that?" she asked.

I looked into her face—a little rounder than pretty, balancing out Daniel's harsh edges—and I felt in that moment how lucky this baby would be. Unlike my mother, Laura would live. And Daniel would know what to do, wouldn't cower under the weight of responsibilities.

"This will be you guys someday," Laura said, and I gently pulled back my hands.

Everett finally pretended not to hear part of our conversation, concentrating on his food. Daniel was doing the same.

"This is really good, Laura," I said.

"It really is," Everett said.

———

I CLEARED THE TABLE with Everett's help. "Join me for a drink out back?" Daniel said to Everett.

"I'll join you out back, but I'll have to pass on the drink." He grinned at me. "Nicolette took me out and got me toasted last night. You guys don't mess around down here."

Daniel laughed. "No, I suppose we don't. Where'd she take you?"

"Murry's?" Everett said. "Kenny's?"

"Kelly's," Daniel corrected as I scrubbed the dishes in the sink. "You don't say."

I spun around. "Daniel, show him the backyard. Seriously, Everett, if you thought our view was nice? This place is amazing.

"Sit," I told Laura as she tried to help.

"Thanks. I didn't mean to get you into trouble with Everett."

"You didn't get me into trouble," I said. "I just don't talk about home much. Probably caught him by surprise."

"Okay. Well, I'm sorry," she said. "I was just shaken. From the cops showing up. And when I'm nervous, I talk too much."

I nodded, and then I did something that surprised us both as she walked to the back door. I hugged her. My hands were soapy, and the ends of her hair held some crumbs, and I felt her abdomen pressing into my side. "You and Daniel will be fine," I said, and when I pulled back, she nodded quickly, tears in her eyes. She cleared her throat. "You coming?" She motioned for the back porch, where Everett and Daniel were sitting under the light, watching the sunset.

"In a sec. Gotta use the bathroom."

I grabbed my purse and waited in the hall until I heard the screen door bang shut. Now that the nursery was almost done, Daniel's office was mostly a storage area under the stairs, about the size of a walk-in closet. I took out the manila envelope full of cash and used a pen to write Daniel's name across it. I didn't think Laura came in here much, but I figured I should leave it inside his desk drawer, just in case.

I owed Daniel money. But if I sent a check, he wouldn't cash it. If I held it out to him, he wouldn't take it. I probably could've given it to Laura, but I was pretty sure she didn't know about it. Telling her now would only make her wonder what other secrets Daniel was keeping.

I hadn't started paying it back for a long time, and it had been hard to scrape together, after rent and lease, on top of school loans. But I was staying here for the summer, and that kid paid me for the sublet up front, and if I let myself get a month behind on the car payment—just this once—I could leave this for him. Before the baby. All debts settled. All ties severed.

He'd given it to me before I left, out of some misguided sense of responsibility. He'd given it to me and let the garage sit, unfinished. *For school,* he said, and he told me to go. A good sister wouldn't have taken the money. But he still had that broken nose, and it was hard not to remember. Hard to say no to his black eyes. He said he wanted me to take it. To have it.

Mostly, though, he wanted me to go.

———

I PULLED OPEN DANIEL'S drawer, pushed the stack of notepads to the side so he'd see the envelope in the bare spot beside them. But the light from the hall caught on something in the back corner. A flash of silver. The gleam of a key. I looked over my shoulder, then reached deep inside. It looked like a house key, and it was attached by a simple ring to an engraved silver key chain, the loops and swirls coming together in an artistic rendition of the letter *A*.

*Please, no.*

I heard laughter from outside. The screen door creaking open.

I took the key. Left the money on top of the desk and slid the key into my pocket.

"Everett?" I called. "I'm sorry, I'm not feeling well."

They slowly made their way back inside, discussing when we might next be in town. Daniel took a business card from Everett, promising to call if he ever needed anything, anything at all. Everett put a hand on my arm as we walked in the twilight to my car. "That was fun."

"Liar," I said.

I cast a quick glance back at Daniel, who watched us from the front window.

The *A* could stand for anything, I told myself.

The key could be for anywhere.

It didn't have to mean anything. It didn't have to be my brother.

———

"SO WERE YOU EVER going to tell me about this Tyler guy?"

If the drive were a straight line on a map, it should take only five minutes. But the roads weaved unnecessarily, cutting around forest and mountain, and it would probably take us closer to twenty.

"You're not about to grill me on ex-boyfriends, are you?" I checked to see if he was kidding. "Oh, you are."

"Stop trying to be cute," he said.

"There's nothing to tell, Everett."

"That's not what Laura thought."

"This is how it is here. Gossip from ten years ago is still relevant. Because nobody ever leaves."

"But you did."

"I did."

He frowned, unconvinced.

"We were just kids, Everett."

He stretched and leaned his head against the window, and the side of his mouth quirked up. "Did you go to prom with him?"

"Stop," I said, but he was teasing, and I was laughing. "No prom."

"Lose your virginity to him at sixteen in the back of his pickup?"

"You're such a jerk."

"Because I'm right?" Huge smile.

"No," I said. *Seventeen. In his room. On his bed that was just a mattress and box spring, with the extra blanket he pulled from the couch because he knew I liked it warmer. It was my birthday, and his hands shook on the buttons of my dress, and I put my hands over his to still them, to help him.*

The car was too cramped, too hot, and I rolled our windows down, the air running through my hair like a memory I couldn't grasp.

"A lifetime ago, Everett."

———

I PARKED THE CAR in my driveway, letting the headlights illuminate the empty porch. "Okay, so could this Tyler guy have done something to Annaleise? What do you think?" Everett asked.

God, were we really still talking about this? I turned off the car, the night dark and alive. "Nobody knows if anything even happened to her. Her brother saw her go into the woods. Nobody knows if she came back. Maybe she did. Maybe she left on her own."

"But could he have?"

*Could* he have done it? That was quite the question.

He seized on my pause. "I don't want you staying here by yourself anymore."

"You're not serious."

"Your ex was the last call on record to a girl who disappeared from the woods in your backyard. And he's been working on your house."

"Tyler wouldn't hurt me," I said as we walked inside.

"People change over the course of ten years, Nicolette."

"I know that," I said. Except not really. *Not really.* People were like Russian nesting dolls—versions stacked inside the latest edition. But they all still lived inside, unchanged, just out of sight. Tyler was *Tyler.* A man who would never hurt me, I had no doubt. But a man who also once loved it when his girlfriend hung off the edge of a Ferris wheel, a man who pushed Corinne in full view of a party and never made excuses for it.

I checked the kitchen chair, wedged under the back door. Was it off just a bit? To the side? Was this exactly how I'd left it?

"You okay?" Everett called.

I felt electricity everywhere. In the air, in the walls. "Just thinking," I said.

"Come to bed."

"Not tired," I said. I watched our reflection in the window. Everett coming closer. His hand brushing my hair over my shoulder. His mouth pressed to the skin of my neck. "Come to bed with me," he said again.

I focused on the distance past our reflections, beyond the trees. "Not tired," I said again.

I felt the weight of the key in my pocket, the ridges pressing up against my skin—all the possibilities, existing all at once.

# The Day Before

# DAY 12

There was something in this house.

*With the skeletons,* my dad had said yesterday. He hadn't been making any sense, but if people got desperate enough, they might try to find meaning in his twisted thoughts, just as I was. And then I wouldn't be the only one searching.

I had called Everett for advice about my dad, and he'd said he would handle it. But he was in Philadelphia and I was here, and I hadn't heard from him since yesterday's phone call. If Everett couldn't tell me how to get this to stop, they'd eventually search this house, just like I'd been searching all night. Until I realized what Dad must've meant: the closet. He'd meant his closet. I'd already gone through mine. And Daniel's was completely bare.

He meant here, in the unlit closet off the master bedroom. He had to.

But all I could find were his old work clothes that he'd never use again, and the ratty slippers that I really needed to toss, and a few coins scattered across the wood floor, strewn with dust.

I yanked all the clothes off the hangers in a desperate last-ditch attempt to find anything, the metal hangers colliding as they swayed. Until I became a girl sitting in the middle of a heap of musty clothes trying to hold her shit together.

*This is what you get for listening to the senile, Nic.*

*This is what you get.*

I stood back up and took a deep breath to steady my hands, but the tremor still ran through my fingers. My head dipped down and I tried again, bracing my arms on the wall in front of me, my forehead resting on the plaster, my eyes focusing on the grains of wood below me.

Dust on the floor, a bobby pin that must've been here since my mom was alive, and two tiny screws beside my left foot, kicked into the corner. *If I were slowly losing my mind, where would I keep things?* I tapped the screws with my bare toe, and as they rolled, I saw that the faces were painted white, like the walls. I checked above me—there was an air-conditioning vent missing its two bottom screws. The top right corner was only partially secured. I sucked in a breath and felt a surge of discovery, of hope. My shaking hands twisted the loose screw until it fell to the floor with the others, the vent hanging at an odd angle, the rectangular duct behind it now exposed.

I couldn't see in from this angle, but I reached inside and felt paper—notebooks with spiral binding. I pulled them out, letting them crash to the floor, a few loose-leaf sheets raining down on top. I stood on my toes, reached deep inside, and scooped what I could out of the vent. Papers and dust and notebooks littering the closet floor. How much deeper did this go? How far into this house did my father's secrets seep? I imagined papers lining the spaces between the walls, like skeletons.

I jammed the heap of clothes against the wall and stepped on top, pushing myself higher so I could see into the darkness. The vent cut at an angle, jutting upward at ninety degrees near the back. I'd reached for the few remaining scraps, my fingertips just grasping the corner of a yellowed page, when the doorbell rang.

*Shit.*

*Shit shit shit.*

Not enough time. Not fast enough. Could they get a search warrant this fast? Would they know what they were looking for? Where to look?

I froze, holding my breath. My car was out front. They knew I was home.

The bell again, and the dull thud of someone knocking. I didn't have to answer. *Out for a walk; in the shower; picked up by friends.* But did it matter if I was here or not? If they had a warrant, they didn't need me to be present to gain entry, I was pretty sure.

I moaned and shoved everything back into the duct. Crumpled the pages and threw them in as far as they would go. Then I replaced two of the screws, but the doorbell rang again and I fumbled with the third screw, so I shoved it into my pocket, then raced down the stairs, my hair a wreck, my clothes a wreck, as if I'd just stumbled out of bed.

Good.

I took a deep breath, made myself yawn, and opened the door.

The sun stood behind Everett, who had his phone out, his hand raised to the door as if about to knock once more. He beamed as I threw myself into his arms with unrestrained relief. *Everett.* Not the police. Everett.

My legs were wrapped around his waist and I breathed in his familiar scent—his hair gel and soap and starch—as he walked us inside, laughing. "Missed you, too," he said. "Didn't mean to wake you, but I wanted it to be a surprise."

I slid down his body, took in his jeans, his lightweight polo, the suitcase on the porch. "I'm surprised," I said, my hands still on him—his solid arms, the strength of his grip—real. "What are you doing here?"

"You asked for my help, and you have it. This is one of those things that needs to be handled in person. Also, I wanted an excuse to see you," he said, his eyes quickly skimming over my disheveled appearance. His smile faltered, and he tried to hide it under feigned confusion. "Where did I put the suitcase? Oh, there . . ." He pulled his suitcase inside the doorway, and when he looked back at me, his expression was typical Everett, calm and collected.

"So what do we need to do?" I asked, shoulders tense, a headache brewing behind my eyes.

"I already stopped by the police station on the way here. Delivered the paperwork and demanded they cease all questioning with your father, pending evaluation."

I felt my entire body relax, my muscles turning languid. "Oh, God, I love you."

He stood in the middle of the living room, taking it all in: the boxes stacked around the dining room and foyer, the rickety table and the screen door that creaked. The floor that had seen better days, the furniture that had been awkwardly pulled away from the walls for painting. And me. He was definitely looking at me. I pressed my palms to my hips to keep them still.

"I told you I'd take care of it," he said.

"Thank you," I said.

And then it was just Everett and me in this place I thought he'd never see, and I wasn't sure what to do next.

His eyes skimmed over me one more time. "It'll be okay, Nicolette."

I nodded.

"Are *you* okay?"

I tried to imagine what he must be seeing: me, a mess. I hadn't showered since yesterday, and I'd been digging through closets all night. I'd had way too much coffee, and my hands kept shaking if they weren't holding on to something. "It's been stressful," I said.

"I know. I could hear it in your voice yesterday."

"Oh, crap, don't you have work?" What day was it again? Thursday? No, Friday. Definitely Friday. "How did you get away?"

"I brought it with me. I hate to do this, but I'll be working most of the weekend."

"How long are you staying?" I asked, brushing by him to drag his suitcase—bigger than an overnight bag—away from the screen door.

"We'll see your dad's doctors today, and hopefully they'll have the papers we need by Monday. But I'll have to go after that."

I thought of the notebooks in the vents. The door that wouldn't lock. The missing people, then and now. "We should stay in a hotel. This place has no air, and you're going to hate it."

"Don't be silly," he said. "The nearest hotel is at least twenty-five miles away." So he had checked, and he wasn't counting the budget motel that definitely had vacancy on the road between this town and the next.

"So, show me the place," he said.

Suddenly, I didn't want to. I shrugged, marginalizing the house and all it represented—no longer thinking, *That's my dad's chair, and my mom's table, that once belonged to my grandparents, that she stripped down and refinished*—instead turning it into a box of wood, trying to see it through Everett's eyes.

"It isn't much. Dining room, living room, kitchen, laundry. Bathroom down that hall and a porch out back, but the furniture's gone and the mosquitoes are killer."

Everett looked like he was searching for a place to put his laptop, specifically, the dining room table. "Here," I said, shuffling the receipts and papers into piles, scooping things up and dumping them into the kitchen drawers I'd just emptied.

He put his laptop on the cleared table, along with his accordion-style briefcase. "Can I work here?"

"Sure. But there's no Internet."

He made a face, then picked up a receipt I'd missed—Home Depot, the nearly illegible date highlighted in bright yellow—and frowned at it.

I took it from his hands and balled it up like it was inconsequential. "Nobody's lived here in over a year. Kind of wasteful to pay for Internet." Not to mention we didn't have an Internet line before that. Around here, service cut in and out from the satellite if there was an inkling of bad weather, and it wasn't worth the annoyance for my dad. Most everyone could check email on a phone, but only one service provider worked, and it wasn't Everett's. "You could use the library? It's near the police station. Not too far. I could drive you."

"This is fine, Nicolette. But maybe we can hit the library on the way to see your dad, so I can send a file."

"Are you sure? Because—"

"I'm here to see you," he said. "Not sit in a library. I missed you."

Now that he mentioned it, we hadn't been apart for this long. Not like we went out of our way to never be separated, but I wondered if we'd just been stuck in the pull of forward momentum, never taking a step back or a step away. What would happen if we paused the track, took a breath?

He missed me, sure. He wanted to help, sure. But I also had the feeling that his case was getting to him. Maybe he needed a break. Distance. I could hear that in his voice on the phone.

"What did the police say?"

He ran a hand through his hair. "Not much they can say. They didn't look too happy to see me, but it doesn't seem to be their top priority at the moment. I'm not sure his statement will help with the current situation." He looked at me from the corner of his eye as he set up his work on the table. "Tell me about this missing girl. The posters are everywhere."

"I wouldn't call her a girl, exactly, but her name is Annaleise Carter. Her brother saw her walk into the woods, and she wasn't home the next morning. Nobody's seen her since." My eyes involuntarily strayed to the backyard, toward her property.

"You know her?"

"Everett, you know everyone in a town like this. We weren't ever friends or anything, if that's what you mean. She's younger than me, but she lived behind us." I tilted my head toward the kitchen, and Everett went to the window.

"I only see trees."

"Okay, well, not right behind us. But they're our closest neighbors."

"Huh." He didn't pull away from the window, and that made me nervous. There were secrets in those woods—the past rising up and overlapping, an unstoppable trail of dominoes already set in motion. I shook my head to clear the thought as Everett turned around. "What's the matter?" he asked.

*The disappearing girls; the police and my father and the things he was saying; the papers in the closet that I had to get rid of before someone else came looking.*

"I lost the ring," I said, my breath coming in shallow spurts as I tried to tamp down the panic. The sting as tears rushed to my eyes, and Everett going all fuzzy. "I'm so sorry. I took it off to box things up, and we were moving everything around, and now I can't find it." My hands started shaking, and he grabbed them and pulled me close. I rested my forehead against his chest.

"Okay. It's okay. It's somewhere in the house, then?"

"I don't know. I lost it." I heard an echo in the house, my ghost, maybe, another version of myself in these halls from another time. I pulled my hands back, balled them into fists. "I lost it." Two missing girls, ten years apart. The fair, back in town. And all of us. Closing the gap of ten years like it was nothing but an inch. Just a blink. A quick glance over the shoulder.

"Don't cry," he said, running his thumb across my cheek, wiping up the tears. *Just a piece of metal,* Tyler had said. *Just money.* "It's insured," Everett added. "I'm sure it'll turn up."

I nodded into his chest. His hands pressed lightly against my shoulder blades. "Are you sure you're okay?" I nodded again. Felt him laugh in his chest. "I never pictured you as a girl who'd cry over a lost ring."

I took a slow breath and pulled back. "It was a really nice ring."

He laughed for real, louder this time, his head tilted back, like always. "Come on." He slung an arm over my shoulder as he walked up the stairs, luggage in his other hand. "Finish the tour?"

I laughed into his side. "You're going to wish you picked the hotel." We stood together in the narrow hall that extended the length of the upstairs. One master with a bath, two other bedrooms, connected by a shared bathroom.

"That's my dad's room," I said, gesturing to the queen bed and the old armoire. I pulled Everett along, shut the door as we passed. "This one was Daniel's," I said at the next door, "but he took his furniture." It had become a dumping ground of things my dad didn't know what to do with: old novels, teaching material, boxes of lesson plans, dog-eared philosophy books, and notes written in slanted script. "We're getting a Dumpster delivered next week. Moving on." I cleared my throat. "This is mine." The yellow bed looked drab. And the room looked way too small now that Everett was here. He didn't like staying at my studio; I couldn't imagine his feelings on this.

"Maybe we should stay in the other room? It's got a bigger bed," he said.

"I am *not* sleeping in my parents' bed. I'll take the couch if it's too small for you."

He eyed me. Eyed the bed. "We'll work it out later."

———

EVERETT HELD HIS PHONE against the car window and muttered a sarcastic "Hallelujah" when we were halfway to Grand Pines. His phone dinged in response, downloading emails now that we were back in the land of the data plan.

He scanned the surroundings quickly before diving into his emails. "We should come back in the fall. I bet it's a sight," he said. *Tap, tap, tap* from his cell as he typed.

"Yeah," I said, even though we knew we wouldn't. Fall comes with a vengeance here after the leaves change—for two days, when the wind blows, they rain down in a storm, coating everything like snow.

"It's prettier in the winter," I said.

"Hmm."

"Except if you're trying to get anywhere. Then this road feels like Donner Pass."

"Mmm." *Tap, tap, tap* on the keypad, and a *whoosh* as his message was sent.

"There's a monster out here," I said.

"Mmm. Wait. What?"

I grinned at him. "Just checking."

———

THE WOMAN WORKING THE reception desk of Grand Pines started preening when we walked in the front door. Back straight, hair flipped, chest out. I was used to it, the unconscious way people reacted to Everett.

Everett is old-money Philadelphia. His whole family is that way, like old stately buildings and cobblestone and ivy. And as with the Liberty Bell, the imperfections only make them more interesting. More worthy of the life that fate has bestowed on them. Everett can hold court, quite literally—even with his friends, even with me. It's a spell, a beautiful spell, the way he's assertive without being bossy, confident without being smug. I imagine his family members were taught this line to walk as they were taught to crawl—*Know thy classics and thy beer.* Finely tuned, all of them, with a father to disapprove instantly if they veered off course.

I stood confidently by Everett's side as he marched into Grand Pines. They never stood a chance, and I knew it.

As he walked off to see the director, the woman behind the desk raised an eyebrow at me, then the corner of her mouth, as in *Nice.*

I nodded. *I know.*

But then her eyes assessed me, like she was picking me apart, and I felt the clothes that didn't fit right, and my hair that wasn't done, and I knew my hands were probably still trembling from the caffeine.

"I'm here to see my dad. Patrick Farrell," I said.

"Okay, sure," she said, picking up the phone.

The nurse I'd seen on the first day led me to the common room, where Dad was playing with a stack of cards, some game that looked like solitaire but didn't seem to follow any rules I understood.

"Look who I found, Patrick. Your daughter."

He looked up, smiled big and real, and I felt my face doing the same. "Hi, Nic."

Such a simple, beautiful sentence.

"You sure are popular today," the nurse said, leaving us.

I grabbed her arm as she walked away. "Who was here? The police?"

"The . . . what?" She stared at my fingers on her sleeve, and I quickly released her. "No, the man who comes for lunch." She brushed her hand over her arm, smoothing out the wrinkles.

"Daniel?" I asked, looking from her to my dad.

She shook her head. "No, the other one. Patrick, who's the man who comes to lunch on Fridays?"

He drummed his fingers against the table and stared past me, a slight grin. "I can't tell you that, Nic."

I grinned at the nurse like I thought this was cute. Funny, even. "Who was here, Dad?"

"I'm not supposed to tell you." He had the audacity to laugh.

The nurse winked at my dad, then turned to me. "Good-looking guy. Blue eyes, brown hair, always in jeans and work boots . . ."

I swung my head back to my father, who was chewing the inside of his cheek. "*Tyler?*" I asked.

The nurse patted my dad's shoulder and walked away. He'd scooped up the cards and was focused on dealing the stack between the two of us. I had no idea what to do with my hand. He played a king and seemed to be waiting for something from me.

"Why the hell does Tyler come here?"

"Why wouldn't Tyler come? Did you lay exclusive claim to rights of friendship with Tyler Ellison? Your turn," he said, gesturing to my cards.

I threw down an ace, tried to relax my shoulders, to keep this conversation from sliding away from him too quickly. "Ha. I didn't realize you guys had so much in common."

Dad frowned as he picked up the stack, then played a five of diamonds. "Pay attention."

"That's exactly what I'm doing. Tell me what Tyler wants with you." I stopped playing, trying to hold his focus.

He shrugged, avoiding eye contact. "He doesn't want anything.

He just comes." He gestured to my hand until I threw out a random card. "He's a good kid, Nic. I think he likes the food." He looked around the room, like he was momentarily confused. "Or maybe the young nurse over there who works Fridays. I don't know. But he comes for lunch." I peered over my shoulder, saw the nurse lingering near the front desk through the doorway. She was shorter than me, her scrubs were nondescript, and her lipstick veered well outside the line of her lips, but she was attractive. Her hair was dark and neat. She was young. Perky.

"And you're not supposed to tell me?" I asked.

"Definitely not." Two of hearts.

"And why is that, if there's not some other reason he's coming? Think about it, Dad." Two of spades.

"You're not paying attention," he said as he swiped up the stack—about the cards or Tyler, I wasn't sure.

A new group of residents wandered in, and a few nurses shuffled in and out, carrying clipboards. We were running out of time. Dad stacked all the cards, and I placed my hand over his. "Dad, I need to talk to you."

"I thought that's what we were doing," he said.

"Dad, listen. We took care of it. The police can't question you. *Do not* let anyone question you. You tell us right away. Or the nurse. Or the doctor. They're not allowed. You don't have to talk to them. You understand?"

"I . . . Of course not. I wouldn't," he said.

*But you did.*

"I wish I'd been a better father, Nic."

"Dad, don't—"

"I really do. I can see it now that it's gone. But you can't go back, can you?"

I shook my head. *No, you can't.*

He tapped the side of his head. "This is my penance, don't you

108

think?" Like losing his mind was the price to pay for being a shitty father.

"You weren't mean. You weren't bad." He wasn't anything. He made me laugh, and he gave me a roof over my head and food in the kitchen, and he never raised a hand to me, or his voice. For a lot of people, that would make him good. A good father. *A good man.*

He leaned across the table, took my hand again. "Are you happy, Nic?"

"Yes," I said. I had everything I wanted waiting for me in Philadelphia. A whole life there.

"Good, good."

I squeezed his hand. "You don't deserve this," I said. "Any of this."

He started drumming his fingers again, double time, leaned toward me, and lowered his voice to a raspy whisper. "Nic, listen to me. I have to pay. I have to."

"I'll take care of everything," I said. "Don't talk about it anymore. Nothing. Not a word. To *anyone.* Got it?"

"Got it," he said.

But I knew it would last only an hour or so. "I need you to focus. I need you to remember this."

"I'll remember, Nic." He lifted his face to mine, his eyes like a child's, waiting for me to explain.

I looked down at my hand over his, at the age spots speckling the back of his hand, the freckles on my own. "Dad, they want to bring you down to the station. You have to stop talking. *Please.*"

He opened his mouth to speak, but I held up my hand to stop him. Over Dad's shoulder, I saw Everett standing just inside the cafeteria entrance, his eyes quickly finding me. I raised my hand, and Dad followed my line of vision. "Dad, I want you to meet someone. This is Everett," I said as he approached. *Remember who Everett is. Please.*

He looked at Everett, then at my bare hand, and smiled. "Sure, sure. Nice to meet you, Everett."

Everett shook my dad's hand. "Same to you, Patrick. Sorry Christmas didn't work out." We were supposed to fly in and out for a Christmas Eve visit before returning to spend the rest of the holiday with Everett's family, but a snowstorm had derailed our plans, and we'd never rebooked. But this was a detail too hard for Dad to pull from his memory. He made a noncommittal noise that to Everett probably sounded like displeasure.

Everett turned to me. "Everything's all set here, unless you want to stay for dinner?"

All at once I felt like I was seventeen again, sitting in the kitchen, with my dad asking if I was staying or going. *Going,* I'd say. Always going. Had my foot out the door as soon as I stopped trying to convince myself my mother might live.

"I've got a lot to do," I said. "But I'll see you later, Dad."

Everett placed his card on the table. "I told the director and the nurses up front, but if anyone comes to talk to you—anyone at all—you give me a call."

Dad raised an eyebrow at me as I walked away. When I looked over my shoulder, he was still watching. I shook my head once, praying he would remember.

I excused myself to the bathroom while Everett chatted with the woman behind the front desk. I closed the door to the stall and dialed Tyler, unease coursing through my veins. "Pick up, damnit," I mumbled, but of course he didn't.

I considered calling information and getting the number for Kelly's to see if he was there. But from outside the restroom, I heard the faint echo of Everett's voice: "What, exactly, was Patrick Farrell saying?"

I raced out of the room. "Everett?" I called, watching him slowly pull back from the reception desk. "Ready?"

—

GOSSIP. THE MOST DANGEROUS part of an investigation. Infectious and inescapable. This was something I was all too familiar with, even before my job as school counselor.

There's a danger to it, because it grows out of something real, a seed in the earth, giving life on its own. It's all tangled together—the truth, the fiction—and sometimes it's hard to pick apart. Sometimes it's hard to remember which parts truly exist.

When Corinne disappeared and we ran out of places to search, people to question, leads to track down, the only thing left for people was the talk.

About Corinne and Bailey and me. Reckless and drunk on life, never thinking of the consequences. How we passed around a bottle in the clearing outside the caverns and invited boys inside. How we lifted candy bars from the convenience store (on a dare, always a dare) and didn't respect property or authority. How we had no boundaries with each other, a tangle of limbs and hair and sun-kissed skin—*They swapped boyfriends, even, you know.*

Because look at the evidence sitting neatly in the box: Jackson kissing Bailey; Corinne hitting on Tyler as I watched. The three of us spinning, blurring, like ghosts in a field of sunflowers. And me, on the outside of the Ferris wheel, watching death rushing by. We lived too close—too close to each other, too close to some mysterious edge, too reckless and invincible, too naive to our own mortalities, just *too*. The talk: that maybe we brought it on ourselves.

Maybe we did.

And on the other side of the talk: Daniel and Jackson and maybe Tyler, the ones to watch with a wary eye. The ones who circled us, watching, waiting. The ones who let their anger break free, who acted. Who broke up with us, who pushed us away when they were displeased and then came back for more.

Who was really surprised, looking from the outside in?

After all the talk, I didn't understand how any of them stayed.

———

I DROVE SLOWLY BECAUSE of the glare coming from the sun, nearly setting, and the roads that wind gradually and then sharply with no warning. And the deer that could be standing there, frozen on the double-yellow line. And because Everett was plowing through his emails and we were about to lose service around that next bend.

I waited for him to start cursing at his phone. "Want to stop at the library again?"

"No," he said, leaning his head against the window. "It can wait until tomorrow."

"Hungry?" I asked.

"Famished."

"Good. I know a place." I cast a quick glance at him. "All I have at home right now are microwave dinners. We can hit the store tomorrow."

"You need to eat better," he said. "You look like you've lost weight."

To judge from the way my pants were fitting, I probably had. I'd been busy, skipping meals, filling my gut with coffee and soda until I could feel the acid churning and rising. Everything else tasted either metallic or stale.

I parked in the lot behind Kelly's Pub because the front streets were already lined with cars, and because that was where the residents parked. Tyler's truck wasn't there, but Jackson's bike was in the corner slot.

The Friday-evening crowd was different from the daytime crowd. The college kids, home and looking for something to do.

The after-work crowd, catching a few extra drinks before returning to their families. But the smell was the same as always: alcohol, grease, perfume mixed with sweat.

There were two people behind a full bar. Jackson at the far end and a woman I vaguely recognized, with a too-tight top and super-straight hair to her waist. She looked in my direction as I entered. "Seat yourselves," she said, nodding toward the tables, as if I didn't know how it worked here.

I slid into a two-person table pressed up against the window, in full view of the vestibule connecting the stairs to the upstairs apartments. "Look at the menu, I'll go get us some drinks," I said, standing. Everett gestured to the waiter and waitresses making the rounds, but I shook my head. "It's faster this way. Trust me."

I walked over to Jackson's side of the bar and knocked on the countertop, since his head remained down.

"Gee, what brings you around today, Nic?" he asked with a smug smile.

"Vodka tonic," I said. "Double."

"Rough day?"

"And a water."

Jackson paused and looked over my shoulder at Everett, who was studying the menu intently in the dim light. "Who the fuck is that?"

"Everett. My fiancé," I said as Jackson's bloodshot eyes stared back at me. "Have you seen Tyler? I need to talk to him."

"So you thought you'd bring your fiancé to his place? That's cruel even for you."

I flinched. "It's an emergency."

"Haven't seen him, Nic," he said, sliding the drinks in front of me. "But this"—he tilted his head toward Everett—"is not the best way to get his attention."

I sipped my drink. "Do me a favor," I said, pointing to the vodka tonic. "Keep these coming."

At the table, Everett watched me as I ordered, and when the waitress left, the corner of his mouth was tipped up, and I didn't think it was the alcohol just yet. "Never heard you talk like that to anyone but me," he said. "It's cute."

My accent was never as strong as most people's here. My father wasn't from here. My mom was, but she left. Got out. Went to school, met my dad, got married. Had a career, a whole life out there. But she came back with Daniel. Said she wanted to raise her kids where she grew up, where her parents lived and died and were buried. She's buried beside them now.

When I left, I learned to mask the accent, faint though it was— to clip my words, shorten the vowels, tighten the *I*'s, sharpen the *A*'s. To speak with a casual efficiency. Until I sounded like I could be from anywhere else.

The accent came out when I was drunk, and I wasn't drunk often. I wasn't drinking now, but it was seeping in nonetheless. "You fixin' to get me drunk and take advantage of me, Nicolette?" Everett asked, and I forced a smile.

I spent most of dinner staring at the open door, made irrationally angry by Tyler's absence. By his visits with my father, by the questions I had to get answered, by the way I could imagine Tyler looking at his phone, seeing it was me, and deciding to ignore the call.

We were almost done with our burgers, and Everett had just finished his third double vodka tonic, when Tyler arrived. He paused for a moment, scanning the crowd from the entrance—caught sight of me, caught sight of Everett—and then he was gone.

"I'll be right back," I said. "Bathroom."

Everett's back was to the door, so he didn't see me push through the crowd and turn right out of the vestibule instead of heading to the other side of the bar, where the bathrooms were.

"Hey!" I called, but Tyler didn't stop moving up the stairs. "I need to talk to you!"

He paused on the steps but didn't turn around. "Is that him?"

I stomped up the steps after him, lowering my voice. "You visit my dad? Why do you visit my dad?" He turned around, and we were way too close. I pressed my back into the railing.

"What? I have a project nearby. I swing by for lunch once a week. He could use the company. I'm right there."

"He could use the company? Are you trying to make me feel guilty?"

"No. I'm not trying to make you feel anything." He seemed to notice how close we were standing, and he took a breath, stepped back. "Your mom died and he checked out. I know, I was there. I get it. You don't owe him anything. Nobody blames you."

"That's not why I don't . . . I have a job and a life. I can't just *stop* because my dad literally drank himself into oblivion."

He nodded. "Fine, Nic. You don't need to convince me. So I visit him. That's my choice, too."

"He said he wasn't supposed to tell me," I said, because that had to mean something. I'd felt like Tyler was keeping something from me, and now I was sure of it. "What do you talk about? What did he tell you?"

He tipped his head back, looking at the ceiling. "Nothing. We just . . . talk. He's not supposed to tell you because of this, Nic. *This* is the reason."

I stuck my finger at the center of his chest. "Don't lie to me."

His jaw twitched. "I don't lie to you. And you know it."

That used to be something I was sure of. There used to be nobody I trusted more. But the fact remained: He hadn't told me that he visited my father, and he didn't want me to know. "Just tell me why, Tyler."

"Give it a rest, there's nothing to tell!" He stepped closer. "He's

115

your family, and you were mine. You left, but he didn't. I don't just cut people off when they no longer suit me. It's that simple, Nic."

I wrapped my arm around my waist. *When they no longer suit me.* "I haven't been *yours* in ten years. He's not your problem anymore. How's that for simple?"

I thought for a second that he was going to argue. Tell me all the reasons I was wrong, all the ways I didn't understand. Instead, he laughed. He laughed with his eyes closed, and it came out like a grimace. "Okay. No problem." He took a step up, then pulled out his key ring. "Ten years, huh? I could've sworn it was sooner." He took a key off his ring—*mine*—and threw it to me, but I let it clatter in the stairwell, echoing as it fell. "Listen, I have to take care of some stuff. Do me a favor and stay away."

And then I felt it—the punch to my stomach—the feeling that there was something worth holding on to, and I was losing it. Again.

I put my hand up to stop him, but his eyes were closed.

"Get him out of here. I want to come downstairs and have a fucking drink, and I don't want to have to look at him."

"Tyler—"

"Don't, Nic." He gestured toward the bar. "I can't—" He dropped his arm. "Look, let's make this easy. You asked me to leave you alone, and now I'm asking you to do the same. It's what we both want, right? See? Simple."

And there I stood, an eighteen-year-old girl breaking up with her boyfriend. The finality of metal on concrete in a dingy stairwell. We'd never had this moment, and maybe it was my fault for slipping away, or his fault for pretending I hadn't, but we'd never officially called us off. Silly to think about now. That those scattered moments made up the longest and most meaningful relationship of my life. That maybe we'd been together these ten years because we never broke up. I just left. *Just cut people off when they no longer suit me.*

This was the feeling I couldn't stomach the thought of back then. Why I slunk off in the middle of the night without so much as a goodbye. But ten years' time didn't change it at all, didn't stop the nausea from rolling through, didn't change the look on his face.

I turned away so he couldn't see what it did to me.

I floundered for my key, stomped back into the bar, and slammed my hand down on the counter.

Jackson watched me out of the corner of his eye. "Went that well, huh?"

"Don't be an asshole," I said. "Please."

He placed one last vodka on the bar. "On me. Time to go." I took the glass, but he grabbed my arm. "Really," he said. "Go."

This time I downed half the drink myself before making it back to the table.

———

"COME ON." I HAD to pull Everett toward the car; he was solidly past his tipping point. I rifled through my purse to find my keys, and Everett put his hands on either side of me on the car roof.

"Hi," he said as I looked up at him. He kissed me, his teeth colliding with mine, his hand sliding up my side.

"Hold that thought," I said, pushing him back. Tyler's apartment had a view to the parking lot, and I was not, as Jackson implied, *that cruel.*

"I think," he said, "I'm drunk."

"That would be an accurate assessment," I said, helping him to the passenger side.

He paused, his hand on my shoulder, his gaze tilted up at the building. "Someone's watching us," he said.

"Get in the car, Everett."

"I've felt it all day, though." He swayed slightly, then eased into his seat. "Like someone's watching. Do you feel it?"

"You're just not used to the woods," I said. But a chill ran up my spine, because I did. I felt eyes in the woods, outside the darkened windows. I felt them everywhere.

———

THE LANTERN WAS MOVING on the front porch again, casting shadows and ghosts.

"This place is trippy in the dark," Everett said, following me up the walk.

"It's trippy when you're drunk," I said, leading him inside.

Everett fell back on the couch, his head tipped toward the ceiling. "This is gonna hurt in the morning."

"I'll make a fire," I said.

"It'll be like a furnace."

"It gets cold at night," I said. "Rest."

While he lay there with his eyes closed and his arm out to the side like a rag doll, I checked the entire house, window by window, the back door with the chair wedged under the handle, my unlatched bedroom window. Nothing looked disturbed. Last, I stood at the entrance to the master closet, shining my phone light inside. The vent in my dad's closet was exactly as I'd left it, but for how much longer?

"Nicolette?" Everett called from downstairs.

There was no time.

"Coming," I called.

I helped Everett up to bed, skirted out from under him as he tried to pull me down with him. "Be right back," I said.

I unscrewed the vent and took the journals and papers downstairs, where I sat in front of the crackling fire. I skimmed everything—the journals turning out to be more like ledgers—and felt the puzzle pieces lining up for just a second. And the spare sheets of paper: descriptions of my mother's jewelry, or receipts of sales, or itemized lists from pawnshops. I tore the pages from the journal, crumpling them up, and tossed them into the fire, watched as the edges curled, turning to black.

Then I pulled the papers from the drawer, everything on the dining room table that I'd been trying to find meaning in. The bank withdrawals. The highlighted receipts. I burned them all. They turned to ash, to nothing, to smoke. I no longer had the luxury of perusal, of a gradual and gentle understanding. It was coming with a vengeance, like the leaves in the fall. Turning colors in warning, and then, with a strong wind, they all fall down.

# The Day Before

# DAY 11

The teenagers scattered throughout the clearing were finally asleep, and I carefully wove through their campsite, stepping over empty cans and sleeping bags, heading for the narrow path to the caverns. Dawn was already breaking through the trees, the sky pink and hazy, but darkness beckoned from the entrance of the caverns. Time didn't exist down there. Too many angles for the light to slip through. Too much distance. You had to move by feel and instinct. My hands on Tyler's waist, following in his steps, Corinne's laughter echoing from deep inside—

Ten years ago, these caverns had belonged to us.

From my house, in a car, they're a good ten miles away, but through the woods, it's more like two, two and a half. Corinne and Bailey and I used to walk here before we were old enough to drive. Not just for the caverns. That came after. That was always the dare. First there was the clearing where we'd all meet up, just like these kids.

This site used to be privately run and maintained, but now it was abandoned, halfway to disrepair, yet with old restroom facilities and plumbing that still worked. The perfect place for bonfires or parties. It belonged to the teenagers and, like a spell, was forgotten as soon as they moved on.

We'd sneak through the rusted cavern gates, following the roped path deep inside, as far as we dared. Our flashlights off, the chill running up our spines, a tap on the shoulder: *Truth or dare . . .*

In the darkness, we were all hands and laughter and whispers. We clung to one another or pressed ourselves against the damp walls, trying to outlast everyone else. Pretending to see ghosts, pretending to *be* ghosts, until someone gave in and flicked a light back on.

———

THE OFFICIAL CAVERN TOURS had shut down a generation before, after an accident. A couple left behind, lost in the total darkness, and only one alive by morning. The woman slipped along the slick rocks, hit her head, and her husband couldn't find her in the dark. Circled the cavern on his hands and knees, spiraling in, calling her name, never making contact. Yelled for help from the locked gate, his pleas swallowed up by the endless forest. It's disorienting down there—might seem unlikely to be trapped in the same cave and never find the other person, but if you've been there, you knew. It could happen.

They found her in a puddle of her own blood and him not twenty yards away.

They'd been exploring a narrow tunnel off the trail. Didn't notice when everyone left until the lights went off. Felt their way back into the main cavern, searching for the path, for the rope to follow back to the entrance. That was when he lost her.

Of course, that was his story. But then there were the rumors, the whispers, that lived on. He killed her. He meant to. Or it was an accident, a fit of passion, a push too hard. Or like Daniel told us: The monster made him do it. It lived in the woods, and this was its home, and it would speak to you only in a whisper that sounded like your own echo.

Either way, this place shut down, the generator burned out, and the trail of lights turned off for good—and with it, the town revenue. There used to be more of a tourist draw. The caverns nearby, the mountains all around, and the river cutting through. Johnson Farm and the sunflowers within driving distance—people pulling onto the shoulder of the road, walking through them like a maze, cameras strung around their necks.

We still had the draw of the mountains, the view, the *way of life* that people found quaint. But the town twenty miles away had a railroad with a cartoonish train and a scenic day trip, and it also had the river and the mountains, the proximity to Johnson Farm, therefore taking all of the remaining visitors.

They bolted the metal gates into the mouth of the caverns, tied it up with chains and a padlock, stuck a sign out front. *Danger. Forbidden. Keep out.*

Like catnip, a goddamn Bat Signal in the sky—*Teenagers! Come!* And come we did.

The gates and the padlock were mostly for show. Everyone knew someone who knew someone who had a key. There were probably eight different copies of that key floating around by the time we graduated, passed down like a rite of passage, senior to freshman—the dares, the bets, the dark privacy of the rooms losing their appeal after graduation. When those seeking privacy and secrets outgrew the cold walls, the damp floor, moving on to the motel halfway between this town and the next.

When Corinne disappeared, the cops couldn't search everywhere. There was just too much area and too few resources, until help from the state arrived. Especially for an eighteen-year-old with no definite sign of foul play. They couldn't rule out the possibility that she'd run.

But the caverns were close to the main road between the fair and our town, a semi-paved access road from when it had county funding. It was a convenient place to leave a body.

Jackson was the one who suggested it as the cops organized us into search parties two days after Corinne disappeared: *Did anyone check the caverns? They* couldn't *not* check. Not with us all standing around, about to head out on our own with flashlights and desperation and an illegal key.

We were there when the cops went in: Bailey beside Jackson, her face resting against his chest, his T-shirt already stained with her eye makeup; Tyler, his fingers laced with mine, his grip too tight; Daniel, his arms folded across his chest, sullen and anxious. The police had this big tool ready to cut the chains, but they didn't need it. The padlock was open, the chains unwound, the gate hanging slightly ajar—the darkness beckoning.

Jimmy Bricks went down with a big spotlight, and Officer Fraize tried to keep us all back as we stood with the gathered crowd. We waited forever, the waiting tightening my throat, the summer air too thick and filled with the scent of decay.

They were down there for over an hour, but the only thing they brought back up was the ring.

The ring was beautiful, one of a kind. Interlocking silver bands with a row of tiny blue stones between them. They'd slid it across a table in front of me the next day in a sealed plastic bag.

"Take a closer look," Officer Fraize had said.

Some of the stones were blackened, coated with dried blood. I'd closed my eyes, shook my head. "Not hers," I said.

In the following weeks, they tried to track down its origin—we heard about it from Officer Fraize, who was married to the school secretary, who told her book club. They tried to link it to Corinne, then to Jackson, with a receipt or an ID from a pawnshop. But the ring appeared just like Corinne had vanished.

From nothing.

Into nothing.

Bailey said it wasn't Corinne's. Jackson said it wasn't Corinne's. But the police clung to the idea of it, that there was something we didn't know about her. Something that had led her here, and she'd seeped into the cavern walls—her bone the smooth rock, her teeth the jagged stone, her clothes disintegrating in the darkness—the only thing left behind, the metal of a ring and the blood it clung to.

Why else would Jackson tell the police to search there? It's what the guilty do when the guilt threatens to drown them. It's human nature to want to tell. To be absolved.

Then they sealed the caverns back up: fresh chains, fresh gate, new lock. No keys. As far as I knew, they hadn't been opened in the last ten years.

———

I THOUGHT MAYBE THAT was what the kids sleeping in the clearing were here to do last night. I thought they were here to look for Annaleise as we once searched for Corinne. That maybe they knew something more, something they were scared to tell. But no.

We'd scoured the earth when Corinne disappeared. When the police couldn't, when they wouldn't, we kept looking. We threw ourselves so deep into her disappearance that some of us never managed to climb back out.

*The monster lives in there,* Corinne used to say. Then she'd grab my hand and pull me in, all breathy laughter. *Come find us,* she'd call, and we'd hear footsteps—from Jackson or Tyler—tiny beams of light cast about the floor as we darted out of their paths.

I stood in front of those gates now, my hands encircling the rusted iron bars, listening to the breeze rush into the darkness and echo back in a low-pitched howl. The lock was closed, the chain covered in a coarse moss that slid off too easily, coating my palms.

I traced the path of the chain to the padlock. I tugged at the bars, but they didn't give at all against the stone. Barely made a noise as the padlock and the chains resisted. My fingers tightened on the bars and I stepped close, my face pressed up against the iron, my eyes focused on the place the light disappeared around the corner. "Hello?" I whispered, listening to the word bounce off the walls. I cleared my throat and tried once more: "Annaleise?"

Nothing but my own voice echoed back.

I tried the gates from a different angle, pulling the metal bars parallel to the rock, seeing if they'd give, slide. I gripped the bars and shook until I heard a girl mumble from somewhere nearby. "Did you hear that?"

I slipped into the trees before she could notice.

———

I HAD A MOMENT of panic—that I wouldn't be able to find my way back home without a path to trace. It had been so long since I'd done it on my own. But it all came back. The downtrodden walking trail to the clearing where I used to meet Tyler, to the sounds of the river, which I followed home.

The heat wave hadn't broken, and I was sweating and dirty by the time I reached my backyard.

Seeing Daniel's car parked in the driveway, I froze at the edge of the woods. I walked to the back door outside the kitchen, trying to get a sense of where he was. Heard him on the phone, his shoes pacing on the hardwood. "Just tell me if she's there."

A pause. More pacing.

"Just no bullshit. Tell me she's okay. We had a fight, and . . . she's . . . I don't know. Not doing well."

The pacing picked up.

"No, I showed up and her car's here and all her shit's here, but she's nowhere."

"Daniel?" I pushed through the back door, same way I came out.

He rounded the corner, the phone pressed to his ear. "Never mind," he said, sliding the phone back into his pocket. "Hey, Nic," he said, all drawn out and slow. Hands on his hips, feigned relaxation. "Where were you?"

"I was out for a walk."

His eyes strayed to my clothes, same as yesterday's, and he frowned. "In the woods?"

"No," I said. "Down the road." I cleared my throat. "Hey, do you know, did anyone check the caverns?"

The line between his eyes deepened, the corners of his mouth tipping down. "What are you talking about?"

"The caverns. Did the police ever look inside?"

Daniel looked me over quickly, and I balled my fists to hide the dirt and moss.

"I think we should let them do their job," he said. "Doesn't do any good getting involved."

"Still. Someone should check."

"Nic," he said, waving his hand, "I came to talk to you." He rolled his neck. For a second I thought he was gearing up for an apology, and I mentally prepared to do the same. "It's about Dad. I've got some good news and some bad news."

*Nope, guess not.*

"First," Daniel said, "we have a court date." We had two affidavits vouching for Dad's general incompetence, and a petition that Everett had helped me draw up that would put Daniel as the primary guardian, then me, on condition of Daniel's death. "But it's not for another two months."

"Two months?" I asked.

"Yeah. And if Dad still refuses to sign the paperwork to put the house on the market, it will take until after the guardianship hearing for us to list it."

"I'll talk to him."

Daniel cleared his throat. "Maybe you should go home."

My eyes latched on to his. He was always telling me whether to stay or go, and I wanted to know why. Why he wanted me gone.

"I thought you wanted my help. You told me. You told me you wanted me to come."

"I can take care of it," he said, his face closed off. Unreadable. Typical Daniel.

"I'll talk to Dad," I said. "He'll sign the papers. We'll sell the house."

He nodded. Stared off into the woods. "Bring your phone next time you're out. So I don't worry."

———

THERE WAS A POLICE cruiser in the first row of the half-empty parking lot of Grand Pines, and I instinctively parked near the back. I knew it was irrational, but still.

The cop walked out of the building just as I left the car, and I stood beside the door, reshuffling the listing paperwork. There was something vaguely familiar about the way he walked, looking down at his feet with his hands shoved in his pockets. Something about his jet-black hair cropped perfectly against his light brown skin—*cinnamon,* Jackson had called it on Bailey. As if her ethnicity had a scent or a flavor.

"Mark?" I called, pushing off my car. "Mark Stewart?" The cop Annaleise had left a message for before she disappeared: *I have a few questions about the Corinne Prescott case. Can we set up a time to talk?*

Mark Stewart. *Here.*

He froze halfway to his car, stranded on the blue lines of a handicap space. I was jogging toward him, my flip-flops slapping against the pavement, the papers slipping from their stack under my arm. I secured them between my elbow and waist and gestured to myself, my heart pounding in my chest. "Nic Farrell. Remember?"

His eyes widened in surprise, but he quickly replaced it with a nod and a smile. "Hi, Nic. Wow, it's been . . ." He let the thought linger in the air between us.

"Yeah," I said. "God, you got tall." I searched his face, but it was completely closed off, both familiar and unreadable. Bailey had always been captivating, the type of person you couldn't tear your eyes from, no matter how many times you'd seen her. Their mom was from Japan—her father had met her there during his four years of navy service—and she had this partially stilted accent that Bailey could mimic perfectly.

The same combination on her brother—the dark hair, the brown eyes, the cinnamon skin—somehow had the opposite effect. He faded into a group, shrank from our focus. I wondered whether he and Annaleise had been close. If he knew something more that he'd kept for himself. Maybe why she'd asked about the Corinne Prescott case in the first place.

Mark had been fourteen when I left. The only thing I really remembered about his personality was that he was exceptionally goofy in that immature-boy way in his own home. Outside, he was morose and quiet. And when I ran into him outside of his house, away from his family, he blushed when he saw me, like he was em-barrassed that I knew the other version.

"What are you doing here?" I asked.

His cheeks tinged red, and I was glad to see I still had that effect. It would make him overcompensate by oversharing. "Got a tip," he said, staring past me. "From a nurse. About a potential crime. We're required to follow up."

I nodded, tried to steady my hand, tried to slow my breath.

*Could be anyone. How many patients are there? What did that brochure say? Six hundred and twenty? Maybe two hundred and sixty. Still, less than a one percent chance.*

"So how've you been? Still living in town?"

"Nah. Just work there. I live a few miles from Bailey. Nice area. You know."

He was acting like I had a clue about Bailey. I didn't know where she lived or what she did. Didn't want to ask around, to draw attention to the uncomfortable truth: Bailey and I didn't speak. Not after Corinne had disappeared. Hardly ever a day since.

That box in the police station, it does things to people. Makes you tell things about each other. Becomes a permanent record of your betrayal, with your signature below.

"Well," I said, "it was really good seeing you, Mark."

I was almost at the door when he called after me. "Hey, Nic," he said, using some voice I'd never heard from him. His cop voice. "You in town for a while?"

I shrugged. "Just taking care of some loose ends." I gripped the papers tighter to keep my hands from shaking.

He didn't ask why I was here or who I was visiting.

He already knew.

As soon as the doors shut behind me, I raced to my father's room.

———

DAD WAS PARTICULARLY DISORIENTED, or rattled, or both.

He sat on the edge of the bed, staring at the wall, faintly rocking back and forth. I knocked on the open door, but he didn't answer. "Dad?" I called. He turned to look at me, then went back to the wall and the rocking. He was shutting down.

There was no imminent danger. No reason for the director to call Daniel or schedule a meeting or explain her concerns. They were probably quite pleased with themselves.

But for me, this was scarier. He wasn't clawing for sanity, or fighting for understanding, or raging against the unfamiliar. He was letting go.

On the wall across from the bed were pictures of us, of me and Daniel and the nurses and doctors, people he shouldn't be afraid of. People he should remember. He was staring right through them now. I stood beside my picture. My hair was shorter in it, and I was smiling, and Dad had his arm slung over my shoulder. It was from when we brought him here last year, taken in this very room, because we couldn't find any recent photos of the two of us. *With daughter, Nic,* it said underneath in Daniel's handwriting.

Dad kept rocking. He was mumbling something—repeating words to himself, all strung together in nonsense. "Dad," I tried again, but he still looked right through me.

Then he stopped, paused, focused. "Shana?" he asked.

I closed my eyes, and he went back to rocking.

There was no picture of my mother on the walls. It had been a hard decision, the one Daniel and I wavered over the most—whether to put her up there and fill him with the hope that she still existed. Or whether to pretend she never did. Which was worse? Daniel and I debated it over dinner the night before we moved him in. I was the one who made the decision, because I knew: The losing. The losing of something you thought you had. That was far, far worse.

I stepped into the hallway, the light too bright, the buzzing from the fluorescence drowning out the low hum of voices in the other rooms. "Hey," I said to the first official-looking person walking down the hall. No scrubs, business casual, hair loose, and a birdlike face. I recognized her from the last time I was here. I grabbed her arm as she tried to walk past with a stiff smile. "What did you do to him?" I asked.

Maybe it was the way I grabbed her arm, or maybe the look in my eye, but she blinked slowly and said, "I'll page the doctor."

"No. I want to speak with Karen Addelson," I said firmly, trying to summon my best impression of Everett, calling the director by her full name.

"She's in a meeting."

If Everett were here, he'd have her pulled out of that meeting without it seeming like his idea. He'd let this woman talk herself in circles: *She shouldn't be long; oh, I see the problem here; well, maybe I'll just peek my head in, see if she can spare a moment.* Make it seem like her idea all along.

"I need to talk to her," I said.

"I'll let her know as soon as she's done."

"Now," I said. "I need to talk to her *now*. Has someone been to see my dad? Is that why he's silently rocking back and forth on his bed right now? Is this what you all mean by"—I raised my hands in makeshift quotes—"exceptional patient care?"

Her cheeks flushed. "Fine. You can sit in the waiting room. I'll tell her you're here."

I followed her determined steps down the hall. "Why were the police here?" I asked.

Her step faltered, but she kept moving. "I don't know. The cops showed up an hour ago—"

"Cops or *cop*?" I asked. "Mark Stewart?"

She paused at the office door, turned to me with a quizzical look. "One cop." She cleared her throat. "Asian, I think?" She blushed again, like that wasn't the PC way to describe someone.

Just a guy. Just a goofy, sullen kid. *Mark.*

"And you let him talk to my dad? I will hold you all personally accountable if this"—I made an arm movement trying to encompass everything my dad was at the moment—"gets worse."

She gestured toward the couch, then sat at the desk in the outer office. "I was in here. I have no idea what happened." She picked up the phone and pressed a button. "I have Patrick Farrell's daughter in the waiting room."

Karen Addelson was outside her office, escorting a couple and making apologies for the interruption, within a solid minute. The director held out her hands. "Nicolette. Please, come in." As if she'd been expecting me.

Her office had potted plants and a little Zen garden on a coffee table, a miniature rake with lazy curving lines through the sand. "What did you do to my dad? I saw Officer Stewart in the parking lot, and my dad is practically catatonic in his room. What the hell happened?"

"Sit, please," she said.

I sat in the straight-back chair in front of her desk, ignoring the couch she was gesturing toward. Tough to feel self-righteous when you're stuffed into an oversize couch in front of a Zen garden.

She took her time walking to the other side of the desk. When she sat, she folded her hands on top of the desk blotter, the blue veins running over her knuckles, making her look about ten years older than I'd originally thought. Sixties. Dad's age. God, he shouldn't be here.

"Ms. Farrell," she began, "I cannot stop the police from questioning a patient, as much as I wish that weren't the case. It was just a few questions. Apparently, your father might've been a potential witness to a crime."

I laughed. "Sure. I'm sure they were hoping he'd be a great witness they could use on the stand."

"Ms. Farrell," she said, "even if he was deemed unfit legally, our hands are tied. It is not our legal right to ban the police from questioning a patient. That responsibility is yours."

"Have you seen him? He's a mess. Nothing he says makes any sense."

"Look. He was talking to a nurse, and the nurse says he called her Nic, and he kept mentioning a missing girl. That he knew what happened. She had to report it, you see."

I fought to keep the surprise from my face, but a wave of nausea rolled through, working its way from my stomach to my throat. "No, don't *you* see? If he thought someone else was me, then he already didn't know what he was saying. Don't you see the fallacy in your logic? Nothing he says makes any sense."

"On the contrary, your father is a very smart man. There's always truth in there somewhere. Maybe you should ask him. Ask him about the missing girl, see what he says."

"Were you there?" I asked.

She took a moment to compose herself, and I recognized her pause as a tactic Everett would use. Be calm, calm the situation. Keep the emotion low, grasp the upper hand. "No. He insisted it be private. They are the police, after all. My hands are tied."

I pushed back from the table. When I got angry, I couldn't stop the tears. As if the two emotions were all tangled up in each other. And that made me angrier, since I seemed weak when I wanted to seem confident and demanding, like Everett. The best I could muster was the grand gesture of storming out of the room.

———

IT TOOK OVER AN hour for Dad to recognize me, and I sat in his room the whole time, waiting it out. Then it all seemed to click. He looked at the picture on the wall and me on the guest chair in the corner. "Nic," he said, fingers drumming against the surface of his dresser. "Nic, your friend. Your friend's brother. Did you know he's a cop? I didn't know—"

"It's okay, Dad. I'll take care of it. Tell me what he asked. Tell me what you said." I stood and closed the door, and he was watching me from the sides of his eyes.

"About that girl. That girl who disappeared."

I shivered. "You don't have to answer. It was ten years ago, and Mark probably doesn't even remember—"

"No, not Corinne. I mean, yes, her. But also. The other. The other girl. The . . ."

"Annaleise Carter? You couldn't possibly be a witness. You've been in here for . . ." I cleared my throat. "You were here when she went missing."

"How long, Nic? How long have I been in here? It's important."

I paused. "About a year."

He sucked in a breath. "I'm late."

"Dad, what did they ask?" I said, trying to keep his focus.

"They wanted to know if I knew her well. And your brother. Always your brother. He never should've done that." He stared at the side of my face as if he could see the mark Daniel left ten years earlier. As if it happened just a moment ago. I felt the sting rise to the surface like a memory, and I ran my tongue along the inside of my cheek, expecting to taste blood. The swing of his arm that had sentenced him to constant suspicion. "And if I thought they were related. Corinne and Annaleise. Yes. That's what he wanted to know. There's too much in that house, Nic."

"There's nothing in the house, Dad. I promise."

"There's plenty," he said. "I need to . . . I keep memories. A record, to help my mind, a—"

The nurse opened the door. "Mrs. Addelson wants him evaluated by the doctor. Come on, Patrick," she said to him without making eye contact with me.

He stood and leaned down as he passed, his heavy hand resting on my shoulder. "With the skeletons," he whispered. "Get it. Get it first."

———

I SPENT THE RIDE home calling people who didn't pick up the phone. Daniel was at work, on site somewhere. Tyler was probably busy at work, too. Everett didn't pick up but sent me a text after saying he was stuck in a meeting and would call later.

When I pulled into the driveway, Laura was waiting on the front porch, leaning back on her elbows, shifting uncomfortably on the wooden steps.

Something was wrong. We didn't have a random-drop-in relationship. We hadn't spoken since the baby shower. And what kind of news couldn't she give over the phone? I held my breath as I walked toward the steps, my heart pounding, before I saw the pots and containers of soil spread out on the porch.

"Hey," she said, slightly unsure herself. "Dan said you guys could use some stuff for the garden. And I'm in full-on nesting mode, but I've run out of things to nest with. I'd do it myself, but I topple over when I try to garden now. It's embarrassing."

"Thank you. You didn't have to do this. But thank you."

"And," she said. "I wanted to apologize for Saturday. For my friends."

I shook my head fast. "Don't. It's fine."

"It's not," she said. "They sometimes don't think. They're good people, really. But that doesn't excuse it."

"Okay," I said, just to get her to stop. I sat down on the step beside her. "I'd invite you in to cool down, but I think it's probably worse in there. Do you want a drink?"

"No, I'm fine," she said. "Are you busy? Or do you have time for me to walk you through some of this?"

Her voice was so hopeful, I couldn't send her away. Not like this. Not right now. Not when everyone else was unreachable and all I had left were my dad's words for company. With the skeletons, he said. I felt my mind wanting to dive down the rabbit hole after him. "Yes," I said. "I have time."

Laura had a scent to her, the fragrance from the garden catching, clinging, taking root in her. Like she herself was blooming or thriving. Her skin had gone transparent, or her veins had darkened as blood rushed under her skin, and I could see the fine map running through her. *Life,* I thought.

"These are full-shade," she said, gesturing to a pot, "so I thought they'd be perfect for the side garden." She paused, frowned. "Some animal really made a mess of it."

I pushed off the steps and reached my hand down to help her stand. She smoothed the fabric of her dress, stretching her neck to look up at the house.

"The place has good bones," she said. "It just needs a little work. Dan's glad you're here."

"He has a funny way of showing it."

She brushed the comment aside with a swipe of her hand. "He's got a lot on his plate, between work, your dad, the property, and the baby. He's just stressed." She grinned. "I'm planning to ask him to put an addition on our house, but figure I should probably wait until all this has passed." She waved her hand around her head, and I wasn't sure whether she was talking about the property or *everything.*

"Good thinking." I picked up the larger flower pots, started walking toward the side of the house. Laura carried a few of the smaller ones, trailing behind.

"I know he's not perfect," she said. "I know you've had your differences. But he takes care of your dad, and he takes care of us. He's going to be a good father—you can see that, right?"

"Of course," I said automatically. It was the expected response, the right thing to say.

Laura frowned, as if she could see right through me. "He was just a kid back then, Nic. Same as you."

As if this was something they had discussed. As if Daniel had drawn her into our family with all of our history—not just as an extension, but something more. A part of our past, as much as our future. She was leaning against the siding, watching me.

I sighed, nodded. "Okay, Laura," I said, brushing my hands on the sides of my pants. "Where do we start?"

———

MY CELL PHONE RANG when I was in the shower, as the soil clumped and swirled down the drain. I reached my hand through the curtain and hit the speaker so I wouldn't get the phone wet. "Hello?" I said, expecting Daniel or Everett.

But the voice. The voice was every bit as sharp as my memory. Tight and quick. Soft and unsure. "It's Bailey," she said.

"Hi," I said, like an idiot. I turned off the water and stood naked, my hair dripping and goose bumps forming across my skin.

"They're bringing your dad down to the station tomorrow for questioning." She let out a slow breath. "I don't know why I'm telling you this."

Nothing keeps in this town. Not in the bed, not over the dinner table, not at the bar, not between family and friends and neighbors. Not even between us.

I was full of panic, full of thoughts, full of a to-do list forming in my head, blurry and unreadable. *Everett. Call Everett.* "I owe you one. I don't know how to thank you." My words echoed through the bathroom, and I had to strain to hear Bailey under my own breathing.

A pause. And then, "Stay away from me."

If these are my debts, if I'm paying them off, then maybe this is hers.

———

I CALLED EVERETT WITH a towel held to my body, dripping on the linoleum. "I was just getting ready to call you back. I'm sorry," he said.

"I need advice," I said.

"Okay," he said. "About the guardianship? You got the affidavits, right?"

"They're trying to question my dad. About a crime. Everett, he's not in his right mind." My voice wavered. "I don't know what he's saying or what he'll say. I have to stop it. Tell me how to stop it."

"Back up. What's happening?"

I told him fragments. A missing girl from ten years ago. Another missing person, dragging the case out for closer inspection. It all came out high-pitched and clipped. My voice was laced with tears.

"I'll take care of it," he said.

"But what do I do? Who do I talk to?"

"I said I'll take care of it. Call the facility, give them my number, tell them to call me if anyone, *anyone,* tries to talk to your father. Tell them we'll sue if they don't. We won't have a case. But tell them anyway."

I did what he said. Called Karen Addelson and left a firm and unwavering message on her voicemail which I'd practiced three times in the mirror. Then I called Daniel and told him what Bailey had told me and what Everett had said.

I tried Tyler again. I considered leaving a message but knew that would be a bad idea. Anything left could be used in an investigation when they broke us all open again, and they were already looking at Tyler for motive. It had happened before. I remembered one of the other things that had made it into the box in Corinne's case:

A recording of a voicemail, Corinne to Jackson. *I'm so sorry,* she'd said, her voice choked, so unlike her. The detective from State played it for me to see if I knew what she was talking about. *Please, Jackson. Please come back. I'll be at the fair. Find me there. I'll do anything. Just don't do this. Don't. Please.*

Jackson swore they never met up. But if he had, if the last thing on record was Corinne and Jackson meeting up . . . It was enough: a pleading voicemail, and nobody saw her after. It was enough to convict in a place like this.

———

I HUNG UP WHEN Tyler's voicemail picked up, and I started searching. I searched the house for skeletons. I had to get them. I had to get them first.

*The Day Before*

# DAY 10

I couldn't sleep in the house, worrying that there was something I was missing—*someone* who'd been in my house, possibly out there right now. I came out to the back porch sometime after midnight for the cooler air, the clearer head. I sat on the back steps but kept the outside lights off—I felt too exposed otherwise, with nothing but my dad's words echoing in my head: *The woods have eyes.*

I stared off into the night—the shadows against the dark—drifting in and out of consciousness. The shadows shifting as clouds passed in front of the moon. The dark shapes in my peripheral vision, creeping like monsters.

———

THE COPS HADN'T FOUND anything yet—no hard evidence. Or if they had, they weren't talking. And that didn't sound like them. Not the ones I knew.

Officer Fraize had been a cop ten years ago when Corinne disappeared. He'd told his wife about Jackson and Bailey and Tyler and me. His wife was the school secretary—maybe he thought she'd know something that would help with the case. Maybe he was looking for information, but he was really giving it away: *Bailey and Jackson? Corinne and Tyler? Do you remember Daniel Farrell? Tell me about them. Tell me everything.*

Jimmy Bricks had been a senior when Daniel was a freshman. In addition to being the first Bricks to attend college, he held the school record for most beers funneled at a time. The record remained unbroken by the time I graduated. We were too close in age. Our circles overlapped. We'd see him at parties when he was home from college. He told rumors about Corinne as if they were facts from a police investigation and not the other way around.

It wasn't until they brought in Hannah Pardot from the State Bureau of Investigation that the case gained traction. Detective Hannah Pardot, who never smiled, not even when she was trying to play nice, with her piercing eyes and the bloodred lipstick that sometimes stained her teeth. She made me the most nervous, mostly because she was once an eighteen-year-old girl. She seemed to know there was more to Corinne than anyone could say.

She was in her thirties back then, with curly auburn hair and gray eyes that revealed nothing. Maybe she'd had kids and settled down by now. Maybe she took an early retirement. Or maybe the cases shuffled in and out and we didn't last with her—not like she'd lasted with us.

Hannah was thorough and tight-lipped, concentrating on the cold, hard facts. If she'd been here from the beginning, maybe she would've discovered what had happened to Corinne.

Maybe if she were here now, they'd find out what happened to Annaleise.

The facts. The facts were difficult to see clearly. The facts were like the view from our porch—shadows in darkness and shapes you could conjure up from fear itself.

———

THERE WAS SOMETHING OUT there. Feet crunching leaves, getting louder, moving closer—someone *running*. Adrenaline propelled me to my feet as the blood rushed to my head. The footsteps were moving faster, approaching from my left. I held my breath, strained to see, but whoever it was remained hidden inside the tree line. He continued past my house, the leaves crunching under his steps at a steady pace before an extended pause as he leaped across the creek that had long ago dried up, onto Carter land.

I looked for my phone—*inside*—and thought of the time it would take for someone else to get here. The footsteps fading as I debated what to do.

*Go.*

I was quick through the grass, but my bare feet recoiled as I entered the woods, turning my steps tentative. I bit back a yelp as a sharp twig caught my ankle, and I held on to a tree, listening for the sound of footsteps. Nothing but silence now. Had he heard me? Was he gone?

I held my breath, gripping the tree, and counted to twenty.

Still no sound.

I stepped carefully, pausing every few seconds to listen, until I reached the hill between our property and the Carters'. I crouched low, climbing the hill on my hands and knees, trying to get a better view of the place through the trees.

There. A light. A shadow moving in front of the gap between the shades from inside the converted studio. I moved closer, side-stepping down the hill. The light was dim—not strong enough to be coming from a lamp, just a flicker through the shades. A flash-light, a television screen, a computer, maybe.

I sneaked closer, but the shades moved aside and the shadow peered out. The way the moonlight angled into the window caught the eyes, set off a glow, and I closed my own eyes in case they were doing the same. I slid behind the nearest tree, kept my back pressed against the trunk, and tried to slow my breathing.

A door latched, a lock turned—the other person was outside now. I heard movement in the leaves, circling around. Slowly at first, coming closer. And then faster, moving away, into the distance.

I waited for minutes, maybe longer, before heading back to my house, my legs shaking, my feet numb to the trail. Someone had been in Annaleise's place in the middle of the night. Someone who knew the woods well. Someone who had a key. Someone who could run in the dark by heart.

———

THE SHOWER RAN COLD, and I wasn't sure whether I was shaking from the temperature or the leftover adrenaline. But the water felt good. The heat of the day had already begun, and I hadn't even started looking for someone to fix the air-conditioning. Tyler had said it was probably the condenser fan, but Daniel wanted a second opinion. A *real* opinion, was what he actually said.

I got dressed, started a pot of coffee, sank into a kitchen chair, and rested my head on my arms while it brewed. I tried to lull my mind, empty it, drift off into a worry-free oblivion. But I had to try to catch Tyler before he left. I had to look into his eyes when I asked. I had to know.

Just one more minute. Just a moment, and then I'd go.

———

THE COFFEE WAS LUKEWARM by the time I pulled myself from the table. *Shit.* I downed a quick cup instead of breakfast and hopped in the car, driving straight to Kelly's Pub.

Tyler's truck was already gone, but I could see the dim lights from the pub through the dirty window. Jackson's bike was in the back lot, like always. Though it was a Wednesday morning, there were a few men at the bar already. Whiskey in a glass. Beer in a bottle. And a bowl of mixed nuts on the counter between them.

The bell rang as I pushed through the front door. Jackson locked eyes with me from behind the bar. "Can I help you with something?"

When I got closer, I could see he was biting back a smirk. "God, do you work here all the time?" I asked.

"It's my job," he said, rough hands pressed flat against the counter, leaning so his muscles strained against his T-shirt, the tattoos on his forearms rippling with life. His nails were bitten down to the quick, and I couldn't tell whether his fingertips were stained with liquor or nicotine. "By the way, you missed him by a few hours." He said this without looking me in the eye.

Jackson and I were always cautious with each other. Even when his words carried the weight of a threat, they were buried under something else. I knew too much of him, and he of me. Too much we learned about each other and Corinne during the investigation. It was only after she disappeared that I realized how little my best friend had shared with me. When I couldn't find the answers to the exacting questions from Hannah Pardot. *What did she think of her parents? What did she say about Jackson? Did you know she had plans to meet him? What was she asking him about in this message?* I could only answer the hypotheticals. Those, I knew. *Would she have gone off with someone she just met? Would she run away? Would she take your boyfriend and pretend it was for your own good?*

But the *What was her state of mind?* The things with substance— the tangible, real answers—those were elusive. I knew only the Corinne who existed in the hypotheticals, the theoretical possibilities: *would she, could she, might she.*

It wasn't until Hannah Pardot broke her open that I knew all of her. Corinne Prescott: more real presumed dead than alive.

Jackson got away with the things he kept hidden: *I didn't see her; she never found me; I don't know what the message was about.*

But only because I never called him on it.

Back then people wanted to believe him. *Jackson Porter, he loved Corinne, he would never.*

There was something about him when we were teenagers. Something about his appearance that made people want to believe him. He didn't look honest, exactly, but his features made him seem trustworthy.

People saw his brown eyes, which were large and framed by eyelashes too long for a guy and made him seem like he was always listening even when he wasn't. And his hair, which was exactly the same color as his eyes, something that seemed perfectly logical, that made you want to trust him. But it was more than that—it was the symmetry of him. Made him seem incapable of deceit. When Corinne disappeared and the questions began, I was seized by the sudden thought that Jackson could—and always had been able to—get away with anything.

And I knew he was lying.

I didn't want to be in a room with him. Or talk about him. And it was this that Hannah Pardot seized on. Not my words but the distance I tried to put between myself and Jackson. This unwillingness to comment on anything Jackson said. To neither confirm nor deny. I switched to *I don't know,* which was all Corinne had left me with anyway.

It didn't matter in the end. Bailey cracked at the first tap, after hearing about the pregnancy test in Corinne's bathroom. Filled that box with each of our betrayals and all of her fears. Told Hannah Pardot what she wanted to hear: *Nic? She thinks she's too good for this place. But she's nothing without us. Nothing.* And *No, we didn't know*

*Corinne was pregnant, but it must've been Jackson's, and that must've been what her voicemail was about, and Jackson didn't want it, obviously.* Bailey followed the pieces Hannah laid out for her, feeding her back the story she demanded: that Corinne was impulsive and reckless—she'd burned down the Randall barn, even—and I was still pissed about her hitting on Tyler at the party. And Daniel was always too harsh on me—emphasis on *harsh. Jackson wasn't going to forgive her this time,* Bailey said. *He told me so.*

It was him. It had to be him. He didn't want her or the baby.

Bailey made it a story, and since she was one of Corinne's best friends, that made it real—everyone else adding layers over the top: *I heard her throwing up in the bathroom; she didn't wear those cropped shirts anymore, because obviously she was hiding it; she was ashamed. Jackson dumped her. The poor girl. That poor, poor girl. Brought it on herself, though, you know.*

I don't know what came over me when I found out. Why I pushed Bailey, why I yelled, why I accused her of ruining Jackson. Why I cared.

Because she did ruin him. That was the story people ultimately believed, even if no one could ever prove it. And that was why he was working at this bar, all alone. And why he never had a girl who stuck around. Now those same eyes with the impossibly long lashes made him seem like he was listening too much, eavesdropping, plotting. His appearance was too coincidental. The symmetry of him was the mask. And he, the monster behind it.

This bar was the safest place to put him.

"Why don't you leave, Jackson?"

He didn't answer. His tattoos rippled as he wiped down the bar between us. But I thought I knew. You wait for people here. For people to come back. For things to make sense.

"Why do you keep coming back?" he asked.

"I'm helping out with my dad."

"So you're only coming back for him?" He smirked again, avoiding my gaze.

I dropped onto a barstool. "Since when did it become socially acceptable to drink at breakfast?" I asked.

Jackson pressed his lips together, looking at me for a beat too long. "It's after lunch."

I checked the clock behind the bar, staring at the second hand jerking to a stop with each movement. I must've been out for an hour or two at the kitchen table. Trading time in the day for the sleep I wasn't getting at night.

"What do you want, Nic?"

I drummed my fingers on the counter like my dad might do, then stopped myself. Held them flat. Willed them not to shake from the caffeine. "Do you know where Tyler works?"

"Same place he's always worked."

"You know what I mean."

Tyler didn't have an office. He and his dad used to work out of their home, where Tyler was happy to live until what I considered way past an acceptable age; he said he'd rather save the money.

"But then you have to spend it on a motel whenever you want to take a girl back to your place," I'd teased him, standing too close.

He'd grinned and said, "I just take them to theirs." And he'd taken me back to my place to prove his point.

But now he lived here. In an apartment above a bar. And I wasn't sure if he still worked out of his parents' house or was on site today.

Jackson threw the rag on the counter and motioned for me to follow him out of the bar, out of earshot. We stood in the vestibule between the front door and the staircase, and he leaned in close. "Stay away from him right now. Trust me."

"What are you talking about?" I felt the men in the bar leaning closer, trying to hear—felt all the rumors that could come from this moment: *Jackson and Nic, whispering about the case. Jackson and Nic, standing too close.*

"Annaleise Carter," he said. "They're pushing Tyler hard on it. And you being here? Doesn't look good for him."

"How do you know this?"

"It doesn't matter. Just don't add more fuel to the rumors, Nic."

"What rumors?"

He cut me off with a look, and I brushed the comment aside. "I'm engaged. I just need to talk to him."

"You need to stay away from him. Annaleise was . . ." He trailed off, thinking. Annaleise was still a thirteen-year-old girl to me. I'd left and missed what she had become.

"Annaleise was what?"

"She was obsessed." He cleared his throat. "With Corinne. She'd been hanging out here a lot. Being way too friendly. Asking questions."

"About what happened?"

"Not really. It's not like she was obsessed with what happened, exactly. Just . . . her." Jackson looked over my shoulder, into the bar, his mouth close to my ear. "She'd say things I swear Corinne used to say to me in the same tone of voice. It was creepy, Nic. Seriously fucking creepy. She could do a pretty sick impression of her." His jaw tensed, every muscle in his body tensed. "I never . . . She creeped me out, more than anything. But the cops still talked to me. They were here just this morning. I bet they're with Tyler now, since they *also* wanted to know where he worked. Bet they'll talk to your brother soon enough."

"Daniel? Why the hell would they talk to him?"

Jackson's lips pressed together and he stared back, unwavering.

"You're not serious," I said. "Daniel wouldn't."

He shrugged. "I hear she called him a lot. She'd come in here looking for him, just like you're looking for Tyler right now. Hear his wife spent a few days at her sister's place a few months back—don't know if it was related. Rumors. You know how it goes."

Rumors. They always start from something. Daniel hadn't told me Laura had left. But then again, would he?

"Just tell me where he works, Jackson."

"I really don't know," he said, his eyes sliding away from me.

*Lie. Again.*

He left me standing in the entrance to the bar. And somewhere along the way, as I felt myself losing a grip on everything I'd fought to hold together—my family—and as the panic surged up and over, I lost all semblance of pride. I followed him in. Raised my voice in the dim quiet. "Does anyone know where I can find Tyler Ellison?"

The man with the whiskey coughed into his fist. I walked over to him, stood too close. "Do you know?" I asked, leaning so close that the liquor on his breath stung my eyes.

He held the glass between us like a shield, smiled as he raised it to his lips. "Nah, I'm just curious what he did to make a girl barge into a bar looking for him." He laughed to himself.

The man with the beer ignored him. He frowned and tipped his glass toward me. "Patrick Farrell's daughter, right?"

The other man went silent. I nodded.

"Ellison Construction's got a project going at the railway. New station. Funded by the goddamn township." He took a gulp of his beer, dropped it to the counter. "For the goddamn tourists." The other man mumbled something about money and funding and streets and the schools. "My guess, you'll find him there. How's your dad?"

"Not good," I said. "Worse. He's getting worse."

"You selling the house? That what I hear?"

"I don't know," I said. Everything was fluid again. Dad hadn't signed the papers. But the house was just the tip of the thing now.

I turned to leave, and Jackson grabbed my arm. "Be smart," he said.

And, like an echo, I heard Tyler whispering to Jackson down by the river. *Be smart,* he said, and then I stepped on a twig, and they both turned around, pretended they were talking about something else.

*Jackson told the police he didn't see her after the fair, Nic,* Tyler had told me later. *He claims he never saw her at all that night.*

But that was a lie.

I *saw* Jackson and Corinne. *After* the fair. But if I said that . . . you had to understand the way things were. The stories people could weave from the few facts they had, the truths they pulled together from that box.

They needed someone to blame. Someone to vilify and put in a cell so they could feel safe again. Someone to play the part, be the monster.

I couldn't tell that. It would be enough to close the box forever. I'd be sentencing him.

Jackson wasn't some pushover who let Corinne wrong him time and time again. He wasn't some angry kid who felt betrayed, like the investigation would have you believe. It had nothing to do with any baby, any fight. When Corinne turned on him, cut him down and made him push back, enough to push her away—he liked it.

I know this because we all did.

He liked it because of what came next—the phone call begging him to return. That phone message they played for all of us: *Please. Please come back.* The way she'd love him, surely, when he did. Nobody would ever love you so fiercely, so meanly, so thoroughly. And the parts of you that you wanted to keep hidden—she loved those most of all.

"Nic," she'd said when my mom died, pulling me to her chest, crying herself. "I love you. I'd trade you one if I could. You know that, right?"

I clung to her, not speaking. Corinne would talk like that, like people were things to trade, pieces on a chessboard that we could move around, that we could control.

"Want to watch something burn?" she'd asked.

That night we went to the Randalls' abandoned barn. She had a red container of gasoline that she shook out, tracing the perimeter.

She let me strike the match, and she held my hand as we watched it burn to the ground. We stood too close to it, so close we could feel each time a piece of wood caught, sparked, ignited.

She called Tyler to come pick me up, and told us to say we'd been together the whole night. "Go," she said, right before she called 911. She took the fall for the barn all on her own. "I told them I was practicing how to make a fire. Like in the Girl Scouts. In case of emergency. It got out of hand." Her smile, huge. The whole thing just a tiny favor. Six months of community service and the wrath of her father, a small gift to help me through my mother's death.

How could I *not* love Corinne Prescott back then? How could anyone not? I liked to believe it was for things like this and not because I was drawn to the mean in her, or how she could destroy things without flinching—a dying bird, an abandoned barn. I liked to believe she did these things because she loved me, too.

I can see it all a little clearer now with the filter of time. How, if you tilt the frame and change the perspective, maybe she wasn't taking the fall only for me. That maybe it was just one more link in a chain of IOUs, emotional blackmail that would one day be called up and cashed in.

I think Corinne believed that life could break even somehow. That there was an underlying fairness to it all. That the years on earth were all a game. A risk for a payoff, a test for an answer, a tally of allies and enemies, and a score at the end. I know now that everything we did or said, and everything we didn't, was kept in a ledger in her mind—and always in the back of ours, too.

———

I CALLED DANIEL FROM the car on my way to find Tyler. He picked up on the first ring. "Hello?" he said, typing in the background.

"Tell me you were not messing around with Annaleise Carter."

The typing stopped. "Jesus Christ, Nic."

"Damnit, Daniel, are you kidding me? What the hell were you thinking? What the hell were you doing? And *Laura*—"

"I know you're not lecturing me on fidelity, Nic. But no," he said. "No." More emphatically. But I didn't believe him. This is what you say when you're being questioned. This is what you cling to against all else, against all evidence. This is what you say, and you pray that someone will back you up.

I'd done it for him once before.

Ten years earlier, I'd heard Hannah Pardot asking my brother in the living room, "Were you and Corinne ever in any sort of relationship?" I pressed my ear to the grate in the bathroom floor and heard him swear: "Never. Never."

When my turn came around, I repeated his words. *Never,* I said. *Never.*

"Nic? Are you listening to me?" Daniel's voice tightened through the phone.

"Jackson said—"

"Jackson doesn't know what the fuck he's talking about. I've got a lot of work to catch up on. So do you need anything else, or were you just calling for the interrogation?"

"Okay. Okay." I hung up, feeling sick to my stomach. Once again, I saw a missing girl in the center of a web. Jackson's words twisting into a warning. Annaleise had been worming her way into the lives of anyone connected to Corinne Prescott. As if she'd been looking for something.

A missing poster lingered in my peripheral vision at the stoplight, her eyes wide and searching. A shudder ran through me, the tremor in my hands coming back.

I was looking for something, too.

I wondered if maybe she'd found it.

———

TYLER WASN'T AT THE railway station. He was about a hundred yards past it, where they were extending the track, a wide frame and cement base already in place. Across the street, even surrounded by men all dressed the same—worn jeans, tan work boots, and a T-shirt, the same uniform he'd adopted eleven years ago—I could pick him out right away. Whereas the rest of the crew had on yellow hard hats, he wore a black baseball cap with ECC in block letters across the front.

A skinny man looked over Tyler's shoulder, gestured with his chin. "I think you got some company."

Tyler turned in slow motion. His face remained passive as he took me in, which was the most un-Tyler-like thing of all. Normally, I'd show up and he'd turn and smile. *Hey, Nic,* like I'd been gone only a day. Not six months, a year, more.

But now his face didn't change. "Hi," he said. The twitch of his thumb, the only indication that I was anything other than a stranger. His eyes shifted quickly to the side, to where the skinny man was watching us. "Can I help you with something?"

"I need to speak to you. It's urgent." I mentally berated myself. *Urgent,* like Everett would say in a business meeting.

"Sure." He gestured to a small trailer, and I worried I'd have to talk in front of his father, but when I got inside, I realized the office was his. Single desk, his truck keys sprawled on top of some papers. A few straight-back chairs throughout. Plans and permits tacked to the corkboard walls. When he'd worked for his dad during school and then after, I'd always thought it was temporary. That he'd want something more, like I did. But he didn't go to college when he graduated, and I should've known it then. Not just assumed he was working for his dad because he was waiting for me.

Ten years later and he was running the company. Ten years later, two fewer degrees than I had, and he was twice as accomplished.

He followed me in, closed the door, and leaned back against it. "Sorry, I wasn't expecting you." He glanced out the window. "This really isn't the best time."

"I'm sorry. But something happened." I tried to get a good look at his face, but the brim of his hat was pulled down low, and I couldn't see his eyes. Just his mouth, a set line.

"What happened?" he asked, his back still pressed up against the door. The distance between us felt tangible, forced and awkward.

"Last night. After midnight. Someone was in Annaleise's place." A muscle at the side of his jaw twitched. I wanted to rip the hat off his head. I needed to see his eyes.

"And you know this because?"

"Because I saw them."

"Nic, you've got to stay out of the fucking woods. You've got to let this go."

"Tyler . . ."

"What?" he asked.

"I have to ask you." I paused, wishing he wouldn't make me.

He readjusted the brim of his hat, turned to stare out the window. "What, exactly, do you need to ask me?"

How many ways could I say it? I stepped closer, but his face remained in shadow. "Was it you?"

He looked back to me, like the whole conversation had caught him off guard. "Was *what* me? What the hell are you talking about?"

I lowered my voice even though we were alone. "Were you in her place last night? After midnight?" I asked.

Tyler turned and fixed his eyes on mine—*What are you saying, Nic?*—until I had to look away.

"Do you have a key?" I asked.

"Are you fucking kidding me right now?"

"You never told me," I said. "You never told me whether you were serious or just screwing her."

He took his hat off, ran his hand through his hair, pulled it back down. He shifted his lower jaw around. "Just screwing, Nic. Happy?"

"No, I'm not happy." My voice wavered, and I took a slow breath to steady myself. "Someone was in there."

"Probably the police. Since they were just here."

Fuck. Fucking Jackson being fucking right.

"What did they want? What did you say?"

He looked out the window again. "They want to find Annaleise. And they want to poke holes in my alibi. They want to catch me in a lie."

I paused, thinking. "What is your alibi, Tyler?"

He grimaced. "That's the problem. I don't have a fucking alibi. My alibi is just that I wasn't there. Except I obviously was a few hours earlier. So my alibi is that I wasn't there when she went missing. That we didn't have a fight that got out of hand."

"That's what they think?"

He shrugged. "That's the story they seem to want. That I called her. We fought. For some reason they haven't quite worked out yet, we agreed to meet up in the woods. She accused me of being with you. I . . . did something." He reached out in front of him, fingers curling in as if closing around her slender neck.

160

"It's up to them to prove that," I said.

"Is it? Is it really? If everyone already believes it and then you show up at my work in the middle of the day?"

"I'm sorry," I whispered, heat rising to my face. "I'm sorry I came. I just needed to know."

He nodded. "No, I'm sorry. I'm pissed. I'm pissed at them. Not at you. It was probably the police in her place, Nic."

"No, not the police. There weren't any cars. Someone on foot." Someone who didn't want to be seen. Someone who had a key. Someone who knew the woods by heart.

"Her family, then."

"Through the woods, Tyler. Someone walked through the woods."

Then he stared again, walked toward the door, readjusted the brim of his hat so it was perfectly centered. Nodded once. "It wasn't me." He looked me over once more. "Go home," he said. "Get out of here before they come knocking on your door, too."

I followed him out the trailer door into the sunlight, the work site too bright, like an overexposed photo.

———

MEALS STARTED BLENDING TOGETHER, along with the hours, losing structure, just as the days had been. Sleep was hard to come by, and I overcompensated with too much caffeine all day. It was after nine P.M. by the time I remembered to eat. There were too many possibilities. All those names and events tied together in that hypothetical box, weaving around, untangling in my mind. And more—the stories that never made it inside the box. The things we never asked each other slowly unraveling.

To solve a mystery, to solve a mystery *here,* you can't come from the outside.

There were people here who knew more than they said, who

chose to keep it silent, like Jackson seeing Corinne. Like me seeing them together. There must be more of us. I had to understand the silence. With Corinne comes Annaleise. With Annaleise comes Corinne.

Apply one filter to the next, watch it all slide into focus.

———

THERE WAS A LIGHT outside the window, in the woods. Someone near her place again. I didn't bother grabbing my phone, just the flashlight that had been in the drawer beside the microwave as long as I could remember.

I was losing them, and I couldn't. I had to know.

The new cop from State, staying at the motel in town? Someone else? Annaleise?

Find them. Find answers.

I sneaked through the yard like I used to when I was a kid, keeping silent and to the shadows until I reached the tree line. I saw the flashlight bobbing periodically in the distance, and I sprinted toward it until I got too close. I kept my own light off. The moon was enough for my footing, or maybe that was my memory.

But the light wasn't moving toward Annaleise's place anymore, or my own. It was heading away. Backtracking. Moving surefootedly and with purpose through the forest. Toward a hiding spot, maybe. Or a car on the other end.

We'd been moving for at least half an hour, and a sliver of panic had wedged itself inside my chest. I was at the disadvantage, I was alone, I was unarmed, unprotected—with no phone, or map, or GPS. My options were to keep following the flashlight or stop with no sense of where I was.

And yet.

I had the sense that I knew where we were heading. Not from the direction but from the timing. I'd taken this trek before at night.

But it wasn't until we reached the clearing that I was sure. Big open space set back from the road. Small narrow path, cordoned off, leading to the caverns. I stayed in the woods, watching the flashlight. Eventually another light appeared on the path, and I willed it closer until it shone on the person I was following.

For a moment I think I expected to see skinny arms and blond hair and huge eyes; pale skin and dirty clothes. Maybe it was nothing but hope, but there it was: I expected to see Annaleise.

But it was a boy. A teenager. *Her brother.* And the person with him was a tall girl with dark hair, an arm held up to shield her eyes. "God, you're blinding me, asshole."

"Where's David?"

"Bringing the drinks. Carly's in the car. She doesn't like it out here when it's just us. Says it's not safe." The girl paused. "Any word about your sister?"

"Nah," he said, lowering the flashlight.

"I'm sorry, Bryce," she said.

Bryce. Right. He didn't look particularly shaken up by the fact that his sister was missing. And they didn't look the same—not like Daniel and I used to. Bryce was stocky, had inherited his father's square jaw and broad shoulders.

"Could still turn up," he said.

Nine days, and that was all he could say. I'd find it suspicious if I didn't already know his type—part of a generation of kids expecting everything handed to them: the missing people, returned. The mystery, solved for them. Ten years ago, we'd torn these woods to pieces. We'd followed the cops to the places they searched, and we'd searched the places they didn't. But not these kids. Apparently, they could just shrug it off, give their condolences, wait for the beer to arrive.

Maybe it was that Annaleise wasn't theirs. A little too old, she'd already left, gone to college, come back. She didn't belong to them or to us. Lost in the gap with no one to seek her out.

I heard an engine and shrank away from the flashlights and headlights. "There he is," the girl said. "Come on, the woods creep me out. My brother used to tell me there was a monster."

Bryce nodded and followed her.

If you let yourself get swept away in legend, let it become more than story, then it's not such a stretch to imagine Corinne disappearing without a trace. It happens all the time, all across the country, especially in the woods, in the middle of the night. And if Corinne did, then so could Annaleise.

Wasn't a stretch to imagine a monster, even. Watching and waiting and making you do things. Breathing in the lick of smoke as the teenagers made a fire. Watching them fall all over each other in a heap of beautiful limbs. Feeling the cold dirt settle under its nails as it waited, listening to the theories and the stories and the bullshit. Waiting until they fell asleep so it could creep back to the caverns and see what—if any—secrets they had to offer.

It's not so hard. From where they were sitting, there was something doing the same, and they had no idea.

Right then I was the monster.

# The Day Before

# DAY 9

**I** *had my back pressed* against the bedroom wall, ear to the open window, like a kid eavesdropping on the conversation outside. Daniel trying to send the police away, to stop them from dragging us into yet another investigation.

*Stay out of it,* he'd said to me, and he was right.

I'd already given my statement to Officer Fraize, useless as it must've been. *Did you see anything in the woods? Hear anything that night? Anything at all?*

*No sir, no sir, no sir.*

I had no relationship with Annaleise. There was nothing on paper tying us to each other, except in that hypothetical box in the police station from ten years ago, and that was just a corroboration of alibi. And yet here was a new cop out front, asking to speak with me.

His voice was gravelly but tentative. Careful. "If I could just ask her a few quick questions about her relationship with Tyler Ellison . . ."

And there it was. *Tyler.* Tyler ties to me and me to Daniel. Suddenly, the whole knotted mess of us is sucked down, prodded and pried until we reveal something unintentional. Something used to break apart the other. Hannah Pardot was an expert at that. This guy, not so much. He was tripping over Daniel, or Daniel was overpowering him. Either way, this cop wasn't getting in to see me.

"I think she's sleeping," I heard Daniel say. "Look, I'm on my way to work, so I can't stick around. Maybe try again this afternoon."

"It's important. A woman is missing, and every day she's not found, she's more at risk. It's our moral duty to track down every possible lead."

Like it had come straight from Witness Questioning 101. What was he, a month out of training? Moral duty. Hilarious. Like it was their *moral duty* to crack open every facet of anyone's life, anyone who came within three degrees of separation. To destroy the living to find the dead.

It had been eight days since Annaleise was reported missing. Asking me questions about Tyler now wasn't going to change the outcome for her. They weren't looking *for her.* They were looking *at him.* Despite Daniel's good intentions, despite his warnings, if I didn't go out there, the police might think I had something to hide.

I pulled on fresh clothes and padded barefoot down the stairs, the conversation muted behind the wood and plaster. I pushed open the screen door and shaded my eyes from the sun. "Daniel?" I called.

The unmarked car was parked halfway up the driveway. This cop wanted it to seem like he was just dropping by, just in the neighborhood, nothing serious. It was navy blue with tinted windows, and it needed to be washed.

"Is everything okay?" I said.

The man wasn't in uniform, and he was bigger than I'd thought, and younger, given his voice. About my age or younger—Annaleise's age—which made him too young to be part of Corinne's investigation. The way he spoke made me think he wasn't from here. Not this town, anyway. An hour east was all it took to make a difference. The mountains and the single winding road kept this place separate, insular.

"Nicolette"—he checked his notepad—"Farrell?" Definitely not from here. Even if he was too young to know me personally, the names go with the houses. It wouldn't be a mystery. The Carter property backs to the Farrell property, and the McElrays own land on both sides, though neither was built on yet. The Lawsons made a bid for the house and land across the lane when Marty Piper, the last of the Pipers, passed on after his third and final heart attack, but the house and the land were unoccupied, tangled in legalese and court paperwork.

I was staring off through the woods, in the direction of Marty's place, when the cop said, "Miss?"

"Yes?" I said.

Daniel rolled his neck and came to stand beside me on the porch.

"You're Nicolette Farrell?"

"I am."

"My name is Detective Charles. I was hoping to ask you a few questions about your relationship with Tyler Ellison." He seemed to be waiting for something—maybe for me to be the Southern hostess, like Laura, open the screen door and beckon him inside, offering him some tea. Outsiders only come in when the investigation shifts. Detective Charles, I was sure, was the new Hannah Pardot.

After he took a few hesitant strides toward the house, I walked down the porch steps, meeting him in the middle of the yard, my feet sinking into the ground, moist from last night's rain.

"How's the motel?" I asked, just to check. "Or are they putting you up someplace nicer?"

His mouth twisted. "I'm sorry, have we met?" he asked.

"You're not from here, are you?" I countered.

"No, ma'am," he said, flipping through his pad. He towered over me, so I couldn't see the writing. He cleared his throat, pen poised over the paper. "This will just take a moment. I'm following up on some questions, here. Heard this might be a good place to start." He didn't look up the entire time he spoke. Not until he said, "Please describe your relationship with Tyler Ellison."

"This will be really fast, Detective. We have no relationship. Sorry you wasted your time coming out here."

His eyes flicked up to mine, then back to his paper. "How about in the past, then?"

"He was my high school boyfriend," I said. "I'm twenty-eight."

He flipped pages back and forth, umm-ing and uhh-ing, before finding what he was looking for. "You've been together since?" he asked. "It's my understanding that you've been seen with him since then."

I smiled up at him. "I live in Philadelphia. But when I used to come visit, sure."

"Not anymore?" he asked.

"I'm engaged," I said, and I saw his eyes drift to my bare finger.

He flipped the pages again. "Uh, he's been seen around your house. More recently. Very recently."

I was getting irritated, and I didn't make any attempt to hide it. "He's been helping—"

Daniel stepped forward, cut me off. "I asked him to. He runs a construction business. We're fixing up the house. Nic's only home for a little while. He's helping *me* as a favor."

Detective Charles faced my brother. "You're friends?"

The briefest of pauses, but I felt it. "Yes," Daniel said. *Be smart.*

Give the most finite possible answer. Close the loop, don't make unnecessary openings, because they will seize them. They will fill them.

"So, the thing is . . ." Detective Charles flipped pages, and I caught a glimpse of a blank sheet. The jerk was playing me—playing us both. The pages were nothing. A few words scribbled in the margins. It was an act to pretend he didn't know who we were and all our history. In truth, he had it filed away in his head. He'd been studying us, and he was playing his angle. God, how long had he *been* here?

I put a hand on Daniel's arm and applied the faintest pressure before Detective Charles looked back up. "The thing is, we can't find Annaleise's cell—and it appears to be off. But we did get a look at her phone records. And the very last call she answered, the night before she was reported missing, was from Tyler Ellison. Around one A.M."

"It's my understanding that they were seeing each other," I said.

He tapped his pen on the page. "No, see, that's the other thing. Tyler said they broke up. And when I looked into why that might be—because that's an awful big coincidence, break up with a girl and then she goes missing—talk around town is that it probably has something to do with you. And why do you think that might be?"

I felt my jaw tighten, my hands tighten. "Because historically, that's what happened. And in this town, what happened in the past is all that will ever happen, Detective. If you were from here, you'd know that."

"No need to get defensive. I'm just trying to understand."

"Then ask Tyler."

"I did," he said. "Though he's a hard man to track down."

There was a time when all I had to do was conjure him to mind—just the wisp of a thought—and there he'd be in the flesh, as if I had summoned him. But now I had to agree. Tyler was starting to feel like a ghost, like if I blinked for too long, he might slip away for good.

Detective Charles tapped his pad. "He says he called Annaleise at one A.M. and that, let me see, he decided to break it off. Because, quote, 'She wanted more than I was willing to give her.' What do you suppose that means?"

"I'm assuming exactly what he said. He doesn't like to be tied down."

He smiled and it was unsettling—the shark ready to play his winning card. "That's quite the opposite of what I've been hearing. Looks like he's tied down really good here."

I shifted my weight from foot to foot. "Look, up until last week, I hadn't talked to Tyler in over a year. I have no insight into the inner workings of their relationship." The detective caught the inflection in my voice, I was sure, and I fought to keep it steady as Daniel put a hand on my back. *Calm down.*

"Ms. Farrell, I'm not trying to get him into trouble or anything. I just want to get a feel for Annaleise's state of mind that night."

*Lie.*

"When were you and Tyler Ellison last . . . together?" he asked, keeping his eyes on his notepad.

"If you're asking what I think you're asking, that's kind of a personal question."

"This is a missing persons investigation. Of course it's personal. Think of the girl, Ms. Farrell."

*Think of the girl.* "Last year," I said.

"Not last week? Not when you returned home?"

"No," I said.

"You return home, and Tyler allegedly breaks up with Annaleise the same night, and then she's reported missing the following morning. You can see how this looks."

I could see what stories they had concocted, and the one they wanted me to feed back to them. But I'd been through this before. We all had. This kid, he didn't have a fucking clue. "I understand that when the police have no leads, they become desperate, trying to find meaning where there's nothing. Trying to connect unrelated dots into a picture they can understand. Whether it's true or not."

Daniel's phone rang and he answered it right then without excusing himself. "Hello?" he said. "What?" He continued listening, and I kept my eyes on his face so I wouldn't have to look at Detective Charles, whose gaze I could feel burning a hole into the side of my skull. "I'll be right there," he said. Then, to the detective, "Our dad isn't well. We have to go. Good luck with the case." He turned to face me. "They need us to come in. Right now."

"Oh, God," I said, running into the house, locking the doors, grabbing my shoes and purse. Daniel already had the car running by the time I was outside, on the phone with the insurance company he was working with as a field adjuster, explaining that he couldn't make it to the site.

Daniel assessed damages for a living. Worked out of his home, going wherever one of several companies sent him in the region. Everything was a checklist—there was a formula to disaster, misfortune, and tragedy. Everything had a value and a cost. I suppose he got accustomed to digging through facts, assigning blame, detecting fraud. Or he found out he was good at it. After he'd lived through Corinne's case, maybe it was a comfort to him—finding the logic in the chaos. Finding the truth.

"No," he said, "I won't make it out today at all. I'll double up tomorrow. Yeah, call it a sick day."

He was calling Laura as we drove down the road. The detective was sitting in his car, making notes to himself, pretending not to watch us as we drove away.

———

DAD WAS IN RESTRAINTS, flat on his back, eyes fixed on the ceiling. The room was full of people, all of whom worked there in one capacity or another. When Daniel and I barged in, the doctor made a show of placing his fingers on the inside of Dad's wrist, which was limp and restrained by a thick ivory strap.

"What the hell are you doing to him?" I asked, pushing past the doctor and working on a restraint that had been buckled around Dad's other wrist.

"Ms. Farrell." There was a hand on my shoulder but the voice sounded farther away. "Ms. *Farrell.*" A woman's voice, more forceful now, and then the hand moved to my wrist, restraining my own movement. "It's for his safety. And ours."

I looked at the hand on my wrist, at the long fingers and cracked knuckles leading to the knobby wrist and the slender arm. Daniel.

It was then that I got a good look at everyone in the room. A nurse looked shaken, half her hair pulled free from a bun. There were two men in the room who didn't appear to be doctors or nurses, and were watching Dad carefully. And the woman who'd spoken my name, dressed in business attire and standing near the doorway.

"He's sedated now," the woman said. "But we don't know what shape he'll be in when he wakes up."

The air was stale and cold and seemed so impersonal. No scents of home. Medicine, cleansers, bleach. It couldn't be good for his memory. He needed to smell the wood floors and the forest behind our house. He needed the exhaust from his crappy car and the grease from Kelly's Pub. "Well, when he wakes up to find himself physically restrained, I can tell you right now it won't be good," I said.

She pressed her lips together and stuck her hand out in my direction, not giving me any choice but to take it. "I'm Karen Addelson, the director here. I don't think I've had the pleasure of meeting you yet, Ms. Farrell. Come, please, to my office, both of you." She didn't let go of my hand, instead taking hold of my elbow with her other hand. "He'll be fine. Someone will stay with him." Her hand on my elbow moved to my lower back, and she led me out of the room, Daniel at my side.

Karen Addelson was dressed smart, like how I modeled myself in Philadelphia. Pencil skirt, black trendy flats, blouse cut to look both professional and feminine. She dropped her hand as we walked in a straight line against the right side of the hall, making room for wheelchairs and service carts. Smiling tightly, she checked over her shoulder to make sure we were following. Her blouse was sheer with a camisole underneath, and it was so at odds with her makeup-free face and hair pulled into a severe bun that I couldn't get a grasp on her.

We followed her into an outer office with potted plants on either side of bay windows and a desk with a secretary who smiled absently in our direction. "Hold my calls," Karen said as she strode past into her office. Three cushioned chairs and a couch on one side, her desk on the other. She gestured toward the couch. Daniel sank into the cushions, but I remained standing. Everett would never sit there—*You'll lose the upper hand, Nicolette,* I could imagine him whispering into my ear. Everett was like that: always teaching me how to handle myself in situations, as if he could mold me into his equal. I imagined his father doing the same for him, teaching him that line to walk, and a miniature Everett nodding, learning, copying, becoming.

Karen sat on the chair across from the couch, and I stood beside the couch, close to Daniel.

"I'm concerned," she said. "Your father had an episode this morning."

"What does that even mean?" Daniel said. "An episode?"

"He became extremely agitated—"

"It's because there's nothing here to help him remember," I said. "I'd be agitated if I woke up in a place I didn't know."

"That may be true, Ms. Farrell, I don't deny his right to those feelings. But his outburst went beyond disorientation. I'm afraid I'd have to call it paranoia. And it makes me question whether this is the right facility for him. Perhaps he would be better suited to a place that can care for those specific needs."

"Paranoia?" Daniel asked.

"Yes. He was yelling that someone was after his daughter, and he refused to remain here. He was unmanageable. He became violent, insisting that he had to get out, get to you. *Help* you." She stared at me, and I looked away, imagining him yelling for his daughter—for me. My spine tingled, paranoia or not.

"It took two men to restrain him so a doctor could sedate him. But all he kept saying was 'My daughter's not safe.'"

I felt Daniel staring at my face. The chill moved up my spine, hollowing out the room and my stomach and my lungs.

"If this was an event in the past, I could understand," she continued. "That would be more in line with what we know of his condition. Was it? Were you once in danger, Ms. Farrell?"

I shook my head. "I don't know what's happening to him." His words echoing over and over, as if I'd heard them myself.

"Well, as I said, the paranoid delusions make me question if he's in the right facility," she said, driving home the point of our meeting.

"It's my fault," Daniel said.

"Excuse me?" Karen said. We were both staring at him; his cheeks were burning as if he'd been working in the sun too long.

"Our neighbor went missing. Annaleise Carter? Maybe you've seen it on the news? I told him. I realize in hindsight that was a mistake. It just slipped out. She disappeared in the woods behind our house, where my sister is staying. I wanted him to hear it from me and not the news. I shouldn't have told him. I'm sorry. It's not paranoia, though. It's confusion. It's a mistake."

Karen tilted her head to the side, assessing my brother's words. She finally nodded. "That's understandable. Upsetting, to say the least. We will need to continue to monitor him, however. If this becomes a pattern . . ."

"I'm sorry," he said. "I'll talk to him."

"Let me," I said. "I'm the one he was talking about." I was glad that I was standing, glad for the confidence in my posture.

Karen stood. "I think that's a good idea."

"Without the restraints," I said.

———

DANIEL WENT TO THE cafeteria to order three lunches to bring back to Dad's room. I was sitting cross-legged on the chair in the corner, drinking a soda from the vending machine, when Dad finally woke. There was an orderly in the room near the door, per Karen's request.

"Hi, Dad," I said tentatively.

He rubbed absently at his wrists, and I could see the red chafing mark against his wrist bone. I leaned over his bed so he'd see me before he saw the room he didn't own and the man he didn't know.

"You're okay," I said. "I'm okay."

He pushed himself up and winced. "Nic?" he said, his eyes focusing, narrowing, roaming.

"You're at Grand Pines, and you're fine, and I'm here, and I'm fine."

He reached his hand, placed it on the side of my face. "Nic, thank God. Nic. It's not safe for you."

"Shh, Dad," I said, looking at the man beside the door. "I'm fine." Daniel walked in with our lunches at that moment, three stacked Styrofoam boxes. "And Daniel's here, see? We're fine."

Dad sat up like a child in bed after a nightmare, both relieved and terrified. He looked at Daniel, at me, at the man beside the door. "You'll take care of her?" he said to Daniel.

Daniel opened the boxes, looked inside each, and passed them out. "Yes, Dad," he said, and I felt a lump rise in my throat. "You can't let yourself get worked up, okay?"

Dad rubbed at his wrists again, like he couldn't remember if something was supposed to be there.

"Dad," Daniel said, "it's important."

I leaned forward, spreading a napkin on Dad's lap. "Dad, everything's fine."

He stared at Daniel. "Promise me," he said. "Promise me you'll take care of her."

Daniel already had food in his mouth. Nothing could kill his appetite. He kept his eyes on Dad. "You know I will," he said as he chewed.

Karen Addelson came in with the doctor. "How's everything going in here? Patrick? Are you feeling better?"

"What? Oh, yes. Yes." He grabbed his sandwich like he was playing a part. "This is my daughter. Have you met? Nic, meet the Lady in Charge. Lady in Charge, meet my daughter."

"Nice to meet you," both Karen and I said. "Now, Patrick," Karen went on, "how about we sleep this off? Have your lunch, and the doctor will give you something. We'll discuss this tomorrow. Okay?"

I nodded encouragingly. Daniel nodded. Dad looked between the two of us and nodded until she left the room. He gripped my wrist. "Promise me, Nic."

"I promise," I said. I had no clue what he was asking or what I was agreeing to. I had a feeling it was better for us that way.

———

KAREN MET US BACK at the front desk. "We'll assess him tomorrow. Determine the best course of action. Let's plan on meeting again next week." She handed me her card. "We'll be in touch."

Daniel and I remained silent, one foot in front of the other, goodbye to the receptionist, thank you to the man holding the door, until we were back in the overheated car, driving with the windows rolled down until the air conditioner kicked in.

"What the hell was that about?" I asked.

"Hell if I know," he said, both hands circling the steering wheel, the afternoon sun reflecting off the pavement like water.

"Did you really tell him about Annaleise? Or was that just the first thing you could think of?"

"No," he said. "I really did."

"That wasn't smart."

"No. It really wasn't." He sighed, his hard-to-read expression even more impenetrable.

"You were wrong to do that," I said.

The pink was creeping up his neck as his knuckles blanched white, like the blood was seeping from one spot to the other. "I am fully aware of that, Nic. Fully. I'll come back tomorrow to check on him."

"Okay," I said. "What time?"

He cut his eyes to me, then back to the road. "Don't worry about it. Get some work done around the house. I'll bring him the listing papers."

"The house isn't ready."

His jaw tensed. "That's why you should stay home."

So much for my momentary swell of emotion for him. This was how we always communicated. In the things we didn't say. We had developed a habit after our mother got sick, fighting in the space between words about anything other than what we meant.

He was with me the day I scratched Tyler's truck with the swing of my passenger-side door, the day we met for real. "You never pay attention!" Daniel had screamed, slamming the driver's-side door. "You parked too close!" I'd yelled back as Tyler looked on.

Nothing about the list of things that needed to be voiced: our dad's growing distance, the fact that Daniel was dropping out of school, about what would happen to us after Mom died. No, we argued about how close we parked to other cars, about scraped metal and whether I was running late or he was early.

This was how we got through. This was the story of me and Daniel.

"I already called out of work for the day," he said. "I'll lend you a hand. Make some progress."

The meaning underneath: that I had not made any on my own.

———

I SAW IT FIRST. That things were not how I'd left them. I stood in the entrance, unmoving, as Daniel brushed by me. "He came in," I said.

Daniel spun around. "What? Who?"

I slammed the door and leaned against it, my breath coming too fast. "That cop. He came in the fucking house." I pointed to the dining room table, scattered with chaos, but *my* chaos. I'd been sorting things into boxes not by item but by time period: things from my childhood, newer things that I'd never seen, and things I could tie to the memory of eighteen—to when Corinne disappeared. And the items I wasn't sure, scattered across the top of the table.

But those items weren't grouped how I'd left them. Things had been rifled through and moved. The home renovation book that I'd found in the kitchen drawer, dog-eared, and left on the table, now open to the marked page when I'd left it shut. Receipts with the dates worn off, reshuffled into the wrong piles.

"How can you tell? This place is a mess."

"He was here, Daniel. Things have been moved. I swear it."

His eyes met mine, and we stared at each other, into each other, until he said, "Check the house."

I nodded and took the steps two at a time to my room. If the cop was looking for signs about Tyler, shouldn't he have checked here? But the room was just as I'd left it. Even the top drawer that I hadn't closed in my rush to speak to the cop. Dad's room was mostly bare, and the closet was sparse—slippers on the floor, empty metal hangers, a few work clothes.

But Daniel's room—the one with Dad's old things—had been searched. Boxes moved and stacked, papers left out, without any attempt to hide it.

I heard Daniel's footsteps coming up the stairs, down the hall, and then I could hear his heavy breathing over my shoulder. "What is it?" he asked.

"Here. Someone's been through here," I said.

Daniel looked at the mess. His old room. Our father's mess. "Not someone looking into Tyler, then," he said.

"No," I said.

Daniel placed his hand against the doorjamb too gently. Since the fair, he never slammed his fists into walls, or kicked at the ground or his car. Lest somebody see him do it. See a pattern. But he was trying too hard, spilling outside his skin, holding himself too still. He spun silently and went back downstairs.

I followed, watching him check the windows, pushing until he was sure the lock was in place.

"Did you lock up?" He turned on me. "Because there's no sign of forced entry, Nic."

"I did," I said slowly. "But the back door lock is broken."

His eyes widened, and he mumbled under his breath, striding through the kitchen, checking for himself. He pulled on the handle and it gave, just like I'd said it would.

"I told you," I said, hands on my hips.

His hand was on the knob, twisting, twisting, in case there might be a different outcome. "It was broken before? Before you got here?"

"Yes."

"Are you sure?"

"Am I sure? Yes, I'm sure, Daniel. God!"

His face had turned so red with the anger he was holding in that it started to go the other way, blotchy spots of white breaking up the rage. "Why the hell didn't you say anything? Why didn't you get it fixed? What the hell are you even doing here?"

"What difference would it make? Come on, Daniel, is a stronger lock going to stop someone determined to get in?" *Be rational. Be calm.* Everett's words, but they were useless in my family. This was how we worked.

"No, Nic, but it would be proof. A broken window, fingerprints on the glass . . ."

"Oh, give me a break. Nobody's going to waste resources on a home break-in for a house we're not living in where nothing went missing. They'll blame it on kids. Nobody. Cares."

"Oh, *somebody* cares," he said.

I swallowed. Took a deep breath. Tried to focus, searching for a reasonable explanation. "Maybe it was Tyler," I said. "He still has a key from years ago—"

Daniel made a deep sound in his throat, though I didn't know if it was for me or for Tyler.

"Maybe he was going to fix the air-conditioning. And maybe—"

Daniel threw his hands up, took a step closer. "What? He got distracted by piles of junk and wasted his day going through Dad's things in my old room?"

"Asshole," I mumbled. I flipped the switch in the foyer to check the air-conditioning, because God if I didn't want it to be true. The other possibilities nauseated me. Made me feel like someone had poked that box in the police station too hard, and it had sprung a leak, and the names were circling, caught up in a whirlwind, vicious and desperate.

Tyler was the only answer that was safe. *Please be Tyler.*

I turned the AC dial down and listened to the walls. Nothing. No catch, no *whoosh*, no rattling vents.

Daniel's knuckles were white. He was right beside me, and his voice was eerily low. "Tyler works. He doesn't need to sneak around or use a key when we're out. I'm sure he can talk his way in here pretty easily. Bet he doesn't even have to talk."

I pushed him in the chest, gently, just for space. Another inch. So we were going to fight about Tyler again. That, at least, was an argument we knew the lines of already.

"He'd call first," he said. "Did he call you?" At my silence: "Did he?"

"No, but we're not . . . he's not really talking to me right now."

Daniel let out a bark of laughter. "Un-fucking-believable. You've actually done it, Nic. You've pissed off the one person who seemed immune. You've finally gone too far. Congratulations."

"You're an asshole."

"And you're so fucking stupid sometimes, it's infuriating."

He stared at me and I stared back, my head tilted to the side—his cheeks bright red, his neck splotchy, his fists balled up, something dark and ugly coursing through my veins. "Are you going to hit me now?" I asked.

He breathed heavily, furiously, and whatever fragile ground we stood on shattered.

One question, creating so much distance between us yet pulling us *right there*. His knuckles colliding with my cheek and the beginning of the end of everything.

Daniel walked around me in a wide berth. He left the front door ajar.

———

I SLOUCHED AGAINST THE wall, cradling my phone to my chest.

This place messed with me. Made me forget myself. I called Everett, but his cell went to voicemail. I called the office and kept my voice practiced and steady as I talked to the secretary, Olivia, who'd become one of my closest friends. A tied-to-Everett friend but a friend.

183

"He's prepping witnesses," she said. "I'd love to chat, but this place is falling apart this week. Can you hear that?" And I could: the ringing phones in the background, the low hum of voices. She went on, "Jesus Christ, I need a girls' night so bad. When are you coming back? Shit. I gotta go. I'll tell him you called."

I stared at my phone, wondering whom to call to ground myself. The truth is, I'm not good at close friends. I'm great at casual, at meeting up after work and bringing lasagna to the potluck. I'm excellent at being friends with Everett's friends. But not at exchanging numbers and calling up just to talk.

I always leave people behind. Holiday greeting cards last one apartment, and then I move, no forwarding address. Emails go unanswered. Phone calls unreturned. It's a habit. It's easier. I'm the friend in the group they'll throw a going-away party for but never keep in touch with. I had ladder rungs to climb, debts to repay, a life to create.

And whom did I have after so many moves? Everett, for a year. My college roommate, Arden, but she was a doctor, and busy, and every decision she made was life-or-death, which made everything I said seem trivial. My thesis adviser, Marcus. I could call him, vent my issues in a normal way. Surface level. Not like this: *My best friend disappeared when I was eighteen, and it's all coming back, and I'm losing my dad, and someone's been in this house. Maybe the cops, but maybe not.*

They were the people you called with news: *I met a guy. I'm engaged. I got a new job.* To share the highs and the lows. But friends to call for the deep things, the things that live in the dark spaces of our hearts? Those people didn't exist for me any longer. Not since I'd left Cooley Ridge.

———

EVERETT CALLED BACK AT night, when I was cleaning the house—guilted into action by Daniel's disapproval. I heard voices in the background, fading as he walked away. "Hey, sorry. I thought it was earlier. You weren't sleeping, were you?"

"Nope," I said. "What's going on there?"

"Boring legal stuff. Boring but relentless." He sighed. "I miss you. How's it going with the filing?"

"Papers have been submitted, and we're waiting for a court date. Working on the house. How's the case?"

"Oh, you know. Be glad you're not here. I'm still at the office. You'd be furious."

I checked the clock, saw that it was nearly ten. "I'd show up and bring you dinner."

"God, I miss you." And then another voice—a woman's. Mara Cross. "Hold on," he said. His hand was over the speaker. "Uh, the Pad Thai. Yeah. Thanks." Then to me: "Sorry. We're ordering food."

"Mara's there?" I asked.

"Everyone's here," he said, not missing a beat. Everett had a painfully healthy relationship with his ex—at least he thought so. But her smile was too forced when she looked at me, and everything about her was too stiff when she walked by him, knees to shoulders to neck. They weren't really friends, despite what Everett wanted to believe. Olivia couldn't stand Mara, the way she talked down to her and then to me. It's probably how we became friends.

I'd asked Everett ages ago why he and Mara had broken up, because she was always smiling and attractive and smart and *there*. "We weren't compatible," he'd said, which made no sense to me at first. They seemed perfectly compatible. Equals, even. She had strong opinions and worked even longer hours than he did, and they could talk about the same things: torts and motions and appellate courts. Words that I understood but that held no real meaning for me.

I liked to imagine they were incompatible in some other way— in bed. Whenever I saw her, whenever I caught her looking at

Everett like she knew him too well, I held tight to the word *incompatible,* picturing something awkward and unsatisfying. Her name became synonymous with this vision, and I found myself legitimately surprised when she won cases. *Her? She's so awkward. Her arguments so unsatisfying.*

Easier than to think that I must be none of those things: strong, opinionated, dominating in a room. Otherwise, we would not be compatible, or so goes the logic. What did he see in me? Someone he could mold, create, introduce, and place in his world exactly like he wanted? What did he see in the painted furniture and the long conversation in Trevor's apartment? A blank slate? *You have to come from nothing,* I'd told him. Maybe he took it too literally. He didn't know I was already something.

I knew things about Everett the same way he knew things about me. From what he chose to share. Or what his family shared in a *Ha-ha, remember the time* way. Where were his skeletons?

He had friends, guys mostly, who varied in degrees of never growing up—which was obnoxious but not harmful. Not haunting. Not defining. They'd tell stories of Everett doing keg stands, and that one time he swallowed a goldfish whole, which was repulsive but not the same as a missing best friend and a family of suspects. If Corinne had never disappeared, maybe we'd meet up for drinks when we were all back in town, share stories like this with our boyfriends, our husbands. *And then Bailey puked on Josh Howell's sneakers . . .*

There was a difference, a chasm, between that type of story and a real past.

Did something like this exist beneath Everett, too?

Where were the stories that defined him, that broke him open, that laid him bare?

Who was this man I had agreed to marry?

"Tell me something about you," I said. "Something no one else knows."

I heard his chair squeak as he leaned back; I imagined him sliding his feet out of his shoes and placing them on the dark wood. Stretching his arms up over his head, the buttons of his shirt pulling, the outline of his bleach-white undershirt beneath.

"Is this a game?" he asked, and I could hear the yawn in his voice.

"Sure," I said. "Or it doesn't have to be."

"Okay. Let's see. Okay. Don't laugh. I tried to use my dad's credit card in middle school to buy porn online. It didn't occur to me that his statements would have the purchased information."

"That's gross," I said, laughing. "But it doesn't count. Your dad knows."

"Ugh. Don't remind me. Still can't look him in the eye when I think about it."

"You're cute. But that's not what I meant. I meant something more, you know? That nobody else knows."

His chair squeaked a few more times, and I didn't think he'd answer. But then he did: "I watched a man die once," he said. The air in the room changed. His voice dropped, and I felt his mouth coming closer to the phone. "I was in high school. There was a car accident on the highway, and I wasn't supposed to be out. There was a crowd of people already around, helping. An ambulance on the way. I couldn't look away."

*Yes,* I thought. *Here he is. Here's Everett. Can he feel it?* "More," I said.

A deep breath. I heard footsteps, a door closing, the squeak of his chair again. I didn't dare interrupt. "I don't know if I have the stomach for my job," he said. "I like dealing in the facts and the law, and I believe that everyone is entitled to the best representation. A fair trial. I do my job well, don't get me wrong. But sometimes there's a moment. A moment when you realize the person you're defending is guilty. And you can never go back. And then justice is this double-edged sword. Like I'm upholding justice with my 'unyielding drive,' to quote my dad. But which is the real justice, Nicolette? Which is it?"

"The Parlito case?"

"Just anyone," he said. He sighed. "I'm a better lawyer when I don't know."

"You can do something else," I said.

"It's not that easy," he said.

"Yes, it is," I said. "I don't care what you do. You know that, right? I don't give a shit if you're a lawyer or not."

He paused. "Right. If you say so. We don't all have that luxury. I'm thirty. I'm a *partner.* This is my life."

"What I'm saying is, it doesn't have to be." *Change your hair, leave everyone behind. Go someplace new and never look back. You can do it. We can do it.*

He laughed as if mocking himself. Putting distance between himself and the conversation. "So tell me, Nicolette, did you always want to be a counselor?"

"No way. I wanted to be a country singer."

"Wait," he said. "You can sing? I feel like this is something I should know."

"Not even a little."

His laugh was soft, like cotton.

Truth is, I was a terrible counselor in terms of actual counseling. Said the wrong things, never had the right advice to give. But I excelled at listening, so I learned not to speak much. I could direct students to the right resource or the resource to them, to find the help they needed. I saw what they were hiding and let them show it to me. They spilled their collective adolescent guts in my office. On paper, I was an excellent counselor.

Perhaps it was because they sensed a kindred spirit or saw something inside me, like what I saw in Hannah Pardot—the feeling that she knew more because she once was one of us.

Maybe they knew I had seen darker things. That I would understand.

Or perhaps they would sense that I am an excellent keeper of secrets.

I am.

———

I ENDED THE CALL when Everett's dinner arrived, already feeling he was unreachable, in a world too far away. With Tyler, it had been the opposite. I'd had to delete his number from my phone to keep from calling him on impulse after a drink at the bar, after a bad date, and especially after a relatively good one.

But one second off the phone with Everett and all I could feel was the distance between us and him turning insubstantial, a figment I had conjured up out of hope that something so good could happen to me.

I slept fitfully, until I gave up. Too many thoughts swirling through my mind, too many names. I thought of anyone who'd have reason to break into this house, to look through Dad's things or to rifle through Daniel's old room. The list spanned ten years. I wasn't sure I was solving what had happened then or what had happened now. Maybe Dad was right, that time wasn't real. Just a thing we created to move on. Just a label to make sense of things.

———

"IF I WERE A monster," Corinne had told us on the front porch with the lanterns swinging and the shadows dancing, "I'd pretend to be human."

Bailey had laughed, and Daniel had smiled. She'd walked up to him, taking his chin in her hand, turning his head side to side, squinting as she stared into his eyes. "No," she said to him, "human through and through."

189

She looked at Bailey next, running her fingers through her long black hair as she did it, which was because Daniel was there and she always put on a show. Her nose touched Bailey's, and Bailey didn't flinch. We'd learned to let her have her way. *Go along for the ride, and it turns out all right. There's a plan that only Corinne knows, and we're a part of it.*

"Hmm," she said. "No, no, not here, but he's been here. He visits sometimes. What does he make you do, Bailey? Does he make you kiss other people's boyfriends?" *That was you, Corinne,* I thought but didn't say. Neither did Bailey. "Does he make you like it?" Her hand was on Bailey's back, under her shirt, her body pressed to Corinne's, and Daniel's eyes had gone dark and hazy, under a spell. "Does he make you dream of him at night? Of boys who aren't yours?"

She stepped back, breaking the spell. Bailey blinked twice, and Daniel walked into the house.

Corinne smiled like nothing had changed. She took my chin, looked deep into my eyes. I could see myself reflected in her pupils from the lantern swinging overhead. She blinked and pressed her cheek against mine, facing away from Bailey, and whispered in my ear, "There you are."

# The Day Before

# DAY 8

**N**ow that we'd emptied the garage, I could see why Daniel had tried to convert it years earlier: windows on both sides and light streaming through, exposed beams inside a steepled roof; a corner tucked away for storage that would be perfect for a bathroom. I stood at the entrance, staring at the unfinished walls, lost in my memory of Daniel and Dad, Tyler and his father, working together out here in the early-June mornings ten years ago. Before everything changed.

The low rumble of an engine cut off, and I backed out of the garage.

"Nic?" a deep voice called from across the yard. One I didn't recognize at first. It tickled my memory, pulling at threads while I tried to place it.

I spun around to find a man down by the road, sliding off a motorcycle, the sun behind him, his face in shadows. I walked toward him, my hand shielding my eyes, until he became less shadow, more person. Where his sleeves ended, dark writing began—scripted and curling—all the way down his thumbs.

"Jackson?" I asked, still too far to see his face.

He nodded. "Yeah, hey. Hi. Sorry to drop by like this. I'm looking for Tyler."

"He's not here."

I stood at the edge of the road and watched as the words on his arm seemed to ripple when he ran his hand through his shaggy brown hair. Erase the tattoos, crop the hair, change his clothes, and he was classically all-American. Strong jaw and defined cheekbones, broad shoulders, lean frame. There was a reason he was Corinne's. Just one version nested inside another now. He had a tremor in his left hand as he brought a cigarette to his mouth, assessing me through the smoke. "You sure?" he asked.

I rolled my eyes. "Do you see his truck?" I looked over my shoulder, cupped my hands around my mouth. "Hey, Tyler, you here?" I turned back to face him, the smoke more pungent now. "I'm sure."

"It's not a joke," he said. "I've *been* looking for him. And I'm not the only one. Haven't seen him since Friday." And today was Monday. Seven days since Annaleise was reported missing.

"What makes you think I have?"

The heels of his black boots dug into the dirt as he leaned against his bike. "I work at a bar, Nic. Where people talk. A bar that Tyler lives above."

"I haven't seen him, Jackson. I swear it. Not since Friday."

He paused, shifted his feet in the loose dirt where the road met the grass. "I can hear his phone from inside his apartment. And . . . I don't want to call the police. I don't think that would be such a good idea. But I was wondering if . . . maybe you had a key? Just to check."

My stomach turned hollow—I hadn't seen Tyler in three days.

Hadn't heard from him at all. I'd thought of many possible reasons for him not showing up in the last few days, but until that moment, none of them had anything to do with his safety.

"I don't have a key," I said. I used to, and then he moved. I was already backing up to the house to get my car keys. "Let me just grab my purse."

Jackson nodded. "Yeah," he said.

———

AT NINE A.M. ON a Monday morning the bar was closed, which I was glad for. Jackson had implied that there were enough rumors already. "His truck is gone," I said, standing in the gravel lot behind the bar. I looked up at the window—the blinds pulled shut.

"I know. It's been gone all weekend. But the phone . . ."

"No, you're right," I said.

"I can call the landlord, but I don't want to leave Tyler with a paper trail. Not with the cops already stopping by. Part of me thinks he's just avoiding them—it's what I would do. But . . ."

"The phone." Ringing inside and no sign of Tyler.

"Right. The phone."

Jackson unlocked the main door, and the vestibule area felt claustrophobic with the bar dark and locked to the side, and the narrow stairway, and the glass door streaked with dirt. He locked the door behind me and motioned for the stairs. "After you."

Our steps echoed in time, and the hall smelled faintly of cigarettes, and his hand brushed mine once on the railing. The floorboards creaked at the landing, and Jackson stood behind me, fidgeting with his phone.

"Let me," I said. I took out my cell and called Tyler, keeping the phone by my side, pressing my ear to the door.

"You hear it?" Jackson asked, leaning way too close.

"Yeah, I hear it." I closed my eyes, straining to hear more.

The slow and periodic drip of a faucet leak. The rattle of the air-conditioning unit as it stirred to life. But no footsteps. No rustling of bedsheets. No call for help. "I don't hear him," I said.

"That's what I've been saying."

There's something distinctly different about being told some-one is missing over the phone, or seeing signs stapled to trees or a picture on the news, and confirming it in person, *feeling* the absence. It's a pinprick of discomfort that grows into a hollow terror. It's a void that gets filled with all the horrible possibilities existing all at once.

I knocked on the door again, in the same way I'd checked the same places for Corinne over and over—back to the caverns, won-dering if there was a corner I'd forgotten, a room tucked out of sight. "Tyler, it's me," I called, my voice wavering with panic. "Tyler." My fist was clenched when Jackson pulled it away from the door.

"Come on," he said, heading back downstairs to the bar. He led me through the empty bar to a storage room and grabbed a ladder. He carried it effortlessly out the door and around back into the parking lot and situated it directly below Tyler's window. "You're my alibi and I'm yours. We weren't breaking in. We were checking on him. Got it?" We nodded at each other, sealing a pact.

He checked the streets behind us, empty now. I put my hands on the rungs, but Jackson placed a hand on my shoulder. "Me. I look like maintenance. You look like a pretty girl on a ladder. Peo-ple won't question me."

I hated that he was right, because I wanted in that room. Needed to be the one to see with certainty that Tyler wasn't there—that the visions in my head of his lifeless body beside his ringing phone weren't real. That he was okay somewhere. I needed to see the phone and know why he left it, look in his closet and know where he went.

I watched as Jackson maneuvered the air-conditioning unit and

196

heaved himself inside along with it. I stared up, waiting, the glare of the sun off the top of the window making my eyes burn. The uncertainty making my breath hitch.

Jackson leaned out the window. "Empty," he called. He spent way too long trying to get the air unit back in. When he eventually came down, he folded up the ladder and wordlessly walked back inside.

"What did you see? Where is he? Do you know?" I asked, trailing behind him. I followed him all the way to the storage closet before he answered.

"Nah, didn't want to go through his shit. He's not there. That's all I know. Maybe he went camping or something."

Useless Jackson Porter. It should've been me. I would've checked for his sleeping bag and canteens. I would've looked for his toothbrush. Scrolled through his phone. Logged on to his computer and checked the search history.

Or maybe Jackson did. Maybe he just didn't want to tell me.

We stood in the middle of the empty bar, the stools on the counter, the panic in my chest slowly unraveling.

"Here," he said, taking down a stool. "Let me make you breakfast. We can catch up."

I slid onto the stool, felt the adrenaline burning through the last of my energy. The crash just beginning. "Coffee," I said. "Strong."

He kept the sign turned to CLOSED and kept the lights off, so all we had was the glare through the window. My eyes were adjusting to the dark. "You serve breakfast at a bar?"

"No," he said. "I make breakfast for myself. We open at noon today. Still, if we turn the lights on, people will try."

"So much for a shitty economy."

"It's beyond shitty, Nic." He cracked an egg, dumped it directly into a pan. "It's great for business."

"Real nice, Jackson. Doesn't it feel like you're taking advantage?"

"It doesn't feel like anything. Unless you think about it too much. Who am I to judge? Meanwhile, I've got the most stable job in the state."

"Good for you," I mumbled.

He slid a sunny-side-up egg on a plate in front of me and I poked it with my fork, the yolk bleeding out. "What's the matter?" he asked. "Don't like eggs?"

I scooped some into my mouth, but it tasted wrong: metallic somehow. Just a little off. "Do you remember Hannah Pardot?" I asked.

"Who?"

"You know. The woman from the State office who was investigating Corinne's disappearance." How could he not remember that?

"Oh, right. Detective Pardot. I had no idea what her first name was. Wow, she let you call her Hannah? God. She must've really liked you."

No, she didn't. And now that he mentioned it, she never called herself Hannah, and I never called her that, either. *Yes, Detective. No, Detective. Thank you, Detective. I'm sorry, Detective.* Yet I remembered her as *Hannah* Pardot.

*Hannah wants to speak with you, Nic.* That had been my father, standing just outside my door. *You don't have to, but I think you should.*

*I already told Bricks everything.*

*So tell Hannah the same thing.*

That was my dad. *Thanks for your help, Hannah.* He's a well-educated man, and he can recite lines of poetry, quote philosophy when the time is right. He's a widower just trying to get by. His son hit his daughter, and I listened to them speaking through the bathroom grate. *Listen, Hannah—can I call you Hannah? This is a family problem, that's all. I have a feeling that Corinne's might be a family problem, too. That girl was always here, trying to get away from something.*

My father was handsome in the way that professors sometimes are, with their mismatching suits and bow ties and penny loafers and hair that they don't bother styling. He had an easy smile and eyes that sparkled from the slight buzz he carried with him through the day.

"I heard someone call her that," I told Jackson. "She didn't like me, either."

"So what about her?" he asked.

"They're gonna bring her in. Or someone like her. And if we're all here, who do you think they'll go after?"

He paused, scooped the rest of his breakfast into his mouth, chased it with half a glass of orange juice. He wiped his mouth with his bare hand. "We should all go on a long trip."

I smiled. "That wouldn't look suspicious at all."

He took my plate and tossed them both into the sink, ran the water without looking at me. "I want to tell you something. You don't have to say anything back."

"Okay."

He focused on the running water, the way it hit the bottom of the silver bin. "I didn't hurt Corinne. I loved her."

"I know," I said.

He glanced up, and his look nearly crushed me. I picked up my glass so my hands would have something to do.

"The thing is, Nic, the baby wasn't mine."

I froze. My cup halfway to my mouth.

"Did Tyler tell you that?" he pressed.

"No," I said, barely any voice coming through.

"I don't know if he believed me when I told him. He was right, though—I couldn't say that. It'd still be a motive. Jealousy, right?"

I nodded, picturing Tyler and Jackson down by the river. *Be smart*, he'd said.

"But I didn't know, Nic. I didn't even *know* . . . she didn't tell me. Why didn't she tell me?" He put his hands on top of the bar, right in front of me. "We never had sex, Nic."

I felt my cheeks heating up, the cup turning slippery. "Okay."

He shook his head, then looked back at me, out from under his long lashes. "Do you believe me? Did she tell you that? Did she tell you who?"

"She didn't tell me anything," I said. "Jackson, this is what the cops want. They want us to start doubting again. To question each other. To drag it all out again. Let it go. Let her go."

He turned the faucet off, his hands dripping as he held them. "I can't. You know what she said to me that night?"

He'd seen her after the fair, I knew that, but this was the first time he was admitting to it, and I wasn't sure why. "She begged me to take her back, and I said no. I said I was done with her. That I'd found someone else. I was so stupid, so stubborn—it never would've worked out anyway, not with Corinne around. Not out in the open. I came second to Corinne for her, too."

"Bailey?" I asked.

He pushed off the bar, leaned against the cabinet of liquor bottles. "Corinne knew, I could tell. She told me she'd take me back, and I said no. She did it to herself, you know. The cuts on her back."

I nodded. I didn't know it then. But I did now.

"God, I should've said yes. I think about that all the time. I was just some stupid kid. I should've said yes, and she'd be here still."

"Why are you telling me this?"

"Because I trust you." He stayed where he was, but his smile made him seem closer. "Because I'd never tell anyone how one night last week, Tyler comes back from a date, sits at the bar, and then your brother comes in and buys him a round and asks him to please leave you alone in no uncertain terms. And then Tyler's phone rings, and he gets this big-ass smile and says to Dan, 'You

200

really should be having this talk with *her*.' And he picks up the phone right there, right here, right in front of Dan, like he's gloating. 'Hey, Nic,' he says, and then his face falls, and he tells you to calm down, and he leaves his drink on the bar and gets the hell out of here, and your brother follows a few minutes later. They both tear out of the parking lot on their way to you, and then Annaleise goes missing."

My hands shook under the bar. My entire body on edge. "It's not—"

"I'm sure it's not," he said. "But you know how shit gets around here. You hear a story like that, or like Corinne begging me to take her back when she's pregnant with someone else's kid—you say something like that, and it's over."

We were silent, pretending to go about our normal activities, like he hadn't both threatened and confided in me. And then I started to laugh. "I hate this place."

"You miss it," he said.

"I miss it like an ex-con misses the other inmates." Like the ice after the fist. They come in pairs.

"Think you'll ever move back?"

"Never," I said. At Jackson's look, I added, "I'm getting married. To a guy in Philadelphia."

"Does Tyler know this?"

"Yes."

"But he's the one you called after midnight . . . No, you're right, none of my business."

I caught a stanza of Poe heading up his forearm, a line from Kerouac slashed across his wrist. As though he had mined my father's old books, borrowed words, and hidden beneath them. "I gotta go. Thanks for breakfast."

"It was good to see you, Nic."

I stopped at the door, turned to see Jackson still watching me. "She's dead, Jackson," I said.

"I know," he said.

———

I DROVE BY TYLER'S parents' place on the way back; his truck wasn't there, either. For all the time we spent together, I didn't know them well. Tyler wasn't the type to bring a girlfriend home for dinner. We stayed indoors only in bad weather. We always had his truck, and there were the woods. On first glance, it may seem like there's nothing to do here, but honestly, the world is yours. And the woods were ours. The clearing where we'd set up a tent. The caverns if we were with friends. And the river. We spent a lot of time down near the river, lying on our backs, fingers loosely linked.

The river cut between our homes, which now seemed more metaphorical than physical. I could get to Tyler's from my own place if not for the river. Technically, it was possible to cross in the narrow section on one of the trees someone had dragged across. But it was out of the way and tricky in the dark. One misstep and you were over. The water cooler than you expected, the rocks sharper, the night indifferent to your plight.

No, it was better to take his truck to the drugstore and go from there. Much shorter, too.

I passed that drugstore on the way back home, and then the elementary school, the police station, the church, and the graveyard. I felt myself getting light-headed at the stoplight, holding my breath until the light turned green.

———

I DIDN'T GO IN my house or the garage; I'd accidentally left the door ajar when I'd left with Jackson in a hurry. I trekked out to the hill behind my house, looking down into the valley, imagining all the possibilities that could've happened out there. The Carter property was to my side, beyond the dried-up creek bed—I could see a sliver of white from the remodeled garage in the distance; the river farther in the distance, now hidden. In the winter, when the leaves fell, and depending on the angle, you could catch a glimpse. Now all you could hear was the low, steady rumble. We could hear it more after a few days of rain.

I used to find Daniel up here sometimes, though I'd thought this spot was mine alone. My haunts, my places, probably belonged to every child who ever lived here. Annaleise must've sat here, too, surveying her world. She must've stumbled upon the clearing with the fort that I thought belonged to us. She must've known all the paths through the woods, all the places to hide, just as I did.

I followed the one I knew best—the one that cut a straight path to the clearing. I used to think the downtrodden underbrush, the exposed dirt, was from the wear of my steps and Daniel's over time, but it probably was begun years earlier and would continue years after.

There was the tree with the hole in the trunk. I stuck my hand in, pulled out a few acorns and a collection of stones we'd stored there years earlier. There was the spot in the corner, the flattest surface where Tyler and I would pitch his tent. There was the joint between two trunks where Daniel and I collected long branches in case we needed to ward off outsiders.

Corinne and Bailey and I took over the clearing once, way before boys, when we were still made for play, and tried to make Daniel and his friends earn it back. Corinne had raised a big stick over her head, pretending to be the *Lord of the Rings* wizard, which the boys had been watching in the living room. It became this big event: me and Corinne and Bailey guarding this site, Daniel and his friends trying to sneak inside without getting caught, and Corinne's booming voice, *You shall not pass!*, disintegrating into a fit of laughter. We'd played until it was dark, and Corinne tried to make them declare their loyalty to her as Queen of the Clearing, waving the stick in front of her body, swishing her hips in a rhythm. Eventually, Daniel swung Corinne over his shoulder—she was skinny and straight, and her hair nearly brushed the ground, and she was yelling, "A curse on you, Daniel Farrell!" because she was Corinne Prescott even back then.

I could feel them surrounding me here before things changed—like the past was alive, existing right beside the present. Daniel abandoned this place first. Always responsible, too mature, no time for kid stuff. Corinne and Bailey didn't want to hang out here by themselves. "It's only fun if someone's trying to fight you for it," Corinne said. "Otherwise, what's the point?"

I tried to hold the memory of all the people who had been here with me. Daniel and Tyler, Corinne and Bailey.

And then I tried to imagine an outsider watching us all.

All those times we used to scare ourselves with sounds—an animal, the breeze. *A monster,* Daniel had said, and we had rolled our eyes. *Nothing,* Tyler had said, pulling me closer in the tent, *I got you.* But what if there were something? What if the monster were a child just watching? What if it were Annaleise crouched in the bushes? I tried to make myself small, make myself timid, make myself *her,* and see our lives playing out through her eyes. What did she see? I wondered. What did she think? Who was I through the filter of her eyes? I stood, wandering to the center of the clearing, trying to picture us.

I was so caught up in the memories of other people, the feeling of people sharing this space with me, that at first I didn't recognize the feeling of someone real. Someone *now.*

The crack of a twig and the shuffling of underbrush. The hairs raising on the back of my neck in response.

I was in the middle of the clearing, completely exposed, and I felt eyes. I was sure I could hear breathing.

"Tyler?" I called.

I hated that he was always my first instinct. The number I'd start dialing after midnight and then stop. The name I'd call when I heard a front door creak open.

"Annaleise?" I called in a voice just above a whisper.

I took out my cell phone, so if there *were* someone, he or she would see I had it.

Sounds—footsteps—from just out of sight, from deeper in the woods.

I backed away, into the trees, closer to home. Heard something from the side and spun in that direction.

I held the phone in both hands. And I had a signal. A beautiful signal, out in the woods, with the one service provider who covered out here. Terrible plan otherwise—couldn't get a break on mobile-to-mobile, the data-service part was murky at best, but I was alone in the woods, and *it worked.*

Everett had taken my phone once while his was in the other room charging. He tried to look up the scores of a game, got frustrated, and said, "Why do you have this service? It's horrible."

"It's not horrible," I'd said. But it was.

Now I thought: *Because. Just in case. For this. For here.* I thought of all the little things I'd held on to. All the little things I'd taken with me when I left. A fine, transparent thread leading all the way home.

I held the phone to my ear, and I called the one person I knew would come, no questions asked.

The phone rang two, three times, and I was teetering on the brink of panic when Daniel picked up. "I'm in the woods," I said. "At the clearing."

"Okay," he said. "Are you okay?"

The faint wafting of a scent on the breeze—cigarette smoke. Gone as suddenly as it had registered.

"I don't know," I said. My hand on the tree trunk with the hole, the bark rough and familiar, grounding me.

I could hear the panic in his breathing, imagined him pushing himself to standing. "What's wrong?" he asked.

My eyes roamed the woods, looking for the source. I lowered my voice. "I don't know. I feel like someone's here."

I heard him curse under his breath. "I'm coming. Stay on the phone with me. Make it known that you're on the phone. Be loud, Nic. And walk straight for home."

It would take him twenty minutes to get here if he were home. Longer if he were on site somewhere.

I had no idea what to talk about and ended up sharing the most idiotic thing I could imagine: "I'm thinking about eloping." Something totally vacant. "I can't stand the idea of a big wedding. All these people I don't know—Everett's family knows everyone. There will probably be two hundred people from his side and five from mine. And Dad . . . what if that day he doesn't know who I am? What if he won't walk me down the aisle? Or maybe we should have a destination wedding, just family. Somewhere warm."

"Where are you?" he asked.

"Yeah. I'm on the trail, there's this cool oak tree, you remember it?" I picked up a sharp rock off the path, spun in a quick circle. Heard a noise to my left. A crackling of leaves. I kept moving, with more purpose now.

"I hear you," he said.

"If Everett's family insists on a wedding, I guess I'd have Olivia—she works with Everett—and Laura, of course, if she wants. And probably Arden from college." I couldn't think of any other names. "Keep it small, you know? Meaningful."

"Keep talking," Daniel said. "I'm on Fulton Road."

I kept moving, kept talking, and had no idea whether someone was still here, still following.

Daniel and I didn't talk about personal stuff, about anything that wasn't an essential conversation, anymore. If he called, it was for a reason. If I called, it was to give him a new address, to tell him my Christmas plans, to let him know I got engaged.

"I once went to this wedding when I was interning for an ex-student's parents. It was so weird. The dad was getting remarried, and the son asked me to come. It was probably totally inappropriate, now that I think of it, an eighteen-year-old bringing a twenty-three-year-old teacher as a date, but I didn't think of it like that at the time. It was in the summer, right after he graduated, and it wasn't like a date—it was just like he got me on the invite list. I thought he was trying to tell me something. Anyway, the wedding was ridiculous. Those people were beyond rich, Daniel. Like, rich is an understatement. A wedding that could pay for college, that could feed a small country. I don't know why he brought me. I don't know what he wanted me to see. I don't know where he is now."

"Cranson Lane, now. Do you see anyone?"

I spun around again but couldn't get a sense where the feeling was coming from. "No. I feel like I should look him up. And ask him. I had this other kid, later, who told me I just *had* to see his football game. I was there anyway—we have to work a certain number of games each semester. But he didn't care about me seeing him play, really. He was showing me something. His father laying in to him after the game. The pressure. He didn't want to say it, right? Sometimes it's easier to show."

"Where are you?"

I checked over my shoulder, but my vision was going a little hazy from the adrenaline, or maybe the panic. "Oh, I'm almost home now. I need to call that kid. Shane something. God, I can't even remember his last name. I've been to his father's wedding, and I can't remember his name? They all start blending together. There are just too many of them. Hey, I can see our house."

"Nic. Get in the house and lock the doors."

I did. I dropped the rock and ran, the phone cutting through the air with each pump of my arms. I ran the remaining distance between the woods and the house, slamming the door behind me and turning the lock, like Daniel had said.

"I'm inside," I said, out of breath, walking to the kitchen window, staring into the woods. I couldn't see anything. No sign of life.

"You're okay?"

"I'm inside," I repeated, my hand over my heart. *Slow down.*

"Stay in the house," he said. "I'm here."

His blue SUV pulled all the way to the garage, and I watched him exit the driver's side, but he didn't walk toward the house. He went straight for the woods.

I ran out front again. "Daniel! What the hell are you doing?"

"Stay inside, Nic." He started jogging away from me.

Like hell. I wasn't about to stay in the house while he went into the woods I'd just run out of in a panic. I walked back to the edge of the woods and stood outside the tree line, trying to keep my breathing quiet and measured. I watched him disappear in fragments—a sliver of him sliding behind that tree, an arm lost to a branch, his footsteps to the wind. I kept my eyes focused on the spot where he'd disappeared, willing him to return.

I waited, my breathing growing louder, my pulse gaining speed, and jumped at the phone ringing in my hand. Everett. I hit the silence button and immediately heard footsteps coming closer. "Daniel?" I whispered, craning my neck to get a better view. And then louder: "Daniel?"

I saw a shock of blond hair first, then a shoulder. Half a face, his long, lanky legs. He came out shaking his head, tucking something in the back of his pants.

"Didn't see anyone," he said.

"Is that a *gun*?"

He didn't answer. Kept moving toward the house, expecting me to keep up. "Are you sure you heard someone?" he asked.

"Why the hell do you have a gun?"

"Because we live in the middle of nowhere and it takes the cops too long to get to the house. Everyone has a gun."

"No, not everyone. That can't be safe, just walking around with it tucked inside your pants."

He held the door for me, waited until we were inside, and took a deep breath. "Nic, are you sure? Tell me exactly what you heard."

I couldn't meet his eyes. "I was at the clearing, the one where we used to make forts, and I thought I heard footsteps." I strained to hear in my memory, but I felt like I was forcing it, making the leaves crunch, turning up the volume. "I thought I smelled some-one smoking. But I'm not sure."

Maybe someone was watching me, but maybe there wasn't. Like Daniel said, there's a monster out there. It's not too much of a stretch when you haven't been sleeping enough, when you've just been threatened, when the people you love have disappeared. It's not too hard to believe in monsters here.

"Maybe you should've figured that out before you called, scar-ing the shit out of me."

I glared at him. "*I* was scared."

He did that deep-breathing technique, trying not to explode at me. I felt my shoulders tightening, like his did when he was tense. "Your eyes are all bloodshot. Have you been sleeping?" he asked. I could tell he didn't quite trust me. As the time grew between then and now, I didn't quite trust myself, either.

"A little . . . I can't, really," I said. "I can't sleep here—"

"I told you to come stay with us, Nic. Come stay with us."

I started to laugh. "Because that would solve everything, right? When did you get the gun, Daniel?"

He picked at the pile of receipts on the table, narrowing his eyes, putting them back where they'd been. "Laura told me what happened at the shower. She feels terrible. Let her take care of you. She's driving me crazy."

"And how would you explain that? Why I suddenly want to stay?"

"Air-conditioning," he said, the side of his mouth quirking up for a second.

"I can't, Daniel. Besides, and no offense, but Laura is really nosy."

He shook his head but didn't argue. "Listen, I have to be on-site tomorrow, but I'll swing by in the morning to check on you. If you can't reach me, you know you can call Laura. She can handle it."

"Right."

"You don't give her enough credit, Nic."

I saw the outline of the gun as he walked away. "It's a family trait," I called after him, but he shook his head and kept moving. "Daniel?" He stopped, spun around. "Thank you for coming."

He turned back around and waved in acknowledgment as he walked away. At the car, he rested his arms on top of it. "Did you get the affidavits?"

"One for two," I said. "Working on the other one."

He nodded. "The gun was Dad's," he said. "I didn't think it was safe for him to have it anymore. I took it from him so he wouldn't hurt himself. Or someone else."

———

SO WE HAD A father who drank too much. So he didn't come home sometimes. So he forgot to get groceries. So he left us to our own devices. We were lucky. In the grand scheme of life, ten years later, I could see: We were lucky.

Corinne was not that lucky. We never knew this. Hannah

Pardot was the one who broke Corinne's father open, let him weep out all his secrets. Hannah Pardot knew how to push and where. Probably because of what my father had told her. *It's a family matter,* he'd said, lowering his voice, giving it meaning.

Corinne had two much younger siblings. She was eleven when her parents had Paul Jr.—PJ, Corinne called him—and Layla followed two years after. They were little kids, seven and five, when Corinne went missing. Silent and stoic, unusual for children— that's what Hannah Pardot told Bricks and what Bricks told everyone else. Hannah asked them questions as they sat on the white sectional sofa in their living room and their mother handed out lemonade and they looked at their father, waiting for their orders. They looked at their father when Hannah asked if Corinne had seemed sad or upset, or if they'd heard her say anything. *Any little thing at all,* she'd said. Anything about her *state of mind.* They looked at their father, questioning. They looked at him like the answer.

———

CORINNE'S MOTHER HAD TAKEN her to the hospital twice. Hannah Pardot read the reports out loud to Corinne's father: once for a dislocated elbow—*climbing out the window,* Corinne had told us, rolling her eyes; another for a laceration at the hairline—*river jumping, damn slippery rocks.*

"Yes," her dad said to Hannah Pardot. "Because of me." Sobbing big, ugly tears. Hannah Pardot called Bricks and Fraize in because she was so sure he was going to confess to everything.

He wasn't the kind of drunk to sit at the bar, like my father, getting lost in himself. He was the kind who drank whiskey in the living room, finding people to be pissed at instead of himself.

"I didn't hit her," he claimed. "I never hit her."

No, her mother said. He never did. Just punished her. Pushed her if she tried to talk back. Once he pushed her down the stairs. Just the once. That was the elbow.

His grip was tight and unyielding. He threw dishes at walls, near their heads. One time he missed. He was full of threat and menace, and at some point, Corinne grew immune. Immune to the sound of a bird flying into a window, its wings beating relentlessly upon the ground.

She'd leave her house, coming over to mine, telling me we had plans. I can see it now, the meaning under her words. *What, did you have a mind-fuck or something? We have plans. I was supposed to sleep over.*

Eventually, I stopped going along with it. I pushed her away, too.

They searched her house for blood. For evidence. For signs that there was another *accident* that her father covered up.

I couldn't imagine Corinne giving the fake stories at the hospital; *I fell. I was sneaking out the window and I fell.* Letting her father win. I couldn't picture that Corinne. The one who cowered, keeping her eyes on the floor. Her power, I realized, was not limitless, as we had all believed. It had borders, and when she left that house, she refused to give another inch. It was a learned trait: how to push, how to manipulate. She knew the line to walk. She learned that from her father—*push but not too hard; crack but do not break.* The darkness lives in everyone. She knew this better than anyone. Everyone had two faces, and she looked deep into us each until she found it.

———

I SEE A CORINNE every year. Can pick her out from the other side of my desk. The strong-willed, the cruel, the worshipped. The sad, sad girl sketched in pencil that you see only when you remove the people surrounding her.

Don't remove them.

Please. Don't.

*She's mean, but she loves you,* I want to tell them. *Wait it out, look closer.*

I see the long sleeves and I know what's underneath.

The uneaten lunch tray, ignored as she cuts someone down.

The boys she pushes away over and over, hoping they'll come back, because they can't get too close. She can't let them.

I want to call her into my office for no reason at all—ignore the one struggling with too much school pressure, or parents getting divorced, or the one literally starving for attention. I want *this* girl, who doesn't show up in my files. I want to call her in just so she knows, as they grow up, and as everyone abandons her—as they inevitably will—that I am here.

This time I am here.

———

TYLER CALLED, JARRING ME awake just as I'd drifted to sleep. His name on the display, and there he was, an image in my mind, safe and nearby. "Hello? Tyler?" I pushed myself out of bed, walked down the hall in case he was in his truck out front, underneath the steady drizzle.

"Hey, Nic."

"You're okay? You're home?" The night was dark, and I didn't see any sign of Tyler.

"Yeah. Jackson said you were worried."

"*He* was worried. I mean, I was, too. Where were you?"

"Taking care of some stuff."

"Why'd you leave your phone?"

A pause like I should know better. "Forgot it."

I hated that Tyler was lying to me. We weren't supposed to lie to each other. We might not say all of what we were thinking, but we never lied—I'd made him promise that. "Tyler," I said. "Talk to me. Please. I thought you were hurt. I thought . . ."

I shifted uncomfortably in the silence that followed.

"I went to Mississippi," he said, his voice quick and hushed. Without his phone, the unspoken understanding.

"To her father's place?"

"I just wanted to check for myself. No sign of Annaleise," he said. "No sign of anything."

I stayed on the phone, listening to him breathe.

Eventually, he broke the silence. "You were right," he said. "We need some space."

I felt him drifting even further as we spoke. "Tyler—"

"Do you need anything, Nic?" Like a professional courtesy.

What did I really need? From him? For him. "Just to know you're okay."

"I'm okay," he said. "See you 'round, Nic."

———

THERE WAS SOMETHING BOTH familiar and discomforting about the rain here. In the city, it hit the windows and streets and flooded the gutters, like it was encroaching on us. It caused traffic jams and made apartment lobbies too slippery. But here, the rain was just another part of the landscape. Like it was the thing that lived here and we were merely visitors.

It made me feel small and temporary. Made me imagine my mother in this very house, hearing this very rain. The same water molecules, recycled and replaying, like the circular diagram in science class. And before that, my grandparents buying this land, building this house from the ground up, standing in front of this window, listening to the same thing. *Some religions believe time is cyclical,* my father had said. *That there are repeating ages. But to others, time is God. A gift for us to stretch out and exist in.*

It was a comfort to me, the sound of my father's voice, trying to make sense of things.

Because the thing about standing here in the middle of the mountains with the rain coming down, in a house your grandfather built, is that it's too easy to notice how insignificant you are.

How quickly you might go from something to nothing.

How one moment you can be a girl laughing in a field of sunflowers, and the next, a haunting face on a poster in a storefront window.

How terrifying, empty and hollow, and then: how absolving.

I brought Tyler outside in the rain once. Asked him, "Do you feel it?" Laced my fingers with his and waited for his whispered "Yes." He could've been talking about anything—the cold on his face, the rainwater in his shoes, the sky whispering to him about love and loneliness and me. But I liked to believe he felt the same. That he was the person who always understood.

I tried to get back to sleep. I lay in bed and closed my eyes, concentrating on the sound of the rain on the roof—hoping it might keep my mind empty, lull me into a gentle oblivion.

But Cooley Ridge was talking to me with each drop, nudging me awake.

*Keep your eyes open. Look.*

Time can weave around and show you things if you let it. Maybe this was how. Maybe Cooley Ridge was trying to show me. Time was trying to explain things.

*Tick-tock.*

# The Day Before

# DAY 7

**T**he house looked brighter, more alive, with the fresh coat of paint that Laura had picked out—pale almond, she'd called it. But the furniture had been pulled away from the walls and sat at unnatural angles, haphazardly covered with sheets of plastic, giving the whole downstairs a fun-house feel. I must've grown immune to the smell of paint sometime during the night. It wasn't until I stepped out to toss the plastic in the trash and went back inside that it hit me—the wall of fumes, sticky and suffocating—that no open windows could alleviate. We needed to run the air, to circulate everything through the filters. We needed the damn air-conditioning.

I positioned Daniel's box fans throughout the downstairs, turned them on, and left the windows open.

And then I left. An accidental catastrophic electrical fire would not be the worst thing that could happen to this house.

———

**THERE'S A SUNDAY BRUNCH** at Grand Pines that makes it family day. Go to church, then visit the family you've sent away. A day of penance. Eat your weight in sins. Guilt by omelet.

It was a buffet, and I was following Dad down the line, my tray sliding along the metal grooves behind his, sounding like nails on a chalkboard.

"Try the bacon," he said, and I obligingly placed a strip on my plate. "Skip the eggs," he said from the side of his mouth. "Biscuits. Take two." I took one—I had no appetite and didn't want to waste them if they weren't really that good.

In the bag slung over my shoulder, I carried a paper signed by a doctor that I'd picked up at the front desk. An affidavit attesting to my father's mental incompetency and his need for a guardian. We needed one more before filing with the court, and the on-site doctor had already gotten me a referral for someone who would visit later this week.

I felt like I was lying to Dad, placing bacon on my plate, taking his advice, acting like I was here for the food, for his company. I wasn't *not* here for those things, but they weren't the primary reason. I wondered if Daniel and Laura made it a habit to meet him here for brunch. Probably. Dad had smiled when I came in, like it was the most natural thing in the world for me to be here, and part of me wondered if the affidavit was wrong. If maybe he *was* getting better. If this was all reversible—a horrible, temporary thing that would gradually unwind itself. *Gosh, Dad, remember that time you couldn't remember us? Really gave me a scare.*

We sat at the table where I'd met him at last week—apparently, his regular spot. "You should see Laura," I said to him. "I went to her shower yesterday. She looks like she's about to pop."

He laughed. "What are they having?"

He knew this. He should've known. "A girl." A slight nod from him. "Shana," I said, and his eyes locked on mine, then slowly drifted to the side. It was the wrong thing to say; I'd lose him to her now. Watch them both disappear.

"You know, when your mother brought me home the first time, I fell in love."

Or this time he would take me there with him.

"With Cooley Ridge?" I asked.

"Well, you don't have to make that face, Nic." He grinned. "But no. Not Cooley Ridge. I fell in love with *her*. Because I could see all of her there. She was like a puzzle piece out of context, but when I put her there, where she was from, it was like I understood. She was so beautiful."

My clearest memories of my mother were the ones where she was fading. Sick. In a wheelchair with a yellow and blue quilt across her legs because she was always cold, Daniel holding a cup with a straw in front of her, both of them getting skinnier, paler, sharper. In pictures, she was beautiful. Before the cancer, she was this perfect mix of sharp and soft, with a genuinely warm smile.

"You really do look like her. You and Daniel both, spitting images of her," he said.

"Daniel looks like you." I tried the bacon, but in rolled the nausea. I broke it into smaller pieces so he wouldn't notice.

"Now, sure, that's what people say. But when you guys were kids, it was all Shana." He looked me over. "Imagine if she hadn't had kids. All of her would be lost now."

"Okay," I said. I didn't like the way he was looking at me, like there was something of her still living—a puzzle piece out of context, part of her stuck over my left eye, to my bottom lip, the ridge of my spine. Concentrating on me like Corinne once had, until she pretended she could find the monster in us.

"We almost didn't, you know. When her parents died in that

accident and she found herself all alone in the world, she told me she would never have just one child. It was none at all or more than one. There was no debating." He chewed his food, rolled his eyes. "So stubborn. For a long time I thought it would be none. I really did. Daniel caught us by surprise, you know."

"No, I didn't know." My parents were older when they had us, but I assumed that was deliberate: careers first, then family.

"That's when we moved back. She was desperate to have you as soon as possible. God, she drove me crazy. I really didn't get why it was such a big deal, but she was determined that what happened to her would never be her child's fate. Alone with no family. She was adamant that you'd have each other always. Now that she's gone, I can see she was right, of course. Daniel needed you."

"I'm sure he wouldn't agree with that." I laughed. "I'm a pain in his ass."

"No, no, Nic. You're exactly what he needs. He knows it. You know how he is, though."

There were no safe topics anymore. Doctors sending affidavits to declare my dad incompetent. Missing girls. A house full of secrets. Accidental children. Daniel. And there were eyes everywhere. Not just in the woods. In this place, too. I felt my eyes roaming, my fingers drumming on the table. I could only tap in to subjects with Dad, circling them from far away, grazing off the top. Not getting him worked up. Not pushing things to the surface that needed to remain below. But I needed him to know some things—I needed him to *understand*.

"Tyler's been doing some work on the house for us," I said, picking at the biscuit.

"That's good. He's a good man."

"You never liked him when we were kids," I teased.

"That's not true. He worked hard, and he loved you. What's not to like?"

"I thought fathers of teenagers were supposed to hate their daughter's boyfriends. It's a rule."

"I never read the handbook. Obviously," he said. Then he pushed himself back in the chair. "I never knew what to do with you, Nic. About you, I mean. You turned out good, though, all on your own."

"I didn't turn out good," I said, half laughing, crumbling the biscuit so it fell into uneaten sections.

"You did, though. Look at you. Look at you now."

I needed to steer the conversation gently back. Carefully. "Tyler said the house would be worth more if we finished the garage," I said. "Remember when you and Daniel were going to do it?"

He looked into my eyes, smiling. "He asked me," he said, thinking about the wrong thing, the very wrong thing. "Or he told me. You know Tyler. Said he wanted to marry you."

I felt warmth flooding my face, my fingertips tingling, trying to imagine that conversation. I hadn't known that, and the surprise caught me by the neck. "He did, huh? What did you say?"

"I said you were just kids, of course. I told him to see the world first. I told him about time . . ." His eyes drifted to the side, and I could sense his mind starting to drift as well.

"What about time?" I asked, pulling him back.

He refocused on me. "That it shows you things if you let it."

I tilted my head to the side. "That's what Mom used to say." When she was sick and I was crying, and she said she could see me, me and Daniel both, the beautiful people we would become.

"Well, that's what I told her. When she was pregnant with Daniel, she worried so much, and the same with you, so we used to make up these stories . . ." Dad was getting sucked into the memories. I'd lose him if I didn't ground him in the now.

"What did Tyler say to that?" I asked. Maybe I just really wanted to know. To see the conversation, a fly on the wall, Tyler sitting on the couch, my dad in his chair.

"Hmm?" He looked up and shrugged. "He didn't say anything. He wasn't asking for my permission. So I told him: Don't be mad when she says no."

I smiled.

"I thought you should know that. It was the day the Prescott girl . . . Well. There were more important things after that, and then you left. But I wanted you to know about that. He's good. He's a good guy. I think he's still mad at me, though. For not giving him your new number."

"You're a good dad," I said. "You really are."

"I'm a shitty dad, and I know it. But I tried to do the right thing when it counted. I'm not sure how that went."

"Dad, look at me. It's done," I said. I stared at his eyes, willing him to remember this conversation. "Whatever happened back then, it's over. It's done. It's time to put the house up for sale."

He sliced into his biscuit, pointed the butter knife at my heart. "Eat your breakfast, sweetheart. You're starting to disappear."

———

I KNEW THAT THE answers to Annaleise's disappearance hinged on what she saw ten years ago, even if the police weren't quite there yet. I knew the answers were going to come all at once. That people wouldn't find out what had happened to Annaleise without finding out what had happened to Corinne, and neither would I.

I had to go back in time.

I had to, while the investigation was still in the *find her* stage. Before it morphed into something more, something worse.

Hannah Pardot showed up from out of town ten years ago, with her stoic expression and bright red lipstick, on a mission. The investigation morphed from *find the girl* to *solve the case*. Those were two very different things. Two very different assumptions.

One week after Annaleise's disappearance and I could feel the shift starting.

I had to understand how everything looked from Annaleise's point of view—all of it—starting at the beginning of that night ten years ago. Starting with what she saw at the fair.

———

THE FAIR DOESN'T REALLY have an official entrance. It has a field that turns into a parking lot that funnels between the buildings that were stables, now used to sell ticket stubs for rides and games. There's a storage shed of first-aid equipment off to the side of the stables/ticket booths, and past that, nothing but trees.

Through the old stables, the space opens up to fields where once a year, for two weeks, the booths come to life and the Ferris wheel looms, proud and majestic. In the fall, hot-air balloons rise up, tethered to the earth. It was the place we went to touch the sky.

The air tonight was full of noise: kids cheering or whining, parents laughing and shouting. Music from the rides, bells from the game booths. Teenagers calling to each other across the grounds— from a picnic table, from the front of the portable restrooms, from the top of the Ferris wheel. My breath caught, seeing it circle from the parking lot. Unlike most things that appeared smaller now that I'd grown, the Ferris wheel looked bigger. More untouchable. I tried to picture a girl hanging from the outside of the cart. I'd be panicked. I'd be sick. I'd be furious.

A girl in a skirt on the outside of the cart, her best friend whispering in her ear, her boyfriend watching from below. Maybe we did bring it on ourselves.

This right here was the closest I'd felt to Corinne in a long time. I could feel her cold hands at my elbows, hear her breath at my ear, smell the spearmint gum on her whisper. If I could just close my eyes and reach across time and hold her wrist. Wrap my arms around her for no reason at all. I wouldn't dare. I never dared.

Someone slammed into my side—a little kid, maybe three years old, colliding with me before changing trajectory, running into someone else on his rush inside. His parents gave me a hurried *sorry* and chased after him. The sun was low, almost gone, and the field lights turned on as I stood there watching. The grounds were garish and exposed, my eyelids slamming closed in response.

I walked between the ticket booths. The grass had always been worn away here; it was mostly dirt with small patches of green. Right near the entrance, right here in this dirt, this was where I fell to my side. This was where Daniel hit me in full view of the Ferris wheel. I spun around, pictured Annaleise leaning against the side of this building, eating her strawberry ice cream. Watching us all.

*Me running for Tyler.*

*Tyler waiting for me.*

*And Daniel grabbing me by the arm, hitting me across the face.*

*Tyler lunging, punching Daniel in the face, then crouching beside me. His hands pulling my twisted arm away from my body. "You okay? Nic, are you okay?"*

*"I don't know. I don't . . ." Frantically scrambling in the dirt, standing, leaning on Tyler, feeling everything realign, the burn of the hit, the sting of the moment. "I'm okay," I said. His hands were everywhere. Pushing my hair aside, over my face, down my neck, my arms, my waist. He glanced over my shoulder, his jaw set, and I saw Corinne jogging toward us. Bailey was in the distance, weaving through the crowd.*

I didn't know if Annaleise was still there. I hadn't looked again. Maybe she was just outside the entrance. Maybe she'd run behind the building, watching through the stable slats that I could see now, with her doelike eyes. Yes, she had confirmed our alibi, but I was wondering if she had also witnessed what came next.

Tyler had pulled me up, checked me again, asking over and over if I was okay. "Wait here," he'd said. He stood over my brother, put a hand down, and leaned toward him, said something in his ear. Daniel looked straight at me, straight into me, so I had to look away. "Nic," he pleaded from across the way, but by then Corinne was already there.

"Bailey, go find some ice," Corinne had called as she approached, and I could feel her presence taking over, taking control.

I'd walked away. I'd left, taking Tyler with me, and we found the first-aid shed where a man sat in a folding chair, a lump of tobacco in the side of his mouth.

"You kids okay?" he asked, not standing.

"Do you have ice?" Tyler asked.

The man opened a blue cooler at his feet, used a plastic cup to scoop some ice into a Ziploc bag for me.

Tyler checked me over again, asked me if I was okay again, his hands running everywhere.

"Tyler," I said. "Your hand." Two knuckles were scraped, as if they'd hit the wrong angle on one of Daniel's sharp edges, and his fingers were discolored. I asked the attendant for Band-Aids.

He eyed Tyler's hand. "Might be broke," he said.

"It's fine," Tyler said, pulling me away. "Come on."

But I could see the man was right; it was swelling and red, and Tyler kept it hanging limply by his side.

"Tyler—"

"I'll take a bag of ice, too," he mumbled.

"At least go wash it off," I said.

He nodded. "Okay. You won't move?"

"I'll be right here," I said. But the second he was out of sight, all I could picture was Daniel sitting in the dirt, his bloody nose, and the way he said my name. The way he looked at me. I had to talk to him. *We* had to talk. About this. *Right now.* Even back then, I could sense how pivotal this moment was. How our entire futures somehow hung in the balance of this conversation.

I'd gone out to the dirt circle to find Daniel, but nobody was there. I thought maybe they'd all been escorted out, or someone had called security on us. I walked past the stables and didn't see him anywhere in the parking lot, either.

I turned to go back in, back to Tyler, when I heard Corinne's soft words somewhere out of sight. I passed the stables to my right—her voice, her laughter, drawing me in.

I saw Corinne first. Behind the building just outside the fair, holding a wet paper towel to my brother's face. Her head on his shoulder. Her other hand under his shirt, at his waistband, trailing over his skin. I watched her gently press her lips to his jaw and whisper something in his ear. And from her posture, from the way my brother was relaxed against the wall, I knew this wasn't the first time. I knew he saw me because he moved his hands quickly and ineffectively, pushing her off, before I spun away. And I heard her words cut into him in displeasure as he pushed her back. But it was too late.

He lied, and he knows I know it. He knows I lied for him, too. *Never,* I said. *Never.*

I wondered if Annaleise saw that. If she was in the trees somewhere. Or crouched between the cars in the parking lot. She was too young to get home on her own. She would have needed an adult. She must've been nearby.

I wondered what it looked like to her at the age of thirteen— what did she think was happening from the distance, from her hiding spot? And if she revisited it as an adult, did the memory shift on her? Grow into a different understanding? I had thought I was the only one who knew about Corinne and Daniel, but maybe I wasn't.

I never knew exactly what happened between the two of them, or with Bailey, after that. I ran back inside, was beside the shed before Tyler came out. We left in his truck, and he let me drive because of his hand, and we passed a bunch of kids from school who teased Tyler. "Damn, letting your girl drive your truck?" A girl added, "Now, that's true love."

I didn't know how Daniel and Corinne got separated, when or how Corinne met up with Jackson, or why Daniel was driving Bailey home. I didn't dare ask. None of us asked.

———

I PEOPLE-WATCHED FROM THE entrance for a long time, trying to imagine how these moments might look through the lens of a camera. What would I see if this moment were frozen? What would I think? Of the mother grabbing the child's arm, one step from disappearing into the crowd; of the teenagers in line for the Tilt-A-Whirl, kissing while the others looked away; of the woman with long black hair, holding the hand of a little girl, frozen in the middle of the crowd, watching me back.

Her face sharpened in my mind, gaining context, and I was jarred into action, walking toward her. "Bailey?" I called. *Bailey.* Her face turning away, black hair cascading in an arc as she spun around . . .

It wasn't in church but in moments like this when I maybe believed in God or something like that. Some order to the chaos, some meaning. That we collide with the people we need, that we meet the ones who will love us, that there's some underlying reason to everything. Bailey standing in the middle of the fair on the one night I was there. Bailey, whom I hadn't seen since I graduated from college. Bailey, who had been here with us the night we all fell apart.

My whole body tingled with the feeling that I was meant to be here, that the universe was laying out the pieces for me, that time was showing something to me.

I knew she'd seen me, had frozen just as I had, but she was moving away through the crowd. I was halfway to her now, pushing through the kids running for the next ride.

"Bailey!" I called again.

She stopped when I'd nearly reached her, looked over her shoulder, made herself look surprised to see me. "Nic? Wow. Long time," she said.

We stared at each other, neither speaking, the little girl still holding her hand. "You have a daughter?" I asked, smiling at the girl. She clung to Bailey's leg, half her face hidden, one hazel eye staring up at me.

"Where's Daddy?" she asked, her face tilted up to her mother.

"I don't know," Bailey said, scanning the crowd. "He should be here."

"I didn't know you got married," I said.

"Well, you missed it. Divorced now. Getting one, anyway." She scanned the crowd again, I assumed for her ex. "What about you?" she asked, still searching. "Married? Kids?"

"No and no," I said, though I didn't think she was listening.

"There," she mumbled as she raised her hand over her head. "Peter!"

Peter was clean-cut, clean-shaven, square-jawed, and taller than average, and I disliked him on sight. Maybe from the way he walked, like he knew he was something worth looking at. Maybe from the way he grinned at Bailey as their daughter ran to him, like he was keeping score of something and she was losing.

"You're late," she said. She thrust an overnight bag at him. "She has swimming lessons at ten."

"I know," he said. Then he looked at me and smiled. "Hi, I'm Peter." I raised an eyebrow at him until his smile faltered. "Okay, well, come on, sunshine. Let's leave Mommy to her fun."

Bailey squatted close to the ground, grabbed the girl, held her tight. "See you tomorrow, love," she said. She stood slowly and watched them move deeper into the fair. "Well, it was good seeing you, Nic. I've got to get going."

"I need to ask you something. About Corinne."

Her eyes widened. Then she turned and walked toward the exit.

"Bailey." I caught up with her at the side of the Tilt-A-Whirl, the cars coming dangerously close to the edge of the track before being yanked back.

"No, Nic. I'm done with that. We're *all* done with that."

I squeezed my eyes shut. "Bailey, just answer the fucking question and I'll be gone." I was talking to her like Corinne would've talked to her, the words out before I could stop them.

And she was waiting, like she always did. I almost didn't want to press her, but I had to know. "Annaleise Carter. Do you remember her?"

She crossed her arms over her chest. "I hear she's missing."

"Did she ever try to talk to you? About Corinne? About that night?"

She started to shake her head, then stopped. Her eyes shone.

"What?" I asked.

"It was weird," she said. "I mean, I barely knew her then. And I don't live there anymore. But a few months ago I ran into her at the farmers' market in Glenshire?" Bailey always ended sentences like that, like she was excusing us for something we might not know. I nodded, waiting for her to go on. "Or I guess she ran into me. I didn't really recognize her. But she said, 'Bailey? Bailey Stewart?' like we'd been friends. Really, I think it was the first time she ever spoke to me."

"What did she want?" I asked. "Did she ask about Corinne?"

"No, not at all," she said. She scrunched up her face. "She asked me to lunch. Asked if I ever needed a babysitter for Lena. It was like she wanted . . . to be my friend."

"Did you do it? Go out to lunch? Ask her to babysit?"

"No. I'm too old for friends like that . . . for people from home." She stared into my eyes. "I grew up, Nic. I'm not the same girl."

"Do you remember—"

She put up her hand. "You said one question. You said you'd be gone . . ." Her voice trailed off and she lost her confidence, her mouth slightly ajar, her eyes following something just past my shoulder.

I caught sight of the back of a man walking alone. Cigarette in hand, hair falling in a mop over his face. Something so familiar about the way he walked with his shoulders hunched forward. "Is that Jackson?" I asked.

"Hmm?" She was jarred back to the conversation. "Oh, I don't know. Haven't seen him in ages."

"Last I heard, he was working at Kelly's," I said.

She shrugged. "I don't go there anymore."

"He didn't do it, Bailey," I said.

Bailey took a step away so her back was up against the side of a hot dog stand. "I know that," she said, which surprised me. It was *her* words that had landed the suspicion on him. *Her* answers to Hannah Pardot. *Her* accusations.

"Then why did you make everyone think he did?"

"They told me she was pregnant! Jackson lied about it. And then the cops came in, demanding answers. I was just a kid!" she yelled.

"No, you were eighteen. We were all eighteen. Everything you said became evidence. *Everything.* You ruined him."

"Everyone had a motive, Nic. If it wasn't him, who do you think it would've been?"

Bailey was smarter than I gave her credit for being back then. But she was just as capable of deceit as I remembered. "Really? What was *your* motive, Bailey? God, you're terrible." But I thought I knew. The man walking behind us. Jackson Porter. *What does the monster make you do? Does it make you dream of them? Of boys who aren't yours?*

"It wasn't *me. She* was the monster. Can't you see that now? We're all better off without her," Bailey said.

"Don't say that."

Truth is, I believed Bailey was lucky. For Bailey Stewart, life with Corinne could've gone two very different ways. Bailey was gorgeous—naturally alluring. But Cooley Ridge was Corinne's. The attention was always hers. Bailey could either submit to Corinne, let her push her around, or Corinne could destroy her. Bailey was lucky she was weak. That she bent and folded so easily. There were worse things than being a door mat.

But Bailey also had a darkness in her that let her be manipulated, that wanted out. She was lucky to be loved by Corinne.

*"Truth or dare, Bailey." Corinne moved the soda straw from side to side in her mouth.*

Dare, *I thought.* Take the dare.

*"Truth," Bailey said.*

*Corinne's smile stretched wide. "Jackson or Tyler? And explain."*

*There was no right answer. There never was.*

*"I changed my mind," Bailey said. "Dare."*

*"No, no, no, Bailey, my dear. Truth or you can leave. Now, tell me, which of our boyfriends would you like to make yours?"*

*I'd leaned back on my elbows, watching Bailey shift in discomfort. Corinne caught my eye and grinned.*

*"Always take the dare, Bails," I said.*

*"Tyler," Bailey said, her high cheekbones tinged red.*

*I laughed. "Liar."*

*She set her eyes on me. "You get a free pass everywhere, Nic. People think you're better than you are because of him. That's my reason. Tyler."*

*Corinne laughed. "Well played, Bailey." She pulled Bailey toward her, wrapped her arms around her from the side, and squeezed. "God, I love you to death. The both of you. You're horrible."*

I hated that Bailey acted so beyond it now. That she would call Corinne a monster as if she could strip out the rest. "Tell yourself whatever you want, Bailey. You always were an excellent liar."

"Don't act like you don't know what I'm talking about. I heard her," Bailey said. "I heard what she said at the top of the Ferris wheel."

I shook my head, pretending not to remember.

"Who says something like that?" she asked. "She was sick, Nic. And she was contagious."

"I don't know what you're talking about," I said.

She laughed like the joke was on me now. "I gotta go."

"Wait," I said. "Can I call you later? We can meet up someplace. Without all this?" Meaning the fair, meaning the Ferris wheel looming above as we talked, turning us harsh and defensive.

"No," she said. "Let it go."

Bailey knew something more, I was sure of it. I wished Everett were here to push her, convince her to lay bare her secrets, to absolve herself. I grabbed a napkin from the nearest booth, found a pen in my purse, and scribbled my number on it. "If you change your mind, I'm in town for a while. Helping out with my dad."

She slid the napkin into her back pocket. God, she was beautiful. Every movement of her body looked choreographed. "Goodbye, Nic."

"Your daughter is beautiful," I said.

She started leaving, tossed her hair over her shoulder, gave me one last searing look. "I hope she isn't like us."

I heard the ride beside us, the gears shifting, metal on metal as the cars came to an abrupt stop and began spinning the opposite way. The squeals of delight from inside. I tried to focus on that, on every individual sound, so I wouldn't think about me and Bailey and Corinne at the top of the Ferris wheel.

I must've seemed so pathetic to Bailey, standing here pretending not to know what she was talking about when that whispered word had become louder and louder over the years. So that sometimes when I thought of Corinne, it was the only thing I heard.

Her cold hands at my elbows. Her breath in my ear. Bailey's laughter, tight and nervous, in the background. The scent of Corinne's spearmint gum. Her fingers dancing across my skin. *Jump,* she said.

She told me to jump.

# The Day Before

# DAY 6

*had a few hours* before I needed to be at Laura's baby shower in the church basement. But every time I thought of that room, I pictured Officer Fraize organizing us into search parties, and I saw the pictures of Annaleise and Corinne hanging from the walls, interchangeable in my mind now.

"So you'll be there at noon?" Daniel was outside the house with a pressure washer, two steps up a ladder leaning against the siding.

"I said I would."

"Give me the list," he said, hand extended.

"Seriously? You're just going to work on the house now? Get it ready to sell?"

He jerked his hand forward a second time. "Come on, I'm not allowed to be there anyway."

I reached up to hand him the paper, and he skimmed the page. "Pressure washer, got it. Okay, I'll do the grouting after, and the painting if Tyler comes to help."

"Tyler's coming?"

"I don't know. He was going to, but I haven't heard from him," he said, cutting his eyes to me. "So do me a favor and pull all the furniture you can away from the walls. I'll handle the bigger pieces. Go get the plastic sheets out of the trunk."

He went back to spraying the house. We were really doing this. Selling the house. Getting it ready. Going about our lives. Moving on.

"Nic," he said. "Trunk. Go."

I felt ungrounded as I walked to his car, as if in a daze. Sleep had been hard to come by the last few nights, and it was doing something to my head—like there was too much space to sort through and I couldn't get a grip on any one solid thing. I pulled the sheets of plastic from the trunk, the smell slightly nauseating, held them against my chest so they billowed up in front of my face. I imagined suffocating inside them, draping them across crime scenes. My mother used to lay plastic sheets across the floor so Daniel and I could paint on easels in the kitchen, and after, they'd be covered in spills and drips, speckles of colors—a beautiful accident.

I couldn't breathe. I dropped them at the bottom of the porch steps, and Daniel turned to look at me. "Nic, really," he said, like I was the colossal disappointment of his life.

"I don't feel good."

He turned off the machine, walked down the ladder. "Well, if you're not gonna help here," he said, "then get to the church and help there."

I nodded. "I'll probably be back late. I have plans after."

"You have plans after?"

"Yes," I said. "I have plans." Plans that consisted of wanting to be anywhere but here.

"You can stay with me and Laura tonight. The paint fumes. I wouldn't want to breathe them in, either."

"Maybe," I said.

He nodded. "Good. See you later, then."

———

MAYBE IT WAS THE church's proximity to the police station, or maybe it was the graveyard behind it, where my mother was buried beside my grandparents, but there was something unsettling about this place, with the wooden pews smelling like earth, and the way you had to walk down the narrow aisle and over the altar to get to the basement steps beyond. I'd spent every Sunday here as a kid, but I'd stopped attending after my mom died, as did Daniel. My dad wasn't usually there, either. Too busy sleeping off the Saturday binge—or just sleeping. And Tyler went only if I asked him to go with me. There was nothing for me under this steepled roof anymore.

Church was just another part of my life here. The thing you did on Sunday mornings, followed by snacks from CVS with Corinne and Bailey and whoever else was hanging out with us at the time. We'd sit on the top of car hoods in the summer, or huddle inside the store when the weather turned, Luke Aberdeen usually behind the cash register, keeping an extra-close eye on us, for good reason.

The last time I'd been to church here was for Daniel and Laura's wedding, three years ago. I had that unsettled feeling back then, too. Standing up beside the altar in a watermelon-pink dress Laura had picked out and guessed my measurements on, because I'd never sent them to her. It was a little too long—hitting at shin level instead of just below the knee—too tight across the top, and gaped at the armholes. I felt out of place. I looked out of place.

I'd sneaked into this basement after, waiting out the crowd. Tyler had found me playing darts by myself in the rec room. I'd heard his footsteps rounding the corner, heard him toss his blazer on the nearest chair, while I took aim at the target with one eye closed. "Nice dress," he'd said.

"Shut up."

"Want to get out of here?" He showed me a secret way out—a set of steps through a closet in the back, a storm shutter, a chain with a master lock holding it closed. But Tyler had the code from when he worked down here after a flood. He had a way out of everything.

Daniel did not forgive me for missing the reception.

———

"NIC!" LAURA SQUEALED WHEN she saw me, waddling away from her older sister and mother, who were hanging decorations.

I smiled. "Daniel said you could use some help here."

"Oh my God, yes," she said. She leaned in closer. "My mother is *crazy*. Katie's trying to keep her occupied, but she's gone off the deep end. I can't tell whether she's excited or terrified of becoming a grandmother."

I nodded too quickly. There were tiny moments, like this, when the grief came on strong out of nowhere. It was sneaky, and tricky, and you couldn't see it coming until it was already there. It came with the mundane, simple tasks: My mother would never be hanging pink streamers at my shower. I would never lean over to someone and conspiratorially whisper, *My mother is crazy*. She would never become a grandmother.

Laura sucked in a quick breath, rubbing her upper stomach as if working out a kink. "Let me get you some punch."

"No, thanks. Just put me to work."

"Okay. Um, Katie?" she called over her shoulder. "What can Nic do?"

I let Katie sweep me up in the details. Hanging a sign, setting up the games, placing the cupcakes just so on the folding tables. Her eyes kept drifting to the board the cops had used in the corner—Annaleise's picture was still pinned to the wall, along with a white grid sheet sectioning off the woods, each box with an assigned letter. Bricks and Officer Fraize had met us all here and organized us into groups. I had been on Team C, which searched the Carter property, stretching to the river. Daniel got A, which was Piper (including the abandoned house—nothing there, he'd told us after), McElray, and us. Tyler was in E, which was nowhere near the Carter place—he had the neighborhoods and property behind the elementary school. And don't think we didn't notice.

I took it upon myself to pull everything off the wall, storing it all facedown under the table.

"Thank you," Katie said. "I felt bad taking them down, but who wants to look at that during a baby shower?" She shook her head. She had hair like her sister's, long and fine, but hers was loaded with material that made it poof up near the top. Katie was twice divorced already, but I saw a ring on her finger.

"Congratulations," I said.

"Third time's the charm," she said in a singsongy voice. "What about you? I hear you're engaged to some hotshot lawyer up north?"

I felt the burn of her gaze on my empty finger. "Yes. The ring's getting cleaned, though."

"If you ever need wedding advice, you know who to ask." She laughed to herself.

"Thanks, Katie."

An hour later and the place looked like a tribute to cotton candy as the guests began to arrive. "Oh!" Katie said. "The present table." She thrust a few wrapped boxes on top of the table in the corner, with pink-and-green-wrapped mints scattered around.

"I left my present in the rec room," I said. The rec room was through the kitchen, attached to the bathrooms, and I heard the toilet flush just as I grabbed my gift bag. I closed my eyes and reached inside to feel it one last time.

I'd gone to Babies "R" Us with the intention of finding the perfect gift, but I'd been completely overwhelmed by the enormity of the place. Aisles upon aisles—an entire industry devoted to the production and growth of tiny humans—and I had absolutely no idea where to start. And I didn't know what Daniel and Laura wanted or needed. I checked the kiosk near the door for their registry, but they didn't seem to have one. So I bought a tiny outfit—a tiny pink gingham dress with a tiny pink hat and tiny pink socks. Later, I asked one of the teachers at work what her favorite baby gift had been. "A breast pump," she'd said. "Oh, and don't get clothes."

That night, as I was boxing up my things for storage, I opened the one bin I'd taken from home. My mother's things, just sitting there, boxed away. Things I'd rifle through and never use. Things I took with me after all. I'd left them inside a gray plastic bin the whole time, too scared that I'd ruin them or that someone would break into my crappy apartment and take them.

And now I realized I'd forgotten a card. Son of a bitch.

Laura came out of the restroom, head tilted to the side, her hair falling over both shoulders. "For me?" she asked.

"I forgot a card," I said.

"Oh, that's okay." She went to take the bag from me, but I couldn't do it—couldn't lose it in the sea of gifts on the table. She moved her hands to my arms. "Can I open it now?"

I nodded, and she smiled. I held the bag while she moved the tissue paper aside, first pulling out the tiny pink outfit, her smile stretching wide. Then she reached deeper, her face twisting as she felt the cold metal, maybe her fingers brushing over the engraving. She pulled out the silver jewelry box with my mother's name engraved on top. It had been a gift from my father on their wedding day. *Shana Farrell,* it said in this perfect script—fancy but easy to read; formal but not pretentious.

Laura didn't say anything. A tear rolled down her cheek as she watched the light catch the name on the surface. "Oh, Nic," she said, her hand up to her mouth and then down to her belly.

"Oh, don't do that. Oh, God. Don't have the baby now. I'm not equipped."

She smiled, shaking her head. "I can't take this. It's yours."

"I'll never have a Shana Farrell," I said. "Please. She would've given it to you if she were here. I know it." It was true. I could picture her doing this, feel her standing in this very spot, reaching for Laura, smoothing her hair.

She shook her head again but kept the box in her hands. "Thank you," she said.

"Laura?" Katie poked her head in back. "The guests are here, babe. You okay?"

Laura wiped her cheeks, held my hand, and squeezed. "We will take good care of this, Nic," she said. "Are you coming?"

"In a minute. Go ahead," I said.

I spent a few moments in the bathroom, which had always been my favorite place for a good cry.

———

THE SHOWER WAS IN full-on party mode, Laura's friends holding punch, grouped together with cupcakes and miniature sandwiches. Her mom and sister restocking the trays and moving effortlessly from group to group. People placing bets on the birth date on a sheet of paper hung over the gift table. I leaned against the entrance, readying myself for the show. *Smile. Be friendly. For Laura.*

"I don't think they're related," I heard one of her friends say as she pulled the papers out from underneath the table. She was in Laura's high school class; I knew her. Knew of her, at least. Same shade of hair, dyed a deep red. Monica Duncan. At least that had been her maiden name. "Annaleise was nothing like Corinne Prescott."

They hovered around the search-party grid and Annaleise's picture, which I'd taken down and hidden to specifically avoid nosy hands, prying words—everything I hated about this place.

Laura stood on the other side of them, her back to us, but she looked over her shoulder and said, "Oh, hush now, Monica."

They waited for Laura to turn back around, and Monica lowered her voice. "What?" she said. "It's true. Don't you remember? That girl used to come around to our parties when she was barely fourteen—*fourteen*—the bunch of them. Remember?" Laura looked over her shoulder again, and I saw her face turning red, her eyes scanning the room. I shrank back into the kitchen. "Hitting on our boyfriends, acting like they owned the town—I mean, what did they think was going to happen? If that was them at fourteen, imagine them at eighteen. Wait, we don't even have to imagine. There were more than enough rumors."

I couldn't believe they were talking like this at Laura's baby shower. Laura, who was married to Daniel, an unofficial suspect in that case. Laura, sister-in-law to Corinne's best friend.

"Annaleise was such a sweet thing. Never made a stir. Knew her place. The Prescott girl, she was different. She was a disaster waiting to happen. Who here is really surprised?"

"I don't know," someone else said. "Annaleise *was* supposedly seeing Tyler Ellison." I heard nervous laughter. "So maybe not so sweet after all." They all laughed.

"Martin said the police showed up at Tyler's place this morning. For questioning. But he wasn't there," a third woman in the group added.

God, the rumors, the conspiracy theories. *This is how it starts. This is how people decide on innocence and guilt.* Time for me to get out there, make them stop because of my presence, and because they have nice Southern manners, after all.

"Can we please not talk about this at my shower?" Laura asked.

"Oh, I don't want to upset you, dear!" Monica said, a hand around Laura's waist. "What I'm saying is, there's nothing for us to worry about. It's not the same thing. No pattern. No reason to think this is all connected," she whispered. I guess they hadn't heard about the text that Annaleise had sent to Officer Mark Stewart asking about Corinne's case. It wouldn't be long, though. I rounded the corner, heading for the punch. Monica added, "Corinne, she got what she deserved. Put them all in their place, didn't it."

Laura had gone pale and was looking directly at me. "Monica," she said.

"What?" Monica said.

Laura pushed away from her toward me, but I backed out of the room again.

"Oh. Oops," I heard Monica say.

There was no way to get through this shower without making a scene. By embarrassing either Laura or her friends.

Laura still looked pale as she followed me into the kitchen.

"I'm so sorry," I said, searching for my purse. "I have to go."

"Nic, don't. Please."

I found the strap to my black bag, swung it over my shoulder. "Congratulations, Laura," I said.

They were right. This wasn't my place. I knew my place, and it wasn't here—wasn't in Cooley Ridge.

Laura couldn't keep up. I disappeared inside that storage room closet, walked up the back steps, and remembered the combination from three years earlier—*Ten-ten-ten, people really are too trusting,* Tyler had said—pushed through the unlocked storm cellar door, and was gone.

———

CORINNE WASN'T AT FAULT, but she wasn't innocent. That's what Monica—and everyone else—implied. Corinne incited passion and rage, lust and anger. Someone couldn't help himself. But she brought it on herself, obviously. That's what you say to convince yourself: *It will never be me.*

*She didn't know her place.*

*She incited too much passion.*

It's typically men who commit murder in the heat of passion. Their fingers tightening of their own accord around our slender necks. Their practiced arm swinging forward in an arc, beyond their own intention, into our fragile cheekbones. Passion. Heat. Instinct.

Women are more deliberate. Adding to silent lists of slights, tallying the offenses, building a case, retreating inward.

Passion belongs to the men. Statistics say an unplanned attack will likely come from them. So the investigation started there: Jackson, Tyler, Daniel, her father.

But the police were wrong to start there, with statistics. They needed to start with Corinne, needed to know her first. Then they would've seen that perhaps there is nothing more passionate than loving someone in spite of yourself. Didn't matter who you were. If you loved Corinne, it was all passion.

What the detectives wanted were facts. Names. Events. Grudges and slights that could boil over into a girl losing her life outside the county fair. Hannah Pardot exposed *that* Corinne—the real one. But I didn't know whether it really mattered. Whether that one was any more real than the one I knew, the one living inside my head. A haunting, blurred image, twirling in a field of sunflowers. I never could grasp her, but she was the realest person I knew.

*Jump,* she'd said. And then she leaned in close, so only I could hear, and whispered, *If I were you, I'd do it.*

But I didn't.

The facts. The facts were fluid, and changed, depending on the point of view. The facts were easily distorted. The facts were not always right.

*What would she do?* they should've asked.

After I said no.

After Daniel pushed her away.

After Jackson abandoned her.

What would she do if we all pushed her away in a single day? If she had nowhere else to go? What would she *do?*

I can feel her cold fingers at my elbows, and her whisper becomes a scream: *Jump.*

You want to believe you're not the saddest person on earth. That there's someone worse, someone there with you. Someone suffering beside you through the unfathomable darkness.

*Jump,* she said, like I had no future.

But she was wrong. So wrong.

Because when I was standing on the edge of the Ferris wheel cart, my breath lost to the wind and Tyler waiting for me down below, everything became so strikingly clear.

———

I WANT TO TELL someone about that night. About Corinne. About what she said.

About me.

But I don't know how. It's impossible, really. They're not separate things. They come in pairs. One event gets tied up in another and you can't tell one story without the second. They're forever entwined in your mind.

Two days before the fair, standing in her bathroom, Corinne holding the test in her hand. "Ninety seconds," she said, not letting me see. The ticking of the clock from her bedroom nightstand. "Tick-tock, Nic."

"I'm glad you think this is funny," I said.

"Moment of truth." She looked first, and I had the sudden urge to rip it from her hands.

She smiled, flipping it around.

The two blue lines, and my stomach rolled again. I sank to my knees on her perfectly white tiled floor, leaning over the toilet. She rubbed my upper back. "Shh," she said. "It'll be okay."

I sat on the floor and watched as she stuffed the test deep inside the box of Skittles already in her trash can. "Don't worry," she said, her mouth twisted into half a smile, "my mom had me when she was eighteen, too."

I shouldn't have let her talk me into taking the test right then, in her bathroom, with her standing over me. She shouldn't have been first. Not before Tyler.

"I have to go," I said. She didn't stop me as I stumbled out of her room, out of her house, down to the river, where I sat and stared at the rushing water and cried, because I knew no one else could hear me. I called for Tyler to meet me there, and I made myself stop crying before I told him.

Two days later, and I see Tyler from the top of the Ferris wheel, and I think for just a moment that I have everything.

Corinne dared me to climb on the outside of the cart, and I wanted to do it. I wanted to know it was as easy as letting go, and say no. I wanted to feel the rush, the power, the hope—everything my life could be.

But then I felt her breath in my ear: *Jump,* she said, and in that moment, I was scared of what Corinne might do. How dark she really was, deep inside. My life was just part of the game for her. A piece to move, to see how far I could bend. How much she must've hated me, hated every one of us, underneath it all.

I was scared that she would push me, that Bailey would never tell, that everyone would think I wanted to die when I wanted nothing more than to live in that moment. For Tyler below, and for the life we might have, all the possibilities stretching before me, existing all at once.

But then I'm thrown off balance, the world skews sideways, the sting of the fist on my face.

Corinne comes running to bear witness to the destruction.

A girl eating ice cream watches on, a memory that never dies for her.

My arm goes instinctively to my stomach as I fall to the dirt, because I've just understood how fragile everything is, how paralyzingly temporary we all are, and that something is beginning for me. Something worth holding on to.

———

I SPENT THE REST of the afternoon after Laura's shower down by the river again, until it turned dark. Until I knew Daniel would be gone. Until the house was empty and the walls were wet and sticky, the paint fumes suffocating.

I ignored Daniel's calls, instead texting him a brief *I'm home.*

*Coming here?* he texted back.

*No. Going to sleep,* I wrote.

But I didn't sleep. I didn't do anything.

I let myself have this one night to feel sorry for myself. Just one night. To mourn for Corinne and my mother, for Daniel and my father, for me and for Tyler and for all the lost things.

Tomorrow I'd pick myself up. Tomorrow there would be no more crying. Tomorrow I'd remember that I had kept going.

# The Day Before

# DAY 5

I *shouldn't be here.* I shouldn't be here. I shouldn't be here.

I was rocking on the couch with the television on in front of me and a fresh cup of coffee in my hands, wearing yesterday's clothes, the fabric stiff and accusing against my skin.

The alarm clock sounded in the bedroom, and I could choreograph the next few moments: He'd hit snooze twice, then curse repeatedly as he raced to the shower, throw on some clothes, pull a hat down over his still-wet hair, fill his travel mug with yesterday's reheated coffee.

I sat on the sofa, legs folded underneath me, sipping my fresh coffee from his ECC mug.

Instead, Tyler came straight out of the bedroom, like he'd heard the television, even though I had it only one notch off silent. He was standing in a pair of black boxers, his blue eyes completely awake. I took in his tanned chest and stomach. He'd put on a little weight since the last time I'd been home, but you didn't notice in clothes.

255

I was the only person who could map the changes over the span of the decade—my hands tracing over every contour, like muscle memory—just as he could with me.

I made myself focus on the screen, and I gestured my mug toward it. "Just catching up on the news," I said, watching the reporter's mouth move. She was standing in front of a poster of Annaleise Carter, outlining the facts once more: last seen by her brother, walking into the woods. Now entering the second day of searching, including helicopters. No sign of her. Nothing ruled out. Nothing new.

"I thought maybe you left," Tyler said. He was almost at the couch.

I kept my eyes glued to the screen. "I need a ride home. I made coffee," I said. "Fresh. In the kitchen."

"Couldn't sleep?" His voice drifted through the apartment as he opened a cabinet. There wasn't much to it—this living room, his bedroom, and the kitchen with the island in the middle. His laptop was closed on the coffee table.

"Not really," I said. Which wasn't entirely true. I'd fallen into a deep and peaceful sleep almost immediately—the best since I'd been back. It was the noise from people leaving the bar at closing time that jerked me awake, and I couldn't find the way back to where I'd been, only Tyler could do that, talking me out of my own head, letting me forget myself. I'd spent the last several hours feeling sick to my stomach.

He picked up the blanket crumpled on the seat beside me and hung it over the armrest, where it had been last night. He sat beside me, a little too close—mug in hand, his right arm behind me, his fingers moving absently in my hair. I felt the tension releasing, my body uncoiling itself. I closed my eyes for a second, listening to Tyler sip his coffee.

This. Us. There's a comfort to it. Something too easy to get lost inside for a weekend.

My phone rang on the table and I grabbed it, expecting Daniel, and felt the blood drain from my face when I saw Everett's name on the display. I set my mug down and answered. "Let me call you right back," I said before I could register the sound of his voice. "Ten minutes."

"I'm on my way in to the office," he said. "I'll try you again at lunch."

"Okay. Later, then." I hung up and leaned forward on the couch, my head in my hands.

Tyler stood. "I have to get ready for work," he said. "I'll drop you on the way." He headed for the bathroom, paused at the bedroom entrance. "Just do me one favor: Don't call him the second I step into the shower."

I narrowed my eyes at his back. "I wasn't going to."

"Right."

"Don't be like this," I said. "Don't—"

He spun around, one hand on the doorjamb, the other gesturing toward me. "You're asking me not to be like this?"

"I was upset!" I said.

"I know, I was here."

"I wasn't thinking."

"That's bullshit."

He glared at me from the doorway to his bedroom. I focused on the reporter's mouth once more. "I don't want to fight with you," I said.

"No, I know exactly what you want me for."

Sharp and cutting, but nothing compared to the look on his face. Everything right about the night before, overexposed in the daylight and undeniably wrong.

"I'm sorry. But what do you want from me?"

His eyes grew wider, if possible. "You're not serious," he said. He shook his head, ran a hand down his face. "What exactly are you sorry for, Nic? I'm just curious. For this, right now? For last year? The one before that? Or for leaving the first time without saying a goddamn word?"

I stood, my limbs shaking with adrenaline. "Oh, don't do this now. Don't bring this up now."

This was our unspoken agreement. We didn't discuss it. Couldn't look back and couldn't look forward.

After I graduated, the plan was to wait a year. Save up some money, leave together. But Corinne disappeared and all the plans went to shit. Daniel stopped working on the renovation, gave me what money he could. I left by myself—one year at a community college, then transferring to a four-year university with student housing and loans and a campus that existed unto itself, segregated from the rest of the world. Someplace safe and far away.

"Or are you sorry for changing your number?" Tyler continued, coming a step closer. "For coming home five months later like it was all nothing?"

"I can't do this," I said. "We were kids, Tyler. Just kids."

"Doesn't mean it wasn't real," he said, his voice softening. "We could've made it."

"Could've. Might've. There's a lot of hypothetical in that. We didn't, Tyler. We didn't make it."

"Because you disappeared! Literally."

"I didn't disappear, I left."

"You were there one day and then you were gone. How is that any different? Your *brother* had to tell me, Nic."

"I couldn't stay," I said, my voice barely making it across the room.

"I know," he said. "But it wasn't a temporary thing. A temporary promise. I meant what I said to you."

*He let me drive his truck because his hand was all messed up. I kept touching my fingers to my face, expecting to find something new, something more substantial than a red mark and a swollen lip. "For real, Nic, are you okay?" he asked.*

*"Yes," I said. "I'm so done with them all. With Daniel, Corinne. I'm done with her games. I'm done with my dad. I'm done with this place."*

*"Pull over," he said.*

*"Where?" The streets were dark and curvy, and there wasn't much of a shoulder, if any, in most places. But there were these outlooks over the valley—guardrails set up around tiny rectangles jutting over the rocks below.*

*"Anywhere."*

*But I thought I knew why he wanted me to pull over, and I didn't want to be caught in the glare of the headlights. "We're almost to the caverns," I said. I pulled his truck into the lot, pulled it off the road, over the lip of rocks and into the clearing, mostly hidden from view by a row of trees.*

*I turned off the engine. Unbuckled my seat belt. But he didn't pull me toward him. Didn't turn to face me at first.*

*"I'll take care of you, you know that," he said. "I'll be good to you. I'll love you forever, Nic."*

*"I know you will," I said. It was the one thing I was sure of.*

*He reached into his glove compartment and pulled out a ring. It was simple. Beautiful. Perfect. Two silver bands woven together. A line of blue gems where they interlocked.*

Forever. It's the kind of thing you say when forever has only been a handful of years. When it's not decades before you become those Russian nesting dolls.

There was a small part of me that was still childish, stubborn in her hope, thinking I could somehow have everything. That Tyler could become Everett, that Everett could become Tyler. That I could be all the versions of me, stacked inside one another, and find someone who would want them all. But that's childhood. Before you realize that every step is a choice. That something must be given up for something to be gained. Everything on a scale, a weighing of desires, an ordering of which you want more—and what you'd be willing to give for it.

Ten years ago, I made that choice for the both of us, ripping off a Band-Aid and taking the skin with it. *A clean break,* I'd thought back then. But I'd never given him that choice, never let him have any say. *You disappeared,* he'd said—

"I left, and I'm sorry, but that was ten years ago," I said. "I can't go back and undo it."

"You keep coming back, Nic."

I wasn't sure whether he meant to Cooley Ridge or to him. "You're going to be late."

He dragged his fingers slowly and forcibly through his hair. "You make me crazy," he said, turning for the bathroom. The shower turned on, and I could hear cabinets slamming, sense him losing his cool behind the closed door.

It happens like this—men losing themselves in moments of passion. We drive them to it. It's not their fault.

I closed my eyes and leaned against the counter beside the refrigerator, feeling my nails digging into my palms, and slowly counted to one hundred.

———

WE HAD TO EXIT through the front door near the bar entrance. I kept my head down to the traffic. I followed Tyler to his truck around back, rested my head against the window as we drove.

We were silent on the ride home. He pulled into my driveway and I hesitated with my fingers on the handle, staring out the window. "Will you be okay here?" he asked.

The house. Skinny and tilted and waiting for me. Beyond that, the Carter property and the search for a missing girl. I left the car, but he lowered the passenger window. "Nic?" he said.

I took a second to look back as I walked away. He'd lost every girl he was with whenever I came home, and the ghost of me followed him everywhere in this town. Not sure why he did it—if he really thought this time would be any different. That this time I'd stay. I was breaking him over and over, every time I left, and this was something I could put an end to. A gift. A debt I owed him for everything I'd lost him.

I couldn't come back after all. The distance only increases.

"I can't see you anymore," I said.

"Sure, okay," like he didn't believe me.

"Tyler, I'm asking you. Please. I can't see you anymore."

Silence as he gripped the wheel tighter.

"I'm ruining your life, Tyler. Can't you see that?"

His silence and his stare followed me across the yard, up the porch steps, until the front door latched shut behind me.

I supposed, when he looked closely, he could see that I was.

———

THE HOUSE FELT DIFFERENT. Unsafe, unknown, too many possibilities existing all at once. Too many voices whispered back at me from the walls. The garage through the living room windows, so unassuming in the sunlight, and beyond, the woods stretching infinitely into the distance.

No, I would not be okay here.

I drove to the church and went down to the basement, where Officer Fraize was organizing about one tenth as many people as the day before. He gave me a map with a section bordered in orange highlighter, and he directed me toward two kids with jet-black hair picking through yesterday's donated baked goods.

"Hi," I said to the girl's back.

She turned and spoke around a piece of pound cake. "Hi," she said. She was a little older than I'd thought—younger than I was but not quite a kid anymore. "You with us?"

*Us* being her and a guy about the same age, two days of scruff on an otherwise unremarkable face. Siblings, I guessed from the hair color.

"Looks like it," I said.

"I'm Britt," she said. "This is Seth." She looked down at the map, and I saw her roots were plain brown, several shades lighter than the rest of her hair. Maybe not siblings. "They have us following the river, looks like. Should be easy enough."

"Let's park at CVS," Seth said. "I need some Advil or something." He winced for impact.

"Hangover," Britt whispered, feeding him a piece of cake with her fingers.

———

I FOLLOWED SETH'S PICKUP and waited for him to come out of the store. Besides the Advil or something, he also got some candy, and the crinkling wrappers accompanied us as we crossed the street and entered the woods. He chewed loudly until we picked up a curve of the river, and then all I could hear was the water trickling along.

I hugged the edge, keeping my gaze on the water, looking for objects that might be hidden underneath. The water wasn't deep, and I could see the rocks and roots below, even in the shade. We reached a clearing, the sunlight bright, my eyes narrowing in response, and the glare of the sun reflected off the surface too sharply, blurring my vision.

"You okay?" Britt had her fingers curled in my sleeve just as I felt my balance start to lean.

"Yeah," I said. "Checking to see if maybe she fell in."

Britt pulled me farther from the edge. "Careful," she said. "I heard they'll get men in the water eventually, but if she's in there"— she pointed down the bank—"it's not like it matters how fast we find her."

Seth unwrapped another candy, shoved the wrapper in the pocket of his pants. "She'd think that was fitting, I bet," he said. "Very Ophelia. Very art. Very *significant*."

"You were friends with her?" I asked.

The girl nodded. "Yeah, I guess. Except not really. I mean, we were, kind of, before she became Art School Annaleise."

"What was she before?"

"Just like the rest of us," she said. Britt picked a slightly worn path a little farther from the river, guiding me along with her.

"I always thought she was quiet," I said.

"Annaleise? I guess. But also not. She was loud with her art. Like, she did the murals for our school play, and she hid all these tiny sick details in them. We didn't notice until after. It was like a tribute to everyone she hated at school." Seth laughed, but Britt wasn't smiling. "It was so subtle—enough to deny. And for us to point it out meant admitting to something, you know? She walked the halls with this obnoxious smile all the time, like she was getting away with something and we all knew it. She had a meanness in her."

We all do. Corinne had shown us that.

"So, no," Seth added, "we weren't friends."

"Any clue where she'd go?"

Seth chewed the candy between his back teeth, grinding as he spoke. "Bet she was never even in the woods," he said.

"Her brother said—" I started.

"Her brother," Seth said. "Useless piece of crap. Want to know why Bryce was hanging out his window after midnight on a Monday night? Probably because he didn't want his mom to smell the pot."

"Heard he's dropping out," Britt added.

A kid with no promise, the opposite of his sister. Watching her image disappear through the smoke.

"Nobody really trusts him, but it's not like there's anything else to go by," Seth said.

"You don't believe it? That she wandered off into the woods?"

"After midnight? She goes for a walk into the woods with her purse? Come on," Britt said.

"Then why are you here?"

Seth shrugged, unwrapped another candy. "Because we were given the day off if we did this instead."

Britt must've noticed the look on my face. "Besides, there are helicopters. If she's out here, they'll find her."

I looked up at the canopy of leaves, and down at the water rushing by, and hoped that was a lie she was telling herself to feel better about not caring.

You could get lost in these woods so easily. You could lose yourself in them. You could live an entire secret history inside of them, a decade's worth, with no witnesses.

———

I HAD COME DOWN to this river the winter after I left, the first time I was home.

I'd enrolled in a school a hundred miles east, used Daniel's money to find a cheap place with three roommates. Got a job in the registration office, which would turn full-time in the summer. Went home for a week over Christmas break, which turned into two because a snowstorm came and I couldn't leave.

I'd put on my snow boots and my down jacket, pulled a hat over my newly red hair. Trudged down to the river, where my lungs burned with deep breaths and the icicles shone against the bank.

And I saw that I was not alone.

We walked slowly down the bank on opposite sides until we reached the log thrown across at the narrow gap. I watched as Tyler balanced on the trunk, and I laughed when he slipped, catching himself with his gloved fingers.

I smiled when he made it all the way across. "I like your hair," he said.

"You don't have to lie."

His gloves smelled like wool and chafed at my skin, just like the scruff of his jawline. His lips were cracked and thirsty, and his skin was warm against the cold. We made a pact that day in our silence. That we would not speak of the things that had happened, we would not speak of all we had lost.

———

BRITT AND SETH FOLLOWED the river until it branched, which was the mark on the map for the end of our search area. Seth spun on his heel, but I stared at the two different paths, remembering where they led. One behind the caverns. The other snaked around the open fields of the fair, cutting close to Riverfall Motel, in all its run-down glory.

"Hey, Nic," Britt said. Had I given her my name? Did she know who I was? "Snap out of it, sister."

"I'm gonna keep going," I said.

"Like hell," she said. "Didn't you get a copy of the rules? We stay together. We return together. We report together."

I followed them back to the road. Followed them back to check in with Officer Fraize. Then took one of the Missing flyers and drove down to Riverfall Motel by myself.

———

RIVERFALL MOTEL WAS A strip of twenty identical rooms, set just back from the road, with a parking lot of slanted spaces in front of each door. It was yellow and falling to disrepair, but there were cars out front. Probably because of the fair. Maybe some of the workers. This was where Hannah Pardot had been stationed for the summer ten years ago. I used to drive by sometimes, just to see if her car was still here.

I parked in front of the office, let myself in, watched the man behind the counter tear his gaze from a soap opera that he didn't bother turning off. "Can I help you?" he asked.

I put Annaleise's flyer down on the counter, felt her eyes staring up at me, twisted the paper around so it was facing him. "Have you seen this woman?"

"Annaleise Carter? The police have already been here. Nope. Never seen her." He was already facing the television again.

"Okay, thanks."

I knocked on each door, getting no response from most, even some with cars out front. People wanting privacy, people who had secrets to keep.

At the third room, I heard footsteps, saw a shadow under the door, knew someone was looking out the peephole back at me, but the doorknob didn't turn. I flipped the flyer around, holding it up to the peephole. "I'm looking for this girl," I said. The door cracked open. The room smelled stale and sour, as if alcohol and milk had been ground into the carpet.

The world was full of people who wanted to give information, who sometimes fabricated it in the hope that it would lead somewhere. But the world was also full of people who had no intention of going anywhere near the police. Who saw things and kept them hidden. A group of people who could piece together the truth if they were so inclined. The man didn't open the door all the way, but I could see his face, bearded and pockmarked. I didn't know why he was here, and I didn't honestly care.

"I'm not with the police," I said. "I'm just her friend. Just looking for her. I thought maybe she'd come here. Have you seen her?"

His eyes scanned me slowly, taking it all in, from my sneakers caked in mud to my old T-shirt and my hair falling from my ponytail. He tilted his head, leaning closer. "Maybe," he said through the crack in the door. "A friend, you say?" Pressing his face closer, his eyes fixed on mine.

I met his stare, refusing to step back. "No," I said. "Not a friend. But I need to find her."

He smiled then, his teeth yellowed but straight, like he'd had braces once. "Maybe there was a girl I saw running from the woods. Maybe she slid open the window to the room at the end down there. Maybe she went inside. None of my business, though."

"Thank you," I said as the door closed. "Thank you."

*See, Annaleise? Someone is always watching.*

I walked around back and tried the window, which wasn't locked. I shimmied through the motel window and found myself in an empty room with no sign of Annaleise. I checked the shower, the closet, under the bed. There was nothing. I closed my eyes and pictured her sprinting through the woods, shimmying inside this room like I'd just done. Why was she here? What did she want?

A place to breathe. A place to gather her thoughts. A place to make a plan. There was no impression in the mattress, no towel askew in the bathroom.

I picked up the phone, listened to the dial tone. Information. I'd call an operator. If I didn't have my phone, I'd call for a number. I checked the pad of paper beside the phone and could make out a few pressure points but nothing more. Couldn't see a number if she'd written one.

I hit redial.

The phone rang four times, and then: *You've reached the Farrells. We're not home right now, but we'll get back to you just as soon as we're in.* Laura's voice. Annaleise had called my brother's house. She'd

267

been at this motel, and she'd called my brother, and then she'd disappeared.

———

I DROVE HOME. FOUND Daniel working on the house, hosing down the ground beside the garage, loading up his car with debris.

"Any word?" I asked, shielding my eyes from the glare in the front yard.

"Nothing." He rolled the free hose on a reel, following the trail toward the side of the house.

I shifted from foot to foot. "What haven't you told me about Annaleise, Daniel?"

He stopped moving, dropped the reel, cut his eyes to me. "Are you saying you don't believe me?"

*What haven't you told me about Corinne?* Would he tell me? Or would he stick to his official statement?

"You can talk to me," I said.

He picked up the reel again. There were voices coming from the woods, and his head whipped in that direction. "The police are in the woods," he said. "Have you eaten? Laura sent me with leftovers. Go on in the house, Nic."

I nodded, went inside. Reheated the stew in a pot on the stove, watched Daniel through the window. Realizing how he knew it was the police just out of sight: He had been watching. Standing out there, watching the woods, and listening.

*What haven't you told me, Daniel?*

We communicated in the space between words. And I wondered: What was he saying now?

# The Day Before

# DAY 4

The rain had trickled to a stop but continued to drip from the leaves, falling on the roof like it was keeping time: *Tick-tock, Nic*. The clock in the kitchen read five A.M., and there was still no sign of Daniel or Tyler's truck.

"Have you heard from him?" I asked, filling a glass from the sink tap.

"How would I hear from him, Nic?"

We stared at Daniel's phone, sitting on the kitchen table. My hands shook as I handed Tyler a glass of water. His fingers stained the base with powder as he gulped it down, rubbing his other hand across the back of his neck. The sky was starting to lighten on the horizon.

"I need to get home," he said. He was covered in dirt and grime, and his hands were white, like mine. "I have to change before the search. I need a goddamn shower. Can I take your car? I'll swing by after, when Dan brings my truck back."

He handed me the glass, and I drained the rest. "I'm not sure how that would look. My car at your place. People will talk."

"People always talk," he said.

"It's different now."

"Why, because you're engaged? We can be friends, can't we?"

We'd never been friends. Not before and not after. I wouldn't even know how to start. "Because your girlfriend is missing," I said. "Be smart, Tyler."

His head snapped to attention. *Be smart.* Then he leaned back, so his head was resting against the freezer. "I can't believe this is happening. Tell me this isn't happening."

"It's happening."

"I'm going to be a suspect if she doesn't turn up, aren't I?" he asked.

"Tyler, you're going to be *the* suspect." Like Jackson had been. *The Boyfriend*—it was the simplest explanation.

He squeezed his eyes shut, and I wanted to run my fingers through his hair, press my thumbs into the base of his skull, like I used to do whenever his neck was stiff from work.

"Use my shower," I said. "I can find something from my dad's room for you to wear. You shouldn't go home like this."

He looked down at his clothes, at his legs, at his hands. "Yeah. Okay."

I cleaned the floor with damp rags—trying to mop up all the streaks, all the footprints—and I tossed them into the washing machine after. I heard the groan of the pipes and then the sound of the shower curtain being pulled aside as I went to rifle through my dad's old things.

Dad's work clothes would be too small for Tyler; he'd have to settle for gray frayed sweatpants that didn't make the moving list, and an old stained shirt from the few times Dad worked in the yard.

I let myself into the bathroom, the moisture of the room clinging to my skin, already coating the mirror. "It's just me," I said, leaving the clothes on top of the sink.

"Hey," he said. "Hold on."

I stood with my back against the door, watching the gray-and-black-striped shower curtain move, the obscured outline of his shadow. It felt easier to talk with the curtain between us, without having to look directly at each other.

"I got a new place," he said.

"Where?"

"Over Kelly's. It's not much. Just an apartment. But there's a couch and a blanket, and you can stay with me, Nic. No strings attached. You don't have to stay here."

I laughed, and it sounded harsh. "That's a terrible idea, for so many reasons."

"Wouldn't be the worst one this week," he said as I scooped up his dirty pile of clothes.

I opened the bathroom door, felt the rush of cooler air as I stepped outside. "I'm washing your clothes. Save me some hot water."

By the time I got back to my room, he was in my dad's clothes, rubbing my towel over his hair. He was looking out the window at the garage, and I stood beside him, doing the same. He turned to face me, used his thumb to wipe the residue from my face.

"I don't understand what's happening," I said. I felt the tears rising unexpectedly, and Tyler tilted my face up. "How—"

"Hey," he said. "Don't do this to yourself. It's taken care of. Okay?"

I tried to let his words work their way into my head—*I've got you,* at sixteen; *I love you,* at seventeen; *Forever,* at eighteen—but the distance was too great. I couldn't get back to it. Instead, the familiar sound of Tyler's truck turning in to the driveway jarred me into action. "Daniel's back," I said, striding out of the room, racing down the stairs.

Daniel drove up the driveway as I hopped down the front steps, Tyler a step behind. Daniel slid out of the driver's seat without looking at us, tossed the keys to Tyler, and went straight for his own car. "I gotta go," he said, not making eye contact.

"Daniel, wait," I said.

"I need to go," he said.

I crossed the yard after him but didn't know what to say once I had his attention. I looked to Tyler for help, but he was loading up his truck, carrying supplies and using a tarp to protect it all.

"What did you tell Laura?" I asked.

Daniel opened the car door. "That I was here. That we were working late."

"See you at the search," Tyler called, hopping in the truck.

I made it inside before throwing up, the kitchen sink coated with water and bile and fine white powder.

I cleaned the kitchen, took a scalding shower, and mopped the floors.

When the dryer finished, I folded Tyler's clothes and stuffed them in the bottom drawer of my empty dresser, out of sight.

———

WE MET IN THE church basement. Everyone was there, nearly all of Cooley Ridge taking off from work, cramped together in the rec room, overflowing into the kitchen, crowding down the steps.

We rally in a crisis. We rise to the tragedy. Suffer a death and we will feed you for a year. Disappear and we will scour the earth until you are found.

Bricks was set up in front, standing on a chair. His hairline was starting to recede, which you could see because he kept his hair buzzed almost to the scalp.

I had to stand on my toes, pushing through the crowd, to see what he was gesturing toward. What was he talking about? I started picking up snippets of conversation, losing Bricks's voice. *Disappeared. Corinne Prescott. Wandered off. Taken. Monsters.*

". . . in grids." There was a hand on my shoulder. I needed to focus. *Laura.* I looked at her over my shoulder, and she raised an eyebrow. *Okay?* she mouthed.

I nodded. Bricks was pointing to a map of Cooley Ridge, the woods beyond, the river snaking through.

"What do they think?" Laura whispered. "That she got lost out there?"

I broke into a light sweat. I couldn't see Daniel, but he must've been nearby if Laura was here. I couldn't find Tyler, either. Bricks was holding up the clipboard we'd signed in on. "We've assigned you to a grid, each with a leader." He held up a purple rectangle. "When I call your name, follow Officer Fraize here."

He started breaking us into teams, and Laura leaned in. "Y'all are working too hard on that house. You really need to take it easier. Both of you."

"I know," I said, keeping my eyes on Bricks.

"Besides," she said, "he's supposed to be painting the nursery. Honestly. I could give birth any moment now."

I whipped my head around.

"Don't worry, I'm *not.*"

"Should you even be here?" I asked.

"Nic Farrell—"

I pushed through the crowd, following Officer Fraize, not knowing anyone else in my group other than by family association. There were eight of us on the team.

"The ground will be wet," he said. "So watch your footing. And always keep a visual on the person to your side. Move as one, at the same rate. And make sure you're all accounted for on your way out. We don't have enough radios, so . . . ." He eyed the group, handed the radio to an older man whom I recognized as the father of someone I went to school with. "Radio back if you find any-thing."

"Hey," I said, and Officer Fraize half looked at me, heading toward the next group. If he recognized me, he didn't let on. "Did you contact her father? Her friends from college?"

"Yeah, we're on it. We know how to run an investigation. Or do you have something to add? Didn't realize you'd moved back, Nic."

The hairs on the back of my neck stood on end. "I didn't. I'm just in town for a little while."

He paused, his mind grasping for something, sorting through the pieces. "You staying at your dad's old place?"

"Yes."

"Happen to see anything in the woods night before last? Hear anything unusual? Anything like that?"

I shook my head. *No sir, no sir, no sir.*

He focused on me for a moment too long. "Off you go, then," he said. He scanned the crowd before moving on to the next group.

I knew exactly who he was looking for.

———

WE STARTED NEAR THE back of Annaleise's house, heading in the direction of the river. The search ended up being tedious work, exacerbated by an older lady who couldn't keep up. We moved at a snail's pace, and then she'd stop to pick up anything that looked out of place. A rock that had been displaced, a pile of sticks, a marker on a tree. The man in charge of our group by decree of holding the radio kept reminding her, "We're looking for *her*. We're not inves-tigating a crime scene."

We weren't close enough to talk to one another in quiet conver-sation; we were supposed to be listening, anyway. For calls for help or something. Every once in a while, the girl on the edge would call,

"Annaleise? Annaleise Carter?" Because there might be more than one Annaleise lost in these woods.

As we approached the river, we ran into another team. "We went too far," I said.

Our leader, Brad, examined the map. "Nah, we've got to the edge of the river. They're out of their zone. Hey! You're out of zone!"

"What?" a man yelled back.

"I said you're in the wrong place!"

They yelled across the expanse, then the two leaders walked toward each other, their maps out, arguing. I sat on a tree stump, waiting it out. This was a waste. We had no idea if the teams were covering the right sections. Not everyone was familiar with the woods. Not everyone knew the right landmarks.

"I think I found something!" The old lady was crouched over a pile of leaves about ten feet from the river. The girl beside me rolled her eyes. The old lady picked up something that glinted in the sunlight, holding it over her head, squinting. "What is it?" she asked.

I rose, slowly making my way toward them.

"A buckle," someone said. "For a fairy. It's tiny."

"Oh," she said. "Like from a bracelet, maybe?" She turned it over in her hands. It had two letters floating inside a circle, the edges coated in mud. "The initials are MK, so it can't be hers."

"Oh, for Christ's sake," I said. "Are we really pulling every piece of trash from the forest? This is ridiculous."

"Should you be touching that?" said a teen who had probably seen one too many cop shows.

The old lady frowned, put it back down, moved the leaves around to make it look natural.

"That doesn't really work," I said. I picked it back up, turned it over in my hand. "It's from a dog leash. Did she have a dog?"

"I don't think so," the kid said.

Brad gestured for us to turn around. "Come on," he said. "Let's start back."

I trailed the others by a few feet, scanning the surrounding ground as we moved. I slid the buckle into my back pocket. It wasn't from a leash or a collar or a bracelet. I recognized that logo. It was from a purse.

----

I TOOK THE LONG way home, stopping at CVS, buying a soda, using the bathroom, dumping the buckle in the trash can, waving to Luke Aberdeen on the way out.

----

I STOOD IN FRONT of my house, tilting my head to the side, trying to see it as a stranger might. Nothing special, nothing to make someone look twice. My feet started sinking in a spot of mud, and I pulled them out, the suction gripping my sneakers before dislodging. I walked toward the porch, my steps slow and labored, as if my feet were sticking to the earth. I waited by the front porch, willing myself to go inside.

The secrets this house had kept locked away, mine included. Daniel's and my father's and those that belonged to the generation before. In the walls, under the floorboards, within the earth. I imagined Corinne shaking out a can of gasoline and me taking a match to the splintered edge of the porch, both of us standing too close as the wood warped and popped, the house igniting, turning to rubble, to smoke and ash. The flames jumping to the extended branch of a tree, taking the woods along with them.

"What are you doing?"

I peered over my shoulder, at Tyler walking from his truck, his legs moving as slowly as mine had.

I turned back to the house—to my window above the sloped roof. "Imagining a fire," I said.

"Ah," he said, his hand on the small of my back as he stood beside me. He watched the same splintered porch, the same window, and I could imagine him picturing the same thing. "When did you last eat?" he asked.

"I don't know," I said.

"Come on. I picked up dinner."

——

THE BAR WAS SOMBER, but it wasn't empty. Tyler stood between me and the door, obstructing the view as we walked past the entrance, the bag of Chinese takeout tucked under his arm. I followed him up the narrow stairwell, took the bag from him as he unlocked the door and held it open for me with his foot.

"So, this is it," he said.

I left the bag of food on the kitchen island directly to my left. The place could use some upgraded appliances, a fresh coat of paint, a throw rug or two over the scuffed wood floors, but in other ways, it suited him perfectly. It had what he needed: couch, TV, kitchen, bedroom. If something didn't matter to Tyler, he didn't do it for the sake of anyone else. He unloaded the food, serving it on ceramic plates, while I wandered the apartment, checking out the details.

His bed was made. He had a queen, and the comforter was plain and beige. The dresser that he'd had growing up was in the corner, and there was a newer one that was so far from matching, it somehow managed to work. The bathroom door was open—shaving cream on the counter, soap in a dish. I checked the closet on the way out. Men's clothes only, camping gear in the corner.

"Does it pass inspection?" he called as I wandered back to the kitchen. He handed me a plate over the island.

"You got my favorite," I said.

"I know I did." He walked to the couch, slid to the floor, his back resting against the cushions, and placed two beers on the coffee table in front of him.

I sat beside him on the floor. "Not a fan of chairs, I see."

"I've only been here six months. Chairs are next on my list," he said, scooping fried rice into his mouth. "Nic," he said, pointing his fork to the plate in front of me, "you really need to eat something."

My stomach clenched as I stared at the pile of food. I took a sip of the beer, leaning back against the couch. "What kind of purse did Annaleise use?" I asked.

I felt Tyler tense beside me. "I don't want to talk about Annaleise."

"It's important. I need to know."

"Okay. It was . . ." He paused, thinking. "I don't know, it was dark green."

"But do you know the brand?"

"No, I definitely don't know the brand. Are you going to tell me why you're asking?"

"We found something in my group. A buckle. From a Michael Kors purse. Down by the river." I took a deep breath. "I'm pretty sure it's hers."

He slid his plate onto the table, took a long pull from the beer bottle. "And where is this buckle now?"

I looked over at him, into his bloodshot eyes. "In the garbage can in the women's restroom of CVS."

He pressed his fingers to the bridge of his nose. "Nic, you can't do this. You can't mess with the investigation or people will wonder why. I really think she's fine."

"I really think she's *not*," I said. "I think when people disappear, it's because they're not okay, Tyler."

"Hey," he said. "Don't cry."

"I'm not," I said, resting my head on my arm, wiping away the evidence. "Sorry. God. I've barely slept in—what, almost three days?—and I'm losing it."

"You're not losing it," he said. "You're here with me, and you're fine."

I laughed. "That's not the definition of fine. I feel like the whole world is off balance. Like I'm losing my shit. Like there's this cliff and I don't even realize I'm on the edge."

"But you do realize it, and that's the definition of holding your shit together."

I shook my head but took a bite of the pork roll, forcing it down. "Are you okay?" I asked him.

"Not really."

Our plates sat on the table beside half-empty bottles of beer.

"I don't know what I'm doing here," I said.

"We're just friends having dinner after a really shitty day."

"Are we? Friends, I mean?"

"We're whatever you want us to be, Nic."

"Don't do that."

"What?"

"Lie," I said.

"Yeah," he said. He rested his arm on the couch behind me, making space for me. I leaned in to his side, and he slid an arm around me, and we sat there, staring at the blank television across the room.

"If it was from her purse," I said, "she's not okay. I should be out there. I should be looking for her purse."

"Nic, you need to relax." I felt his slow exhale against my forehead.

We sat in silence, but the sounds of people leaving the bar drifted up from the window.

"I don't know what to do about the house." Taking a bite of the dinner had been a mistake. I took a deep breath, trying to hold my shit together. "I can't sleep in that house," I said.

"So don't," he said. "This couch pulls out. You can have my bed. You really need to get some rest."

"People will—"

"Just for tonight. Nobody knows you're here."

I rested my head on his shoulder. Closed my eyes, felt his fingers absently near the bottom of my hair, which suddenly seemed too intimate, even though he was barely touching me.

But maybe there was nothing more intimate than someone knowing all your secrets, every one of them, and sitting beside you anyway, buying your favorite food, running his fingers absently through your hair so you can sleep.

"By the way," he said, "I like your hair."

I smiled, trying not to think of tomorrow. One day I could come back here and he could be gone. One day I could walk through the woods, fade to nothing, leaving behind nothing but the buckle from a purse. All of us eventually stacked up in boxes in the police station or under the earth, passed over, passed by, with nobody left to find us.

I lifted my head off his shoulder, shifting so I was on top of him, one leg on either side, my arms sliding behind his neck, my fingers working through his hair.

"Wait. Don't think this is . . . That's not why I—"

I pulled my shirt over my head, saw his gaze drift to the scar on my shoulder and then away, as it always did.

Tyler gripped my thighs, holding me still. Rested his forehead against my bare shoulder, his breathing shallow.

If there's a feeling to coming home—something comforting and nostalgic: a mother's cooking, a family pet sleeping at the foot of the bed, an old hammock strung between trees in the yard—for me, it's this. It's Tyler. Knowing that there's someone who has seen all the different versions of me; watched as they stacked themselves away inside one another; knows all the choices I've made, the lies I've told, the things I've lost, and still.

"Are you going to make me say please?" I asked.

I felt his breath on the space between my shoulder and my neck, his lips moving as he spoke. "No," he said, "never," and he pulled my head down to his.

Because the thing about Tyler is he always gives me exactly what I'm asking for.

# The Day Before

# DAY 3

Annaleise was unofficially declared missing when the police station opened that morning, but the storms rolling through the mountains meant there would be no searching today. She was twenty-three years old and had been missing only a day, but it was the circumstances that got the police curious: Her brother said he saw her walk into the woods sometime after midnight. Her mother went to get her for their trip to visit a grad school around lunch, but she wasn't there. Her cell went straight to voicemail. Her purse was gone.

And then there was the text message. The one she sent to Officer Mark Stewart, the one that asked if they could set up a time to discuss the Corinne Prescott case.

Tyler showed up at my place just after breakfast, dressed in khakis and a button-down. He was pacing the downstairs, leaving rainy footprints across the floor. "That message is going to make everyone uneasy around here."

"Do the police have any idea why she sent it?"

"Not that I heard. Doesn't matter, though. It's one hell of a coincidence, don't you think?" He opened his mouth to say more, but we heard tires crunching gravel under the rain.

"Someone's here," I said, walking to the window.

A red SUV I didn't recognize had pulled into my driveway and parked behind Tyler's truck. A woman about my dad's age stepped out—hair gray like his, face round and soft—and pulled an umbrella over her head, keeping her eyes on the woods as she walked up the front porch steps. She was built thicker than Annaleise, but her eyes were as large and unsettling.

"Annaleise's mom," I said, heading for the door. I pressed my back to the door, watched him stare at the wall past me as if he could see through it. "Why are you here, Tyler? *Why are you here?*"

He blinked twice before responding. "I'm fixing the air-conditioning," he said.

"Then go fix it," I hissed before pulling open the front door.

Her mother was facing the driveway, her umbrella still up even though she was under the protection of the porch; the rain dripped off the spokes in slow motion. "Hi, Mrs. Carter." I pushed open the screen door and stood on the threshold.

She turned her face slowly toward me, her eyes lingering a moment behind. She was looking at my driveway, at Tyler's truck. "Good morning, Nic. It's nice to see you home." Manners first, always.

"You, too. I heard about Annaleise. Any word?"

She shook her head, let the umbrella rest against her side. "My son says he saw her walking in the woods. She's like that, you know. Keeps her own company, goes for walks. I've seen her out there; it's not too unusual, really. But she and I had plans yesterday . . . and her phone . . . Well." She pressed her lips together. "It would've been late, after midnight. Since we share property, I wanted to check. Any chance you saw her? Or anyone? Anything?"

"No, I'm sorry. I was cleaning the house, and I fell asleep early. I didn't notice anything."

She nodded. "Is that Tyler Ellison's truck, dear?"

"Oh, yes. My brother hired him to do some work on the house for us."

"I don't have his number, and I need to talk to him. Do you mind?" She moved forward, forcing me to back up, and stepped inside my house, placing the open umbrella on the ground.

"Sure, I'll just go find him. Sorry about the heat. It's the air-conditioning unit. Busted. That's why he's here. Tyler?" I called from the hallway. "Tyler, someone's here to see you!"

He came down the steps, and before we could see his face, before he could see us, he said, "I think it's the condenser fan. If you buy a replacement part, I can— Oh, hi," he said, his steps slowing.

"I've been trying to reach you," said Mrs. Carter.

"I'm sorry, I've been working. We've got a project with a crazy deadline. I've actually got a meeting at ten down at the county clerk's office. I should probably be heading that way."

"Of course. I was just wondering if you've heard from Anna-leise?"

"I haven't."

She took another step into the house. "When did you last see her? What did she say?"

Tyler paused, removed his hat, ran his hand through his hair, pulled the hat back down. "We went to a movie after dinner Monday night. I dropped her off a little before ten. Had an early morning myself the next day."

"Did she mention anything else? What she was planning?"

"No, I haven't seen her since."

"Did she mention going to look at grad schools?"

"No," he said.

"Do you know whât she was doing in the woods?"

"No. I'm sorry."

Her questions came fast, but Tyler's answers came faster. "I'm so sorry," I said, opening the screen door for her. "Please let us know if you hear anything."

"Okay," she said, dragging her eyes from Tyler. "If she doesn't turn up by tomorrow, they're going to organize a search—" Her voice broke.

"I'll be there," Tyler said. "But I'm sure she's okay."

She picked up her umbrella, her eyes shifting between me and Tyler as she backed out of the house.

———

CORINNE'S MOTHER HAD COME to see me a week after she went missing, after we'd scoured the woods, the river, the caverns. "Just tell me, Nic. Tell me the things you think I don't want to know. Tell me so we can find her."

I remembered the feeling of wanting to tell her something, to give her something. I remembered thinking she was so young, too young to lose a full-grown daughter.

But I shook my head because I didn't know. This was before Hannah Pardot broke Corinne open, and all I had to tell her mother was *She had a meanness. A darkness. She loved me and hated me, and I felt the same.* I couldn't say that to the broken woman on my front porch, not with my father in the kitchen, not with Daniel upstairs in his room, probably listening out the window.

"Tell me this," she'd said. "Do you think she's okay?"

A week was too long to keep up the charade, even for Corinne. "No," I'd said. Because that, too, was something I could give her.

A year later, when the investigation was fading to a memory for everyone else, Mrs. Prescott got divorced. She took those kids, and she left Cooley Ridge. I don't know where they went. Somewhere there aren't any woods to cut through or caverns to crawl inside. Or a river to cross and logs to slip from. Where a man does not push her down stairs or throw plates near her head. Where her other children will not hold dominion over a town and where, I hope, they will never be abandoned.

———

TYLER STOOD BESIDE ME on the porch as Annaleise's mother drove away. "I have to go," he said. "I have to be in a meeting about a land survey. But I'll come back later."

"Okay, so go."

He stood too close, like he was going to kiss my forehead, and had to change movement at the last minute. He put an arm around my shoulder and pressed down, like Daniel might do. "Don't look at me like that. I can't bring you with me to work."

"I didn't ask you to."

"No, you just looked at me *like that.*"

I pushed him in the arm. "Go."

He changed his mind, pulled me to his chest anyway, and said, "Everything's okay." I wanted to stay like that indefinitely. Everything was not even close to okay, but that was the thing about Tyler—he made me think that it might be.

I clung to him much longer than what might be considered appropriate for a girl with a fiancé and a guy with a missing girl-friend.

"I'll be back tonight," he said, pulling away.

"Maybe you shouldn't," I said.

"Why not? Her mother just showed up and saw my truck here. There are going to be rumors anyway," he said.

"Your missing girlfriend really isn't something to joke about."

"She's not missing. She's just not here. And I think it's safe to say, whenever she shows up, that we're over."

"Oh my God, stop joking."

He sighed. "I don't know what else to do, Nic."

I nodded at him, squeezed his hand. And then I watched him go.

As soon as his truck was out of sight, I went back inside and pulled open the kitchen drawers, dumping the contents on the floor, trying to piece together my father's life over the last ten years.

———

THE RAIN WAS SUPPOSED to break the heat, but it didn't. It was a hot rain, as if it had manifested out of the humidity, the air unable to hold it any longer. The only thing it did was keep us all from searching the woods.

I drove to the library after lunch, sat at one of the computers in the corner, and pulled up the Yellow Pages site, looking for pawn-shop listings. I scribbled down the number and address for any within an hour's drive, then stepped into the back courtyard of the library, which was essentially the backyard of a home encircled by a high brick wall, plants along the sides and benches in the middle. It was abandoned in the rain. I stayed pressed against the wall, under the lip of the roof overhang, the water streaming down six inches in front of my face, and dialed the first number on the list.

"First Rate Pawnshop," a man answered.

"I'm looking for something," I explained, keeping my voice low. "It would've come in sometime yesterday, probably. Or maybe today."

"I'm going to need a little more information than that," the man responded.

"It's a ring," I said. "Two-carat diamond. Brilliant setting."

"We've got some engagement rings," he said, "but nothing that's come in recently. Have you filed a police report?"

"No, not yet."

"Because if you don't, if this was stolen from you and it turns up in a shop somewhere, we're not just gonna hand it over to you. That's the first step, honey."

"Okay, thanks," I said.

"Do you want to leave a number in the meantime, in case it shows?"

I paused. "No," I said. "Thanks for your help."

*Shit.* I shoved the list deep in my purse to keep it from getting wet and headed through the library back to my car. I would have to see for myself. Navigating the roads in the rain, browsing the crappy stores on the corners. *Just looking,* I'd say. *Just passing through. The sign just caught my eye, is all.*

———

FIVE HOURS LATER AND I needed dinner. I hadn't found the ring, and I was irritable, and I knew it was partly because I was hungry, but also because of the ring, and also because Daniel's car was in the driveway and I wanted quiet. I needed time to think, to work this all through. I needed to understand.

I ran through the rain, holding my purse over my head. "Daniel?" I called from just inside the front door. The only noise was from the rain on the roof, the wind against the windows, the distant rumble of thunder. "Daniel!" I called from the bottom of the stairs. Getting no reply again, I took the steps two at a time to the second-floor landing and paced the hall, calling his name.

The rooms were empty.

I went back downstairs for my phone, called his cell, and heard the familiar ringing from somewhere in the house. I pulled the phone from my ear and followed the noise into the kitchen, saw his phone on the edge of the table, beside his wallet and car keys. "Daniel!" I called louder.

I threw open the back door, eyes drilling into the woods. Surely he wouldn't be out there in this storm. I switched on the back porch light and stood in the rain calling his name. Down the steps, around the side of the house, and no sign of Daniel. I ran to his car, peering in the window, now completely drenched. I saw a few tools in the backseat but nothing too out of the norm. Then I heard a sharp thud, like a hammer, just under the thunder—from the garage. A faint light seemed to be coming from the side window. I shielded my eyes from the rain, walking closer.

The sliding doors to the garage were shut, and Daniel had hung something over the windows. I pounded on the side walk-through door. "Daniel!" I yelled. "Are you in there?"

The noise stopped.

"Go in the house, Nic," he called through the door.

I pounded more. "Open the fucking door!"

He unlocked the handle, pulled it open. His hands were covered in white chalk, and the floor was fractured and splintered—chunks of concrete off to the side, the earth below it exposed.

"What the hell is this?" I asked, pushing past him into the room. "What the fuck are you doing?"

He closed the door behind me. "What does it *look* like I'm doing? I'm digging." He ran his hand over his face, the white chalk streaking down with his sweat. "I'm *looking*."

"You're looking . . . for what?" I asked.

"What do you think, Nic?"

*For something buried. Something that's been buried for ten years.*

"And you think it's *here*? You *know* this?" I stuck my finger in his chest, but he backed away. "Why do you know that, Daniel? Daniel, look at me!"

"I don't know, Nic. Not for sure."

"Really? Because you're tearing up the goddamn floor. You seem awfully sure of yourself."

"No, but I already dug up the fucking crawl space and the garden, and this is the only place left I can think of. We were getting ready to lay the floor the day Corinne went missing. But it wasn't done."

"You didn't finish it?"

"No, I didn't finish it. I assumed it was Tyler and his father, but don't know for sure who finished it. And isn't that a little troubling?"

His face was all shadows. I was shaking from the rain, and I wanted to be anywhere but here.

"Now, get out of here," he said. "Go check on Laura. Tell her I'm working on the house. Tell her not to worry."

I ran through the rain, back into the house, pacing the downstairs. I dialed Tyler, and he answered on the first ring. "Hey," he said, "I'm just finishing up here. I'll be over in a bit, okay?"

"Daniel lost his shit. He's digging up the garage."

A pause, and his voice dropped lower. "He's doing what?"

"He's digging up the garage, because he doesn't know who finished the floor ten years ago." I gripped the phone tighter, waiting for him to provide a safe explanation, an answer that made sense.

Silence.

"Was it you, Tyler? Did you lay the concrete? With your dad?"

"God, that was ten years ago. I don't really remember."

"Well, think," I said. "Was it you?"

I heard him breathing on the other end before he answered. "I really don't think so, Nic."

"He's got a sledgehammer and a shovel, and he's *digging* all over the property. He's lost his mind."

"Hold on," he said. "I'm coming."

———

I WAITED THE FORTY-FIVE minutes for Tyler to show up so we could handle Daniel together. I couldn't go back in there and have a real conversation with him alone—I had no idea how to talk to him about anything. He was paranoid. He was crazed. He had a sledgehammer, and I didn't know if I believed him about why he was digging up the floor.

I stood on the porch when I heard Tyler's truck. He pulled something out of the back of the truck and headed straight for the garage. I took off after him. "What the hell is that?" I asked.

He was already at the door, knocking. Daniel flinched when he opened it, scowling at me over Tyler's shoulder. "You called Tyler? What the hell, Nic?"

Then he saw what was in Tyler's hand, just as I had. A goddamn jackhammer.

"Let him finish, Nic. He already started," Tyler said, walking into the room, his eyes slowly taking it all in, then drifting closed. "Okay. Let's do this."

I threw my hands in the air. "You're both completely out of your minds."

"We have to know," Daniel said.

"No, we don't!" I said. I had my head in my hands, searching for understanding, for answers. "Why is this happening? How did this happen?"

Daniel slammed the spade into the concrete. "You're not asking the right questions. You want to know *why* and *how,* and you're getting strangled by it! Listen to what Dad's saying. *Don't sell the house.* What do you think he means? He means this. The garage floors. It wasn't me. I came in one day after, and they were just *done.*"

"That doesn't mean it was him. It doesn't mean he did it," I said, storming out of the garage.

I slammed the door on them, the thunder directly overhead, muffling the sound of the jackhammer. Daniel had emptied the garage, and all the material sat behind it, out in the rain. The gardening supplies, the tools, the wheelbarrow.

I grabbed the wheelbarrow and pushed it back to the door, silently cursing them, and myself, and my dad, and Corinne for disappearing in the first place. Tyler and Daniel paused to stare at me when I threw open the door again. I started picking up chunks of concrete, hauling them into the wheelbarrow. "Well? What should I do with this?" I had my hands on my hips, trying to focus on the task. Just the task.

Tyler met my eyes. "Back of my truck," he said.

I wheeled it out into the rain, lifted the tarp, and hauled the pieces underneath, my hands turning chalky, like Daniel's. When I turned back for the garage, Tyler was standing a few feet away, watching me. "You should go to Dan's place," he said. The rain fell from his hair, soaked his clothes, came down in a torrent between us.

"Did he send you out here to tell me that?"

He stepped closer, and I couldn't read the expression on his face in the dark, in the rain. "Yeah, he did." Another step. "Look, it might be nothing."

"If you believed that, you wouldn't be here."

He came closer, put a hand on the truck behind me. Dropped his head, letting out a breath I could feel on my forehead, resting his own against mine for a second. "I'm here because you called me. It's as simple as that." And then his lips were sliding over mine in the rain, my back against his truck, and my fingers were in his hair, pulling him impossibly, desperately closer, until the jackhammer started up once more. "I'm sorry," he said, pushing himself away. "I wish we could go back."

My hands were shaking. Everything about me was shaking, and the rain was coming down harder.

"You really should go," he said, striding back to the garage with his head tucked down.

I should've listened. I wanted to. I wanted nothing more.

But it wasn't fair to them or Corinne. I had to bear witness. I had to pay my debts.

———

THE NEXT FEW HOURS consisted of Daniel and Tyler dislodging fragments of the floor and me moving the pieces in a wheelbarrow to Tyler's truck, all of us covered with white powder.

None of us spoke. None of us came close to touching each other again.

The floor was in pieces, and Tyler stood back, hands on his hips, breathing heavily with exertion. The earth was exposed and waiting. Tyler got a shovel from his truck, Daniel used the one in the corner, and I used the garden spade from out back, softening the earth until it crumbled, coming up in chunks.

The only sounds were our breathing, shovels hitting earth, dirt hitting dirt, and rain and thunder.

And from deep in my memory, Corinne's words in my ear, the scent of spearmint, her cold fingers, and my skin rising in goose bumps as I dug in once more, hitting something that was not earth, not rock.

My fingers reached in, touched plastic, and I jerked back. Used my shaking hands to brush aside some dirt. It was a blue tarp, like the one Tyler had in the back of his truck at this very moment.

Of course it was me.

It was me with the tiny shovel and the corner of the garage.

It was me, and it was fitting—that I should be the one to find her.

I stood too quickly, my vision swirling as I pressed myself against the wall. Tyler and Daniel had stopped, moved to see what I had uncovered. Stood around the spot I'd left. Daniel used the side of the shovel to brush more dirt off the tarp, to nudge it a bit to the side, exposing a corner of quilt.

Daniel sucked in a quick breath. "Oh, fuck."

Blue material and yellow stitching.

My mother's blanket that she wore around her legs in her wheelchair. Long, dull hair, matted and spilling out the top.

Like whoever had put her here, in the earth, couldn't bear the thought of her being cold.

———

MY MOTHER DIDN'T DIE in this house. She intended to, but I guess at one point she also intended to live. Intention is nice, but it's a thing sometimes based more on hope than on reality.

It had been winter, and with winter comes the common cold, and we all had it. My father came down with it first, which wasn't something I'd typically remember; Daniel and I had the chicken pox together, and I remembered my mother dunking us into oatmeal baths, dousing us with calamine, but I couldn't remember which of us got it first. This cold, I remember: Dad's dry cough echoing at night, and the hospital mask we attached over our mom's ears, and him sleeping on the couch. And then Daniel coming down with it, and then me, and then her.

The cold quickly running its course through all of us but becoming pneumonia for her. Packing her up to the hospital, the onslaught of fluid in her lungs and ineffectual IV treatments, and her sudden death.

She was terminal—had been terminal—and yet her death was unexpected. Caught us all unprepared. I guess I imagined last words of wisdom from my mother, something meaningful to hold on to, something worthy of a story to tell my children. Something with weight that would belong to me alone.

I felt robbed.

It was my dad's fault. Even he knew it. I suppose if I'm being honest with myself, I know that it was a virus's fault and cancer's before that. And she could've caught it from any of us. But if my dad traced back the threads—which of course he had, as he was the type of person to follow every thread no matter what rabbit hole it led him down—it would end with him.

Maybe he knew where it came from, that virus. A student at school, a colleague from the workroom. The man behind the counter of the coffee shop, or the woman who asked for directions. Maybe he had his own point of blame. Maybe he saw this person with his girlfriend, or laughing next to his car, or staring out the window absently, and thought: *You killed my wife.* And they never knew. How many people out there are responsible for some tragedy and don't even know it?

————

THIS WAS WHAT I was thinking about when I saw the quilt. This was what I did to protect myself for just one more moment. Focusing on my anger, on my mother, on who was to blame—the fault, and the suddenness, and maybe even its bitter insignificance—and not on what lay underneath the blanket.

A rustle of plastic as Daniel moved the tarp again, and then it hit me with its own suddenness. *Corinne.*

I lunged outside the garage, knees in the grass and sickness in the earth. I wiped my mouth with the back of my hand.

Daniel was standing over me, a hand on my shoulder. I shrugged him off. He dragged the hose from the side of the house, even though it was already raining, to clean up the mess. And for once, just once, I wished we would discuss what was actually happening. At least mention it. Acknowledge it. *What should we do? What?* My mouth formed the *W,* but no sound would come forth.

Daniel was already making a list: *Clean up the mess.* "We'll burn it down," he said.

"And what," Tyler said from inside, "get the cops here so they can find a body? Get an investigation started?"

Inside the door, in the dim light, I could just make out Tyler's profile—still staring down at the blanket, which would implicate someone in this house. And the plastic tarp, and the concrete floor, which might implicate him.

He cursed, kicking the tools on the floor. Stormed past us and tore the tarp from the top of the truck bed. He threw it over the exposed plastic, used the shovel to tuck it under at the edges. I stayed outside while Daniel helped Tyler roll the tarp up.

Daniel peeled back the corner to check and ended up in the grass beside me.

"Is it Corinne?" I asked.

He didn't answer at first, just dragged his arm across his mouth, spitting out anything left, which was answer enough. A body with long hair buried under our garage. Of course it was her. "It's her clothes," he said, and then he gagged again, retching over the grass.

"Nic," Tyler said, "watch the woods."

I watched the woods. Tried not to notice the rolled-up tarp, and the blanket underneath, and Corinne underneath that, being carried from the garage to the back of Tyler's truck. Tried not to picture the girl she had been or the times I had stood in that very spot, the truth just inches below the surface.

Daniel put a hand on Tyler's shoulder. Took the keys from his grip. "Not your responsibility," he said.

Tyler rubbed a hand down his face. "We've got work sites."

"This won't come back to you," Daniel said. "Thank you."

"Daniel," I said.

"I know plenty of places, Nic. This is my region. It's full of abandoned sites."

We were doing this. Really doing this. Moving a dead body with no idea how it truly got there. I thought of police and lawyers and all the ways her body being under this house might get twisted around. And then I thought of Everett trying to get the phone records thrown out in the Parlito case. "Leave your phone," I said. "It's a GPS."

"It's in the kitchen," Daniel said. And then, tilting his head toward the mess, "Will you take care of this?" He looked at Tyler, since I am unreliable, apparently. Tyler nodded.

He drove away, and I began to cry, hoping the rain would cover for me.

"I need your car," Tyler said, pretending not to notice. He kept his gaze focused on the garage as he spoke to me.

"For what?"

"Gravel. Concrete. We need to pour a new floor."

"Shouldn't we wait until morning?"

"I don't think that's a good idea. We need to clear the area. Level it. Can you do that?"

This was a task. I could do the task. "Okay," I said. "Yes."

Stop crying.

Focus on the pieces of concrete. Focus on the dust. On the pressure washer. On the thunder.

Focus on the tiny insignificant details.

Leave out what's happening

*Pull yourself together, Nic.*

*Pick yourself up and move.*

*Tick-tock.*

*The Day Before*

# DAY 2

**I**t *was just after* midnight. *A new day,* I thought. The long drive home behind me. Me and Cooley Ridge, slowly adjusting to each other once more. I'd get some sleep before sunrise and see it again with fresh eyes, and I'd do what I had to do to get Dad to talk, to remember what he'd seen. I'd come at it from a different angle. Work my way back to it. Find out what had been hiding, buried, for the last ten years. The ghost of Corinne, spinning and blurring in my mind.

*I need to talk to you. That girl. I saw that girl.*

I turned off the hall light, and the house was completely dark. I put my hand against the wall, feeling the familiar chips in the paint at the corners. Five steps from here to the stairs. I knew the way by heart.

*Shit, the ring.* I forgot the ring again. I'd left it in the middle of the kitchen table so it wouldn't get lost amid the cleaning supplies.

Two steps back to the light switch, and the give of the floorboards at the kitchen entrance, and the faint flickering of something out in the night. I kept the light off, took a step closer to the window.

There was a shadow moving up on the hill. I could see it because there was a light in front of it. A narrow beam cutting through the trees. I pressed my face closer to the window. It was descending the hill, and for the briefest moment my heart soared and I thought, *Tyler, like always.*

But the shadow was too small. Too narrow. In my backyard, her blond hair caught the moonlight, and she flicked off the flashlight with her delicate fingers.

It occurred to me, as she stared at the darkened windows, that she couldn't see me watching her.

She had an off-white packet of some sort under her arm, and I watched her bend down, disappearing from view. Then the gentle sound of paper wedging itself under the back door. It wouldn't come completely inside, even as she tried to jimmy it a few times. She stood, and the door handle slowly began to turn. *What the—*

My hand went to the knob on instinct, pulling the door open before her. Then I hit the light switch, bathing us both in light. She jumped, gripping the envelope to her chest, her eyes wide and innocent. She blinked slowly, her face stoic.

"Hi," I said, stepping back so she could enter. "Annaleise." *What can I do for you?* or *What's up?* seemed inappropriate now that I realized how late it was and that she'd been about to open my back door without knocking.

She stepped inside tentatively, her fingers pressing into the envelope, her knuckles blanching white.

"Is that for me?" I asked. I saw my name in boxy print, done in a ballpoint pen. Just *Nic.* Nothing more. "Is this a 'Back off my boyfriend' letter? Look, I could've saved you the trip. Tyler and I are done. He's all yours."

She cleared her throat, relaxed her grip on the envelope. "No, it's not," she said, sliding her phone from her back pocket and resting it on the kitchen table. She sat at my table, crossing her legs, her hands fidgeting in her lap. "That's not what this is at all." Her large eyes met mine, and her smile stretched wide, and I was taken aback—how different this Annaleise was from the thirteen-year-old girl I remembered. She pulled apart the envelope seal and flipped it over, dumping the contents on my kitchen table.

I saw the typed piece of paper first, *the cost of silence* and *the price for the flash drive* and *leave at the abandoned Piper house,* and my mind was scrambling to keep up with the dark, shadowy images strewn across the kitchen table.

"I don't understand," I said, my hands touching the glossy surface of the rest of the sheets. Pictures. Shades of black and gray, grainy and pixelated. Everything dark. So dark. I leaned closer, could make out almost nothing but the way the light shone out of a window and the shape of the tree branches. But I knew it was my house.

"I don't— What is this?" I asked.

"Our agreement," she said, her voice firm and measured.

I leaned closer, focusing on the backlight, the way it reflected off something—something lower, on the porch. A lump—a carpet? A blanket? There was a shadow hovering near the side of the frame. And at the edge of the blanket, something bronze and willowy. Hair. *Hair.* Bronze hair spilling out of a dark blanket. I threw the picture back on the table, jerked my hand back. "What—"

"Wrong question. *Who.* Looks to me like the body of Corinne Prescott. There's no statute of limitation on murder, you know," she said as my face gave way to a horrified understanding. Here, finally, the answer we'd sought for so long. Here was the body of Corinne Prescott—at my house.

"And you think I—"

She waved me off with a brush of her hand. "I don't think anything. Actually, you're going to pay me not to think."

I picked up a picture with my pointer finger and thumb, strained to see the shadow off to the side. I could make out an arm . . . a dark shadow . . . nothing more. For a moment I thought, *Daniel.* Because there was a girl's long hair and our back porch and it was dark. But it could've also been Dad—no, it could've been *anyone.* Maybe I just didn't want it to be them.

"That part would be for the police to decide," she said, tapping the shadow in another picture.

"Where did you get these?" The room had hollowed out, and my voice sounded tinny and far away.

"I've always had them, just didn't know it," she said. I had to struggle to focus on her words, which were slipping through the room like smoke. "I got this new camera the week before Corinne went missing. I was messing around with the settings, trying to figure out how to take pictures at night. Your house always seemed like this haunted place to me through the trees." She shrugged. "Maybe because your mom died, but then the flowers went, too. I used to think it was contagious somehow." Like death was leeching from the center, spreading out. "So I took these pictures that night after the fair, but I couldn't see anything. Then my senior year, I got this new software, and a new computer, and I transferred everything—about to purge these old things. But I was tinkering with the setting and the software, and look what appeared."

As with a Polaroid picture, shadows coming to life.

"You look sick. You really didn't know?" she asked. "You never suspected?"

I *was* going to be sick. There wasn't enough air in the room. Annaleise had seen these pictures at eighteen, a dangerous age. Boys and their uncontrollable passion, impulsive and coiled to snap. Girls, with the uncontrollable yearning for something intangible. Something else.

"No," I said, trying to get a grip. And then to Annaleise, "Get the fuck out of here."

She tilted her head to the side. "You think I won't tell?" She picked up her phone, a mean smile on her face, her fingers flying across the keypad—

"Wait. Stop. What are you doing?"

She turned the phone around so I could see. "I went to school with Bailey Stewart's brother. Officer Mark Stewart?"

The edges of my vision turned hazy. I struggled to focus on the screen. *I have a few questions about the Corinne Prescott case. Can we set up a time to talk?*

"You have until he wakes up and sees this tomorrow morning to change your mind."

My throat burned. I stared at the images once more. This was happening. This was really fucking happening. The room was buzzing, the air electric. "How do I know you won't send these out anyway?"

"Because," she said, "I haven't yet."

"Yet?"

"I left these for your father years ago with this same note," she said. She leaned forward in her chair. "And he paid. He *pays*. Why do you think he does that, Nic?"

My father had paid for her silence. Why does anyone pay? You have to pay your debts.

I picked up the note again; it trembled in my hand. "I can't pay you this much." Ten thousand to keep quiet. Twenty thousand for the flash drive.

"Tyler said you're getting married. Said your ring was worth more than this house. Said you're a counselor at some fancy private school and you're off for the summer."

"I don't have any money, Annaleise. I have nothing to my name. Bet I'm worth less than you, even."

She rolled her eyes and stood, but I still had to look down at her. "You're here to sell the house, isn't that right?"

I nodded.

"I'll give you some time, then." She slid her phone into her back pocket.

"You're fucking crazy," I said. "Does Tyler know you're this fucked up?"

She held her hands up, like I'd done from the window as she peered at me. "I just need a way out, Nic."

"Get a job," I said, then remembered the money my brother had given me to help me get out. I had someone. I had help.

"Yeah, I'm working on it." She stood at the door. "Two weeks, Nic. I'll give you two weeks."

"I can't—"

"Really," she said. She grabbed the ring from the center of the table. "I bet this is worth that amount alone, isn't it?" I couldn't answer. I didn't know. She slid it onto her pointer finger. "I'll keep it safe until you pay."

"You're making a mistake. You can't take that," I said.

She opened the door. "Call the police. I dare you. I'll hold this as insurance."

She really was daring me. *What will you do, Nic? The past or the future? Run away again, or stay and pay your debts?*

I couldn't figure out why Annaleise was doing this to me. Why she thought she *could*. She was a quiet girl, a timid girl, a lonely girl.

That's what I could see of her from the fragments of my memory.

And what must she have seen of me?

Me on the other side of the door, after my mother died, as she delivered food and I stood there, silent and broken. Me at the fair as Daniel hit me, as I remained on the ground, weak and shaken.

Sad and quiet and pushed around.

She saw me as the broken girl.

She didn't know the other parts of me. She didn't know me at all.

———

AFTER I HAD PARKED Tyler's truck behind the caverns, and after he'd slid that ring on my finger and I'd crawled across his lap—

I saw Corinne. Saw Jackson's car come to a halt at the edge of the cavern parking lot, over Tyler's shoulder, through the trees. *What is it?* he'd said. *Nothing,* I'd said. *Just Jackson and Corinne. Ignore them. They can't see us.*

I saw Corinne throw open the door and yell something at Jackson. Heard Jackson's muffled voice yelling something back, then him pulling away, the tires kicking up dirt. Through the woods, that's the way she'd go to my place. But she disappeared around the curve, walking down the road.

"Should we go after her?" asked Tyler, twisted around in his seat, watching the same scene.

But I was full of her words, telling me to jump, and seeing her with my brother, which seemed like the ultimate betrayal after he'd just hit me. She went to comfort him, not me. She knew, and she leaned against his side. *Ignore her,* I'd said to Tyler, turning his head to face me, and Tyler had been all too happy to oblige.

We left for home not long after. I eased the truck out onto the road, high beams on in the dark, Tyler's ring on my finger. We took the first curve, and there, thumb out, skirt blowing with the breeze, stood Corinne Prescott.

She stood at the edge of the road with nothing. She'd left her bag at my house earlier, a common Corinne maneuver to see who would pay for her. Whether she could talk the vendors into covering the cost, whether she could convince one of us. I'd paid for her Ferris wheel ticket. I'd paid for everything. Because on the tip of

Corinne's tongue was a truth I wasn't ready to share. A trump card. Emotional blackmail. A dare.

Bailey had sneaked in a few miniature vials of whiskey from her dad's collection. She pulled one out at the top of the Ferris wheel, took a gulp, passed it to Corinne, and Corinne handed it to me, her eyebrows raised. I took it from her outstretched hand, held it to my mouth, felt the burn of the liquor on my tongue, on the back of my throat. I was starting to make a decision right at that moment, as I let it slide back into the bottle instead.

She'd grinned at me. "Tyler's here," she said, pointing him out in the crowd.

I leaned over the edge with her. "Tyler!" I called.

She took another swig, then followed it up with a piece of spearmint gum. "Truth or dare, Nic," she said, slowly rocking the cart back and forth as Bailey giggled.

"Dare," I said too fast. There were too many truths, too close to the surface.

"I dare you to climb on the outside of the cart. I dare you to ride it like that. On the outside."

And then later, with her thumb sticking out, her eyes meeting mine through the windshield: *I dare you to drive on by. I dare you to pretend you don't see me here. I dare you.*

Annaleise didn't know—I always took the dare.

———

I STILL KNEW TYLER'S number by heart. He answered his phone, and I could tell from the low hum of noise in the background that he was at the bar. "Hey, Nic, what's up?"

The kitchen light shone off the glossy surface of the pictures, and I squeezed my eyes shut. "Did you know your girlfriend blackmailed my dad?"

"What?" he asked.

"Oh yeah," I said. "Want to know how I know? Because she just came to my house, trying to blackmail me."

"Calm down. Hold on. What?"

"Your girlfriend! Your fucking girlfriend! She has pictures, Tyler." I saw them again on the table, and I sucked in a sob with my breath. "Pictures of a girl. A dead girl. A dead fucking—"

"Oh, God," he said. "I'm coming."

I stared at the pictures for so long, they turned blurry. Trying to talk my way out of what they were. What they meant. Everything was grainy and indecipherable. But it was my porch. And that was a girl, wrapped in a blanket.

That was enough.

———

I WAS WAITING ON the front steps in the dead of night when Tyler's truck pulled in, and I led him straight back to the kitchen. "Look," I said.

He picked up a picture, held it to his face, twisted it back and forth. "I don't understand," he said. "Annaleise gave you these?"

"She's had them for the last five years!"

"Is that—"

"What do you think, Tyler? Of course it is." I choked on a sob. "What the hell is she doing on my porch?"

But wasn't that what Dad had told me when I asked? *She was on the back porch, but just for a moment . . .*

"Whose shadow is that?" I asked. Wondering whether my dad was the one who put her on the porch, or whether he knew about it from the pictures. Because if it wasn't Dad, then it was—

"Nic?" The front door swung open and I dove for the pictures, brushing them back into a pile on the table as Daniel walked in.

"What the hell is going on?" he asked.

Tyler rubbed his face, looked between the two of us. "He was sitting next to me at the bar," he said. "I'm sorry."

"You should go," I said, my back to the table, desperately hiding the pictures.

"Nic. Move away from the table," Daniel said.

But I thought of the shadow, which could've been from one of two people. "Go home to Laura," I said. We were all about to break open. The final crack. It was time to understand.

The line between Daniel's eyes deepened, and his steps took on a slow and dreamy quality, like he wasn't sure he wanted to walk over and see what was on the kitchen table. He reached around me, picked up a photo off the top, narrowed his eyes as he twisted it back and forth in front of his face. "What is this?" he asked. Then, louder, "What is this?," like it was my fault. And then Tyler was pushing Daniel out of my face, and I was pushing Tyler, because I had to do *something*.

"It's pictures of Corinne!" I yelled back, tears stinging my eyes.

Daniel stared at the picture, his hand trembling, and his eyes slowly, slowly, rose to meet my own. We stared at each other over the dark corner of that photo. Even now I had trouble asking. Silently, I mouthed: *You?*

He shook his head just once.

Tyler turned around and looked at Daniel over his shoulder, then at me. "Who is this?" he asked, pointing to the shadow.

"It's Dad," Daniel said.

It had to be, because otherwise, it was him.

"Did you know about this?" I asked.

"No," Daniel said, frowning at the other pictures. "No, I swear."

*The woods have eyes.*

"Where did you get these?" he asked.

Tyler was silent, staring across the lawn, deep into the woods.

"Annaleise Carter," I said.

Daniel's face hardened. "Burn them," he said.

"She has a flash drive," I said. "Dad paid before. And now she wants me to pay. She sent a text to Officer Stewart asking about Corinne, said I had until he saw it to make up my mind. I had to say yes." I felt the tears rising again, and I fought them back down.

Daniel dragged a hand down his face, shaking his head. "Okay," he said slowly. "Okay, tell me. What does she want?"

"Ten to stay quiet. She'll give us the flash drive for twenty."

"*Thousand?*" Daniel barked. "How the hell does she think we can get twenty thousand dollars?"

Tyler looked down at the floor, but not before I stared at him for too long. "Because, Daniel. We're selling the house. Everyone knows."

"We need the money," Daniel said. "We can't afford to pay her off and pay for Dad."

"I know that."

"Do you?" he asked.

Great. We were going to start fighting about something that had nothing to do with the pictures of a dead Corinne Prescott. We were going to fight about how I didn't understand basic finances, how I'd checked out of family affairs for the last ten years, how I'd left all the responsibility to him, like always.

"These are just pictures," Tyler said. "And really hard-to-see pictures. They don't prove anything."

"Except they're enough to investigate," I said.

"Okay, okay," Daniel said, pacing the room. "Well, we have some time. Even after we get an offer on the house, it can take months to close. Buy us some wiggle room. I'll talk to her. We'll talk to Dad. We'll figure something out."

I started laughing, my chest heaving, my eyes tearing over. I held up my left hand. "She gave me two weeks. And she took my ring."

"What?" Tyler yelled.

"Yep. As insurance, she said. Thinks maybe I'll get her the money faster. Thinks I won't report it missing."

"How much is it worth?" Tyler asked.

"You're not serious. I can't just tell her to sell it and keep the money. It's appraised and insured, and trust me, Everett's not just going to *let it go*."

"Everett," Tyler mumbled.

"Really, Tyler," I said, "she thinks I have money because of you."

"This is ridiculous. It isn't like her," Tyler said.

"Are you sure? What's she like, then?"

We all have two faces. I learned that from Corinne.

"Call her," Daniel said.

"What?" The panic made my voice too high, too tight.

"Call her. Get her over here. This shit ends now," Daniel said.

"Oh, right," I said. " 'Hey, baby, you know how you've been blackmailing the Farrells? Can we talk about that?' "

Tyler stared right at me as he pressed his phone to his ear. "Hey," he said. "Did I wake you?" He lowered his eyes from mine and left the room. "I know it's late. I'm sorry. I've got a favor to ask." More pacing. "I left my truck at the Farrells' place so Dan could cart some stuff to the dump in the morning. I left the keys, but now I'm thinking I might've left my wallet. I can't find it." He leaned his forehead against the window while he listened. "Can you drive it over if it's there? Do you want me to stay on the line? Okay. Thanks."

He hung up. I didn't know what was about to happen, but it was happening now, whether we were ready for it or not. The three of us clumped into the kitchen.

"Turn off the lights," Daniel said.

Tyler came up behind me in the darkness. "I'm sorry," he whispered.

"Let's go," Daniel said.

———

I SAW HER COMING from the corner of the house I was pressed against, her purse slung over her shoulder, in yoga pants with her hair in a ponytail, as if she'd just rolled out of bed. She had a flashlight, and she strode across the backyard, around the side, straight for the driveway. I saw the moment she realized: when she noticed not only Tyler's truck but Daniel's car behind it. She slowed and stopped, and I could sense her debating. She took a tentative step back.

"Wait," I said. I had circled behind her, and Tyler was standing beside the truck. He opened the door, switching on the overhead light so we could see each other better. I could make out her outline but not her face—couldn't tell whether she was surprised or scared, pissed or sad. I couldn't see Daniel at all.

She whipped her head back and forth between me and Tyler. "What the hell?" she said, but she knew. She knew *exactly* what the hell.

"You made a mistake," Tyler said. "The ring. Give it back."

She hitched her purse up on her shoulder, folded her arms across her stomach. "Did she tell you?" she asked. "About the pictures?"

"You made a mistake," he repeated.

"Seriously, Tyler?" She looked over her shoulder. "Where's Dan? Why am I not surprised? Are you out here, too?" she said. And then louder, "You know what I realized? You *all* lied that night, didn't you? All of you. You have to know. You're all covering for someone."

I saw Tyler's head snap up, his whole body wound tight.

"Those pictures don't prove anything. But blackmail is illegal," I said.

"That's what anonymous letters are for," she said. "Anonymous packages with pictures of a dead girl on your back porch."

"Give me the ring, and give me the flash drive, and I'll pretend you didn't suck my father's life away."

"Really, Nic? You'll just . . . let it go? Why's that?"

"Annaleise, cut the shit. Give her the fucking ring, and get the fuck out of our lives," Tyler said.

*Our lives.*

She laughed, mean and sharp. "Tyler, be real. *One* of the Farrells is a murderer."

"You're wrong," he said. "You can't prove anything with grainy pictures that were probably doctored, with no time stamp. You know what you *can* prove? Blackmail. You've been taking money from a confused, mentally impaired man for years. There goes your future, Annaleise."

"You can't prove that, either. But you know what *is* proof? A body. Ever think of that?"

I froze. *She was on the back porch, but just for a moment.* Where did she go? Where did he take her? "You stole my ring. I can prove that."

There was a noise behind her, from the edge of the woods, and she spun just as Daniel emerged from the trees. "We'll work it out. But not like this," he said. Always the reasonable one, always the responsible one.

"Oh, look at you, all self-righteous. You're such a fucking hypocrite."

"Give her the ring back and we'll talk," Daniel said.

Her body was rigid. We were at an impasse. Two crimes, and neither of us could call the police without dragging out the other. "I don't have it on me," she said, hitching up the strap on her designer purse.

Daniel nodded. "Then let's go get it."

"Fine," she said, slowly moving away from us. She walked a few steps ahead of Daniel, with me and Tyler trailing behind, his hand on my lower back, promising me, *Everything's okay, everything's working out, we've got this all under control.* I don't know whether it was that three of us were following her and she was scared, or if she felt her options running out, felt her world and her future growing smaller, but she stepped into the tree line—*the crunch of a branch, the darkness like a cloak*—and she ran.

"Fuck," said Tyler as he took off after her.

"Wait here, Nic," Daniel said, and he took off through the woods at another angle.

I stood on the hill in sight of both our houses—dark, except for the light from Tyler's truck. I sneaked closer to hers so I could see her front door better. And I listened to the woods. For the monsters and the demons and the eyes. For a struggle, or a whisper, or a scream.

I crouched down when I heard footsteps slowly coming toward me. My muscles twitching, ready to snap.

"Nic?"

I relaxed at the sound of Tyler's voice. "Up here," I said. "Did you find her?"

"No. You?"

I shook my head as he crouched beside me, watching her house.

It was another twenty minutes before Daniel came back from the other direction. "I lost her," he said, reaching out one hand as if grasping a ghost. "Got as far as the river, and then I lost her."

"She'll be back," Tyler said.

"Go," I said to Daniel. "Go home to Laura."

Daniel checked his watch and frowned. "Call me when she

comes back." He stuffed his hands deep into his pockets as he walked away.

"You, too," I said to Tyler. "Go home. I'll watch for her."

"Nah," he said, sitting beside me on top of the hill. "I'm not going anywhere."

———

WE STAYED THERE UNTIL sunup, but she didn't come back.

Back in my kitchen, I made a pot of coffee while Tyler paced. "Fuck. *Fuck,*" he said.

I stared out the window, biting my nail. That feeling like static, like something thrumming, pressing down on us, was thick in the air—the feeling that something was about to happen. And we were waiting for it. Sirens, the police, a phone call from her, just *something.* I started a fire, threw the pictures into the flames, watched as they bubbled and curled, willing them to disappear faster. When nothing had happened by the time Daniel stopped by on his way to work, I started to think that maybe it wouldn't.

"Anything?" Daniel asked.

"She's not back," I said. "What did you tell Laura?"

"Nothing," he said. "Never got the chance. When I didn't come home, she left. Probably went to stay at her sister's. God. Now she's giving me the silent treatment."

"Just tell her you stayed here," I said.

"And what was so wrong with you that I had to stay here?" he asked.

I sighed. "I'm sure you'll think of something."

"Goddammit," he said, running his hand through his hair. Then he cursed repeatedly under his breath, gripped the edge of the table, breathing deeply, getting himself under control. "We need to talk to Dad."

"I'll do it," I said.

"You need to be careful," he said, and I understood. I couldn't let it become something Dad fixated on, couldn't let him get lost in it, couldn't let him work himself up about this. I had to graze the surface, come at it from the side, ask him about it in pieces.

"Go to work," I said. "Both of you. Everything's normal. Everything's fine. Only call if you know something."

I watched Annaleise's empty apartment until noon. Watched as her mother knocked on the door and knocked again. Watched as she took a key from her pocket and let herself inside. Until she came back out, standing in the entrance, her phone in her hand, staring at the ground. I watched until the very moment she realized her daughter was gone.

———

MY BODY WAS ON edge the entire car ride to Grand Pines, my muscles twitching with too much energy, even though I hadn't slept since the day before. I couldn't feel my feet; they tingled with heaviness.

I gave my name at the entrance and was escorted by a young male aide to Dad's empty room.

"He wanders," the aide said. "Probably out in the courtyard. It's a beautiful day. Hear we're getting some nasty storms tomorrow, though." He was leaning against the window beside me, and I saw him looking me over in the reflection. His gaze flicked down to my hand. "Hi," he said, sticking out his hand. "Andrew. I work here." His eyes were blue, and he was probably younger than I was, and he had a nice smile that probably had the same effect everywhere.

"Nicolette," I said. "I live in Philadelphia, actually."

"Shame," he said. "You in town for a while?"

"No," I said. I pointed out the window. "There." Dad was reading a book on a bench near the edge of the courtyard, his elbows resting on his brown pants, like he was deep in thought, searching the words for more meaning. "Thanks for your help, Andrew." I forced myself to flash him a smile as I left the room.

Out in the courtyard, a few women sat around a café table with lunch in Styrofoam boxes. Two men were playing chess. A few people were pacing in what appeared to be slow, endless circles around the perimeter. I settled in beside my father on the bench. "Hi, Dad," I said.

He pulled his face out of the book, glancing in my direction.

"What are you reading?" I asked.

"Nabokov," he said, showing me the cover. "For next semester." He wasn't here. But he wasn't far.

I cleared my throat, watching him from the corner of my eye. "Yesterday," I said, "you told me you saw my friend Corinne. A long time ago. On the back porch."

"Did I tell you that? I don't remember that." He ran his thumb over the page edges, fanning them slowly.

"Yes," I said. "I was just wondering . . . I was just wondering if you knew how she got there."

He didn't answer, his head still in the book. But his eyes weren't moving across the lines; they were staring, his mind elsewhere. "I was drinking too much," he said.

"I know you were. It's okay."

"I mean, I went to get you. I got a call. About you. My daughter and some stunt on the Ferris wheel. I said I couldn't come. But I did. I got mad, and I got in the car, and I drove, because it was all escalating, and it had finally come to this." He put the book down and squeezed his eyes. "You were pushing more and more because I never stopped you. I never did. So I got in the car. I was going to be a *dad*."

I started shaking my head because I didn't like where this was going. And it was too much. Too direct. Nowhere to hide for either of us.

"So I got to that bend before the caverns, and I thought: *This isn't how to be a dad. Driving drunk. This isn't how.* So I pulled over. I just . . . pulled over."

"Where, Dad?" It came out as a choked whisper.

"Just before the caverns, there's this access road, a dead end. I pulled in and I parked." He looked over at me. "Don't cry, doll. I wasn't in a good state. I needed some air. I just needed some air."

He needed to stop.

"I had the windows rolled down—I just needed to sleep it off." He folded his hands in his lap, his fingers drumming against his knuckles. "I heard people yelling . . ."

I had to know. It was time. "Dad," I said. "What did you do?"

I felt his body tense, parts of him twitch. "What do you mean?" He looked around, narrowing his eyes. "This place is a rabbit hole," he said.

And Corinne was the rabbit. We followed her down, down, down, and she left us here.

Then, to me: "I don't like it here. You need to go. I want you to go now. Nic, you need to leave."

I stood, the air too heavy, his words like static. My memories, spinning and blurring like our pictures, like our ghosts. I couldn't look him in the eye when I left.

———

TYLER'S TRUCK WAS IN my driveway, but he wasn't in the house. I found him around back, sitting on the edge of the porch, his feet on the grass. "Anything?" I asked.

"No," he said. "Did you see your dad?"

I sat beside him. Pulled my knees up, dipped my head down so I could see only the blades of grass under my shadow. "I don't understand what happened. I don't understand that picture. It doesn't make sense. He said he was driving near the caverns. He said he was *there.* But that's all he said. That's all." Tyler reached out, took my hand. "Did you lie to me?"

"I don't lie to you, Nic," he said.

"But . . . what do you think happened to Corinne?" The hairs on the back of my neck stood on end as I imagined her on this porch, inches away—her hair falling out of a blanket, the shadow hovering near the edge of the frame.

He cut his eyes to me, held tighter to my hand. "Don't you see? I don't care what happened to her."

"Well. It's time to start caring." I took a deep breath. "There are pictures, and she's dead. So tell me. Tell me what happened."

"You didn't do anything wrong. I promise. Let it go."

I nodded, let him wrap an arm over my shoulder. And I let myself believe him.

———

I HAVE TO TELL it this way, in pieces. I have to work my way up to it. Work my way *back* to it. I have to show you the beautiful things before I get to the ugly.

You have to understand that she was messed up.

First, I have to promise you that I loved her.

Corinne stood on the side of the road, her thumb sticking out. I didn't slow down.

"You're not gonna stop?" Tyler said.

"No," I said.

My eyes went to hers; her thumb was down, and she was staring right back. I pressed the gas harder—*Screw you, Corinne*—and I blinked. Just once. Once, and she was already stepping into the road, right in front of the truck.

Tyler's hands went out in front of him just as I slammed on the brakes—I cut the wheel hard and squeezed my eyes shut as the tires screamed for traction. The seat belt felt like it was cutting me in half, and I couldn't breathe as we spun, the window cracking, then the thud of metal as we came to rest.

I struggled for my bearings as the adrenaline sharpened everything into focus at once, and then there was too much to process. We were facing the wrong way, pressed up against a guardrail, hovering too close to the edge. A branch jutted through the window in front of me, the edge slicing my shoulder, where it would leave a scar. Tyler's voice, not making any sense, not coming all the way in. I couldn't move. I couldn't feel.

Until I could—everything all at once.

I felt a wave of nausea and a pain that began in my stomach and worked its way up my back. My hands were desperate and ineffective at the seat belt button. Tyler had to do it for me. We were too close to the edge, near a drop-off, so Tyler pulled me out his side.

There was a ringing in my ears, and the earth kept spinning on me, or I was spinning, looking for Corinne. I put my hand on the hood of the truck and realized it was running, hot to the touch. Everything tingled.

"Where is she?" I whispered.

Tyler had his hands on the hood of the truck, too, his arms shaking like he was about to fly apart.

"Corinne!" I screamed. "Answer me! What the fuck is wrong with you!"

In a panic, Tyler checked under the truck, and my stomach ended up in my throat. The road was dark and empty, the woods even darker, our headlights pointing back toward the caverns.

"Corinne!" I yelled again, bent over as I screamed her name.

Tyler peered over the edge of the drop-off, jogged down the road a bit before coming back. "I don't see her," he said.

"Did I hit her? *Did I hit her?* No, no, no," I said, frantically making my way down the rocks. I tripped, my knees catching the sharp edges, my palms gripping the cold stone. The drop-off was dark and steep, and I couldn't make out any shapes in the shadows.

"Stop, Nic. Stop." Tyler was following me down the rocks. I couldn't see her.

"Why would she do that? She jumped in front of me!"

"I know, I saw." He grabbed my arms to keep me from going any farther. "Your shoulder," he said, pressing his hand to it. But the pain was in my abdomen, radiating across my back.

My hands were shaking. "She stepped in front of me. They'll believe me, right?"

His grip on my arms loosened for a moment as something twisted in his face.

"Call 911," I said, because I couldn't find her and she wasn't answering.

He took his phone out with his uninjured hand and looked deep into my eyes as I felt another wave of pain roll through me. "I was driving," he said.

"What? No. *I* was driving. Look at your hand. You shouldn't be driving!"

"You were drinking. You can't."

"I didn't swallow any, I swear."

"You reek of it. No, it was me."

"How can you even be talking about this right now? *I was driving.*" I was yelling now. "Not you. I won't let you say it. People saw me driving when we left. Remember?"

He shook his head again. Slid his phone back in his pocket. I heard movement in the trees, and I whipped my head in that direction.

"Corinne?" I called. No response. No movement.

Tyler narrowed his eyes at the trees. "Just the wind," he said.

"Where is she, Tyler?"

326

He looked into my eyes, but the world was still spinning. "You didn't hit her," he said. "This is all one of her fucked-up games."

"Where is she, then?"

"Hiding. Fucking with us. Laughing right this second. Because she's fucked up."

I closed my eyes, picturing it. I could see it so easily. It was so her. *Of course* she would do that. Of course she would try to ruin every good thing in my life.

"I can fix the truck," he said almost silently.

I sucked in a breath from another wave of pain, and I nodded.

And in that moment, we made a decision, a pact. We nudged a domino, and it set something off.

"Stay here," he said. He handed me the key to the caverns. "Go wait for me there. I'll get my dad's car. I'll come back for you."

"I can make it from here," I said. "I know the way."

But I wasn't going to make it home in time. As another wave of pain rolled through me, I knew I was losing everything tonight.

He looked over his shoulder, his body on edge. "Are you sure?" he asked.

"Yes," I said.

I waited until I heard him in the truck, and then I ran. I headed for the caverns, because it was the way I knew how to get home. But I pictured her calling *Come find us,* and racing into the depths, like she always did, like we used to do together. I unlocked the chain— would she lock it? If she was fucking with me—*Yes,* I thought, *yes, she'd do this.* Then I slipped inside, called her name as I gripped the rope. I yelled her name into the dark again and again. "Joke's over, Corinne!" I left the rope, used my phone to illuminate the space in front of me, searching for her in the darkness, so sure I could hear her breathing but seeing nothing. No one.

One more wave of pain, and the fear gave way to anger. She was ruining me without even flinching.

I gripped the rope as I pulled myself back out.

It wasn't until much later that night, when I was all alone, that I realized I had lost Tyler's ring.

———

SHE HAD TO HAVE jumped out of the way. She had to have hidden. She had to have been killed in some other way—another car, another accident, throwing herself from the ledge to the rocks below. It cannot be that my dad heard us and knew it had been me. It cannot be that he found her after we left. Not that he took the body and moved it so I wouldn't be found out, so my life wouldn't be ruined.

Tyler promised I had done nothing wrong. And so it must be something else.

Otherwise, it's too brutal in its simplicity.

Ten years later, and the past is still here. A picture shifting into focus. A memory gaining clarity. Something whispering to me in the dark: *Look, Nic, do you see?*

It was time to open my eyes.

*The Day Before*

# DAY 1—
## *Night*

I **was tired from the** long drive and the visit with Dad, and dirty from an afternoon of housecleaning, but there was still so much to do. *Be the responsible one,* I thought. But I already was—I just wished Daniel could see that. I'd made promises, and trades, and decisions that Daniel could only begin to understand.

The sink faucet and the drain had turned brown with rust. I rummaged through Daniel's box of supplies, poured the rust remover down the drain, listened to the crackle of the chemical reaction.

I slid the thick yellow gloves over my hands and took out the scrub brush, but the ring was twisted, the rock catching on the inside of the rubber any time I bent my fingers. I removed the glove, slid the ring off my finger, and placed it in the middle of the kitchen table, in my direct line of sight. Something to tie me to the outside, a reminder that I had moved on from Cooley Ridge.

I tackled the sink and the counters, vaguely satisfied with myself, meticulously scrubbing and buffing it all to a shine. The ringing phone was a welcome relief. My eyes had started to go blurry, and I wiped my arm against my forehead to brush the hair back, pulled one of the gloves off my hand. "Hello?"

"Hey. Sorry I'm calling back so late," Everett said.

I sank into the kitchen chair, pulling off the other glove with my teeth. "No worries. I know you're busy."

"So, you made it."

"I made it," I said.

"How's it going so far?" he asked.

"Pretty much as expected. Dad's the same, Daniel's the same. Dropped off the paperwork for the doctor. I'm tackling the house already." I stood, doing a quick tidying up before heading upstairs.

"How long until you can list it?"

"Not sure. I don't want to list it until everything's fixed. First impressions are everything." I saw that it was almost midnight and yawned.

"Get some sleep," he said.

"I'm about to." I turned off the downstairs light, backing out of the room. Turned to face the window, to see the trees and mountains illuminated in the moonlight as I stood in the dark. *Goodbye,* I thought.

And thought for a moment that I saw a flicker of light between the trees.

"I'm going to try to get my dad to sign the papers on his own. Doesn't feel right, taking it out from under him," I said.

"Well," Everett said, his own yawn making me smile, "do what you need to do."

"I always do," I said.

———

TEN YEARS AGO, I'D stumbled through these woods, trying to get back home. Desperate for the safety of the walls—*just make it home.* As if that could prevent the inevitable. Dad's car and Daniel's car were gone, and I sprinted across the yard, holding my arm to my stomach, pain shooting through both. The porch light swinging, and the screen door creaking, and me gasping, alone in the house.

I was alone.

The rest of the night I can handle only in flashes. I'm not sure what that says, that I can stare back at Corinne for minutes on end but not at this. I have to come at it from the side, grazing pieces here and there. Not looking it directly in the eye. I've never told it before. This is the only way I know how.

I'm getting there.

———

STRIPPING OFF MY CLOTHES in the bathroom in a wild panic, trying to stop something I had no control over—furious that I could not—and the fury giving way to something quiet and hollow the moment I surrendered. When I remembered that the world would not bend to my will, that it never had, and it certainly wasn't about to start now.

Turning the water on hot, leaving the clothes on the floor, folding up my knees and sitting in the tub, my head resting on my arms, my eyes squeezed shut, letting the water hit me everywhere.

*Two days.* It had been a hypothetical two days ago in Corinne's bathroom, had just barely morphed into something real and hopeful in my mind, and now it was gone. Like it had never truly existed.

———

DANIEL, KNOCKING ON THE door a while later. "Nic? Are you okay?" More knocking. "I can hear you."

Holding my breath so I'd stop crying.

"Answer me or I'm coming in."

The door handle turning, and a cold gust of air, and Daniel sucking in his breath as his shadow stood beside my clothes in a heap on the floor.

"Are you okay?"

Letting out the breath along with a sob. "No, I'm not okay."

"Tell me what to do. Tell me how I can help." Tyler had told Daniel I was pregnant after hitting him. I knew from the way Daniel had looked at me with so much regret.

"It's too late."

"Get out of the tub, Nic. I can't help you unless you get out of the tub."

"I don't want your help."

And him: "I'm sorry. I'm sorry."

His shadow retreating. The door closing.

The water eventually running cold, pulling myself up, grabbing a towel from the bar.

My clothes off the floor and the laundry running downstairs. Wrapping myself in the fleece pajamas I used in the winter, sinking into the center of my bed, hearing Daniel on the phone in his room. "No, Tyler, you don't understand. You have to come."

Me calling back through the bathroom between our rooms: "He can't."

Daniel hanging up, standing in the doorway to my room, looking as helpless and lost as I felt. "What do I do? What can I do?"

Me, crying again—everything from that night too tangled together—and wanting to go back years, a decade, to a time when every possibility could exist. Saying, "I want Mom." The most unreasonable request.

And Daniel, expression unreadable, with his chin set, his nose swollen, his eyes faintly bruised, saying, "Well, I'm all you've got," as he came to sit beside me.

—

TYLER MADE IT ANYWAY. On foot. Over the river. I heard him downstairs later, with Daniel.

I'd tell him in the stairwell, on my feet. I'd stop crying.

I'd lost his ring. I'd lost everything. And I wasn't sure if his offer still stood. If he still meant it. It was easier to pretend it just never happened at all.

—

EVERYTHING IN THAT BOX in the police station had belonged to me: the pregnancy test, the ring, the stories, even. And in a way, it was fitting. That girl faded to nothing from the curve of the road on the last night of the county fair. She disappeared. She changed her hair and her accent, her phone number, her address. She did not look back.

*Do what you need to do, Nic.*

*Pick yourself up.*

*Start over again.*

# PART 3

*Going On*

It is quite true what philosophy says; that life must be understood backwards. But then one forgets the other principle: that it must be lived forwards.

—SØREN KIERKEGAARD

# Two Weeks Later

# DAY 15

**T**he sirens were faint in the distance but growing louder, and Tyler was halfway across the room, and his words—*body at Johnson Farm*—echoed in my mind. I pictured sunflowers. The ghost of Corinne, spinning in the field. Her body resting there now, ten years later.

But Daniel had said he was taking her to a job site. It couldn't be Corinne.

"Annaleise?" I asked. "Is she dead?"

"Yes," he said. "She was just lying there in the middle of the field."

"Was she shot?" I asked, because Daniel had access to Dad's gun, and he'd been chasing her through the woods. Because I'd found that purse buckle near the river, where Daniel said he'd lost her, and he had her key, which must've been inside her bag.

Tyler nodded. "This family found her—the kids had run off after pictures and . . ." He tugged his fingers through his hair, leaving

341

the thought. "This guy I work with, his wife works dispatch, and she got the call. I tried to get there first when I heard. I tried."

"Oh, God," I said. "Daniel?"

"I don't know, Nic," he said, but he wouldn't look at me when he said it.

Everett was probably at the airport by now. I couldn't call to ask for advice again—not about this, and not after everything else.

What was Daniel *thinking*? The body, all the evidence, leading right back to him. And *Annaleise* . . . Jackson had told me there were rumors, that Laura had left Daniel for a time because of them. The rumors would spin to fact, into motive, in someone else's hands. I knew my brother could fall for the wrong person—he'd done it once before—but I couldn't imagine Daniel allowing Annaleise to take his picture if he'd truly been seeing her. Except someone had gone through her computer late at night, deleting images from months earlier. I'd heard his steps through the woods, seen his shadow in her home. Someone who knew his way in the dark, in these woods, by heart. Daniel. Annaleise must've taken them when he wasn't looking or when he was sleeping. Like all those pictures I'd seen in her files, pictures of girls caught unaware. They had no idea someone was watching. Annaleise, with her big wide eyes behind the camera, fading into the background. You'd never know she caught you.

He should've been smarter than this.

Daniel had reached her at the river and grabbed her purse, and the buckle broke. He took her purse, her phone. He must have buried it all somewhere or ditched it in his car, because I knew he didn't have it when he met up with us again behind the house. He'd kept her house key, which was now tucked away in my father's slipper. Add my brother to the missing gaps, and the story begins to take shape.

He must've found her and . . .

But no. *Wait.* I knew Annaleise had gotten away from him.

Followed the river. Reached the motel and shimmied through the back window before calling Daniel again. From the hotel phone, because hers was in her purse.

I didn't understand. Why had she called Daniel's house? She'd been trying to get *away* from him. Daniel was probably here, anyway. It made no sense. But I'd stood in that motel room, and I'd hit redial, and I'd heard the machine: Laura's voice, cheerful and welcoming, dancing through my head: *You've reached the Farrells . . .*

Laura. Not Daniel's cell. Annaleise had called the house, knowing Daniel wasn't there.

She had called Laura. My hand rose to my mouth in sudden understanding.

"It's not Daniel," I whispered. Tyler nodded, staring at the mess around him, but I wasn't sure if he believed me or if he thought this was just me, hoping.

But I could feel it all coming together—could see all the pieces lining up in reverse.

Annaleise's whole world was shrinking to a point, and this must've been the only card she had left. Her only way out. Tell Laura. Tell her about her dangerous husband, his dangerous family. No need for the blackmail pictures to come into it if she could convince Laura to come forward instead.

*Where's your husband right now? I can tell you. Chasing me through the woods to keep me silent. He has my purse. My phone. It's not safe for you. Someone in that house killed Corinne Prescott. You must know that.*

I tried to imagine Laura picking up the phone, listening to Annaleise. Would she believe her? Would she listen? Daniel had said Laura wasn't home when he got back—that she'd probably gone to her sister's place. That she was upset. She'd done that before, if rumors were to be believed.

But what if she hadn't? What if she'd answered that call and listened? What would she *do*?

What if my brother had been telling the truth: that he followed Annaleise to the river, and then he lost her. His arm reaching out, fingers grasping the edge of her bag, and yanking. The handle breaking, the purse dropping, the buckle lost in the mud. All he had was her purse, her phone, her key. And he'd hidden it all, and waited.

As the days passed and she didn't reappear, he must've felt that net closing. All the secrets, threatening to shake loose—then and now. He used her key to check for evidence at her place, to go through her files, deleting himself from her history as the investigation gained force. Hid the key after in his desk just in case, where he figured Laura wouldn't look—and where I'd found it. The only thing my brother had been trying to cover up was the rumored affair. He knew, as well as I did, what it could lead to.

But somehow Annaleise ended up dead in a field of sunflowers. Just *lying there.*

Daniel would've buried her. Brought the body to one of his abandoned sites. But Laura . . .

I closed my eyes and saw it all sliding into focus:

Laura picking Annaleise up from the motel—*Where are you? I'll come and get you*—with Dad's gun in the glove compartment. Laura driving her out toward Johnson Farm, away from town, just driving around—*so we can talk*—listening to Annaleise accuse her husband and her husband's family. Laura, who had already started a list of slights. The rumors about Annaleise, or maybe more, that had made her leave Daniel for a while months earlier; and now *this.* This woman, threatening to take down everything Laura had planned. Laura, who was eight months pregnant and had an entire life stretching out before her: one that included Daniel. She was so close, she could see it. The life she wanted, the life she was owed.

Laura, who could not dig a garden, let alone bury a body, but needed a place to get this woman away from her family.

Daniel was right—I underestimated Laura. I underestimated

how fiercely she loved my brother, my family, her future. I under-estimated the lengths everyone here would go to for each other.

I underestimated how much I wanted to come back.

———

TYLER LOOKED OUT THE window because the sirens were getting louder. A shudder ran through him.

"I tried to get there first, Nic. I *did* get there first. I was trying to find the ring, but I heard the sirens, and I ran . . . I ran out of time."

"It's okay," I said. The sirens were closer, moving with purpose, and Tyler was trembling in the middle of the kitchen.

"No, it's not okay." His hands shook. Did he touch her? He must have. "They found—" He ran both hands down his face.

"They found the ring?" I asked, my vision turning hazy.

He shook his head. "A letter."

"She sent a letter?"

"No. No. It was tucked inside her waistband. I didn't see it. I heard the sirens and I ran."

"So then how do you know?" I asked. He had run, he said. And it looked like he had driven straight here.

"Everyone knows!" he said. "Jackson called just before I got here. To make sure I'd heard." He winced, dropped his head in his hands. "To make sure I'd heard about the piece of paper folded over and addressed to the Cooley Ridge Police Department." He fixed his eyes on me. "No envelope. Like she meant to leave it for them somehow. An anonymous letter."

I pictured the blank pad of paper from the hotel, imagined her scrawling a note in desperation. Pictured her tucking it away when Laura pulled up to get her, saving it for later. "What did it say?" I whispered. All the terrible possibilities echoing in my head. All the reasons Daniel had just called in a panic, telling me to get out.

Nothing keeps in this place.

Tyler paused. Lowered his voice. "That they could find the body of Corinne Prescott on the property of Patrick Farrell. Advising them to take a hard look at Nic Farrell and Tyler Ellison."

I felt my body start to tremble, mirroring Tyler's. "Oh, God."

Annaleise had not meant to be tied to the letter. An anonymous note and Laura. She was counting on both in a desperate effort to come out unscathed.

"Listen, I'm sure someone saw my truck. The family who found her was waiting out on the road. Even if they didn't see *me,* someone saw the truck. They can place me in the field. I'm covered in pollen. It looks bad. I need to go. I have a cabin in Tennessee. It's not registered under any name, just this place I built on my own a few years back. I need to disappear for a while. I set it up this weekend just in case."

Tyler had been in the field of sunflowers with Annaleise's body, with a note implicating us. Maybe he could explain away Annaleise. Maybe he could even prove it. But not without revealing what had happened ten years ago. Corinne comes back to us.

To me.

His truck, which I had been driving. He's always known. But he let me believe that I wasn't at fault. That something else must have happened to Corinne on the side of the road after we left. He let me believe I was innocent.

The box is full of lies, but none of them has the same type of power. There is nothing more dangerous, nothing more powerful, nothing more necessary and essential for survival than the lies we tell ourselves.

I stuck my finger in his chest, a desperate plea rising in my throat, coming out in a gasp. "You swore I didn't kill her. You promised I didn't do anything wrong. You swore."

His eyes closed and he took a slow breath—time stretching, pausing, giving me one more moment, just one more. "You didn't,

Nic. She threw herself in front of the truck. She killed herself. *She did it.*"

*There's a moment when you know,* Everett said. *When you can't explain it away anymore. And you can never go back.*

Up until the moment I saw those pictures, all the possibilities could still exist. She left. She ran away. Someone else hit her. She jumped.

*She jumped.*

I believed she would do that. Hearing her whisper at the top of the Ferris wheel. Seeing her step out in front of my car. After Hannah Pardot broke her open, I believed it even more. Corinne Prescott was the most deliberate person I knew. She would've done it.

But it had been me—me behind the wheel, Corinne dead, and Tyler the one who would pay for it.

"Get out of here, Nic. Right now. Drive straight back to Philadelphia. There's still time. Don't look back."

No, I suddenly saw what I needed to do.

How to ask for Cooley Ridge to let me come back. How to pay my very last debt.

*It's your turn now, Nic.*

"You were never at Johnson Farm," I said. "Whoever saw your truck is wrong. You've been here. Listen to me, Tyler. Listen, and do exactly what I say."

———

THE SIRENS GREW INSISTENT, but Tyler was wrong, we had time. I could make time work for us. Right now it could save us.

I could see it so clearly, the debts I was meant to pay. Ten years. That's the cost. That's the trade. Corinne has weighed and assessed and assigned it a value. The ten years I've fought for. That's what was owed. Like it's a blink. Like nothing.

*Pay your debts, like everyone else.*

My father for hiding her body. Jackson for not taking her back. Tyler, my enabler.

The fairness of it all, the give-and-take, like a ledger of rights and wrongs. I could feel her in this house. How could I not see it before? Of course she had been here. Of course.

And it was so clear that I would do it. I would pay. But not for Corinne.

"Get in the shower," I said.

"Nic, it's too late—"

"Leave your clothes in the bathroom and get in the shower."

"It's the middle of the day, and it's not my house. This makes no sense. I came to say goodbye."

I gripped his arm. "I know you did. And I'm telling you to get in the goddamn shower, Tyler. Please trust me."

I used a paper towel to wipe up the mud he'd trailed through the kitchen, as the sirens got closer. They were coming here. They were coming for us. "Run," I said. And he did.

I left his work boots in the back of Dad's closet, as if they were his. Took the key in the slipper and tossed it into the vent, as far as it would go.

Then I ran to my bathroom. His clothes were on the floor, like I'd asked. I picked them up and ran them down to the laundry room with a pile of my own clothes, starting the machine. Tyler's clothes from last week were still in my dresser drawer, and I threw them on the floor of the bedroom. Slid out of my own and left them on the floor, too.

"Okay," I said, stepping into the bathroom. "Everything's okay."

The first thing they see is everything. The first thing we say. An investigation lives and dies by first impressions. The story takes a life of its own from there.

The first thing they need to see is me and Tyler coming out of the shower together. It's the story they wanted in the first place.

The motive they wanted to nail Tyler with. Me and him together and Annaleise dead because of it. Now jealousy would be Annaleise's motive instead.

———

I HEARD THE KNOCKING, could see the lights coming through my bedroom window from the bathroom, flashing red and blue against the far wall. I grabbed a towel, wrapped myself in it, handed one to Tyler to do the same. I threw on a bathrobe, padded down the stairs, and opened the door to Mark Stewart, Officer Fraize, Jimmy Bricks, and that guy from State—what was his name? Detective Charles? It didn't matter. It really didn't.

Water dripped from my hair in the silence that followed. Mark Stewart blushed, looking away from my robe.

"What's wrong?" I asked. "Did something happen? Is my dad okay?"

Tyler came down the steps behind me, dripping wet, buttoning his pants. "What is it?" he asked. He, too, froze. "What's going on?"

"Nic. Tyler." Officer Fraize nodded at each of us.

The detective was frowning behind him. "I thought you hadn't been seeing each other," he said.

I folded my arms across my chest. "Hardly seems like any of your business."

"Lying during an investigation . . ." His words trailed off as a car pulled up behind them. I craned to see Daniel's car over his shoulder.

"Why is Daniel here?" I said. "Is anyone going to tell me what you're all doing here?"

"We have a few questions. We'd like permission to take a look around," Detective Charles said.

Tyler put a hand on my shoulder. "What's this about?"

"I'm afraid we've got some bad news," Bricks said. "We found Annaleise. She's dead."

Tyler's hand curled into the fabric of my robe. "So you came to question me?" he asked.

"No," he said. "That's not why we're here." Detective Charles looked over his shoulder again, at Daniel jogging toward us, at Tyler's truck parked behind mine. "When did you get here, Mr. Ellison? If you don't mind me asking."

I tried to calculate how long it had been since Everett had left. Tried to give Tyler as much of an alibi as possible. "About an hour ago? Maybe more?" I said, peering up at Tyler. His eyes locked with mine, his lips slightly parted, like he was watching the story in my head playing out, becoming real.

He nodded. "Yeah. About then," he said.

Daniel pushed his way through the crowd, tried to hide his surprise as his eyes darted between me and Tyler, both of us dripping wet, on display. "Everett's on his way back," he said. "I caught him just as he was getting to the airport."

My stomach hollowed out, and I felt Tyler tense beside me.

Daniel turned to the detective. "Our lawyer told us not to talk. Not to let you in." He held up his hands—*Not my call, just following orders*—"Sorry."

———

I LEFT DANIEL AND Tyler on the porch with the police while I got dressed, cracking open my bedroom window. I heard steps on the porch as Bricks and Officer Fraize circled the house, pausing to peer inside the windows. Eyes, eyes everywhere.

Detective Charles was near the garage, also peering in the windows, occasionally crouching low to examine something on the ground. My heart was pounding, and I couldn't even ask Daniel about Laura, as he was busy keeping watch on the front porch.

It wasn't long before Everett's cab returned, leaving him halfway up the driveway. He froze as he exited the taxi, then took a second collecting his luggage. Composing himself, I knew. Processing the scene. His fiancée's brother and another man on the porch. Two police cars and an unmarked car along the road. Officers in and out of uniform, circling my property.

I stepped outside, and Everett's eyes swung toward mine with the creak of the screen door. He introduced himself to the police, all businesslike, very curt and *Philadelphia,* which wasn't the best approach, honestly, but it got the point across. "Do you have a warrant for the premises?" he asked the detective before acknowledging me. Business Everett. Efficient Everett.

"We're in the process of securing one," he said.

"So that would be no, then," Everett responded.

"We'd like to ask them some questions. You're free to sit in. The warrant will be granted, I can assure you."

"Great. Then *at that time,* you can come back. They're not answering, and you all need to back up. Off the property, gentlemen." To me, "Get inside, Nicolette." Nobody moved, me included. "Okay, or stay on their property and I'll file a complaint with the state."

*That's not how it's done around here.* It makes us look guilty. Appearances are everything.

"It's not my property," I said. "Not yet. I don't know what my dad would want—"

"Nicolette," Everett snapped, "get in the house."

Bricks raised his eyebrows but backed away. The group walked slowly toward their cars. But they didn't leave. The unmarked car remained on the street; Officer Fraize spoke to the detective through the window.

"Inside," Everett said, motioning for all of us to follow him. "And you are . . . ?" he asked as the door shut behind him.

"Tyler Ellison." The silence that followed was long and excruciating, until Daniel started pacing, pulling Everett's focus.

"They're not leaving," I said.

"They're waiting for a warrant to come through, and in the meantime, they're making sure you don't ditch anything. Jesus Christ," Everett said, dropping his bags near the door. "Care to fill me in on what started this shit storm? I just left, for fuck's sake." The prescriptions were unopened on the table, and I saw him taking that in, and my wet hair, Tyler's bare feet.

"They found Annaleise's body," I said. "She was shot." I saw Daniel tense. "And she had a letter. Accusing us in Corinne's disappearance."

"Accusing *who*?" he asked. "Your dad? Or all of you?"

"It's complicated, Everett."

"Try me," he said.

I couldn't look at his face. I could tell he wanted to understand. I could tell he was still hoping.

But you have to pay your debts.

I turned to Daniel, who was standing against the wall. "You should go home. You should check on Laura," I said. I wondered if he knew. If he suspected. He must know the key was missing from his desk; maybe he just assumed Laura found it and took it, silently punishing him. She'd been out that night, after all. I wondered if he'd ask. Or if he'd go home and check his gun. If he'd say anything at all.

I walked over and hugged him. "Thank you for coming," I said. And then, with my mouth pressed close to his ear: "You went home after the bar. Laura was there. You were together." He moved his hands to my back, pressing his head closer to my shoulder to show he was listening. "Make sure Dad's gun is never found."

I felt Daniel's whole body change in that moment of understanding. He didn't look at me, kept his head down, ran his hand through his hair as he walked slowly out the front door.

I watched him go, watched Officer Fraize put his hand out as Daniel approached his car. Watched as Daniel slowly spread his arms out from his sides.

"What are they doing to him?" I pressed my palms to the window as Officer Fraize patted his hands up and down Daniel's body before stepping back and nodding.

"Looks like maybe the warrant is for a weapon," Everett said. "They're making sure he didn't leave with it." He paused. "Are there any weapons here, Nicolette?"

"What?" I turned to face him. "No, there aren't any *weapons* here, Everett."

He looked out the window again, squinting against the sun. "Time to tell me what the fuck is happening here."

I stepped away and turned to Tyler, who was sitting on the couch in silence. "You should go home, too," I said.

He shook his head, glanced from me to Everett, and said, "I'll be out front." The screen door banged shut behind him, and I saw him sitting on the bottom step, chin in his hands.

Everett followed as I walked into the kitchen. He was too close when I turned around.

"Okay. Here's what's happening. Annaleise Carter is dead," I said, "and she's trying to bring us down with her. She left some note that said the police should look into me about what happened to Corinne. The note said Corinne's body might be here."

"And why would Annaleise want to do that? Why would she make something like that up?"

"Because she's fucked up. The world is full of fucked-up people, Everett. Do you know how many I see a day? And those are just the ones I can *see.*"

"But Annaleise is dead, Nicolette. Somebody killed her with that note on her. Do you see how that looks?"

"Oh, I see. Do you think I'm stupid?"

"They're getting a warrant. A *warrant*. What do they think they'll find?"

"I don't know!" I said.

Everett got closer, and I backed up. "What was your father saying? Why did you need the cops to stay away from him? Why do you need him silent?"

"Back up," I said, my hand on his chest. I opened the fridge, grabbed a soda, buying myself time, clarity.

He paused, hands hanging at his sides. "Okay, let me put it to you this way," he said. "You're called up on the stand. A lawyer asks, 'What happened to Corinne . . .'"

"Prescott," I said.

"'What happened to Corinne Prescott?' What would you say, under oath, on the stand?"

I tipped the can of soda to my mouth, but he didn't back away. The carbonation fizzed against my lips. "Well," I said, "I guess I'd plead the Fifth."

"This isn't some cop show, Nicolette. And the Fifth Amendment is only admissible to protect yourself."

I looked out the back window, lowered my voice. "Everett? You're bound by oath, right? This is confidential?" I put the drink on the table, eyes on his, and hated the way he was staring at me, his head tilted to the side. What was he looking for? What would he see?

He staggered back, or maybe I'd pushed him—my hand was charged, numb, and I couldn't tell.

"What did you do, Nicolette?" he whispered.

Everett lived in a world that didn't touch mine. In a place where he saw the injustices elsewhere—somewhere lesser than his place in life. His moral compass did not falter. His world was black and white. He could not look into the darkness, or take it home with him, or love it. He'd never welcome the monster into his heart.

Would he hide a body for his daughter? Move one for his sister? Everett's world was all on paper, because he'd never been tested. What was it he'd told me? The terribly dark thing that nobody else knew about him?

He'd seen someone die.

And what had *I* done? he wanted to know. So many things. I'd killed Corinne—it was the only explanation remaining, no matter whose fault it had been. Abandoned her on the side of the road. Lied to the police then and now. Lived with her underneath my house. Run away from Tyler and home because of it. Left them all to pick up the pieces.

But I didn't owe Everett that truth.

*Pay your debts,* she insisted. *Pay them all.*

I thought of my apartment with the painted furniture and the desk with my nameplate, waking up and feeling for Everett beside me in his darkened room.

"I slept with Tyler," I said.

Everything about Everett hardened, and I realized this was a blindside. Not something he'd anticipated. I waited for seconds, moments, as it sank in.

"Tell me again," he said.

I backed up, felt the cold, impersonal wall. "I slept with Tyler," I said again, my heart pounding, my skin tingling.

Tyler was outside, and it was just us now. I waited to see what Everett might do. If he was going to rush out front and hit Tyler. Grab my shoulders and shake me. Call me words that would burn in my memory. But he closed his eyes and lowered his head as he backed away. Everett wasn't like that. He wouldn't kill, or move a body, or lie to take the heat or blame. He was a better person than the rest of us.

"I'm going to be sick," he said.

Let us both believe it was because I'd been unfaithful.

355

———

HE CALLED A CAB—HAD to ask for my phone because he didn't have a signal—and even speaking those words seemed to kill him. He didn't look at me during the wait, didn't speak to me as I sat across the table from him, drumming my fingers.

We heard the car pull up. He grabbed his luggage, headed for the entrance, didn't look at Tyler as he walked through the door. Not a violent bone in his body.

"I'm sorry," I said as I stood at the top of the porch beside the screen door.

No, I was wrong. As he was leaving, he took my upper arm in his hand and whispered in my ear, something about how he had really loved me, and something more, like *How could you* or *I hope you're happy*—some empty platitude—but I couldn't hear him clearly because I was focused on his fingers, digging and digging into my skin, grinding into the tendons, pinching a nerve, my knees giving slightly as my mouth opened in silent pain.

He left, and the bruise was already forming.

———

I SAT BESIDE TYLER on the steps, watching him go.

"You okay?" he asked.

"Come on," I said. "Come inside."

They'd be back. That's what Everett had said. They'd be back with a search warrant, and they were watching us now. As soon as the door shut behind us, I leaned in to Tyler, felt his arms slowly come up around me. "There's a key in the vent. I need to get rid of it," I said.

Tyler and I decided we'd flush the key, using a plunger to make sure it wouldn't float back up. But first I studied the intricate pattern of the *A* of the key chain, and I told him I'd found it at

Daniel's—told him everything I believed about Daniel and Laura. I whispered all of it under the sound of running water as he scrubbed the mud from his boots.

I noticed now that there was a thin line bisecting the key chain, and I instinctively pulled the two halves in opposite directions. A lid slid off, revealing a flash drive.

My ring for the flash drive. In the end, it turned out I'd paid that debt, too.

I wondered when Annaleise had felt that unbreakable thread growing between her and Corinne. If it was after she saw the pictures. If it was before. If it started all the way back that night at the fair.

I imagined Corinne looking away after Daniel pushed her back, and Annaleise standing there watching, their eyes locking for a moment too long. I imagined Annaleise seeing Corinne cry, all alone, maybe, something I'd never witnessed. Or maybe Corinne looked deep into Annaleise and saw something dark and appealing inside. Something that bound them together.

Or maybe it was brief and one-sided, like most moments we assign weight to. Maybe Corinne didn't even notice her standing there, but Annaleise saw something she needed. A likeness or a comfort. That even Corinne might fall. Even the strong are lonely. Even the adored are sad. I hoped she loved her in that moment—when no one else did.

Or maybe it wasn't until later. When she saw the photos shifting back into focus.

I know what it's like to leave, to come back, to not fit. To feel that distance between you and everything you've ever known. But Annaleise couldn't find a place out there. Couldn't let go enough. A lonely kid, a lonelier woman. She came back to what she knew.

You want to believe you're not the saddest person in the world.

Annaleise found her there, in the pictures. The sad, lonely girl.

She found her in the old, dark photograph, covered in a blanket. But still she wanted more. To find her in Jackson and Daniel, Bailey and Tyler. To pull her from my father's guilt. One more thread when I showed up. To take her from me.

I pictured Annaleise staring deeply at the image of Corinne's limp body with fear, with longing. *Am I you?* she asks. *Is this what we become? How we fade away and disappear?*

The woods have eyes and monsters and stories.

We are them as much as they are us.

———

ANOTHER CAR PULLED IN before sunset but not much earlier. The fireflies were flashing in the yard. Detective Charles walked up the porch steps, warrant in hand, detailing what they were searching for.

Everett was right—they were looking for a gun. A gun and a body. I stepped aside, grateful that I had burned my father's ledgers and all the receipts. The history of his debt to me, his money for Annaleise's silence. *I'm late,* he'd said to me at Grand Pines. Late on hush money. *My daughter's not safe.*

Mark Stewart sat at the dining room table with me and Tyler, like a babysitter, but he wouldn't look directly at either one of us.

I moved out to the front porch an hour later, when a new team showed up with machines. They tore up the new garage floor, as if the fresh concrete was evidence enough. Dug through the garden. Brought out a dog to sniff around the rest of the property from the road to the dried-up streambed. But eventually they left, too.

And in the late evening, when I was sitting in the kitchen with Tyler as the officers finished dismantling the house, Hannah Pardot walked into the room. Her hair was longer, the curls dyed darker, and she'd traded her red lipstick for a muted maroon. Her body was softer, but her face harder. And she still didn't smile. "Nic Farrell," she said. "So it all comes back to this." As if no time had passed at all. We were merely picking up a conversation left midsentence just a moment ago.

"There's nothing here," I said.

She sat down in the chair across from me and said, "Annaleise Carter, I remember her. She was an alibi for your brother, you remember that? For all of you, really."

"I remember."

She pulled out a piece of paper sealed inside a Ziploc bag. Evidence removed from the scene. "She was killed with this note on her, Nic. Explain that." *I dare you.*

It was written on a small rectangle of paper in neat handwriting—probably from the pad at the motel. But the ink had bled out from the rain, softening the paper, tearing it in places.

"I came home, Tyler dumped her, she blamed us both. She wasn't a nice person, Detective."

Hannah tilted her head to the side as Detective Charles came to stand behind her. "You lied to me about your relationship with Tyler," he said. "Either you're lying then or you're lying now. Either way, hard to believe you."

"You lied first, Detective. Standing in my front yard, putting on this schoolboy act. Telling me you didn't want to get Tyler in any trouble. Please."

Hannah frowned at him, then turned her attention back to me. "Explain it to me, then. Who, besides the two of you that she implicated in that note, would have a reason to kill her?"

"Oh, you don't know Annaleise very well, do you?" I asked. "Annaleise had a lot of enemies." I turned to Hannah again. "Ask the people she went to school with. She liked to expose them, tell their secrets. Like she was daring them to do something in retaliation.

I'm sure she got tangled up in some mess she had no business being a part of. Thought she was so much better than everyone else. Break her open, just like you did to Corinne. You'll see."

"Is that so," Hannah Pardot said.

"Yes," Tyler said.

*Do you hear what I'm saying? She incited too much anger, too much feeling. She's not at fault, but she's hardly innocent.*

*Brought it on herself, you know.*

"Okay, let's get down to the details then, shall we? You know how this goes." Hannah placed the recorder between us on the table. "Where were you, the both of you, the night she disappeared?"

"Right here, cleaning the house," I said.

"Anyone who can vouch for you?"

"Tyler. I called him, he was at the bar, and he came. Broke up with Annaleise standing right across the room from me, to do the right thing. He stayed here the whole night."

"So you're each other's alibi, is that it?"

Tyler leaned back in his chair. "Jackson Porter was with me when Nic called. He saw me leave. Knew I was coming here."

Hannah leaned across the table. "Your father has a gun registered in his name."

"He does?"

"Yes. Any idea where it might be?"

"I haven't seen it anywhere." I shrugged. "We moved him out last year. The back door lock's been broken for a while—I need to get it fixed. Someone was actually messing around in here the other day." I stared at Detective Charles. "It could've been anyone."

Hannah's jaw shifted. "The concrete was fresh in the garage. What were you doing in there, Nic? Tyler? I'm assuming she had help."

"We're refinishing it," Tyler said.

"To bring my dad home," I added. I smiled at her. "He always liked you, Hannah."

She frowned. "I thought you were getting married to some lawyer in Philadelphia."

"Do you see a ring?" I asked.

She shifted in her seat. "You're filing guardianship to sell the house. We've seen the paperwork."

My mind drifted, but only for a second. I shook my head, smiled to myself. "No, not to sell. There's no sign. It's not on the market. We have a court date for guardianship. I'm bringing him home with me." As if this had been my plan from the start.

The distance, like time, just a thing we create.

All the pieces falling in a beautiful crescendo—lining up to bring me safely home.

*Three Months Later*

S omewhere there's a storage unit full of painted furniture. And when the money runs out and they can't reach me because I've left no forwarding address, they will auction it off or cart it out to the Dumpster in the parking lot behind the building.

That person will disappear. A ghost in their memories.

I changed my number. It's just easier this way.

The ring hasn't turned up. Maybe Annaleise's brother found it before the police swept through. Maybe her mother hid it to save her from something she didn't understand. Maybe it's buried in her purse along with everything else, wherever Daniel left it. Maybe it will turn up one day in the form of a new car, or a redone garage, or a year of college.

Nothing stays lost forever here.

———

THEY TOOK ANNALEISE'S LIFE apart, put it back together again. Broke open her family and the people she went to school with, tracked down leads from college, dug into her past. As for me, I was done talking. I didn't have to speak again. I knew that much from Everett.

Tyler stopped talking, too, and then Jackson and Daniel and Laura, until we slowly became a town without a voice. Could they really blame us after last time?

There were whispers about us. But the whispers I could deal with.

If the entirety of Annaleise's investigation existed in a box, I imagine this would be all you'd see: a folded-up letter, addressed to the Cooley Ridge Police Department; an autopsy report with the findings: gunshot wound to the chest, bled out, clean and simple; all other evidence washed away; her phone records, which Daniel explained away—*I told her to stop calling. She was harassing me*—as he rocked his baby in his arms; and lies: *He was home with me,* Laura swore. *Came home from Kelly's just after midnight. We were here together. I was up sick with heartburn from the pregnancy. He made me pasta to settle my stomach. We were here together the rest of the night.*

———

THE HOUSE WAS COMING along. We completed the garage first, for Dad. Sometimes I thought maybe there was nothing wrong with him—he was doing better back home, surrounded by the things he knew. But occasionally, he'd wander off, end up across town. Someone always brought him back. And sometimes he'd walk inside in the morning and sit at the kitchen table and call me Shana, like he was existing in some other time. His eyes might drift to my stomach those days, and he might say something like *I hope it's a girl this time. He needs a sister. Someone to protect. It will make him a better man.*

———

IT WAS A WEEK after we brought Dad home when I noticed I was four days behind on my pills. It was two weeks later when I noticed the same nausea, the same feeling of bone-tiredness, that I'd felt in Corinne's bathroom two days before everything changed.

Tyler's been renovating room by room, making a place for us. My bedroom will be the nursery. Daniel's old room will become Tyler's office. He had to gut my parents' room before I could sleep in it—repainting it, putting in carpet and new furniture. I thought of Laura, of the hoops she made Daniel jump through, and I thought I understood.

Despite the tiredness, I still have trouble sleeping in long stretches. Sometimes I can't differentiate night and day, sleep and wake.

And sometimes the tremble comes back in my right hand. So I press it to my stomach to keep steady. I'm still scared. I feel like it's all too close to the surface. That it would take only a nudge and our fragile story would tumble down, crack open, exposing us.

But it hasn't yet.

I think we'll be okay.

————

HOW DO I SLEEP at all? After everything?

I don't know who it would help at this point to tell: Corinne was beautiful, and a monster, and I loved her once. But in the end, I abandoned her, like everyone else. In the end, she made me kill her.

There. There's my confession. But she was the most deliberate person I knew—she knew what she was doing. She had to. That's how I sleep at night.

But sometimes she's all I can think about. And that night, barreling straight for me. Sometimes when I'm falling asleep, I see her eyes in the headlights, locked on mine.

On those nights, as on this one, Tyler pulls me closer, like he knows.

If there's a feeling to home, it's this. A place where there are no secrets, where nothing stays buried: not the past and not yourself. Where you can be all the versions of you, see it all reflected back as you walk the same stairs, the same halls, the same rooms. Feel the ghost of your mother as you sit at the kitchen table, hear the words of your father circling round and round over dinner, and your brother stopping by, wishing you'd be a little better, a little stronger. Just checking in to be sure. And Tyler. Of course Tyler.

It's four walls echoing back everything you've ever been and everything you've ever done, and it's the people who stay despite it all. Through it all. For it all.

Where you can stop fearing the truth. Let it be part of you. Take it to bed. Stare it in the face with an arm tucked around you.

The truth, then.

The truth is, I'm terrified of all I have to lose and how close I will always be to losing it. But it happened before. And I survived it.

I like to believe that's what Everett saw in me and what Tyler knows. That I survive. It's only one thing. But it's also everything.

*Pick yourself up.*

*Start over again.*

# ACKNOWLEDGMENTS

Thank you to my agent, Sarah Davies, who encouraged this idea when it was just a one-sentence pitch, who offered invaluable advice along the way, and whose unwavering support and belief in this project helped bring it to life.

Thank you to my editor, Sarah Knight, who saw exactly how to make this book stronger and showed me how to get it there. I'm so grateful for your sharp eye and your insight. And to the entire team at Simon & Schuster, especially Trish Todd and Kaitlin Olson.

Thank you to Megan Shepherd, who read so many drafts of this book that I've lost count, and to Elle Cosimano, Ashley Elston, and Jill Hathaway, for all the brainstorming sessions, the feedback, and the friendship. Huge thanks also to everyone at Bat Cave 2014, for your insight and encouragement on this project.

And last, thank you to my husband, Luis; my parents; and my family, for all of your support.

# ABOUT THE AUTHOR

Megan Miranda is the author of several books for young adults, including *Fracture, Hysteria, Vengeance, Soulprint,* and *The Safest Lies.* She grew up in New Jersey, attended Massachusetts Institute of Technology, and lives in North Carolina with her husband and two children. *All the Missing Girls* is her first novel for adults. Follow @MeganLMiranda on Twitter, or visit www.meganmiranda.com.

Simon & Schuster Paperbacks
Reading Group Guide

# ALL THE MISSING GIRLS

## MEGAN MIRANDA

*This reading group guide for* All the Missing Girls *includes an introduction, discussion questions, ideas for enhancing your book club, and a Q & A with author Megan Miranda. The suggested questions are intended to help your reading group find new and interesting angles and topics for your discussion. We hope that these ideas will enrich your conversation and increase your enjoyment of the book.*

# INTRODUCTION

When Nicolette Farrell receives a phone call from her brother, Daniel, with the news that their father is declining, she immediately heads back to her hometown of Cooley Ridge. Although she has established a new life elsewhere and is engaged to a successful young attorney, her homecoming causes memories of her adolescence and the mysterious disappearance of her friend Corinne Prescott ten years earlier to come flooding back. As Nicolette runs into the people from her past—her ex-boyfriend Tyler, her old friend Bailey, and Corinne's high school boyfriend Jackson—she ruminates on the fateful days that changed the course of each of their lives and realizes that she is inextricably tethered to the people and place she thought she had left behind. When the woman that Nic's ex-boyfriend has been seeing suddenly goes missing during her stay, Nicolette can't help but search for the connection between the two disappearances. In a mind-bending twist, the story of Nicolette's return to Cooley Ridge is told in reverse, keeping readers on the edge of their seats until the very last page is turned. This tale of buried secrets and a "town full of liars" cleverly explores the distance that people will go to protect those they love and poses haunting questions about the powerful grip the past can have on us and how well we can really know other people—and ourselves.

# TOPICS AND QUESTIONS
# FOR DISCUSSION

1. Consider the epigraphs printed ahead of each part of the story. Why do you think the author chose these epigraphs? What do they reveal about the major themes of the book, and how do they help to unify the various sections?

2. Who narrates the story? Is he or she a reliable narrator? Why or why not? How do the choices in narration support a dialogue about how we come to understand or believe the stories we are told and how we determine what is or is not the truth? For instance, how might our understanding of the story be different if the author had chosen to employ more than one narrator or a different narrator?

3. Why does Nicolette Farrell return to Cooley Ridge? What is her experience of homecoming like? What seems to be the same about the town and the people in it and what seems to be different? How has Nicolette changed or not changed since her time growing up in Cooley Ridge?

4. Consider the motifs of myth and superstition in the story. Who is the monster in the woods? What does the story seem to suggest about how myth and superstition shape our fears and sense of what is—and is not—menacing?

5. Who is responsible for the disappearance of Corinne Prescott? Explain. How are the victims of each disappearance treated?

How do the people in town react to their disappearances? What roles do reputation, gossip, and opinion seem to play in the investigations?

6. Why do you think the author chose to tell the story in reverse? How did the reverse telling of the story affect your interpretation of the situation and your assessment of the characters therein?

7. Evaluate the theme of truth in the story. What lies do the characters tell, and why do they tell them? Do you feel that any of the lies were justified? What role does perspective seem to play in the determination of what is true and what is not?

8. Everett says that people can change, but Nicolette seems to believe that people do not change in any substantial way. Does the book ultimately suggest who is right? Do you agree? Explain.

9. How would you characterize the relationship that Corinne had with the other characters? How did each of the characters seem to feel about Corinne? How do we know this? What does Nicolette reveal about Corinne that gives us insight we might not otherwise have? How does this point of view—and the point of view of the other characters—shape or influence your assessment of Corinne's fate?

10. Evaluate the themes of morality and the dual nature of humans. Can readers distinguish who is a "good" or "bad" character as the story unravels or at the book's conclusion, or is a more complex view of morality presented? Explain. What motivates the characters to make the moral choices they each make? Do you feel that they made the right choices? Discuss.

11. What does the book seem to suggest about how well we can know others? What does the story indicate about the way we come to "know" another person? What influences our assessments of others and what prevents us from knowing other people—and ourselves—better?

12. What does Nicolette say is most necessary and essential to our survival? Do you agree with her? Why or why not?

13. At the conclusion of the story, what does Nicolette say defines *home*? Is her concept of what makes a home surprising? Do you agree with her definition? Explain.

14. Evaluate the theme of memory in the book. Are the memories of the characters reliable? Why or why not? What does this suggest about the way that time influences our perspective and how the past affects our future?

15. Since the majority of the action takes place in Nicolette's memory, how does the author create suspense and tension? What are some of the most surprising elements of plot and character and why are they surprising? Were you surprised by the conclusion of the book? Why or why not? How did your opinion of each of the characters change by the story's end?

# ENHANCE YOUR BOOK CLUB

1.  Read and evaluate *All the Missing Girls* alongside Gillian Flynn's *Gone Girl*. What do these books have in common? How are the characters alike? Who narrates the stories, and what points of view are represented? Does one point of view stand out over the rest? What common experiences do the characters share? What overlapping themes appear in these works? What role does genre play in treating these themes?

2.  Use *All the Missing Girls* as a starting place to discuss victimization and the portrayal of victims. Nicolette gives us a sense that there was a feeling in Cooley Ridge that Corinne may have "deserved" and "brought on" what happened to her. Discuss how reputation and gossip affect an investigation and shape how we perceive crimes and their victims.

3.  Consider an event from the past that you feel shaped or heavily influenced the course of your life. How has your perspective of this event changed with the passage of time? What do you understand about the event now that you did not then?

4.  Write a story about your adolescence. Then write the same story in reverse beginning with the conclusion and working back to the beginning. How does it change your perspective?

# A CONVERSATION WITH
# MEGAN MIRANDA

**Can you tell us about your inspiration for *All the Missing Girls*? What were the novel's origins? Where and how did you begin, and why were you interested in telling this story?**

When I first began writing *All the Missing Girls*, I called the draft *Disappear*, because thematically, that's what I was really interested in exploring. The ways in which people can disappear—not just literally, but the other versions of themselves as they grow and change over time. I wanted to explore how things that happen in adolescence can change and define people. How we are equally shaped not just by how we see ourselves, but by how others see us. And I'm fascinated by memory—the pieces we hold on to, and why we hold on to them, and how those pieces can shift and change over time.

The heart of the story idea actually began with the backstory, where I first got a sense of who the characters were, and the mystery that haunts them. But when I sat down to write, the scene that first came to me was ten years later, with Nic returning home. So I knew I would be playing with two stories, that the theme and the story would both become integral to the structure, and that they all would need to develop alongside each other.

**Why did you choose to write the story in reverse rather than in a linear fashion?**

I knew I wanted to tell a story about a disappearance where the "reveal" of the mystery would not only be the narrator discovering what happened, but the reader experiencing it for themselves. And I wanted that structure to be there for a reason. So I thought a lot about why a narrator would choose to tell a story in reverse, which is how the idea finally came together for me: that Nic, who is recounting the story, is (as she says at one point) working her way up to something, *back* to something, giving pieces of both the past and the present as she does. And, for me, the structure was also linked to the fact that she's going into a much deeper past to pull all the answers together, unearthing memories from ten years earlier that she'd rather leave alone.

**When you began writing the story, had you already decided what the ending would be or did the story lead you to its own conclusion?**

Partly. I had worked through a bit of the backstory first, so I knew where I was generally heading in the past story line, about what happened ten years earlier. But the present story, with Annaleise's disappearance, led to its own conclusion as I wrote, which then changed a bit of the past as well. The story evolved a lot as I wrote—I had a few pivotal scenes in mind, but other than that, I let the story and the characters lead the way.

**How did you decide upon the narrator of the story?**

For me, this was always Nic's story—she came to me first, and the story filled in around her. I started to hear her voice clearly on the drive she describes in the opening section, on her way back home. While Nic grew up in North Carolina and moved north, I did a bit of the reverse: I grew up in New Jersey, and now live in North Carolina. And it's a drive that I, like Nic, now know by heart. The route itself feels like a character shift as the scenery changes around you, how you can feel the person you are become the person you were as you go—with all the people who know you that way, waiting for you there.

**What kinds of sources did you consult in order to prepare for writing a book of this kind?**

One thing I've done for the past several years is attend a hands-on workshop for writers, run by former and current members of various law enforcement branches, where we can ask specific questions, learn about protocol, but more important, listen to their stories. I also spoke with an attorney who specializes in elder law to get a grasp on the logistics of Nic's father's role in the story. But I connected most strongly to place. I spent some time surrounded by the mountains, letting the setting take over while I wrote.

**Everett and Nicolette seem to disagree over whether a person can really change in any substantial way. Where do you stand on this?**

At first glance, I'd have to agree with Everett: Yes, I think people can and do change. But what I see in Nicolette's thoughts is her belief that, change as you might, the other versions are still *there*. It goes to her feelings of being unable to escape the past. How place and people can tie you to time. And how Nicolette herself can almost slip back to the person she was when surrounded by all the people and memories of the past as well.

**How has *All the Missing Girls* influenced your current writing projects or changed the way you write? Do you think that you will revisit any of the characters or themes from this novel?**

It has made me more willing to take risks. Writing this book involved a lot of trial and error, but when I finally reached the end of the first draft, it was probably my highest writing moment to date.

As for revisiting these characters, my first instinct when finishing a book is that I've left the characters as I hoped to leave them. Anything I write about them afterward is going to alter the whole balance of who they are for me. But inevitably, down the line, I'll start thinking about them and wondering how things have turned out. So I won't say never, but I don't have any plans for them right now.

Themes, on the other hand, yes. I see themes as questions to explore—not necessarily with an answer in mind. And I think there are many, many ways to explore the same themes that seem to particularly resonate for me.

**As a reader, who are some of the storytellers you find inspiring and why?**

I am a big fan of Gillian Flynn, Tana French, and Megan Abbott—they write sharp-edged character-driven stories, with haunting prose, brimming with tension. I love the mysteries they construct, but even more than that, I'm always so fascinated by their characters.

**What do you think the suspense or thriller genres offer that other genres do not?**

I think there's something particularly revealing about suspense or thriller stories due to the immediacy of the action, and the urgency. Morality is put to the test in single moments that force characters to reveal themselves in split-second decisions. That sense of danger, or ticking clock, elevates every emotion and puts even the seemingly mundane under a microscope for closer inspection. Every phrase or interaction can carry the meaning of something else, and I think these types of stories can bring the reader even closer, into a more active role.

**Are there any significant events from your own adolescence that you feel ultimately shaped the course of your life and your identity?**

I think the moments that have most influenced my life happened later for me. Though I am struck by how much of our outer lives seem to hinge on decisions we're supposed to make when we're sixteen, seventeen, eighteen years old. I had been thinking a lot about this, how we make these decisions in adolescence that really do affect the trajectory of our adulthood. I was thinking that there are the decisions people expect you to make—if and where to go to college; where to live; what field to pursue—but that there could be all these hidden ones as well, that no one else bears witness to. Or, if they do, that it somehow bonds you all closer, tying you to each other, regardless of time and distance.

Read on for a sneak peek at Megan Miranda's
electrifying new thriller

# THE PERFECT STRANGER

on shelves in May 2017.

# PROLOGUE

**he cat under the** front porch was at it again. Scratching at the slab of wood that echoed through the hardwood floors of my bedroom. Sharpening its claws, marking its territory—relentless in the dead of night.

I sat on the edge of the bed, stomped my feet on the wood, thought, *Please let me sleep,* which had become my repeated plea to all things living and nonliving out here, whatever piece of nature was at work each particular night.

The scratching stopped, and I eased back under the sheets.

Other sounds, more familiar now: the creak of the old mattress, crickets, a howl as the wind funneled through the valley. All of it orienting me to my new life—the bed I slept in, the valley I lived in, a whisper in the night: *You are here.*

I had been raised and built for city life, had grown accustomed to the sound of people on the street below, the car horns, the train running on the track until midnight. Had come to expect footsteps overhead, doors slamming shut, water in the pipes running through my walls. I could sleep through all of it.

The silence in this house, at times, was unsettling. But it was better than the animals.

Emmy, I could get used to. She slipped right in, the sputtering engine of her car in the driveway a comfort, her footsteps in the hallway lulling me to sleep. But the cat, the crickets, the owls, and the coyote—these took time.

Four months, and it was finally shifting, like the season.

———

WE HAD ARRIVED IN the summer—Emmy first; me, a few weeks later. We slept with our doors closed and the air turned on high, directly across the hall from each other. Back in July, when I first heard the cry in the middle of the night, I bolted upright in bed and thought, *Emmy.*

It was a muffled, low moan, like something was dying, and my mind was already filling in the blanks: Emmy struggling, grasping at her throat, or keeled over on the dusty floor. I'd raced across the hall and had my hand on her doorknob (locked) when she'd torn it open, staring back at me with wide eyes. She looked for a moment like she had when we'd first met, both of us barely out of school. But that was just the dark playing tricks on me.

"Did you hear that?" she'd whispered.

"I thought it was you."

Her fingers circled my wrist, and the moonlight from the uncovered windows illuminated the whites of her eyes.

"What was it?" I asked. Emmy had lived in the wild, had spent years in the Peace Corps, had grown accustomed to the unfamiliar.

Another cry, and Emmy jumped—the sound had been directly below us. "I don't know."

She was roughly my size but skinnier. Eight years earlier, it had been the other way around, but she'd lost the curves and give in the years since she'd been gone. I felt I needed to be the one to protect her now. To shield her from the danger, because there was nothing to Emmy these days but sharp angles and pale skin.

But she moved first, noiselessly walking down the hall, her heels barely making contact with the floor. I followed, keeping my steps light, my breathing shallow.

I put my hand on the phone, which was corded and hooked to the kitchen wall, just in case. But Emmy had other plans. She grabbed a flashlight from the kitchen drawer, slid the front doors slowly open, and stepped out onto the wooden porch. The moonlight softened her, the breeze moving her dark hair. She arced the light across the tree line and started down the steps.

"Emmy, wait," I'd said, but she'd eased herself onto her stomach in the dirt, ignoring me. She shone the light under the porch, and something cried again. I gripped the wooden railing as Emmy rolled onto her back, faintly shaking with laughter before it made its way from her gut, tearing through the night sky.

A hiss, a streak of fur darting from under the house straight into the woods, and another following behind. Emmy pushed herself to sitting, her shoulders still shaking.

"We're living on top of a cat brothel," she'd said.

The smile caught on my lips, a stark relief. "No wonder the price was so good," I'd said.

Her laughter slowly died, something else pulling her focus. "Oh, look," she'd said, a skinny arm pointing to the sky behind me.

A full moon. No, a supermoon. That's what it was called. Yellow and too close, like it could affect the pull of gravity. Make us go mad. Make cats go crazy.

"We can put up cinder blocks," I'd said, "to keep out the animals."

"Right," she'd said.

But, of course, we never did.

———

EMMY LIKED THE IDEA of the cats. Emmy liked the idea of old wood cabins and a porch with rockers; also: vodka, throwing darts at maps while drinking vodka, fate.

She was big on that last one.

It's why she was so sure moving here together was the right thing to do, no second thoughts or second guesses. Fate leading us back together, our paths intersecting in a poorly lit barroom eight years since the last time we'd seen each other. "It's a sign," she'd said, and since I'd been drunk it made perfect sense, my thoughts slurring together with hers, wires crossing.

The cats were probably a sign, too—of what, I wasn't sure. But also: the supermoon, the fireflies flashing in time to her laughter, the air thick with humidity, as if it were engulfing us.

Any time we'd hear a noise after that, any time I'd jolt alert from the worn brown sofa or from my seat at the vinyl kitchen table, Emmy would shrug and say, "Just the cats, Leah."

But for weeks, I dreamed of bigger things living underneath us. Took the steps in one big leap when I left each day, like a kid. Pictured things coiled up or crouched down in the dark, in the dirt, nothing but yellow eyes staring back. Snakes. Raccoons. Stray and rabid dogs.

Just yesterday one of the other teachers said there was a bear in his yard. Just that: a bear in his yard. Like it was a thing one might or might not notice in passing. Graffiti on the overpass, a burnt-out streetlight. Just a bear.

"Don't like bears, Ms. Stevens?" he'd said, toothy grin. He was older and soft, the skin around his wedding band ballooning from either side in protest, taught history and seemed to prefer it to reality.

"Who likes bears?" I'd said, trying to skirt him in the hall.

"You should probably like bears if you're moving to bear country." His voice was louder than necessary. "This is their home you all keep building right up on. Where else should they be?"

The neighbor's dog started barking, and I stared at the gap between the window curtains, waiting for the first signs of light.

On mornings like this, despite my initial hope—the scent of nature, the charm of wood cabins with rockers, the promise of a fresh start—I still craved the city. Craved it like the coffee hitting my bloodstream in the morning, the chase of a story, the high of my name in print.

When I'd first arrived in the summer, there had been a period of long calm when the stretch of days welcomed me with a blissful absence of thought. When I'd woken in the morning and poured a cup of coffee and walked down the wooden front steps, feeling, for a moment, so close to the earth, in touch with some element I had previously been missing: my feet planted directly on the dirt surrounding our porch, slivers of grass poking up between my toes, as if the place itself were taking me in.

But other days, the calm could shift to an absence instead, and I'd feel something stir inside of me, like muscle memory.

Sometimes I dreamed that some nefarious hack had taken down the entire Internet, had wiped us all clean and I could go back. Could start over. Be the Leah Stevens I had planned to be.

# Also by
# Megan Miranda

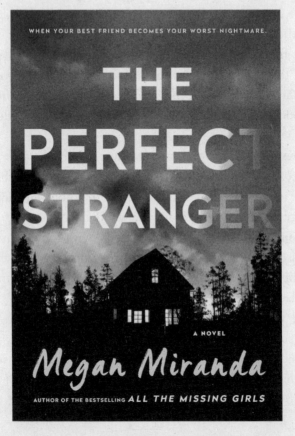

When your best friend becomes your worst nightmare . . .
Megan Miranda's next gripping thriller, *The Perfect Stranger*,
follows a journalist who sets out to find a missing friend, but
what she finds will gradually put everything she values in jeopardy.

## Pick up or download your copy today!